ALSO BY RANDALL SILVIS

WALKING THE BONES

A Ryan DeMarco Mystery

RANDALL SILVIS

sourcebooks
landmark

FOR MY SONS,
BRET AND NATHAN,
HEART OF MY SOUL, SOUL OF MY HEART

Published by Sourcebooks Landmark, an imprint of Sourcebooks, Inc.
P.O. Box 4410, Naperville, Illinois 60567-4410
(630) 961-3900
Fax: (630) 961-2168
sourcebooks.com

Library of Congress Cataloging-in-Publication Data

Names: Silvis, Randall, author.
Title: Walking the bones : a Ryan DeMarco mystery / Randall Silvis.
Description: Naperville, Illinois : Sourcebooks Landmark, [2018]
Identifiers: LCCN 2017027748 | (trade paperback : alk. paper)
Subjects: LCSH: Police--Pennsylvania--Fiction. |
    Murder--Investigation--Kentucky--Fiction. | Cold cases (Criminal
    investigation)--Fiction. | Psychological fiction. | GSAFD: Mystery
fiction.
Classification: LCC PS3569.I47235 W36 2018 | DDC 813/.54--dc23 LC
record available at https://lccn.loc.gov/2017027748

Printed and bound in the United States of America.
VP 10 9 8 7 6 5 4 3 2 1

Oh, love is the crooked thing,
There is nobody wise enough
To find out all that is in it...
                                     —*William Butler Yeats*

I

He who does his duty as his own nature
reveals it, never sins.

—*Bhagavad Gita*

ONE

Late July, eastern Kentucky

Shortly after entering the forest on the first day, midafternoon, Ryan DeMarco's cell phone went dark, battery depleted, and since he was no longer able to estimate his progress up the mountain by checking the time or the GPS, he stowed the phone in a pair of socks at the bottom of his backpack. He briefly considered stowing his off-duty weapon as well, a .40-caliber Glock 27, lighter and more concealable than his SIG Sauer .45 service weapon, but decided against it for protection against black bears, timber rattlers, copperheads, and wild dogs. He was less likely to encounter a mountain lion or drug trafficker, and it was too early for ginseng hunters to be doing anything but checking on the sanctity of their beds, but each of those could be dangerous too. Besides, when unarmed he felt off balance somehow. So despite the extra weight of his Glock and pocket holster pulling at his sweat-slickened waistband, he kept the handgun within easy reach.

Throughout the rest of that day there was only the waxing and waning of the light to mark his climb, and the changing currents of heavy, steamy air—this one cooler by a few degrees and smelling of moss, this one warmer and thicker and smelling of wood rot, the ancient scent of decay—and the scent and snag of his own relentless movement, and the thirst, the weariness, the resistance of muscles unused to such routine, and the niggling but incessant torment of gnats and mosquitoes drawn to the sweat of his neck and face and arms and ears and to the allure of blood coursing just beneath his skin.

Each of these sensations was experienced with an acuity and detachment a second part of him found intriguing, as if a second DeMarco was following the first, grinding his way uphill through deep forest, this second one close behind and incorporeal, taking note of and registering not only all the other man's sensations but eavesdropping too on his thoughts, the self-recriminations and remorse, the stinging replay of the previous day's mistakes. The second DeMarco regarded all this with curiosity, a mild amusement, and sometimes a touch of pity.

Thanks to the heaviness of the top canopy some forty feet up, and the second canopy provided by saplings and smaller trees, the forest had no full unfiltered light, only gradations of dusk. The sun, when it briefly revealed itself, appeared only as a splash of white halo, or as a glowing lacuna spotted through the perforation of leaves. Throughout that day he marched toward one slender, streaming shaft of mote-filled yellow after another, the neglected sky like a sputtering fluorescent bulb hidden somewhere high above.

Those high leaves, when DeMarco stared into them for a few seconds while resting, would become like leaves afloat upon first milky and later inky water, and he would remember his childhood and the woods to which he had so often escaped, and how the anger in him in those distant times had given way to a debilitating sadness that usually culminated in tears. This, in turn, would remind him of the seven murdered girls whose childhoods had been no doubt even sadder than his, and consequently he would push upward again, his weariness assuaged by another surge of resolve.

The high canopy was a living mosaic of leaves, mostly oak and other hardwoods, from which came the shrieks of crows and the nighthawks' cries, and the scolding chitter of squirrels. The animals were never more than fleeting shadows, though chipmunks he saw in abundance, both on the ground and in the lower branches. He heard turkeys calling from the distance. He flushed rabbits and grouse and had once stood not ten feet from a doe and fawn watching him watching them. Twice he heard the drone of airplanes, and once the *whuff* of a helicopter in the high unseeable clouds.

He could associate no scents with that higher realm, unless perhaps for the unexpected freshenings, those rare, brief drafts of cooler air that crossed his path without so much as a riffling of the ferns. But from the lower realms of understory and ground came an abundance of odors, of humus and fungi, of blossom and fern and moss, of leaf mold and rotting wood and rotting carcass and the scent of his own sweat. Once, on the first day, he smelled cigarette smoke in the air, but since then there had been only the forest's varied fragrances, of which he now included his own.

Those scents too took him back to his youth, those many days through all seasons when he had escaped into the solitude and safety of the woods, felt shielded and protected in their dimness. And now he realized how much he had missed that scent of dry leaves underfoot, and under them a damper layer, the rich, loamy fragrance of decomposition, and the sweeter scents of ferns, of tree bark, of deadfalls rotting and falling apart. They were all a part of the past yet here distinct, scents all these years living silent in his memory, waiting to be opened, a window to the past unshuttered.

And the sounds of the forest. After the first hour, he had left the trails behind, and so too the tourists, the day hikers, the noisy teenagers drunk on their freedom, even the solitary millennials trudging toward a favorite campsite. His own footsteps and the dry scrape of leaves were the loudest noises now, all else hushed and natural.

For a long time after Thomas Huston's death, DeMarco had been plagued by a low rumbling sound of unknown origins. It was as much felt in his eardrums as heard, a low-frequency intrusion that played as a discordant bass line to whatever else he was doing, whether trying to sleep, listening to music, or sitting at his desk and staring out the window. It was almost always there with his coffee in the morning. Sometimes he would lose track of it during the day, but in quiet moments, it inevitably returned. Time after time he would open a window or door and look outside, thinking a truck was sitting idly nearby, or a neighbor had his music turned too loud, or a plane was too low, a chopper hovering, a distant storm approaching, a high-altitude thunder. But no source was ever visible. Sometimes it seemed to be coming from deep within the earth. When the noise became especially bothersome and no outside source could be identified, he would walk around the house and put his ear to the refrigerator, or stand with the basement door open, his body leaning into the dimness; something must be wrong with a condenser, a fan, an overstressed motor.

Anytime he was quiet, looking for quiet, desperate for quiet, the rumbling sound would be there. When he awoke alone in the middle of the night. When he lay awake in bed in the morning wishing he could sleep longer. In the shower. Alone in his office with the door closed. Alone in his car with the engine and radio shut off. Alone. Alone. Alone. The rumbling sound was always there.

He finally decided the sound must be inside his own head. A tumor pressing against a nerve. A synapse in short circuit. Or maybe there was something rolling around in there like ball bearings on a lead track. A thickening. A misdirected flow. A hardening of something not meant to be hard.

But now, hundreds of feet up on the side of a forested mountain, the rumbling was no longer detectable. There were birds flitting, some calling out. Squirrels leaping from branch to branch. Insects buzzing, lighting on his skin, drinking his sweat. But no rumbling. Thank God, there was no more rumbling.

And after those first five hours of dragging himself uphill through this dimness and hush and damp, through the ponderous heat of the forest in summer, of being lashed and cut like a flagellant by branches and vines, of tripping over roots and deadfalls and sliding to his knees in bogs of hidden leaf muck, of being ambushed by growls and squawks, boulders and stones, and of being bitten and stung every minute, the demarcations of day and night were merging into one unbroken ordeal.

The change occurred the next morning, on what he expected to be the final morning of the uphill climb. The total elevation was only 3,100 feet, so he had never imagined the search would take even half so long. But he had also never imagined the forest's darkness could be so deep and disorienting, that it would be so easy to spend an hour or more walking laterally while imagining he was moving in a vertical line, or how much time he would lose crawling over boulders and up and down slippery gullies, or how many rests he would need, or how slow and halting his pace would actually be.

On that first morning in the forest, he rose from his sleeping bag, rolled and packed the bag and tarp, and stood against a slender oak to urinate before shouldering the pack to hazard on. He planned to chew a few coffee beans while he walked. His breakfast would be the last four strips of jerky in the bag. By noon, he hoped, he would find some sign of habitation. A piece of litter, the hint of a trail, a butchered animal carcass, the scent of a cook fire.

He relieved himself against the tree, and then, while zippering up and thinking he should get the coffee beans out and put them in a pocket, a gunshot ripped into the side of the tree, peppering his face with shards of bark. In an instant he pulled the Glock from its holster and, face stinging and eyes watering from the bark, dove for cover behind the forked trunk of a thick oak six feet to his right.

The slide through the dead leaves carried him a few feet farther than intended, and then he was tumbling, rolling, bouncing and sliding down a steep ravine. Along the way he raked the back of his head across the sharp facet of a rock buried in leaves, and with that blow lost both his weapon and his consciousness.

And now, some timeless while later, he lay not yet fully conscious, in fact conscious of only three things: the mosaic of leaves swimming high above, and the stuttering light between the leaves; the searing throb of pain shooting from ankle to knee with the regularity of a frenzied pulse; and the sense of being observed.

Moment by moment he remembered more. The gunshot. The dive. The long helpless tumble to the bottom of the ravine. Now he lay on his back atop sodden leaves and, buried beneath them, a slow but cooler rivulet, thousands of years old, that had carved that gash in the earth. Soon he remembered his weapon, flexed his empty hand, then touched his leather holster, which was now stuffed with leaves.

He was as good as naked lying there. The Bowie knife with its ten-inch blade remained strapped to the pack left leaning against the tree. There was no use trying to flee; he doubted he could even stand. He did not want to look at the leg just yet, afraid of what he might see. So he lay motionless, waiting and listening. An acorn ticked down from a tree. Something small rustled under a leaf. The forest clicked, creaked, fluttered drily.

In a moment, everything had been lost.

He thought, If a man dies in the woods, does anybody hear?

And the thought brought a smile, but a self-mocking one. You're fucked, he told himself.

TWO

Ten days earlier, southwestern Kentucky

I t was 2014 they were discovered," the man told DeMarco. "Seven young females reduced to bone."

"Name's Hoyle," he had said, but without extending his hand. His throaty voice moved with a distinctly southern lilt, but his articulation was precise, educated, a halting delivery that suggested an agile mind racing far ahead of every word.

He stood half a foot shorter than DeMarco, but twice as wide. A round, slow-talking man of seventy or more, his nearly bald head and face beaded with perspiration. He breathed heavily, though he had not moved an inch since meeting DeMarco. A worn black suit, twice buttoned, a white shirt damp with sweat around the collar, a dark-blue tie. Plain black brogues shiny with morning dew. The frayed cuffs were wet too, as were DeMarco's running shoes, the grass in the unkempt lot as high as their ankles.

"Mid-July," Hoyle continued. "Just like now. Hot as Hades. If not for the termites, the poor girls might never have been found."

The man's eyes remained fixed on DeMarco's face, and the slow, infrequent blink of his gaze added another element to the strangeness of the morning—the man's appearance, the heavy solemnity with which he spoke. Even the buzz of insects and chirp of birds seemed incongruous now, the world slightly askew.

"Seven skeletons in a four-by-fourteen-by-ten-foot space between walls," Hoyle said. "Each one cocooned in clear plastic sheeting. The kind painters use to cover a floor. Each cocoon sealed with silver duct tape. Each skeleton meticulously flensed, probably through cold water maceration."

"That will remove everything?" DeMarco asked. "Strip the bones clean?"

"Ninety-eight percent. The rest can be easily picked away. A short bath in a Drano solution is equally effective."

DeMarco winced. "All of similar age?"

"Fifteen to nineteen."

DeMarco stood there thinking. Too few pieces. How to make them fit?

And then a bright-yellow blur glided between the men, downward past DeMarco an inch from his nose. He jerked back suddenly, and in the next instant recognized the creature now fluttering past Hoyle's broad midsection. Butterfly.

Hoyle had not flinched, had not lifted his eyes off DeMarco's.

"Here's the interesting part," Hoyle said. "Not a single Caucasian girl in the bunch. African American one and all. Light-skinned. What do you make of that?"

"Either a fetish for girls of color…"

"Or?"

"A hatred of them."

Hoyle smiled. Finally he looked away, following the butterfly as it floated across the quiet street to land on a summersweet bush. "Cloudless sulphur," he said. "*Phoebis sennae.* Female."

He pulled a white handkerchief from his pocket, dabbed at his face and scalp. "Butterflies and hummingbirds," he said. "Every summer we suffer the same infestation."

And then he did, to DeMarco's eyes, the oddest thing. Extending both short, heavy arms, one hand still holding by finger and thumb the white handkerchief, Hoyle moved his arms in a slow and sensuous wave, as if hoping, against all odds, to lift himself, too, aloft.

| |

I love the man that can smile in trouble,
that can gather strength from distress,
and grow brave by reflection. 'Tis the
business of little minds to shrink; but
he whose heart is firm, and whose
conscience approves his conduct, will
pursue his principles unto death.

—*Thomas Paine*

THREE

The previous winter, western Pennsylvania

Sundays DeMarco sat beside Baby Ryan's grave. Sundays he didn't drink. He didn't pray. He didn't ask for forgiveness because any God who would allow such banal cruelty as had befallen his son, such savagery as had befallen Thomas Huston and his family, such a monstrosity as Carl Inman had proven himself to be—pleas for mercy and forgiveness to any such God would only be laughed at and derided. So DeMarco asked for nothing, and deliberately withheld what he needed most, as if his own stubbornness might outlast God's.

On this Sunday afternoon in early December he sat in his parked car with the engine off, the door swung open, his feet in the snow. Between his hands he held a metal thermos cup of steaming coffee. He listened to the naked trees creak with cold. He listened to the dry wind scrape across marble, metal, and crusted snow.

Before his fingers could grow chill and stiff he reached into a hip pocket and withdrew the round silver locket he carried everywhere he went. Each night he set the locket on the stand beside his bed where he could reach for it if a dream startled him awake. The night his son was pronounced dead, a thoughtful nurse had presented him with a small envelope containing a cutting of the baby's fine blond hair. The next day DeMarco purchased two silver lockets and one silver chain. Laraine wore her locket around her neck. She had not thanked him when he gave it to her, and said less and less to him with each passing week. Then one day he came home from work and all her clothes and the baby's clothes were gone. He tracked her down finally in a small rented house in Erie, and though she never turned him away at the door, and sat patiently each time he spoke in a pleading and sorrowful whisper, she refused him a single word of comfort or blame, and therefore it all felt like blame to him, all well-deserved.

And now in the cemetery, this Sunday and every Sunday, he held a metal cup of coffee in his left hand, the locket in his right. From time to time he looked up at the frozen sun, clouded and dim, and monitored its descent into the horizon. Now and then an eighteen-wheeler Jake-braked out on the highway, releasing a rat-a-tatting pulse of air that made him grit his teeth. Sometimes a crow screeched, or the thumping rumble of overloaded woofers swelled and then gradually receded. Every anomalous sound jarred and made him stiffen. When no identifiable sounds were present, there was always the faint rumbling that seemed to come from all directions at once.

DeMarco wished for nothing but silence inside and out. A silence absolute and eternal.

He would sit like this long after the cup had been drained, after his feet were numb and his bare hands scarlet and stinging. The only thing warm would be the silver locket clutched in his right hand.

Only after he had shivered and wept himself empty, had relived and questioned and cursed every fatal decision he'd ever made, only then would he admit to himself that pain could never cancel out pain, could never erase memory or alter the past. Pain wasn't fire, it wasn't magic, it was only human suffering. And it would be with him all the days of his life.

FOUR

After Huston's death, and Inman's, Bonnie's, the whole Huston family's, DeMarco agreed to speak with a psychiatrist. His station commander and several of the troopers had begun to treat him gingerly, as they might a brick of C-4 or some other explosive—a treatment that, he told himself, maybe *could* make him explode. He wanted everything to be as it had been months ago. No, years ago. Thirteen and a half years ago, to be exact. To have his son, his namesake, in his life again... That would change everything.

During the first session, the psychiatrist wanted to know how DeMarco felt about Huston's death. And what about Bonnie's murder, her throat slit not far from where he had been sleeping? Did he blame himself for any of those tragedies?

DeMarco felt as if he were watching an episode of *The Sopranos* after three double whiskeys. He didn't laugh or get angry, just watched numbly as the scene transpired.

SHRINK
Do you resent having to talk to me?

DEMARCO
It's what you get paid for.

SHRINK
But you feel it's unnecessary. An intrusion.

DEMARCO
I'm not an extrovert.

SHRINK

Excuse me?

DEMARCO

Psychiatrists are how extroverts are forced to
look at themselves.

SHRINK

And by look, you mean examine? Self-
critique? That's something you don't need?

DEMARCO

Everything I see is a mirror. You or the wall,
it's all the same to me.

In the second and last session, the shrink tried something different,
an attempt to incite more than shrugs and curt responses. The shrink
was not a bad guy, well-meaning, no doubt, but DeMarco felt nothing
toward him, neither animus nor felicity, neither interest nor contempt.

SHRINK

Let's talk about Carl Inman. The one person
you actually pulled the trigger on. Do you
feel remorse for that act?

DEMARCO

I had no choice.

SHRINK

We always have a choice.

DEMARCO

Kill or be killed. You call that a choice?

SHRINK

Not a good choice but a choice nonetheless.
You choose to take a life, or to sacrifice yours.

DEMARCO

I wouldn't sacrifice a snail's life for a man
like Inman.

SHRINK

You don't value human life more than a snail's?

DEMARCO
(after a pause)
Have you ever been threatened?

SHRINK

Let's keep the focus on you.

DEMARCO

I'll take that as a no. In which case you
have no contextual understanding of such a
situation.

SHRINK

I've read your report. I've read your file. I
think I have a fair understanding of what you
experienced.

DEMARCO

All you have is story. Story and theory.
Words written by other people. Some of
whom, like you, have never known what it's
like to have their lives threatened.

SHRINK

Why don't you tell me what it's like.

DEMARCO

How could you understand if you've never
experienced it?

SHRINK

Well, we're not here to talk about me,
though, are we?

DEMARCO

Are you sure about that?

SHRINK

What does that mean?

DEMARCO

(stands, crosses to him, leans down, grips
 the arms of the shrink's padded chair)
If I were to put my hands around your throat
right now and start to squeeze, what's your
theory going to tell you to do?

SHRINK

Please return to your seat, Sergeant.

DEMARCO

(leans closer, whispers)
How do you know I won't do it? How do
you know?

The shrink presses back against his chair…leans awkwardly to the side…reaches for his briefcase…fumbles to unsnap it.

DeMarco smiles, draws back… He turns away, returns to his seat. He sits there smiling, hands placid atop his lap.

By now the shrink has his pistol out, a Beretta .380 semiautomatic, the short silver barrel showing above his hands, hands clasped atop his groin, trembling.

> DEMARCO
>
> Let's say you do it. Let's say you pull the trigger on me. Will you feel any remorse afterward?

> SHRINK
>
> This session is over.

> DEMARCO
>
> Theory and reality, Doc. Not the same thing. It's best not to confuse them.

> SHRINK
>
> This is all going into my report. Every second of it.

> DEMARCO
>
> (smiles, stands)
>
> I'll look forward to reading it.

FIVE

As per their understanding, never stated aloud, Jayme was gone when he returned to the house after visiting his son's grave. Four Saturdays in a row she had spent the night with him, languorous and wonderful nights. Often when she slept he searched for words to tell her how much those nights meant to him, but in the morning when he rehearsed the words they sounded false inside his head, and he let them fade unspoken. He was a man unused to gentle language. His job and history had made him a stranger to it, and he had grown easy with that agreement. But Jayme's regular presence in his life was forcing a reappraisal.

On their first Sunday morning together, Jayme had noticed a change in him midmorning, a restlessness while they cleaned up the breakfast dishes, him fully dressed, her still in panties and one of his black T-shirts. Later, when she refilled their coffee cups and carried them into the living room, where she then sat and patted the sofa cushion next to hers, and held out the paper, he hesitated, looked almost panicked for a second, then took the paper from her hand and sat down.

She waited a few minutes before speaking. "You have plans for the day?"

Again he hesitated. "Not really."

"You seem a little anxious to me. If you have something to do, it's okay."

"It's not important," he said.

"I don't want to interrupt your routine. Just tell me and I'll go."

"I don't want you to go."

"But you don't want me to stay either."

"I want you to come back."

"And in order to do that, I first have to go away."

He smiled. "That's not what I meant."

She set her cup on the coffee table, then swung a long naked leg across his lap and straddled him. "I understand. All you want is a sex toy."

He slipped a hand under her shirt. "I've always wanted a sex toy."

"You can buy them online, you know. Express shipped from Japan."

"I only buy American-made. Local, when possible."

"And what are your specifications, sir?"

Now he withdrew his hand from the warmth of her waist and cupped it gently against the side of her neck. "Somebody smart," he told her. "Smarter than me. Nicer than me. Sweeter than me. And prettier than me."

"That covers just about everybody," she said. "How about physical attributes?"

"We talking ideal scenario here?"

"Absolutely. We ship made-to-order."

"Hmm. Five seven, five eight would be nice. A firm yet womanly bottom. One breast for each hand. One very delicious mouth. Two green, hypnotic eyes. And a thick mop of—" He lifted the hair off her shoulder. "What color would you call this?"

"It's a deep shade of strawberry blond. Verging on honey blond."

"That's how I want my sex toy. Verging on honey blond."

"I'll place your order immediately. Oh, one last thing. How do you like your vajayjay, sir?"

"I'm a little embarrassed you didn't notice, but I don't have one."

"On your sex toy, Sergeant. Do you prefer natural, shaved, or landing strip?"

"That's what yours is called, a landing strip?"

"Correct. It serves for both takeoffs and landings."

"With signal lights in case of heavy traffic?"

She answered with a lighthearted slap.

"Sorry," he said. "Out of line?"

"And almost out of business. Shall I place your order or not?"

"Please," he said.

"Done. Now tell me why you're so anxious to get rid of me today."

He slid both hands down over her shoulders, along her arms, and covered her hands with his. "Sundays I go to the cemetery."

"Oh baby," she said. "To see Thomas Huston?"

"My son," he said.

She inhaled deeply, then leaned into him, slipped her hands around his back.

And they sat like that for a long time. She asked no more questions, and neither did he.

After a while she kissed his cheek, slid away from him, stood, and went into the bedroom to dress.

When she came back out he was standing at the kitchen window, gazing across the yard. She kissed him again. "I'm keeping the T-shirt," she told him.

"What do I get to keep?"

"Me," she said. She put both hands on his cheeks and pulled his face down to hers and kissed him on the mouth.

She held him a moment longer, then stepped away. "Tomorrow, love," she said, and headed for the front door.

Moments later he stared at the empty doorway and wondered, *How does she do that? How does she give herself to love so easily, no questions asked, no doubts, no litany of fears?* He had done that for only a short time in his life, and it had been spontaneous, a sudden outpouring of love impossible to restrain, that tiny face, that tiny soft bundle, seven pounds, four ounces, a miracle to behold.

And look how that turned out, he thought. Then busied himself with unnecessary housekeeping until his time for the cemetery arrived.

SIX

And after that first Sunday, he relaxed through the subsequent sleepover mornings. Sometimes they watched a movie or took a walk or made a trip to the mall. He learned that he could look out the window in the afternoon and say, "I guess I better get going," and she would smile without getting up from the bed or the sofa and say, "Okay, baby. I'll see you tomorrow." And when he later returned to the house in the deepening dusk, every room would be empty, her scent following him wherever he chose to sit, another ache of hollowness like an old gunshot in his chest.

At those times he reverted to the stillness of sitting in his silent house, unreclining on his recliner in the living room. He closed his eyes and tried to empty his mind of thought but that was never possible. Sometimes unwanted thoughts of his days in Panama arose and sometimes of his life as a boy in a trailer court in Youngstown. When he felt his body stiffening in reaction to those thoughts, he turned his mind to Jayme instead, and remembered their previous night together and the way she had smelled in the soft sunlight of morning.

He did not know if what he felt for Jayme was love or only gratitude. As a trooper she was first-rate, intelligent and perceptive, flawlessly reliable no matter what task was assigned. And when she unbraided or uncoiled her hair for Saturday night and when she stepped out of the gray-and-black uniform, she was something else too. She was beautiful and loving and more than a little magical whether in moonlight or in the soft pink glow of sunrise.

So he told himself that gratitude is a kind of love. And that the tenderness he felt for her was a kind of love. And the emptiness when she was gone, and the nervous anticipation of being alone with her again. And the sickening, hollow fear that one day soon she would change her mind and he would be left with an incrementally deeper, never-healing ache.

It was the inevitable punch line to a cruel cosmic joke, but one he knew he deserved: to be the recipient of such love when he, the only other time he loved, had loved so poorly.

SEVEN

That same winter, in southwestern Kentucky, the man named Hoyle sat alone on the front bench seat of his Ford Bronco, his feet swung into the passenger side as he switched out his standard black brogues, size 9.5 EE, for a pair of black Skechers Energy-Downforce cross trainers whose white *S* logo he had blacked out with a permanent marker. The customized bench seat allowed him not only more room, but also easier entrance and egress from the vehicle, and the tinted windows provided a degree of anonymity.

The January night was cold, a few degrees above freezing, so beneath his black suit coat Hoyle wore a black fleece pullover with the collar zipped. Because of his bulk, putting on a pair of new shoes was never easy, but even more so bent double in the front of his vehicle.

Seated behind him, Rosemary Toomey, a small Caucasian female wearing a jogging suit of indigo velour, kept watch out the side window, alert for anomalous lights or movements in the trees between the vehicle and the McGintey trailers. Beside her, a tall African American male, David Vicente, outfitted more casually in a pair of dark-brown corduroy slacks and a drab olive-green cardigan sweater, held in his hands the binocular night vision goggles Hoyle had purchased online. All three individuals were well into the eighth decade of their lives. From the moment the vehicle was parked along the side of the dirt service road, all conversation took place in voices hushed to half whispers.

Hoyle said, "Please do not put that on over your head, David."

"I am simply examining it," Vicente said. "Besides, my hair is clean."

"I have adjusted the straps precisely."

"I shampoo every day."

"All hair contains oils. As do shampoos."

"Rosemary," Vicente said, "has this thing touched my head?"

"It has not," she said without turning to look.

Vicente said, "I thought you were buying the monocular unit."

Hoyle continued to struggle with his left shoe, head bent near the dashboard. He said, between huffing breaths, "According to research conducted by the United States Army Research Laboratory in Aberdeen, Maryland, the binocular goggle provides the best ocular configuration for visually directed activity."

He finished with his shoe finally, sat up, and caught his breath.

Vicente held the goggles toward him. "You're out of breath already. If you weren't such a germophobe, either Rosemary or I could do this one."

Hoyle reached for the goggles and fitted them on over his head. "Mysophobia is a pathological condition. My concerns are wholly practical."

He swung his legs back to the left, under the steering wheel, and then toward the door, which he quietly opened. The interior lights remained off, all bulbs removed.

"Ten minutes in, ten minutes back," Vicente said.

"At whose pace?" Hoyle asked.

"All right; thirty total." He clapped Hoyle once on the shoulder, even though he knew that his friend would flinch from the touch. "If the dogs start up, hotfoot it back here. Rosemary will blink the flashlight on and off to guide you. I'll be ready at the wheel."

"Wear gloves, please," Hoyle said. He then turned to his left, feet dangling outside the vehicle, and, gripping the steering wheel with his right hand, eased himself down as slowly as he could. Then he closed the door, switched on the goggles, and headed into the now green-lit woods.

His movements were slow and precise, only a slight reduction of his usual pace. He knew his limitations. As a younger man, even then a hundred pounds overweight, he had studied and practiced the movements of other large men, and discovered that the difference between ponderous, as evinced by Orson Welles, for example, and graceful, as demonstrated by the comedian Jackie Gleason, rested in the patience with which they moved. In patience is grace, he used to remind himself, until the habit became inherent to his nature. Only his mind moved quickly.

Now, as he stepped deliberately through the green landscape, he was thinking several thoughts concurrently, some fleeting, based on moment-to-moment observations, and some lingering, recognized by his consciousness and then left to stand like a pedestrian waiting for a break in the traffic: *a strange, eerie green everywhere I look, as in a Roger Corwin movie; Lucas's trailer dark, a single blue light in Chad's; should have at least tested the binocular and monocular units; Skechers are indeed quite comfortable; sixty yards, more or less, to go; fingers numbing, should have worn gloves...*

Eventually, the tree line loomed. Beyond it, a scraggly yard. Then the rear of the trailers. *Dogs out front*, he reassured himself. Still, his breath quickened.

The device, which eavesdropped on internet usage, recording up to five hundred gigabytes of data, had been attached to the cable descending from the satellite dish at the point it entered Chad McGintey's trailer. Vicente, before installing it two weeks earlier, had stenciled the Dishnet logo and an imaginary serial number on the black surface. Now Hoyle slipped a hand into his breast pocket and removed the wire-cutting tool.

He walked laterally until directly behind the rear corner of the trailer. Leaned into a thick trunk. Fifteen yards of open lawn lay ahead. If such can be termed a lawn, he told himself.

Thirty seconds to the trailer, he calculated. Snip snip. Thirty seconds back to the trees. If he could make it that far without waking the dogs, all would be well. A leisurely stroll back to his vehicle. Drive home, plug the USB cord into the device, download the data onto his computer. If Chad had viewed any child pornography in the past two weeks, particularly of a kind featuring African American girls, he would advance to the top of their list. If not, they would concentrate on Henry and Royce, try to eliminate one or the other. They were also hoping to find email communication between Chad and Virgil Helm. Either discovery would be culpatory.

Hoyle fully expected the case to open up now that Vicente and Rosemary had agreed, reluctantly, to employ the latest technology. Legality be damned, he had argued. Thankfully, frustration finally won the day. Any evidence gained could be submitted anonymously to the authorities, search warrants secured, computers seized, arrests made. Fait accompli.

Hoyle closed his eyes in an attempt to quiet his heart. Watched his breath going in through his nostrils, out through his mouth. "Ehyeh asher ehyeh," he whispered into the bark. "I am that I am. I am that I am…"

And then away from the tree, forward to the trailer. Wire cutters extended in his right hand like the fighting claw of a coconut crab. Fourteen yards to go. Thirteen. Twelve.

When he was ten yards from the trailer, motion sensor lights flared on, drenching the entire lawn in blinding white. Immediately the barking began, fierce and malevolent. Hoyle was stunned for but a moment, then whipped the goggles off his head and hurried forward to the trailer, reaching toward the cable, searching for the unit.

But it wasn't there. In its place, a large clear plastic ziplock bag was affixed to the cable. And in the bag, a sheet of paper. Hoyle tore the bag free, flipped the goggles down, turned, and, as best he could, ran.

He was halfway to the car when the barking grew louder and fragmented in voice. Unleashed, he thought. Three large, vicious dogs now hot on his scent.

A flashlight beam cut through the trees ahead and to his left. Blink blink. Blink blink. He veered toward the light, heart thundering, every gasp scalding his throat and lungs. Long, lurching, graceless strides. The dogs, by their sound, close on his heels.

The car. Engine running. Headlights on. Rear door open. He dove inside, head landing in Rosemary's lap.

Vicente gunned the engine. Dirt flew beneath the wheels. "There were no lights last time!" Vicente said. "When did he install those lights?"

He received no answer. Then asked, "Did you get it?"

Hoyle, a hand pressed to his chest as he grunted "Unh...unh... unh" and tried to fill his lungs, raised the bag to Rosemary. She took it, shined the flashlight upon it. Opened the bag and removed a single sheet of notebook paper, on which a short message had been typed in bold black script. She read aloud.

"'Dear FBI slash CIA slash NSA slash DIA slash all USSA Nazi Cabal Federal Reserve trespassing ass wipes...'

"Oh my," she said.

Vicente asked, "What else?"

"Just two words. The first one is 'eat.'"

Vicente blew out a breath. Banged a fist atop the steering wheel. Looked in the rearview mirror and saw three vociferous dogs being swallowed in the dust.

Two miles later he came to the highway. Hoyle was still saying "Unh" with every breath, still clutching his chest.

Again Vicente looked in the rearview mirror, this time at Hoyle, who was sitting with his head laid back over the seat, eyes closed. "You're wheezing like a leaky accordion," Vicente told him. "You doing okay?"

Hoyle's only answer was another groan.

Vicente looked to his right down the dark highway, then to his left. "Okay," he said. "Where to now? Restaurant or home?"

Hoyle sucked in a deep breath, held it for a moment, and then, exhaling, said, "Hospital."

EIGHT

As a boy Ryan learned to cultivate stillness—the appearance of stillness—whenever his father was home. Early mornings were easy because the boy had only to lie motionless in bed, face to the wall, until the heavy presence filling his doorway stomped away and into Ryan's mother's bedroom instead, where that harsh, demanding voice would continue for a while until silenced by the softer, soothing one. And then the headboard would bang and his father would groan and lapse into sleep, allowing Ryan the opportunity to escape to school or into the woods.

Late afternoons were more tenuous for the boy. Then his father sometimes came banging in suddenly, throwing open the trailer's cheap aluminum door which even in winter had no glass in the panel, then the thicker but no more substantial wooden door, and Ryan might be caught doing his homework at the little banquette table, or playing Old Maid with his mother. Immediately he would stiffen and fix his gaze anywhere but on his father's face. His father would go to the kitchen first, opening and banging shut cupboards and drawers as he searched for a few errant dollars. Then he would find Ryan's mother's purse and rifle through it and sometimes dump its contents onto the table right under Ryan's nose. With luck his father would find enough change for a shot or a couple of beers and be gone without further harm. Ryan's mother tried to keep a few dollars just for such emergencies, but money was never plentiful and sometimes she spent what she had squirreled away, pressing it into Ryan's hand for lunch money, or buying a bottle of wine to share with their neighbor Paul when Ryan's presence was insufficient to abet her need for affection and approval.

Sometimes his father's noisy search would leave him empty-handed, and he would turn to Ryan then and demand, Where's yours? Ryan, without lifting his eyes to his father, would will his body to be still and answer: I don't have anything. And then his father's face would come close, the stubbled cheeks and sour breath and stink of smoke and old sweat, and with the words spitting into Ryan's face he would say, Don't you lie to me, boy. Where you keeping it? Ryan would say nothing and give no sign of recognition and wait for what he knew would happen next, which was to be grabbed by the arm and dragged back to his bedroom and tossed inside and told to start looking. And you better hope you find something.

He would find a nickel and a few pennies atop his dresser, a quarter in the dust underneath his bed. Ryan would lay these coins on the corner of the bed and his father would snatch them up in his fist but remain in the doorway blocking the opening. Then crawling across the floor on his hands and knees, Ryan would dig through his pile of dirty clothes and search every corner of his tiny closet. Then pull the small thrift store dresser away from the wall and search behind it. Maybe even lift his mattress and show the emptiness underneath.

I guess that's all there is, he would say, and sometimes his father's eyes would fill with contempt and he would stomp away, back to ransacking the rest of the house. But sometimes his father would say, There sure as hell better be more, if you know what's good for you, and hold his position, in which case Ryan would pretend to think and scrutinize his room and then feign recollection and hurry to his backpack hanging from the headboard, unzip and turn it upside down over his bed shaking out the pencils and notebooks and a solitary quarter. I forgot about that, he would say, and his father, snatching up the coin, would glare at him and mutter, I bet you forgot.

Ryan would look at his father's chest but not into his eyes. I was saving it for pizza day at school, he might say, and with luck the big hand would only cuff the back of his head and knock him sideways onto the bed. With luck his father would leave the bedroom then and after another ten minutes of ripping up cushions and screaming

at Ryan's mother, would then storm out the door with his final pro-
nouncement: It's a damn sorry state of affairs when a man is reduced
to picking up bottles along the highway just to get himself a beer!

Only then would Ryan relinquish his stillness with a smile. He had
already picked up and redeemed every bottle on the streets leading
away from their home, and he had already stashed those coins in a
tobacco tin Paul had left on his concrete patio one day, and he had
already buried and reburied that tin a dozen times beneath his favorite
tree in the woods behind the house. At last count the tin contained
eleven dollars and forty-seven cents. Before long he would have to
find a second container. He had no idea what he intended to buy with
the money. He only knew that his father would never have it.

NINE

In other ways, too, the winter bruised and laid its welts upon DeMarco. He was hounded by the media to recount Thomas Huston's final hours. This he adamantly refused to do. A production company offered him three years' salary for the rights to his story. "It's not my story," he told them. "So I have nothing to sell."

He made the mistake one time of agreeing to sit down with a writer from *Cleveland Magazine* who claimed to be writing a memorial piece about Thomas. She was young and full of enthusiasm and DeMarco agreed only as a tribute to his friend. After taking notes for thirty minutes, the writer had asked, "Can you tell us about how you finally tracked down the murderer? How you put all the facts together and finally figured things out?"

He wanted to walk away then, but he also wanted to do right by his colleagues and their profession. So he answered truly, if obliquely. "It's never just a matter of gathering the facts," he said. "Facts are just a part of the story. Sometimes not more than an outline. First you have to know what happened. That's the easy part. Then you need to know why it happened. That's the hard part. There's the tip of the iceberg, and then there's the rest of it hidden below the water."

He waited for her to ask, *Didn't Hemingway say something like that?* But she only smiled and nodded, kept her eyes open wide as if he were about to impart an ancient wisdom.

"There's text and there's subtext," he said, and struggled to remember the full conversation with Thomas and all the writer's words. "There's implication and inference. There's story and there's backstory. In fact, there's no story without backstory. There's no you, for example, without your mother. Without your father. There's no present without the past."

"Wow," she said while scribbling furiously. "Just wow. That's really good."

He excused himself then and went back to his office and closed the door. When the piece was published, he refused to look at it.

And throughout that winter he also thought of Laraine again and again, always questioning if he had made the right decision. Their relationship after the separation had been toxic, yes, but was leaving her alone with the poison the best thing to do? Every weekend he fought the urge to drive to Erie and check up on her, and managed to talk himself out of it with the logic that she picked up strangers at bars and took them home and had sex with them only because she knew he was watching; therefore, if he stopped watching, the behavior would cease. This was a good logic after the sun went down, but in full light it fell apart. There was also an element of self-destruction to her activities. She probably wanted to wipe out her memories as badly as he wanted to erase his own.

The psychiatrist he had met with after Huston's death had attempted to broach those memories, and a part of DeMarco had been rooting for the guy to succeed. But the other part, self-schooled in silence since the age of four or five, found itself immune to the litany of carefully phrased questions, so that the only effect of those questions was to make DeMarco drowsy. *How has the incident affected your relationships at work? Do you have trouble sleeping? Do you think you drink too much?*

Most times DeMarco had wanted to answer truthfully, but heard only half-truths coming from his mouth. Just the mention of Baby Ryan made him wince, made the scar on his silence shrink tighter. The psychiatrist had called the baby's death an accident, which made DeMarco angry. Was stupidity an accident? Was inattention, no matter how brief, an accident? No, that so-called accident was *his* doing—not the other driver's, not God's, not Fate's, not anybody or anything else's fault but his own. And he refused to be denied that guilt.

In the end he returned to active duty, back to the routine of helping to maintain a semblance of order throughout the villages and hamlets and farms of a rural county where the social high point of the year was the end-of-summer farm show.

And there encountered the most onerous irritation of that dangerous winter. The way the other troopers treated him...the way his station commander always looked at him when he thought DeMarco wouldn't notice, as if DeMarco were about to split down the middle and...and what? Release the demons? Set the entire barracks aflame with the fury of his misery?

Thank God for Jayme. This became his mantra each time he slipped toward anger or, even worse, into a mute and impotent despair. She had no idea how desperately he clung to her, for he was careful to ration out his attention through the week. A touch on her arm, a cup of coffee, a gesture here, a smile there. And always felt guilty, as if he was playing her somehow, exploiting her for his own survival.

Saturday nights were different. He made love as if he fully believed he would lose her in the morning. And if he lost her, he would lose that last small part of himself that was maybe worth keeping.

TEN

During the first warm days of March in southwestern Kentucky, the yard and garage sales began. Aaron Henry, disgraced eighth-grade teacher and registered pedophile, made his rounds every weekend. He focused on first-edition books, old jewelry, women's handbags, DVDs, band instruments, working iPods and MP3 players, carnival glassware, ceramic figurines, dolls and action figures, and any other items that could be cleaned and sold on eBay for a profit. He always wore a ball cap and mirrored aviator glasses, stayed away from trailer courts, where most of the items were worn-out junk, and from affluent neighborhoods, where most items were priced too high for profitable resale, and never shopped in the school district where he used to teach.

On their third such surveillance of his activities, with Hoyle and David Vicente watching through binoculars behind the tinted windows of Hoyle's Ford Bronco, Rosemary Toomey attempted a more direct approach.

"This is interesting," she said while standing opposite Henry at a folding table crammed with children's toys. She picked up a rubber troll doll with flame-orange hair, held it up for him to see, and said, "My granddaughter loves things like this."

He looked up only briefly, nodded, and looked away. Took a step farther down the table.

Rosemary walked apace. "I keep telling her it's junk, but she says it will be valuable someday. What do you think?"

He glanced at the doll. "How much?"

"Four dollars," Rosemary said.

"She might get ten for it now. Hard to predict its future value."

He turned away from the table then, walked to the next table. Rosemary followed.

"What about Beanie Babies?" she asked. "She has at least a hundred of those. She's been saving them since she could walk."

"The market's saturated," he told her. "Only the rare ones have any value."

Again he tried to walk away from her. Again she kept apace. "She has them all, I think," Rosemary said. "Which ones are most valuable?"

He said, "There are price guides online."

"I'll tell her," Rosemary said. "She's thirteen now. Such a beautiful girl. Let me show you a picture of her."

Aaron Henry turned away once more, abruptly this time, and strode toward the street empty-handed. She watched him walking half a block to his car parked along the curb, then returned the troll to its proper table and crossed to the Bronco.

Vicente opened the rear door from inside, then slid over to make room for her. She closed the door and said, "He wouldn't bite."

Hoyle asked, "He showed no interest whatsoever?"

"None I could detect."

Vicente leaned back in his seat and closed his eyes. "The man is voluntarily subjecting himself to Depo-Provera. He doesn't warrant any further attention."

Hoyle said, "Current behavior is not necessarily relevant to past behavior."

"Then why," Vicente asked, "are we wasting another Saturday morning?"

Hoyle turned the key, started the engine. "I've ordered a listening device," he said. "It should arrive within the week."

ELEVEN

D eMarco's decision to retire from the Pennsylvania State Police had not been a sudden one except to his employer and colleagues and everyone else who knew him. None were aware he had been considering retirement ever since last November, when he had watched his friend die, and then had fired a bullet into the heart of a madman. Ever since that day, the fact that he had been unable to save Huston sat like a crushing weight at the top of his spine, even though he knew how cleverly Thomas Huston had choreographed his own death.

Then, eight days before the summer solstice, DeMarco walked into Jayme's office at the barracks, closed the door, and told her, "I wanted you to know before I make it official. I'm hanging it up."

She stared at him for ten long seconds before pushing away from her desk, standing, then crossing to sit on the desk's front edge. Even in uniform, she took his breath away—her long hair pulled back and double-braided like the mane of a sorrel filly; her long, slender, talented legs; the long, delicate fingers; the eighteen pale freckles spread across her cheeks…the scent of her neck, the taste of her skin.

"You're retiring," she said.

He nodded. "That's the plan."

"To do what?"

He shrugged. "Catch up on my sleep, I guess."

She straightened her back, took in a deep breath. Her breasts beneath the starched gray shirt pulled his gaze. They were lightly freckled too.

He remembered their most recent Sunday morning together. "Let there be light," Jayme had said after climbing naked from the bed and sweeping the heavy curtains aside, flooding the room and her own pale body with the pink hues of sunrise. Her fair skin glowed even brighter than the light through the window.

And DeMarco, from the bed, had blinked like a man arising from his grave. "Hallelujah," he had said.

But now, in her office in the final days of spring, her glow seemed more of a glower. "Is this some ploy of yours to get rid of me?"

"I'm not going anywhere," he told her.

"You're damn right," she said. And then, a few seconds later, "You've thought this through?"

"Extensively."

She chewed on the inside of her cheek. "So now what?" she asked.

"You mean us?"

"Of course us."

"Now it gets better, I hope. Now we don't have to hide this."

"And?"

"I'm not sure what that means."

"It's a conjunction. It's not the end of a sentence. More words are required."

"Yabba dabba do?"

She smiled. "Very appropriate, Mr. Flintstone. But I don't speak Neanderthal." She raised her hands in front of her body, fingers cupped inward. "Are you saying you want more of this?"

"Yes, please."

"Good. I like you when you're docile. But how do I know you won't get bored doing nothing, and buy a motorcycle, and go off without me in search of some hairy-chested adventure?"

How do you tell a woman that the only thing you know for certain is that you cannot survive without her? He had not yet learned how to fit such words to his mouth. "Like I said, I'm not going anywhere."

The tiny pools in her eyes glittered with their own light. He waited for her to say more, but when she looked away from him and down at her desk, and a tear splashed onto the varnished wood, he said, "I promise. Nothing will change."

When he moved toward her, she raised a hand and held it motionless in the air, head canted down now and turned to the side, so he retreated to the door as quietly as he could, and he left her alone with his silence.

TWELVE

O n his tenth birthday Ryan DeMarco was walking the tracks that ran alongside the river two miles from his home. The tracks were never used anymore and were rusted, and in some places spikes had been removed and a length of the rail pulled up. He liked to walk along the tracks because he could do so without making much noise and could sometimes steal up close to a turkey or grouse or ring-necked pheasant that would then burst into the air with a loud whumping of wings that always startled and pleased him.

On his birthday he did not flush any birds so he decided to follow a wide, slow feeder stream to see where it might take him. He hadn't walked for very long before the hot sun scents of scrub grass and Indian tobacco and dry summer day began to stink of rotting carcass. He kept walking and the stink grew stronger and he finally had to pinch his nose and breathe with a hand cupped over his mouth. He had never before smelled such a powerful stink of putrefaction, so he wanted to see what was making it. No dead possum or squashed cat along the road ever smelled like that. No pile of rotting garbage or dead rat on the kitchen floor.

This stink had a physical presence too and it felt like grease on his face and like some kind of sour stinging smoke in his eyes. He wondered if what he smelled could be a human body or maybe two of them and he started thinking about all the ways something like that could happen in the woods. A couple of drunks could have passed out and been attacked by a bear or a flock of buzzards so big the drunks died under the weight of the birds. A man might have chased some woman into the woods to do sex and they had ended up killing each other with knives or guns. Maybe somebody hunting deer out of season had tripped and shot himself in the head and accidentally blew his brains out. Something like that could generate a powerful stink. He wasn't sure but suspected that rotting people would somehow smell far worse than roadkill or rotting rats, the only other corpses he had any experience with.

Then after twenty minutes or so the stream made a turn into a kind of shallow cove full of stagnant water, and suddenly there was a swollen brown-and-white cow with its rear end in the filmy water and its white belly looking impossibly huge in the sunlight, and its eyeholes pecked clean and its long, dead tongue hanging out the side of its mouth looking black and obscene. He was surprised that something as common and innocuous as a cow could produce such an overwhelming odor. Every hole and rip in the hide trembled with fat black buzzing flies and silent white maggots. He wondered why there were no buzzards and no signs of dogs or other animals having eaten from the cow. Nobody but the maggots and flies wanted anything to do with it, and the flies were making a sound like a thousand hummingbirds in a field of sweet yellow flowers.

THIRTEEN

Fewer than thirty minutes after DeMarco informed Trooper Jayme Matson of his plan to retire, she stepped into the office of Kyle Bowen, the barrack's station commander, and closed the door behind her. She moved quickly to the chair facing the corner of his desk, sat down, leaned back, crossed her arms, and looked at him.

Fifteen seconds passed before he spoke. "I tried to talk him out of it."

"You tried?" she said.

"It's his decision. What am I supposed to do?"

"You know what state of mind he's in."

"I'm not any happier about this than you are."

"Then talk him out of it somehow."

He blew out a breath. "I was hoping you would. You're the one he cares about most, Jayme."

With that her posture went tight; her hands dropped into her lap.

"You thought we didn't know?" Bowen said. "Everybody knows. The only time he isn't scowling or bitching or muttering to himself is when he's around you."

"It wasn't like we planned it or anything."

"Hey, I'm happy about it. You're good for him. At least now we can all stop pretending we're too stupid to notice the obvious."

She leaned forward and clasped her hands between her knees. "When was the last time you were at his house?"

"Me? Never."

"It's full of ghosts," she said.

"I can imagine."

"Really? Do *you* blame yourself for your baby being killed in a car accident?"

He said nothing.

She sat hunched over, voice breaking. "Do you blame yourself for the end of your marriage? For your wife turning into some kind of sadistic nymphomaniac? For your best friend's family being slaughtered, and for your friend dying in front of your eyes?"

"I know," he said. "I know."

"It's been one trauma after another for what—ever since we've known him? His psyche is *in pieces*, Kyle. This job is the only thing that's holding him together."

"Then why does he want to retire?"

"Because he feels like he can't make a difference anymore. Like everything ends in failure."

"So it's a better solution to just quit?"

"Did you say that to him?" she asked.

He offered a wincing smile. "You know he kind of scares me, right?"

"He loves you like a son."

"Love might be just a bit too strong a word."

"He loves everybody in this place. And he used to love his work. He needs his work. You can't let him retire."

"I don't know what to do, Jayme. He's determined to go."

Both were leaning forward now in the same posture of helplessness, shoulders hunched, hands between their knees.

A few moments later, Bowen cocked his head, then sat upright again. He put his hand on the wireless mouse and woke the computer, then clicked to move from screen to screen. Jayme waited.

Finally he spoke. "He has two hundred and ninety-three sick days saved up."

"Yeah?" she said.

"So what if I tell him the maximum buyback is two hundred days?"

"Is that true?"

"I don't know, I'd have to call HR. The point is, if he believes it's true, maybe we could convince him to go on extended medical leave for a while. Instead of retiring. He stays on the payroll, he doesn't lose his insurance."

"Okay," Jayme said, thinking it through. "So he's sitting at home in his dark house while on medical leave. Drinking too much and surrounded by ghosts and wallowing in a sea of failure and grief. But at least he still has insurance coverage. Yay! Good save, Kyle!"

"You know, you're even starting to sound like him. I'm trying my best here, and all I get is sarcasm."

"Your best sucks."

They sat in silence.

Then she said, "I have at least a couple months of sick leave and vacation days saved up myself."

"Yeah, but…I'm pretty sure I can get a psychiatrist to sign off on him. But where's your PTSD?"

"Don't try to tell me you've never fudged a report."

"Fudged? This would be insurance fraud, Jayme. For the sick leave, anyway."

"You think I wouldn't go to jail for him?"

"And maybe we can get adjoining cells. While my wife takes a job at the Dollar Store."

"He'd do it for you. He'd do anything for any of us."

In frustration Bowen whacked his fist on the edge of the desk, then winced in pain and massaged the fingers with his other hand.

When the pain subsided, he asked, "So be honest with me. What do you really think will happen to him if he retires?"

"He's forty-nine years old, multiply traumatized, and clinically depressed. He self-medicates with excessive coffee during the day, excessive alcohol every night. He doesn't eat right, doesn't exercise, and doesn't get enough sleep. What will he do if left alone with no purpose in life? He'll disappear. One way or another."

Bowen thought for a moment. "So he's a danger to himself?"

"It might be a very slow suicide, but yes, he is gradually killing himself. Right before our eyes."

He thought for a few moments. "Okay. Fudge I will do. Exaggerate I will do. But not fraud."

"Meaning what?"

"Meaning you're still the best medicine for him I can think of. Starting now, I am assigning you to full-time surveillance of Sergeant Ryan DeMarco."

"Get serious," she told him.

"Your job is to bring him back to us healthy and sound. How you do that is up to you. But like I said, he scares me a little. So if this conversation ever gets back to him, I'll deny we ever had it."

"He would hate me if he ever found out I'd agreed to something like that."

"He would hate both of us."

"It's insulting to him. You know that, don't you?"

"Look," Bowen said. "Would you rather we turn him loose on his own?"

She considered her options. "Maybe I should just take a leave of absence. Unpaid."

"How long?"

"However long it takes."

"Can you afford to be without a salary?"

"I live alone," she reminded him. "I've saved my money."

"It's not like he's going to be on another planet or something. Even if you're here at work, he's only what, eight miles away? So you meet for lunch. You spend weekends with him. You check in by phone a couple times a day. I mean really. Nothing personal, but would a guy like him even want a full-time nanny?"

"Now you're insulting *me*," she told him.

"He's not a sociable man, Jayme. You surely know that by now."

She sat with her eyes down, lower lip pouting. Then said, "And what if he decides he wants to take off somewhere?"

"You talk him out of it."

"That's the thing, though. I think it might be the best thing for him. Get him away from that dark little cave full of bad memories."

"The cave is in his head," he told her.

She sat motionless for a few moments, then put her hands on her knees and stood. "This conversation is getting us nowhere."

He shrugged. "Let me know if you come up with something better."

FOURTEEN

Jayme had to wait until Saturday, after dinner, after lovemaking, and halfway through *The Three Burials of Melquiades Estrada* on Cinemax, to hear about DeMarco's conversation with Kyle Bowen the previous Thursday. They lay scrunched pleasantly together under a faux fur blanket on DeMarco's La-Z-Boy, DeMarco in boxers, a T-shirt, and clean white socks, Jayme naked but for her freckles.

"So Kyle thinks I should use up some of my sick leave before officially retiring."

"Really?" she said. "You could do that?"

"Apparently I can sell back two hundred days of sick leave. I have two-hundred ninety-three."

"Wow. That sounds like a no-brainer, doesn't it?"

"I don't know. Medical leave. It kind of feels like cheating."

On the TV screen Tommy Lee Jones as Pete was talking with a blind old man who wanted Pete to shoot him. The old man was alone in a desolate land, with no one to take care of him. He wanted to die but did not want to offend God by committing suicide. Pete did not want to offend God by committing murder.

Only when Pete and his prisoner were riding away with the decaying corpse of Melquiades Estrada did Jayme and DeMarco return to their conversation. Jayme said, "Would it really be cheating, though? I mean…I know you're still sort of struggling with everything that happened. Though I'm assuming that everything went fine with the psychiatrist."

"Super fine. We're bosom buddies now."

"Uh-oh. What did you say to him?"

"It's in my personnel file if you want to read it."

"I would never ask to do that."

His hand, resting under her thigh, squeezed lightly. "He recommended continuing cognitive behavioral therapy and stress reduction training. Both in the form of sex. As frequently as possible."

She chuckled. "Okay. So are you getting enough of that?"

"For now," he said. "I might need some more after the movie's over."

She turned her head against his shoulder, her mouth to his T-shirt. He felt the warmth of her breath going into him.

"Thing is," he told her, "my health insurance would stay active."

"That's a good thing," she said. "So you think you'll do it? Take the medical leave?"

"It's hard for me, you know?"

"In what way?"

"It's like admitting that I...I don't know. Can't handle things."

She was glad he couldn't see her face just then. She tried to keep her breathing steady.

"I don't think it's like that at all," she said. "Medical leave just gives you a little extra *time* to handle things. You can handle anything. You always have."

DeMarco watched the television screen. "Tommy Lee Jones certainly can. Was this movie before or after *No Country for Old Men*?"

"I'm not sure. He looks younger in this one."

"You know he went to Harvard? He was Al Gore's roommate."

"Seriously?"

"He was an English major. And an All-Ivy guard on the football team."

"You're making this up, right?"

"His father started out as a Texas cowboy, ended up working in the oil fields."

"You must admire him to know so much about him."

DeMarco watched the screen a while. Then he said, "I was twenty-four years old when I saw him in *The Fugitive*. That's when I decided I wanted a career in law enforcement."

"Twenty-four," she said. "And before that?"

"Nothing significant. Graduated high school by the skin of my teeth. Then a year and a half of drinking, fighting, working in a steel mill in Youngstown. Then I beat the crap out of a guy for insulting a girl I was with, and that got me arrested. The judge gave me the choice of a year in prison or a hitch in the military."

"Where did you serve?"

"Five months in Panama, one tour in Iraq. The rest of it stateside. Then back home to nothing and nobody. I spent the first day home alone in the movie theater."

"*The Fugitive.*"

"The U.S. Marshals program required a college degree. So did the FBI. That left the state police. I didn't want to end up arresting any of my old acquaintances, so I moved thirty miles east."

"And here you are," she said.

"In the arms of a beautiful woman."

They held each other close and did not speak for a while. Telling her about his past, spontaneously and without coercion, was not something he had expected to do, but now, having done it, he felt both relieved and embarrassed.

Then he asked, as the credits rolled, "You want me to rewind the last half of the movie? I apologize for talking so much."

"You're better than any movie," she told him.

He smiled. "Even *Apocalypse Now?*"

"Except for Marlon Brando's death scene," she said. "That's pretty hard to top."

He pulled her against him, his mouth to her ear, and whispered, in his best Marlon Brando voice, "The horror...the horror..."

FIFTEEN

Sometimes when they were making love she would think about the very first time with DeMarco, and how, when it was transpiring, she had thought, This is just like my very first time when I was fifteen.

The first time with DeMarco had been more than a year earlier, before his final break with his wife, Laraine, before the terrible shock of the death of Thomas Huston and his family. Had she left that night up to DeMarco, the date would have ended with a peck on the cheek in the restaurant's parking lot. Instead, she followed him home not secretly but playfully, never trying to hide her car from his rearview mirror. Then, at his garage, after he pulled inside, she had blocked the door with her car and climbed out. When he came walking up to her looking puzzled, she took his hand and said, I want to see where you live, but was thinking *how you live*, because she wanted to know everything she could about him and was afraid he would never make himself available to her again.

Inside the house he poured a short drink of whiskey for each of them, carried them into the living room and put her glass on the coffee table in front of the sofa, then carried his glass to the La-Z-Boy where he sat down. This is it, he'd said as if there was nothing more to his house or to him. At the restaurant he had been funny and attentive but now inside his house with only a dim kitchen light on behind them he was serious again. So she picked up her glass and sipping from it she did a slow dance over to his chair, then straddled his knees and sat down.

He looked surprised but otherwise did not move or speak, and it was just like her first time when she was barely fifteen and seduced an older man. Back then she had tickled the man's ribs and he had laughed uncomfortably and said, Aren't you a little big to be sitting on me like this? And now she touched her glass to DeMarco's cheek and he said, Maybe this isn't a good idea, Jayme. She knew both times that they wanted her but didn't want to want her, and that only made her want them more. It made her want to make it happen whether they were willing or not. To make it happen even though they were fighting their own desires and she was the object of those desires. No matter how they protested she just kept smiling and touching them until there was no way she would give up or agree to their denials.

That first time, she was only guessing when it came to blowjobs. All she knew about them was from the older girl next door who, before she was killed, showed Jayme on her arm how to give what she called the perfect blowjob. But with DeMarco, Jayme had no doubts that she was doing it right and in both cases it got her into their beds and into their heads and their hearts, where she wanted and needed to be.

After the first time when she was fifteen they had not stopped for the next seven years, meeting whenever and wherever they could and even choosing her college so they could be close enough to get together for weekends. It only stopped because he could not believe it wasn't wrong and he always hated himself for it afterward, he said. With DeMarco the first time wasn't pleasant afterward because he hated himself for past deeds and hated having good feelings for anybody else.

But then a year later he relented for a reason she still could not understand and now they were together. She did not feel bad about any of it and refused to admit any wrongdoing, either the first time or with DeMarco. She knew he was hurting himself by wanting her but the desire must have been stronger than the pain because she was with him always now and his hunger for her was as real and tangible as hers for him. Both hungers came from a place she didn't fully understand and told herself she didn't need to understand. But there was nothing wrong with love and she would never agree that any kind of love could ever be wrong.

SIXTEEN

Sunday morning. DeMarco was at the sink, scrubbing out the skillet in which he had made their huevos DeMarco—scrambled eggs seasoned with adobo, then mixed with chopped poblano pepper, chopped onion, and sweet Italian sausage, topped with melted provolone, salsa verde, and a dash of hot sauce, and served on half a toasted everything bagel. Jayme was seated at the small table near the window, sipping coffee.

"I've made an observation," she said.

He looked over his shoulder. "It's about my butt, isn't it?"

"Your butt and the rest of you," she said. "You're a contradiction."

He smiled. "We're putting our master's in psychology to work, are we?"

"On one hand you're a creature of routine," she told him. "You rely on old habits and routines to get you through six days of every week."

"You being the seventh day?"

"Correct," she said. "Which only shows that you can be adaptive when necessary."

"Or when properly motivated."

"Every Sunday morning you make breakfast for me. And, by all appearances, you enjoy doing so."

"I do enjoy it," he said, and rinsed the skillet under the tap.

"Invariably you start with some established recipe, such as huevos rancheros, and then you…"

"Screw it up?"

"Improvise. You look in the refrigerator, you look in the cupboard, and then, twenty minutes later, huevos DeMarco. Now tell me the truth. Have you ever made that dish before this morning?"

He placed the skillet in the drying rack, dried his hands on a dish towel, then turned to face her. "With precisely those same ingredi-ents? I honestly don't remember."

"Most times you like to present yourself as a stodgy old curmud-geon. But you're not stodgy and you're not old."

He crossed to the table, pulled out a chair, and sat across from her. "I'm still waiting for you to say I'm not a curmudgeon."

"Oh, you can be curmudgeonly. But you're not a curmudgeon."

"I'm still in training," he said with a smile.

"Have you really thought about how you will fill those five and a half days of former routine if you retire? You're not even fifty yet, Ryan. What will you do with all those empty hours? Go sit beside somebody's grave?"

DeMarco flinched. He sat back in his chair. "Don't pull any punches on my account," he said.

"I care about you."

"And I care about you."

"Do you?" she asked.

"Why would you ask such a thing?"

"Does the word *love* frighten you?"

He felt an urge to stand, get up and walk away. But he forced himself to remain sitting. "It's not a word I take lightly."

"Is that why you won't use it with me? Because you don't love me?"

Without thinking, he laid a fist against his chest. Suddenly he was having trouble breathing. "Why does it have to be said? Don't I show how I feel about you?"

"Every Saturday afternoon through Sunday afternoon, yes."

When he offered no response, she said, "You've made me a part of your routine, that's all. My question is, what happens when you have no routine? What happens to us? And more importantly, Ryan, what happens to you?"

It took him a long time to answer. "I'll adapt," he said. "We'll adapt."

She smiled and reached out her hand, laid it atop his. "In other words, my love, you have no clue what you're going to do when you retire. Or what will happen to us. Do you?"

He turned his hand beneath hers, fitted their fingers together. "I'm going to take the medical leave," he told her. "Ninety-three days. After that, what happens happens."

"*Que será, será.*"

"Something like that."

She held his hand a little tighter. "And what if you had a companion for those ninety-three days? How would you feel about that?"

"I have been thinking about getting a dog."

"Asshole," she said as she gave his hand a jerk. "What if I go on leave too? A three-month sabbatical with you? We can travel. We can stay in bed all day. You can create a hundred new egg dishes. And we will have all three of those months to figure out what this relationship of ours is going to be. Because I can tell you what it's not going to be. It's not going to be a Saturday night and Sunday morning–only relationship."

He wanted to do two things then. First, to tap his fist against his chest so as to get more air into his lungs. Second, to slowly reclaim his other hand, stand up, and slink away. He did neither. He said, as evenly as he could, "Why would you do that, Jayme? You have twelve, thirteen years in. A few more and you can be the admiral on that ship of fools."

"So I take a little time off. No big deal."

"I'm not even sure the department will allow it."

"If I can, I will. If I can't, I won't. What are you afraid of?"

He said, "What are you afraid of?"

"Unlike you," she told him, "I'm not afraid to answer that question. What frightens me is you sitting around in this dark little cave of yours all day. Doing what? Brooding over your tragic past? One big pity party for the rest of your life?"

"Jayme," he said.

"Uh-uh. Just stuff it, Ryan. I'm going to take some time off, and—"

"I can't let you—"

"What? You can't *what*? Since when do you make my decisions for me?"

He reclaimed his hand then, but only to hold up both hands in surrender.

SEVENTEEN

That same Sunday morning, six hundred forty-nine miles away in Illinois, Hoyle, behind the wheel of his parked Ford Bronco, watched parishioners filing through the front door of Evansville's huge Resurrection Baptist Church, the women in heels and colorful dresses, the men in crisp suits of every imaginable style and hue.

"By my estimate," he said to his companions, "at least a thousand so far."

"Seating capacity in the sanctuary is fifteen hundred," Vicente said. "Times three services every Sunday." He attempted to speak without moving his lips, remaining very still in the backseat as Rosemary applied glue for his mustache and shaggy beard.

"Times an average contribution of…to be conservative," said Hoyle, "ten dollars per capita."

"At least," Vicente said.

Rosemary told him, "You're going to get this in your mouth if you don't stop talking."

"Amounting to, at a minimum," Hoyle said, "forty-five thousand per week exempt from federal income tax. Most impressive."

Vicente waited until Rosemary had pressed first the mustache, then the muttonchops and matching beard, into place. "Impressive in a despicable way," he said. "The very thought that a man like him should profit from the spiritual desperation of—"

"Did you turn off your phone?" Rosemary interrupted. She had heard his incipient tirade too many times already. She did not disagree with his sentiments regarding Pastor Eli Royce, but neither did she wish to be subjected to them yet again.

Vicente reached into his trousers, took out the cell phone, silenced the ringer and vibration. She handed him his wig, the same dirty gray as the beard and mustache. He set it atop his head, she repositioned it, then handed him a battered brown leather Ben Hogan–style cap. He set it low on his forehead, then removed a pair of sunglasses from his coat pocket and put them on. The orange-tinted polarized lenses, perfect for fishing and driving at night, gave the sunny morning a sharp but jaundiced pallor.

"How do I look?" he asked.

She leaned away, studied the overall effect. Cracked leather golf cap, orange lenses, unkempt hair and beard, vintage brown pin-striped suit, scuffed brown loafers. "Like a half-blind wino," she answered. "I'll be surprised if they let you through the door."

"It's a church," he told her. "They have a moral obligation to serve my spiritual needs."

Hoyle swung a heavy arm over the back of his seat. Between finger and thumb he held a small black box, half an inch wide by an inch long, and wrapped in a thin cellophane film.

"This end holds the microphone," he said.

Vicente leaned closer. "Which end?"

"This one. With the pinhole."

"How am I supposed to see a pinhole?"

Hoyle turned the other side toward him. "This is the USB port. The opposite end has the microphone. Make sure it is not obstructed in any way. Here on the underside is the power switch."

Vicente squinted. "I can't tell if it's on or off."

"It's off. When you move it, it will be on. The device will then record for twenty-five hours. After which, the battery will be depleted."

"What's this wrapped around it?" Vicente said.

"A protective film. Do not remove it until you are ready to install the device. The top side of the device is coated with an adhesive, so do not touch the top side. Peel off the film on top, attach the device, peel away the rest of the protective film, and use your fingernail to switch the device on. Bring the protective film back with you, else you will be leaving your fingerprints behind."

Vicente slipped the device into his coat's side pocket. "Twenty-five hours doesn't seem like a lot."

"He will be here, in this building, until ten or later this evening. During that time, how frequently will a man of our age urinate?"

Vicente said, "I could urinate a thousand times and never once say anything incriminating. Who's he going to be talking to in there—his pecker? Oops, I'm sorry, Rosemary."

She blew out a little puff of air and waved his apology away.

"David," Hoyle said, "while I fully understand, and even share your lack of confidence, I must also concede that we are left with few practicable options. Traditional means of surveillance have gotten us nothing. Other than a new stent in my heart. So if you would rather we forego this tactic, and throw in the towel, so to speak, I will not attempt to argue otherwise."

Vicente watched the last of the morning's parishioners enter the building. Everything he looked at was a sickly yellow.

"For the sake of our seven little sisters," Vicente said, "I shall hazard yet forward. One of my nephews can retrieve the device next week." He popped open the rear door, climbed out, and shuffled toward the church.

Inside, he queued up behind the last five parishioners at the entrance to the sanctuary. Then, when a deacon touched him on the arm and said, "Follow me, brother. I'll find you a seat," Vicente pulled up short and whispered, "Ahh jeez, I gotta go. I'm gonna pee my pants if I don't. Which way is the restroom?"

With a hand on Vicente's elbow, the deacon guided him back into the lobby and turned him to face a corridor. "Public restroom third door on your left."

"Thank you, brother, thank you. I feel a tsunami coming on."

Vicente walked as briskly as he imagined a feeble man could, found the men's restroom and stepped inside. Counted to five, peeked out into the hallway, saw no sign of the deacon, and then continued more briskly down the long hall.

Near the end of the corridor he found the pastor's private office, its door locked. But adjacent to it was a door marked *Private, No Admittance*—exactly where he had been told it would be. He turned the gold-plated handle, and the door swung open.

Inside was a spacious, well-lighted bathroom. Pink-veined marble tile on the floor and walls, a full-length mirror, twin bowl sinks set into a long black marble counter, an electric hand dryer, a shower stall large enough for three people, a Jacuzzi tub, a toilet with a padded seat and backrest, soft instrumental hymns playing through concealed speakers, a long bench seat covered in wine-colored leather, and, atop a marble pedestal, a bronze seraphim with outstretched wings.

Vicente fingered the listening device. Where to place it? Would Royce do most of his talking on the toilet or standing before the mirror?

He was a vainglorious man, this much Vicente knew. So, the mirror. The frame, flush with the wall, offered no concealment. But it ended a foot above the floor. Who was likely to look down there?

Hurriedly, though not as deftly as he would have preferred, Vicente lowered himself to his knees, removed a portion of the protective film, stuck the device to the bottom of the frame, pulled away the rest of the film, and struggled for most of ten seconds to move the power switch to On. Then, just as he was about to shove the protective film into a pocket, the door swung open behind him. A man's full frontal image filled the mirror. The deacon.

Vicente clasped both hands to his chest and leaned forward, the rim of his golf cap touching the glass.

A hand on his shoulder. He looked up in the mirror.

"What are you doing in here?" the deacon asked. "This ain't no public bathroom."

"Praying somebody would find me," Vicente said. "I don't know where I am."

"You're where you don't belong," the deacon said, and took him by the arm. "Stand up here."

He pulled Vicente to his feet, turned him around, and leaned close to stare into his eyes. Behind the orange lenses, Vicente let his eyes go sleepy, half-closed.

"You come here drunk?" the deacon asked.

"I don't even know where here is," Vicente said. "Where am I?"

"You're in the Resurrection Baptist Church."

"Praise God," Vicente said.

"I ain't letting you in the sanctuary like this."

"Put me outside," Vicente suggested. "I'll be all right. The sunshine will show me the way home."

"You remember where you live, old-timer?"

"Of course I do. Three blocks straight, four blocks right."

"You sure you can walk that far?"

"You just get me started in the right direction, young man, and I'll be fine. My head's clearing up already."

The deacon guided him back to the lobby and out the front door.

"Praise God," Vicente said again.

"You sure you're gonna be all right on your own?" the deacon asked. "Maybe you can call somebody to come pick you up."

"God bless you, brother," Vicente said. He gave the deacon a pat on the cheek, then walked away singing "Shall We Gather at the River."

From the Ford Bronco, Hoyle and Rosemary watched Vicente and watched the deacon. Vicente came singing out to the sidewalk. Hoyle lowered his window to listen. "I didn't know he could carry a tune," he said.

Rosemary said, "He sang in a blues band in college."

Hoyle turned to face her, eyes wide.

"It's true," she said.

They watched him continue down the sidewalk, still singing.

When the deacon disappeared back inside the church, Hoyle started the engine and pulled out of the parking lot. He caught up with Vicente, who, shambling along at a snail's pace, was no longer singing, but holding his side and breathing heavily.

When the vehicle stopped beside him, Vicente pulled open the rear door and climbed inside. "Mission accomplished," he said.

Sweating profusely, he pulled off the Ben Hogan, the beard, and the mustache, but not without a few grunts. He scratched at his cheeks and upper lip, the skin flushed and pimply.

"You must be allergic to the glue," Rosemary said.

He kept scratching. "It feels like it's burning my skin off."

To Hoyle she said, "Stop at the first drugstore you see. We'll get a jar of Pond's."

Fifteen minutes later, in a Walmart parking lot, his face white with cold cream, Vicente leaned back against the seat while Rosemary used tissues to gently wipe the cream away.

"I almost lost my cookies back there," Vicente admitted. "It's such a pain being old."

Hoyle said, "Try it morbidly obese."

Rosemary cleaned the cold cream from the corner of Vicente's nose. "Waa waa waa," she said.

EIGHTEEN

The following Saturday, Jayme took DeMarco shopping for a recreational vehicle. "Three months," she had told him. "If we can survive three months together in an RV, then we'll know, right?"

When she talked, she had him. When he could smell her delicate scent, feel her warmth against him, no argument was available. "You smell like morning," he'd told her once, by which he meant like sunrise, always clean and fresh and new. But when alone, the stale dark heaviness returned, and trepidation assailed him. He was too old for her; he could never keep her happy; she would dump him some day and break his heart; he didn't deserve the happiness she offered.

They were sitting alone in the captain seats of a motionless four-year-old Fleetwood Storm when he finally expressed those doubts. The sun glared down on the wide windshield, the leather smelled like Armor All. The steering wheel grew slick under his hands. Twenty yards across the parking lot, a smiling salesman in a blue suit waited in the dealership doorway, pen in hand.

"I just think it's maybe too soon," DeMarco told her. He was thinking about all those Sundays he would miss, those hours of dusk with his son. It felt like bad luck to break that routine. It felt like neglect, an abandonment of duty.

She leaned toward him so quickly that he flinched. But instead of knocking his head into the side window, she seized his chin, yanked him across the console, and put her mouth to his ear. "Get over it, my love," she whispered. "We are buying this mo-bile home."

NINETEEN

Mid-July, southwestern Kentucky

DeMarco had been jogging down Poplar Street—if his slow, lurching, heel-to-toe locomotion could be called jogging—when the pain in his side convinced him to stop. He used his phone to check the time. 8:36 a.m. He had been jogging for only seven minutes. Seven minutes that felt like thirty. Pathetic. Already his pulse was pounding, chest on fire, eyeballs feeling swollen with the summer heat. Jayme was already out of sight, probably a mile and a half ahead of him by now. Miles he had no intention of covering, not unless he keeled over and an ambulance crew scooped him up before he melted into the pavement.

This was all her idea anyway. No more beer, no more whiskey. A glass of red wine or two in the evening. Easy on the fried food. Easier on the fast food. Exercise daily.

Some of the exercise he enjoyed. Some of it made the rest of this ordeal worthwhile. An hour ago, for example. Jayme cool and naked beside him on the RV's allegedly king-size bunk, her morning scent every bit as sweet as her midnight scent, her fingertips light against his back, her small breasts hard and cool against his chest...

Stop it, he told himself. *Not here.* He pulled the front of his jogging pants away from the protrusion, took a quick look from right to left, and was glad to see all but two of the residential yards empty, a man washing his car in the driveway three houses away, a woman kneeling in a flowerbed two houses nearer but with her back to DeMarco.

Good boy, he told his erection. *Down.*

The previous night they had landed in this little town in southwestern Kentucky, maybe twenty miles from the Tennessee border. They had been south of Hattiesburg, Mississippi, three hours from New Orleans, when she got the call, *Grandma's gone.* So they immediately reversed direction, swung northeast to Birmingham, then due north on Interstate 65 up through Tennessee to Grandma's neat little Craftsman home in Aberdeen, Kentucky, population 1400, minus one.

They had already spent thirteen days on the road, with some lovely layovers in Ocean City and Rehoboth Beach. Then down to the Outer Banks, hang gliding in Kitty Hawk—a thrill for Jayme, but twenty minutes of sphincter-squeezing past-life appraisal for DeMarco—and hand-lining for blue crabs off Manteo's Little Bridge. "More my speed," in DeMarco's words, a cold beer in one hand, a dangling chicken neck skewered to a fishing line in the other.

They had listened to an audio book of *Midnight in the Garden of Good and Evil* all the way to Savannah, but found the city charming despite the book's ominous whispers, and opted to prolong their stay in lieu of a long drive down the Florida peninsula to Key West. After Savannah they swung inland because DeMarco was uncomfortable on the beaches in his T-shirts and shorts, and even more uncomfortable when, to please Jayme, he briefly exchanged them for swim trunks.

"You know what we need?" she said somewhere outside of Hinesville, as if she had only then thought of the idea. "We need to start getting some regular exercise. Start eating right. We might be on the road for a long, long time. We need to start taking care of ourselves."

DeMarco groaned as if she had moved up the date of his execution.

"It will be fun," she said.

"Fun for somebody already in good shape. Perfect shape, in fact. As for El Lardo here…"

She reached for his hand atop the steering wheel. "You are by no means fat, babe. You just need to move things around a little."

"Right," he said. "Like completely off my gut and into thin air. Which won't be thin anymore after my contribution to it."

The unpleasant exercise started the very next morning, and every morning thereafter. A quarter-mile slog for him, three or four graceful miles for her. But he was determined to work his way up to a full mile. If only so he could ditch the T-shirt when they made love.

Then came the phone call from Jayme's brother, and late yesterday afternoon they swung off the interstate and onto a two-lane state road leading into Aberdeen. The road ran parallel to a wide, shallow stream with high, forested bluffs on both sides. With the roar of the big highways still echoing in DeMarco's brain, he slowed to forty miles an hour and powered down his window. He took a long, deep breath.

"What do you smell?" Jayme asked.

"Trees," he said. "Water. It sort of reminds me of home."

She said nothing. Smiled. Watched the glint of water out her window.

"See up there?" she said a minute later, and pointed to a large stone building perched near the edge of a bluff. "When I used to visit here, that place was empty, just a stone shell. A bunch of us would sneak up there on summer nights."

"And do what?" he asked.

"Scare ourselves mostly. The place was supposed to be haunted."

DeMarco took a last glance at the bluff. "It doesn't look empty now," he said. "I think I see some lights on. Or just the sun reflecting off the glass."

"Some rich guy bought it a while back. Put millions of dollars in it, Grandma said."

"Just think," DeMarco told her. "If you had played your cards right, you could be living up there in luxury. The queen of all she surveys."

"Now you tell me," she said.

Two miles later they entered Aberdeen. The short driveway and both sides of the street in front of Grandma's house were lined with cars from six states, and the covered porch was overflowing with Matsons and their heirs and in-laws, most of them with a beer or iced drink in hand. DeMarco brought the twenty-eight-foot Fleetwood Storm to a stop directly in front of the house. "Grandma was popular," he said.

"That's just family," Jayme told him, and waved toward the house.

When she popped open the passenger door, a spice-scented heat washed inside. "Oh God," she said. "I've missed that smell."

"One of your relatives?" he asked.

"Hummingbird summersweet. See those bushes with the white bottlebrush flowers? Everybody grows them around here."

DeMarco leaned toward the open door and inhaled. "Sweet as tupelo honey, honey."

"Sweeter. So listen; if you drive about three blocks down, there's a convenience store on the right. There's plenty of space to park out behind the store. Just tell whoever's working there that you're with me, and we're here for Grandma. We'll need a place to park for at least two nights, maybe three."

"Three nights?" he said. "Parked behind a convenience store?"

She gave him a look, then climbed down, turned, and faced him. "And I'll see you back here in ten minutes or so. Right?"

"I should maybe check the fluids and the tire pressure and, you know…"

"You should maybe get back here and meet my family."

"Aye, aye, Captain," he said.

"And try not to be a smartass, okay?"

He smiled. "I have been trying."

"And someday you're going to get the hang of it. See you soon." She closed the door and sprinted up to the porch and into a sea of sweaty hugs. The mourners not embracing Jayme kept squinting in his direction.

"Uffa!" DeMarco muttered, and gave all the strangers a wave.

TWENTY

After guiding the RV into the rear corner of the gravel lot behind Cappy's Meat, Milk & Bait Mart in Aberdeen, Kentucky, DeMarco entered the little store and introduced himself to the clerk.

"You with Jayme?" the man asked. "No shit? You married or what?"

His age was difficult to determine beneath the greasy black hair and week-old scruff of beard. He wore torn jeans and a dingy black T-shirt with the Metallica logo nearly flaked away. DeMarco ball-parked the clerk at fortyish, the T-shirt at no younger than thirty. The man's arms bore crudely drawn tattoos—a skull and crossbones on one forearm, a snake on the other.

"You know her?" DeMarco asked.

"Do I know Jayme Matson? She spent every summer here till she was seventeen or so. So yeah, I know her. I surely do."

DeMarco wished he had access to his baton or flashlight. One sharp whack would knock that smirk off the clerk's lips.

Instead, DeMarco reached for his wallet. "I'm happy to pay what-ever you think is fair."

The man stroked his scruff. "For Jayme," he said, "I'll give you my best discount. Make it twenty…naw, better throw in another ten. I've got some regular customers you're going to piss off for using their parking space."

DeMarco unfolded his wallet, withdrew two twenties. He pressed the bills into the man's hand.

"I take it you'll be sleeping out there?" the clerk asked.

"Possibly," DeMarco said.

The man smiled and stuffed the bills into a pocket. "All right then. I expect I'll be seeing you two later. Say hey to Jayme for me."

DeMarco had turned away, his hand reaching for the door, when the clerk asked, "Jayme still got that smart mouth on her? I never knew what it was turned me on more about her, that sassy mouth or that tight little ass."

DeMarco paused; blood surged into his face, made his eyeballs ache. Then he turned and smiled. "She still has both. Only difference is, she backs them up now with a master's degree in psychology and a combined rating of ninety-six percent in the use of pistol, shotgun, tear gas, and three forms of martial arts."

The clerk blinked. "I heard she went into law enforcement of some kind."

"Only female cadet I've ever seen take down a two-hundred-forty-pound man using nothing but a choke hold. Had him on his knees in three seconds flat."

"I thought them choke holds got banned."

"Not the lateral vascular neck restraint. Shuts off all blood to the brain. Puts your lights out just like that," DeMarco said with a snap of his fingers.

Seeing the look in the clerk's eyes, DeMarco stepped closer, then leaned forward and softened his voice. "Of course, if the guy really deserves it, we can maintain the hold as long as we want. It can get tricky, though, calculating just how many brain cells we want to destroy. Jayme and I both like to err on the long side, you know? Why send him back out onto the street when ten more seconds of pressure will have him slobbering in his soup the rest of his life?"

The clerk's Adam's apple went up and then down as he swallowed hard.

"By the way," DeMarco said, "I didn't get your name."

"Richie," the clerk said, and looked away for a few seconds.

"You get those tats in prison?"

"County jail. I never did hard time. Nothing serious, just…juvenile shit."

"Everything we do is serious, pardner."

Richie nodded and rubbed his arms. "I hear that. I surely do."

TWENTY-ONE

After parking the RV, DeMarco took his time walking back to the house on Jackson Road. He had been hoping for another year or so to prepare himself for meeting Jayme's whole family. Mother, three brothers, so many aunts and uncles and cousins that even she had trouble remembering them all. Just the thought of that suffocating crush of people all giving him the Matson hairy eyeball made his legs heavy.

For over a dozen years he had lived alone. Had been on the verge of turning feral when he met Thomas Huston. The brief friendship had started some alchemical change in him, and then Jayme's embrace had galvanized the change, made it all but irreversible. The hard part was in dropping the trooper stoicism in groups larger than two. He wanted to shed it, truly wanted to be open and lighthearted and full of joie de vivre. But how to become what he could not remember ever being?

So he walked slowly and admired the wide, clean streets of Aberdeen. The neat yards and homes. The vivid greens and pinks and yellows of the manicured landscaping, all of it scented by the flowery heat of full summer. In five minutes he saw more butterflies than in a whole summer in Pennsylvania. And found himself smiling. Feeling lighter somehow. Thinking, if all those butterflies could metamorphose, why couldn't he?

Grandma's front porch loomed through the leaves of a birch tree. Suddenly he was overweight again, sweaty and unshaven from the long drive, his stomach sour from the truck stop food they had resorted to since learning of Grandma's death.

By the time he made the turn up the sidewalk and headed for the porch, fourteen eyes were fixed on him, every conversation silenced.

"How's it goin'?" DeMarco said as he mounted the four wide stairs.

"You get that boat parked?" a grinning man asked. He was tall and slender, his short-cropped hair more orange than red.

DeMarco held out his hand. "Ryan DeMarco. You've got to be Cullen. Brother number three."

"I prefer to think of myself as brother number one," Cullen said, and took DeMarco's hand. "Last born male but best of the litter."

"Best at the bullshit," said another man, slightly less tall and less orange than his brother. DeMarco's hand was barely free before being seized again. "Bryan. And you're the man who's shaggin' our sister."

"Well," DeMarco said, and blushed.

Bryan laughed and slapped DeMarco on the shoulder. "As long as she's happy."

"It's when she's not you'll need to watch your back," Cullen told him.

And then everybody was laughing, and DeMarco shook five more hands, and soon found a cold beer in his left, an awkward smile on his face as he was relentlessly teased.

"Jayme says you used to live in a cave till she came along."

"Is that true, Ryan? And what's with this Italian surname anyway? Ryan is Scottish. What are you, some kind of alien hybrid? If you came here looking for lasagna, you're going to go home hungry."

"Actually," a cousin said, "there is a platter of lasagna in there."

"Made with haggis, of course."

"We make everything with haggis. Even that beer you're drinking."

"You know what haggis is, don't you, Ryan?"

DeMarco said, "I can't say that I do."

"Why, it's sheep pluck. Ground-up lungs, liver, and heart, mixed up with oatmeal and stuffed back into the stomach. Let's go inside and get you some."

The look on DeMarco's face brought all the men nearly to tears with laughter.

Finally Cullen took him by the arm. "Come on; I'll help you find Jayme in that mess inside."

TWENTY-TWO

It was a long afternoon for DeMarco. He was introduced to another twenty people, even the little ones. Was kissed and questioned by Jayme's mother, still a beauty at nearly sixty, and half a dozen aunts, and shook hands with every male. Every natural-born Matson woman looked like Katharine Hepburn's sister, while the Matson men ran from plump to stout to gangly, from bald to brown to chestnut to orange of hair.

Conspicuously absent among the Matson males were Jayme's father, four years deceased, a small-town lawyer dead at sixty-six from congestive heart failure caused by an undiagnosed mitral valve prolapse, and Jayme's oldest brother, Galen, an anesthesiologist living in Seattle. Both men were present only in photographs, both tall and slender and long-limbed, noses a bit sharper than Jayme's, eyes a bit darker, smiles less easy, and faces less open.

"I'm sorry Galen isn't here to meet you," Jayme's mother, Nedra, told DeMarco. "His work, you know. He couldn't leave his work."

"Of course," DeMarco said, but did not fail to notice how her gaze faltered when she offered her son's excuse.

"We don't get to see him much these days," she said.

"It's very demanding," DeMarco offered, "the medical profession."

"It is, it is. Still, it would have been nice. He and Jayme were particularly close. Has she told you that?"

"I got a bit of the family history from her. I know she adores every one of you."

"That's our Jayme," Nedra told him. "But it was Galen she was closest to. He took such good care of her. Protecting her from the other boys, you know. They used to torment her so."

"Bryan and Cullen did?"

"Oh my, it was awful. They teased her mercilessly. Unless Galen was around. He'd put a stop to it. I do wish he could be here to meet you."

"Someday," DeMarco said.

"And what of your family?" Nedra asked. "Jayme tells me you're divorced?"

Reluctant to lie to her, DeMarco answered with a smile.

Around five that evening, neighbors started showing up with hot casserole dishes and steaming foil pans full of even more food to crowd onto overloaded tables and counters. Again and again he was introduced to these strangers, most of whom became a blur in his memory the moment they turned away. A small, white-haired woman with piercing gray eyes was the one exception. She not only stared intently at him throughout the brief introduction, but every time he came into her view. When he had a chance he pointed her out to Jayme. "The one with her back to the doorframe," he said. "She keeps staring at me. Is she like a psycho great-aunt of yours?"

"Close," Jayme said. "But not a relative. And psychic, not psycho. She's a retired librarian. She'll read your tarot cards if you want."

"Can I leave now?" he asked.

"Don't be rude."

"I can't eat another bite or drink another drink of anything. And I'm fairly certain my face is permanently deformed from all the smiling I've been doing."

"It will be an improvement," she told him, and patted his cheek. "Get a cup of coffee and a dessert plate, and keep both of them full. Women can't stand to see a man with an empty plate."

"Can you at least ask old Miss Elvira to quit staring a hole into my forehead?"

"Relax. She's probably just reading your dirty little mind," Jayme said, and left him alone again with a kiss on the cheek.

As DeMarco wearied and sagged over the hours, Jayme grew more energetic. Around eight that evening, she found him asleep in a living room chair. She knelt and awakened him with a whisper in his ear. "Wakey-wakey."

He jerked awake, blinked, looked around. "Sorry," he told her.

"Don't be. You had a long drive, and now this. You've been a fine little soldier."

He blinked again. "Is everybody here except me on an amphetamine diet?"

She squeezed his hand. "Mother's insisting we spend the night here, but all that's left is an air mattress in the basement. Why don't you slip out and head back to the RV? We'll have brunch here tomorrow and then go to the funeral home."

The thought of a night without her brought his eyes open wide.

"Don't worry," she whispered. "I won't be long."

He sat up. "I don't want you walking back in the dark alone."

"Please," she said. "I'll borrow a baseball bat. I can handle myself, you know."

He said, and was surprised to hear himself say it aloud, "But I don't want you to have to."

She leaned close, put her cheek to his. "See how good this has been for us? You're a member of the family already."

"And I didn't even have to eat haggis," he said.

"Yet."

TWENTY-THREE

That night he lay awake a long time, feeling more than thinking about or remembering the incidents of the previous days, some pleasant, some uncomfortable, but most strangely empty, hollow of meaning. What had he done of lasting import over the course of those days?

He traced back through his memory to locate his last meaningful action. He had thought at the time that packing away his uniform and the duties that came with it was a meaningful act, but now saw it had been just the opposite; it had been a walking away from the last remaining definition of who and what he was, a surrender to meaninglessness.

He was a floater now, little more than a corpse drifting along on the current. Physically the corpse retained all indications of life, could smile and eat and make love and... No. Wait. He truly was alive when making love. There was nothing fraudulent about the connection he and Jayme shared. But afterward the emptiness always returned. So how could love alone, adrift in a sea of meaninglessness, have any meaning?

Maybe retiring really had been a mistake, even under the guise of the temporary leave Kyle had talked him into. Kyle was a good man. DeMarco shouldn't have teased him so mercilessly. They were all good troopers, Carmichael and Lipinski and Morgan and all the others, each with their own strengths and shortcomings, but all intending to accomplish some good, to keep the madness of the world in check. All except him. He had thrown in the towel. Burned out. Washed up. Not even fifty yet and already irrelevant.

And here he was, dragging Jayme into oblivion with him. She lay sleeping on her side, one hand beneath her cheek, the other touching his arm. He thought of Thomas Huston and the exit he had chosen. A magnificent exit. DeMarco's single shot into Inman's heart had been little more than a period at the end of Tom's final line. God, how he admired that man. And how he missed his friendship.

All the people he had let himself love were gone. His mother gone. Laraine gone, at least from his life. Ryan Jr. ineluctably gone. Thomas gone.

Duty gone. Purpose gone. Meaning gone.

Only Jayme remained. A vibrant, intelligent, ambitious, and relevant woman, now reduced to this, companion to a floater.

He moved an arm across his chest, let his fingertips touch hers. Closed his eyes and thought, *Please, God. Tell me what to do. Don't let me ruin her life too.*

TWENTY-FOUR

DeMarco was awakened by the cackle of a blue jay. Or maybe it was by Jayme's hand between his legs, a light, tickling touch that sent an electrical charge into his scrotum, up through his spine, and into his wearied brain, where it produced a static discharge that shocked him awake with a sound remarkably similar to a blue jay's cackle. Whatever the source of the sound, he opened his bloodshot eyes in a tight squint. Dim pink light stung his retinas. "I hate you," he mumbled.

"You disgust me," she said softly, then brushed her lips slowly down over his chest and stomach and down the length of his lengthening penis. When she took him into her mouth, he felt himself falling, so he put his hands in her thick hair and held on until she lifted away and sat atop him, her back to his chest, right leg bent at the knee, left foot flat against the floor as she rose and fell atop him in languorous, gentle waves of movement.

Later she lay against him chest to chest, heels hooked under his ankles, her mouth to his neck. He waited until their breathing slowed. "That was exhausting and wonderful," he told her. "I'm going back to sleep now. If I'm not awake by noon tomorrow, do that to me again."

She chuckled. "I'm headed for the shower, babe. And then it's your turn. And then we'll go run and get sweaty. And then we'll shower again and go to Grandma's for brunch, and then we'll go to the funeral home. Then you can take a nap."

"There's not enough water for four showers," he said.

"Then we get up and run."

"Nooooo," he said.

She rolled over and sat up. "Come on, it's good karma. A man's body is his temple."

"Your body is my temple."

"Nice. And if you ever want to worship there again, get your sweet butt in gear."

TWENTY-FIVE

Only seven minutes into his first sluggardly jog in Aberdeen, he gave up the pretense and slowed to a trudge. Jayme was probably at the far end of town by now, maybe cooling her feet in Lake Barkley. How could she run so lithely, so gazelle-like, after such a grueling day and unrefreshing night? Were it not for the sexy wake-up call, he might still be dead to the world. He had to admit there were perks to not living in solitude. But there was also a price to be paid. He intended to keep paying it but worried that he was quickly running out of currency.

It was not yet 8:00 a.m., and the sunlight off the pavement stung like vinegar in his eyes. So did the blue of the sky. The thousands of blooming flowers punctuating every lawn seemed to explode upon his retinas in silent little bombs of color. Only the still-dewy grasses did not irritate his eyes. So as he walked, he kept his gaze just to the left of his feet, just beyond the curb.

It was the anomalous length of the grass after all those manicured lawns that caused him to look up. An empty lot, long untended. And centered in the lot, standing nearly motionless behind the low, weedy mound of a filled-in foundation, was another anomaly: a man in a black suit. A very round man, who was looking his way.

DeMarco, out of embarrassment, smiled and nodded. Both gestures hurt. And that was when the day turned strange for DeMarco, took on a kind of dreamlike unreality though everything remained visibly the same. A minute ago the day had been utterly real and concrete for DeMarco, the unpleasantness of jogging, the steamy, heavy air. But now, with the appearance of a rather odd-looking man in an empty lot, DeMarco felt as if the world had made a tilt of some kind and shifted off balance.

The man responded to DeMarco's smile with the one response DeMarco did not welcome. Speech. "Shameful," he called out.

DeMarco tried to stand a little straighter. That hurt too. "Pardon me?"

"What happened here. It's shameful. You agree?"

Damn, DeMarco told himself. Now you've gone and got yourself into a conversation.

He weighed his options: begin jogging again, or explain later to Jayme that he had just hit his stride when a stranger interrupted his run.

He lifted one foot and then the other over the curb. It would be easier to trudge thirty feet than to project his voice the same distance. He crossed to the man.

"Sorry," he said, and held out his hand. "Ryan DeMarco. This is only my second day in town. So I have no idea what happened here."

"Name's Hoyle," the man said, but kept his hands at his side.

After an awkward few seconds, DeMarco lowered his hand too. "So what shameful thing happened here?"

"Used to be the First Baptist Church," Hoyle said. His throaty voice moved with a distinctly southern lilt, but his articulation was precise, educated, a halting delivery that suggested an agile mind racing far ahead of every word.

"Why is it gone?"

"Would you recognize the name Eli Royce?"

"Doesn't ring a bell," DeMarco said.

"He was the pastor here till they tore it down. Up in Evansville now. Calls himself the voice of the people. Once a charlatan, always a charlatan."

There was something broken and surreal about the conversation. DeMarco wondered if maybe he was still dreaming. "So this Royce fella… Not a real pastor?"

"A degree in divinity does not make one a man of God. You should know that, sir."

"I should?"

"You are Miss Matson's beau, are you not? Former colleagues from the Keystone State?"

DeMarco's eyes narrowed even more. "How would you know that?"

"Small-town grapevine. Faster than ever thanks to email."

Was that a smile Hoyle gave him? Hard to tell beneath those heavy jowls. DeMarco had a peculiar feeling the man had been lying in wait for him. But how could he have known DeMarco's jogging time and route?

"Okay," DeMarco said. "So what does Eli Royce have to do with the church being gone?"

"That is precisely what I have been standing here pondering."

DeMarco blinked and blew out a sour breath. "I'm sorry, Mr. Hoyle. But I had a rather difficult day yesterday, and no coffee yet this morning, and I'm having a heck of a time understanding where this conversation is headed."

"Seven young females reduced to bone," Hoyle said. His eyes remained fixed on DeMarco's. "Seven skeletons in a four-by-fourteen-by-ten-foot space between walls. Each one cocooned in clear plastic sheeting. The kind painters use to cover a floor. Each cocoon sealed with silver duct tape."

"And Eli Royce was responsible for this?"

"No responsibility has yet been assigned."

"But you think it was him?"

"My thoughts are my own business, Sergeant."

"Then why am I standing here talking to you, sir?"

A few moments passed.

"Just Ryan," DeMarco said. "I'm on leave from the department. But you already know that, don't you?"

Now Hoyle averted his gaze to stare at the weedy mound. "It was 2014 they were discovered," he said. "Mid-July. Hot as Hades. Just like now."

"It is hot. I'll give you that."

"Are you familiar with the homilies of Mr. Samuel Clemens?"

"I've read a couple of his books."

"Everybody complains about the weather, he said. But nobody ever does anything about it."

Hoyle followed this remark with another attempt at a smile. Then followed it, jarringly, with, "If not for the termites, the poor girls might never have been found. Each skeleton meticulously flensed, probably through cold water maceration."

"Jesus," DeMarco said. "That will remove everything? Strip the bones clean?"

"Ninety-eight percent. The rest can be easily picked away. A short bath in a Drano solution is equally effective."

DeMarco winced.

"Or they might have been buried for a while. Let the maggots do the work."

DeMarco tried to push the image away by staring at the grass. "All of similar age?" he asked.

"Fifteen to nineteen."

DeMarco stood there thinking. Too few pieces. How to make them fit?

He asked, "Have any of them been identified? Any DNA matches?"

"Each and every one."

"And the dates of their disappearance?"

"1998 through 2004."

"Seven years, seven bodies. One per year?"

"Interesting, is it not?"

"So whoever did this," DeMarco said, "he stopped after '04. Maybe he died."

"Or found a different place to hide the bodies."

A shiver ran up DeMarco's spine. "All local girls?" he asked.

"None within two hundred miles of here."

"Good Lord," DeMarco said. "And you think this Eli Royce is involved?"

Hoyle lifted his gaze to the horizon then, out across the rooftops. "I frequently doubt my personal assumptions unless verifiable by fact. I do dislike the man intensely. The opinion of an acquaintance of mine, however, a lawyer, is even more pertinacious."

"May I ask why?"

"Royce is an agitator. Uses his pulpit to incite racial discord. From which he profits handsomely."

"A white supremacist preacher?"

"Anti-white supremacist."

DeMarco nodded. He knew the type. "But you, unlike your lawyer friend, you have other suspicions?"

Again Hoyle faced him. "The world is full of suspicious individuals, sir."

"That it is. What is it you do for a living, Mr. Hoyle?"

"For a living? I breathe, I eat, I defecate, I keep myself well hydrated. In this heat, the last is a necessity. You should carry water when you exercise."

"I'll remember that. In the meantime—"

"If, on the other hand, you mean to inquire how I provide for myself financially, I was the coroner of Graves County for a number of years."

"Graves County? Really?"

"It is droll, isn't it? The coroner of Graves."

"Are we in Graves County now?"

"We are not. Though it is contiguous to our east."

"And you are now retired from that profession?"

Hoyle's half smile spread to three-quarters. "Your skills as an interrogator are much in evidence, Sergeant."

"My apologies. Old habits die hard."

Hoyle waved the apology aside. "What you are wondering is if my interest in this case is merely that of an aesthete."

"I'm afraid I'm not certain of the definition of that word."

"If I find a certain art and beauty in the details of this heinous crime."

"That's not what I'm suggesting."

"That's unfortunate, because you would be correct. To a certain extent. One has to admire, even respect, a seemingly perfect execution in any endeavor. Am I right?"

"Even when it comes to killing girls? I'm sorry, but I find no beauty or art in that."

"The difference in our chosen professions, perhaps. Yours is to apprehend in one meaning of the word, mine is to apprehend in quite another."

"All right," DeMarco said. "I suppose I can see your point."

"On the other hand, Sergeant, my intention is never to apprehend in merely one meaning of anything."

DeMarco's squint tightened. "You keep setting me up for the punch line, don't you? Are you working for Jayme's family, by any chance? Trying to determine if I'm worthy of her?"

"I trust that Miss Matson will be the best judge of that."

"Then perhaps you wouldn't mind explaining why you drew me into this conversation."

"Are you a believer, Sergeant?"

"Sir?"

"You employed the name of Jesus to express disdain, I believe. Earlier in this conversation, into which you feel so involuntarily drawn. Do you subscribe to the mythos?"

"By which you mean…Christianity?"

"It's all lies and distortion, you know. The true Jesus, Yeshua in Hebrew, was an Essene. A gnostic."

"I'm a little fuzzy on that denomination."

It was then a bright-yellow blur glided between the men, downward past DeMarco, an inch from his nose. He jerked back suddenly, and in the next instant recognized the creature now fluttering past Hoyle's broad midsection. A butterfly.

Hoyle had not flinched, had not lifted his eyes off DeMarco's. "Is this conversation making you tense, sir?"

"You might say that."

"Then here is the interesting part," Hoyle said. "Not a single Caucasian girl in the bunch. African American one and all. Light-skinned. What do you make of that?"

DeMarco felt like he was getting whiplash from Hoyle's sudden changes of direction. "Well," he said, "either a fetish for girls of color…"

"Or?" Hoyle asked.

"A hatred of them."

Hoyle smiled, a real smile this time. And then he looked away, following the butterfly as it floated across the quiet street to land on a summersweet bush. "Cloudless sulphur," he said. "*Phoebis sennae.* Female."

He pulled a white handkerchief from his pocket, dabbed at his face and scalp. "Butterflies and hummingbirds," he said. "Every summer we suffer the same infestation."

And then he did, to DeMarco's eyes, the oddest thing. Extending both short, heavy arms, one hand still holding by finger and thumb the white handkerchief, Hoyle moved his arms in a slow and sensuous wave, as if hoping, against all odds, to lift himself, too, aloft. And in fact, he did begin moving, walking leisurely toward the street, up and over the weedy mound, his arms still waving.

"I suggest you begin your deindoctrination with *The Gospel of Thomas*," Hoyle called without turning his head. "In the original Coptic, if possible."

DeMarco's head was spinning. He took a few steps in pursuit of the fat man, but then paused, sat down atop the mound, and waited there for Jayme's return.

TWENTY-SIX

DeMarco lay on his back atop the low mound, hands crossed over his stomach. He had thought briefly about getting up and jogging so as to meet Jayme on her return, but doubted he would get far, and she would scold him nonetheless for his lack of progress. So he went horizontal instead and sent his gaze into the depthless blue. The sun on his motionless face and hands felt kinder than it did bearing down on the top of his skull when his brain was bouncing up and down.

There had been a time when he used to love running, as fast and far as he could. As a boy he would race the school bus home the last quarter mile from the bus stop, and often he would keep running long after passing his home, especially if his father's profile could be spotted through a window. If it was summer and his father was nowhere to be seen, he might continue running until he came to the wild tiger lilies that grew up through the guardrail, and he would pick two or three newly budded and take them home to his mother, who would put them in a jelly glass or Mason jar filled with water and set them on the windowsill above the sink.

At sixteen he was still fleet of foot, and by then had gotten a name for himself as a street fighter thanks to his quick hands and footwork. His knuckles were still scarred from some of those fights.

In the army he could do five miles with a full pack and still be the first man to the showers. But he had been forty pounds lighter then. And unburdened by the elephantine weight of a conscience that rendered all unnecessary movement futile.

These days all the important movement took place inside his head. And to keep that movement from devolving now into a dark downward spiral, he thought about the girls. Seven unfortunate girls of color, all from miles and hours away, all ending up here in quiet little Aberdeen with the butterflies and hummingbirds.

He wondered if Hoyle had been aware of the metaphor he had created by describing the girls as *cocooned* in plastic sheeting. Hoyle, as strange as he was, did not strike DeMarco as a man who chose his words lightly.

And it made DeMarco sad to think of those girls as unformed butterflies. They had never been given their wings, had never tested the sky. And now every time DeMarco saw a butterfly, he would think of those girls.

He had failed to inquire as to the cause of death. Hoyle's sudden shifts of topic had unfocused his concentration. But now everything was quiet and still. He did some of his best thinking on his back.

Precise identification of the cause of death is problematic with skeletal remains, he reminded himself. Approximate stature and sex can be identified with greater probability than ancestry, which is suggested by skull morphology. Sexual dimorphism is most prominent in the skull and pelvic bones. Approximate age can be determined from bone development.

Using known age, stature, and sex, investigators would have compared that data to missing persons reports, then narrowed down possible matches to a fairly long short list. Dental records, X-rays, and other nutritional or skeletal anomalies would have resulted in a presumptive identification. Finally, DNA from the bones would have been matched with familial DNA, leading, eventually, to positive identifications.

It must have been a painstaking process, DeMarco thought. Painful for everyone involved. It was painful for him to contemplate.

And what about cause of death? When working only with bone, he told himself, perimortem trauma by projectile, sharp force, or blunt force are easiest to identify. Strangulation can be identified too by damage done to the tiny hyoid bone in the neck. But not all cases of strangulation break the bone. Or a choke hold could have been used. Or a garrote. The girls would have been unconscious in fifteen seconds, dead a few minutes later.

And now DeMarco winced remembering how he had teased Richie at the convenience store. Teased and threatened. It hadn't been a very mature thing to do. He started replaying the incident in his head, thinking of better ways he might have handled that flare-up of jealousy, but then reminded himself that this was precisely the kind of thinking he needed to avoid, this constant analysis and rescripting, as if the past could somehow be rewritten.

Cause of death, he told himself. How else might the girls have died?

There is poisoning, drug overdose, smothering…a thousand and one variations on the theme. Too many ways to die. Sometimes the bones talk, and sometimes they hoard their secrets.

And what about the killer? How much could be known?

In all likelihood, a male. Someone who knew about the false wall in the church. And about how to access it. So either a local or a regular visitor, or, as Hoyle had implied, the pastor. Or maybe the false wall was well-known throughout the community. That would be easy enough to check out.

But the girls themselves were not local. The investigation team would have created a map. Maybe Hoyle had seen it.

One a year for seven years. Very odd. A rigidly disciplined sexual predator? Or were there more bodies in other places?

He wished he had questioned Hoyle more. The man hadn't been easy to talk to. DeMarco thought maybe he could visit the local police department, request a copy of the forensics report and any additional information. But even if they allowed him access…

Then what? he asked himself. What makes you think you can do what dozens of others have already failed to do? And don't forget, you're on vacation. You're just traveling through, final destination unknown.

And then her voice. "Hey!"

He turned his head to the side. Jayme was jogging in place out on the street, skin glistening. "Is that all the farther you got?" she called.

He rolled onto his side, rose onto hands and knees, pushed himself up. God, what a blob, he thought. He walked out to the street, feeling fatter than ever.

Jayme kept jogging in place. "Seriously?" she said.

He offered a sheepish smile, but received no smile in return. Then he too started jogging in place. "Up here?" he told her, and pointed at his head. "I've already run a marathon."

"Right," she answered. "So now I'm going to use all the hot water."

She turned away and sprinted, and he followed at a ponderous jog, punishment accepted.

TWENTY-SEVEN

L ate for brunch, DeMarco and Jayme had little time for conversation. She, as promised, had used up most of the hot water by the time he came shuffling inside. His body was covered with goose bumps when he stepped out of the shower stall after only five minutes of frantic scrubbing.

"How was it?" Jayme asked from behind the table, which she had claimed for her makeup and mirror.

"Refreshing," he said as he toweled off before the bathroom mirror. "Like a spritz from a garden hose in a broom closet."

She chuckled. "Think of it as behavioral therapy."

He spread a handful of shaving cream over his face. "I was waylaid," he told her.

"You were what?"

"Waylaid. By a man named Hoyle. You know him?"

"Hoyle?" She paused to apply her eyeliner. Then, "Doesn't ring a bell."

"Retired coroner. Graves County."

"Still no bell. What did he want?"

"Yesterday at your grandmother's house," DeMarco said, talking between strokes of the razor. "Did you mention to anybody where and when we'd be jogging this morning?"

"Somebody suggested the route, I don't remember who. I was going to take you to the high school track. But this was better, don't you think? The last mile especially. Fields and trees all the way. Lots of shade. Too bad you missed it."

DeMarco grumbled to himself and finished shaving.

A few minutes later, with one towel wrapped around his waist and another draped over his shoulder, concealing as much of his chest as possible, he hurried past Jayme and into the bedroom.

She asked, "So who's this Hoyle person you mentioned?"

He stuck his head out of the bedroom. "Do I have time to iron a shirt and slacks?"

"Lickety-split," she said. "Just do the front of the shirt. Nobody will see the rest."

"I didn't bring a suit," he told her.

"A sport coat?"

"Sorry. I wasn't counting on a funeral."

"A white shirt at least?"

"Yellow oxford?"

She stared at herself in the mirror, asking herself, he assumed, *What was I thinking?* Then she said, "Did you at least bring a tie?"

"I won't roll up the sleeves," he told her.

On their walk to Grandma's house he filled her in on the conversation with Hoyle. Jayme admitted to having heard about the discovery at the church a few years earlier. Some of the residents had wanted the church burned down, the scandal and shame obliterated by fire, but the town council could not come to an agreement. A few days later an unknown individual or individuals torched the church. The volunteer fire company, housed only minutes away, arrived too late to save the building.

"Grandma was a Methodist," Jayme said, "so I didn't know Pastor Royce. But some of the kids I hung around with summers did. And there were stories about him."

"Such as?"

"He liked money, and he liked women. Of all ages. I don't recall ever hearing that he went after children. Or that he limited himself to any one race."

"Was he investigated?"

"I'm sure he must have been."

"The strange thing about Hoyle," DeMarco said, "is that he knew both of us. You, I understand. But me? He even knew my rank back home. You didn't see him when you ran past that empty lot?"

She shook her head no. "But you know who I did see? Rosemary Toomey. The librarian."

"The scary one?"

"She lives a few…let me think…five houses *before* the empty lot. She was watering her flower bed when I went by. Waved and called out good morning to me."

"And then made a call to Hoyle sitting in his air-conditioned car somewhere down by the lot. What do you want to bet?"

"The question is, why? Why would a librarian and a coroner conspire to engage you in a conversation? Are you sure you weren't suffering from heatstroke?"

"It didn't feel like a conversation as much as a… I don't know. A test of some kind."

DeMarco walked a few paces in silence. Then he asked, "Am I going to look out of place at the funeral? Without a coat and tie?"

"We do take our funerals seriously down here," she said.

"Great. DeMarco the uncouth Yankee."

She grinned. "It's bad enough you're shagging a former Peach Festival princess. But showing up at a funeral in khakis and loafers and no tie? I bet you didn't know Grandma was a Daughter of the American Revolution, did you?"

He said, "I should have worn my American flag bandanna."

"Definitely uncouth," she told him, and took his hand.

He loved holding her hand. He wished he could hold both of them at the same time and still walk in a straight line. He said, "I think I might have lost a pound or two from all this sweating I've been doing."

"Like that's going to help," she said.

TWENTY-EIGHT

A t brunch with the Matsons, he limited himself to a small helping of scrambled eggs, a bowl of fresh fruit, and three cups of coffee. He asked Bryan about the false wall in the church, which caused Bryan to ask everyone within ten feet if they, unlike him, had had any knowledge, prior to the termite infestation, of the wall's existence. Nobody did. Nor was Hoyle known to any of them, but after hearing Bryan's repetition of DeMarco's description—"sort of like Humpty Dumpty in a faded black suit"—two of the cousins who still lived in Aberdeen thought they might have seen such an individual once or twice, though they could not say where. All admitted that the murder of the seven girls was a heinous act that had tarnished the little town's good name.

"You probably don't know we got us a pair of registered sex offenders living within twenty miles of here," Cousin William told him.

"Seriously?" Jayme said.

"One of them's up north a bit. Lives in a double-wide on forty-some acres with a woman and his brother. Some kind of antigovernment group. I forget what they call themselves."

Another cousin asked, "Is that the bunch had a fifteen-year-old living with them?"

"She was fourteen," Cousin William said. "Only one of them took the fall for it. Served six months or something like that. But from what I hear, they were all in on it. The girl too. Share and share alike, you know what I mean?"

"What happened to the minor?" Jayme asked.

"Hard to say. This went on when? Four, five years ago?"

DeMarco asked, "And you say there's another one in the area too?"

"Sex offender?" said Cousin William. "He grew up about eight miles out on Lakeview Road."

"That's where we went jogging today!" Jayme said. Then, with a wink to DeMarco, "I did, anyway."

"Well," said Cousin William, "if you went far enough you would have seen a run-down old dairy farm. Except there's nothing there anymore but for a dozen or so dogs and cats and free-range chickens, plus the two old folks. I don't know what became of their pedophile son."

"All three of them collecting government checks, no doubt," Cousin William's wife said.

"No doubt, darlin'. No doubt."

The chatter continued another ten minutes or so, with DeMarco listening closely, noting not only the information dispensed, but also the subtle variations in speech patterns and enunciation. Those of the clan who had moved away from Aberdeen, including all of Jayme's immediate family, and those older individuals who had not, the senior citizen aunts and uncles, spoke with either no discernible accent or with a more genteel fluidity to their words, almost songlike, not as loud or coarse as the under-fifty locals. Until that moment he had thought of Aberdeen as a kind of Brigadoon, a magical little town caught in a time warp. But it had its ugliness too, he realized. A contemporary darkness encroaching from all directions.

Bryan held up his cell phone and pointed at the screen. "It's almost twelve thirty, folks," he announced. "Better wrap things up here. It's time to go say goodbye to Grandma."

TWENTY-NINE

After the funeral, the family queued up for one last look at Grandma before the casket was closed. DeMarco, waiting in line with Jayme, looked back to see the librarian seated alone in the fourth row of folding chairs, her piercing eyes fixed on him. When he met her gaze, she gave him a little nod.

He leaned down and whispered in Jayme's ear. "Okay if I step away for a minute?"

"Too much coffee?" she said.

"I'll be right back."

So as not to encourage conversations from those in line behind him, DeMarco kept his gaze at belly-button level as he crossed toward the librarian. He passed numerous well-dressed women in shades of gray, black, and navy blue, and just as many similarly colored suit coats and slacks. Not even the teenagers were dressed in khakis. He made a mental note to buy a black blazer at the next mall they passed. He hoped Jayme would agree to leave Aberdeen by the day after tomorrow at the latest. In the meantime, his curiosity nagged at him.

"Ms. Toomey," he said from the end of the row. "Do you mind if I sit for a moment?"

"Mrs.," she said. "Please do." She turned slightly in her chair so as to face him more directly.

He said, "I had an interesting chat with a Mr. Hoyle this morning."

"Dr. Hoyle," she said.

"Oh. So he's actually a medical examiner?"

"Retired," she said.

"Yes, that's what he told me. What interests me, however—"

"Yes," she said.

"Yes?"

"Yes, he was waiting for you. I helped to arrange it."

"I see. So the only other question I—"

"Why," she said.

"Exactly. Why that conversation? Why me? Why there?"

"We had hoped you would feel the horrible weight of the crime. They spent several years imprisoned there, you know. Stacked up like firewood. All that misery percolating into the ground. And you did feel it, didn't you?"

"I always feel the victims' misery," he said.

"I know," she answered.

Her gaze was so unsettling, those blue-gray, unblinking eyes, that he looked away momentarily. When he was a boy, one of the neighbors had kept a dog chained up close to their trailer, a German shepherd–husky mix they called a police dog. The dog never barked, never growled, but always stood alert whenever young Ryan was outside. Always pulled its chain taut and stood leaning forward, its blue-gray eyes fixed on the boy. Ryan had never known whether the dog wanted to play with him or tear him apart, and he had always been too afraid to venture close enough to find out. The librarian's gaze chilled DeMarco with the same ambiguity.

Jayme, he now saw, only two mourners from the casket, was motioning for him to return.

The librarian put her hand on his knee, startling him. "You have obligations today," she said. "And tonight. Tomorrow will be fine. There's a little place on the road to the reservoir. Zia's Trattoria."

"Excuse me?" he said. "What reservoir?"

She stood. "One thirty will be fine. After the lunch rush."

Jayme was motioning more frantically now, and she wasn't smiling. The librarian made her way between the empty chairs, out the other end, and toward the door.

DeMarco stood and walked briskly to stand beside Jayme as she leaned over the casket.

"This is him, Grandma," she said softly. "Do what you can for him, okay? God knows he needs the help."

DeMarco looked down on Grandma's wrinkled face. As far as he could remember, he had met only his maternal grandmother when he was a boy, and then only twice. He had no memory of his other grandmother. Yet the face of Jayme's grandmother looked familiar to him, as if this was how a grandmother should look—peaceful, composed, serene, and calming.

He turned to Jayme then. Her cheeks were streaked with tears. He slipped an arm around her shoulders, and looked at Grandma a final time, and this time saw the striking resemblance between the young woman and the old, the fine angular features, the high cheekbones, and he knew in an instant they had the same green eyes, that Grandma's hair too had once been strawberry blond verging on honey brown, that her fingers had once been long and thin and elegant too, her tongue sharp, her heart huge with love. And all he could think to tell either of them, and both, was "I'm sorry."

THIRTY

If Ryan happened to be in the same room when his father started laying into her...if his father started out asking some question that could trick you into thinking he was teasing, his voice sounding almost playful with his Hey, this piece of crap refrigerator must've drank my last beer!...if Ryan was watching *Batman* or maybe *Get Smart* and wasn't really paying any attention to the arguing that had become like the rumble of big trucks out on the four-lane...and if his father took up a position between him and his bedroom so that Ryan, now sensing the danger, would have to risk squeezing past his father or else heading for the door...in which case his father would probably take a couple long strides and grab him by the scruff of his neck and jerk him off his feet...if this happened as it had many times before, there would come a moment when Ryan would feel the anger turning toward him instead, his mother cowed and whimpering...and then his father would hunker down with his red, sweaty face close to Ryan's and scream so loud Ryan would think his eardrums would burst, and then it was too late to go anywhere safe and his father's spit would be hitting him in the face with every word and curse, and then it was only a matter of standing there and counting, one one thousand, two one thousand, three one thousand, four one thousand...until his father's big, hairy, dirty-fingernailed hand would *bam* across his face or *boom* against his chest or worst of all would grab a handful of Ryan's hair and drag him dancing on his toes from one end of the room to the other, shaking him like the mewling puppy Ryan had brought home one time and tried unsuccessfully to hide from his father.

THIRTY-ONE

A fter the somber procession to the cemetery, with Jayme and DeMarco riding in the backseat of Bryan's Altima, and after the solemn thirty minutes at the gravesite, then came a subdued two hours back at Grandma's house. The brunch table was cleared, the dishes washed, neighbors arrived with more food, wine was opened, and stories shared.

Sometime after five Jayme came to the sofa and squeezed in between Cullen and DeMarco. She leaned up against DeMarco and closed her eyes. "Carry me home," she told him. "I'm exhausted."

Cullen said, "You guys need to stay here tonight with the rest of us."

"I need a bed," Jayme told him, "not an air mattress."

"We'll give you our bed tonight."

She pulled away from DeMarco, leaned close to Cullen, and kissed his cheek. "I need to be alone with Van Morrison and my trooper man," she told him.

Cullen leaned forward to look at DeMarco. "It takes two of you to make my sister happy?"

"At least," DeMarco answered. "Sometimes we need Sting too."

Cullen nodded. "An Englishman, an Irishman, and an Italian with a Scottish name. No wonder you need a bigger bed."

THIRTY-TWO

They undressed side by side at the foot of the RV's bed, with only a small reading light illuminating them. He stepped out of his loafers, placed them in the narrow closet, then removed his belt, slid his slacks off and folded them at the crease and hung them with his other clothes. She watched as he faced the bed again and unbuttoned his shirt, finger and thumb moving unhurriedly down his chest, then the right cuff, then the left. He moved back to the closet, turned away from her, and removed his shirt, which he placed in the laundry hamper. Half shielding himself behind the closet door, he leaned close to the shelves to pick out a T-shirt.

But she came up behind him then and laid her hands around his belly and pressed her breasts to his back. "Don't wear one tonight," she said.

"But you know I'm—"

"Shhh," she told him, and turned him toward the bed, her body pressed to his.

"Then let me turn out the light," he said, and she said softly, "Just please shut up."

And at the bed she moved to his front and sat down and removed her panties quickly and placed her legs outside of his. She drew his boxers down over his thighs and knees and ankles and he stepped out of them and she pulled him close and took him into her mouth, her hands gripping his buttocks. He put his hands on her shoulders and ran his fingers down over her spine as far as he could reach and back up again, and she moaned and arched her back with pleasure like a cat being stroked, and there was a little catch in her breath and then another and he realized she was crying.

He pulled away and knelt and lifted her face to his, but before he could speak she pulled him forward and atop her and said, "Don't say anything, please. I want you inside me."

"But wait," he whispered, and she said, "Please. Just please come inside me. Just please."

She pulled at him hungrily with legs and hands until he was standing again with her ankles crossed behind him against the base of his spine. He wanted to be gentle because now she was letting the emotion of the day roll out of her and he only wanted to give her what she needed, but she said, "Don't wait for me, baby, please. I want you to come."

"You first," he said, but she said, "No, don't wait. I need to feel you come in me."

It was not how they usually made love but it was what she wanted. She pushed herself hard against him and increased the pace for him to follow, and soon it was building fast and hard for both of them, and when his breath quickened hers did too, and then he was falling against her, their bodies tight, all muscles tensed, her fingernails and teeth sharp against his skin.

They held each other until the trembling passed. Then she sniffed and swallowed and turned her mouth to his cheek. "I bit you too hard," she whispered.

"No you didn't," he said.

Another minute passed. He said, "I forgot to close the blinds. Richie was probably watching all that."

"I don't care," she said.

He wanted to ask if she was all right, to say he understood her grief, to say I know exactly how you feel. But those were useless words and untrue and they could not soothe as well as silence and a lover's touch. So for a long time he lay motionless and said nothing and felt her tears against his cheek, and he thought of all the people they had buried, and of all the sorrow yet to come.

THIRTY-THREE

She watched him at the coffeemaker, filling her cup without spilling a drop, adding a splash of almond milk, three stirs with a spoon, the spoon laid on a paper napkin neatly folded in half. He was dressed in sweatpants and a light-blue T-shirt; she, fresh from the bed, with the faux fur blanket wrapped around her as she half sat against the edge of the table.

He handed her the cup. "I can turn down the air conditioner if you're cold," he said.

"It feels good," she said, and sipped the coffee. "You been up long?"

"Thirty minutes or so."

"Doing what?"

"Drinking coffee and waiting for you."

She smiled. "What's it like outside?"

"Steamy," he said.

She took another sip. "I gotta say, Sergeant, you make a fine cup of coffee. And how do you keep that carafe from dripping coffee all over the counter?"

"You have to hang the lip over the brim of the cup. Then pour slow and steady."

"Slow and steady," she repeated, and smiled again.

"What?" he said.

"You remind me of my father and oldest brother, that's all."

He returned to his seat at the corner of the table, and reclaimed his own coffee mug. "Both of them?"

"We used to call Galen 'Ed Jr.,'" she said. "Whatever Dad did, he did."

"Your mother told me you were very close."

"With Galen?" she said, and nodded. "He was eight when Bryan was born. Which made him twelve years older than me. He was my protector."

"So I heard."

He waited for her to continue, but she sipped her coffee and said nothing more.

"Is that why you like me?" he asked.

And she said, "Probably. Does that bother you?"

"No reason it should. Is there?"

She gave him a curious look then, a curious smile. So he added, "I take it he's divorced. Nobody ever mentions a wife or family when his name comes up."

She held the cup close to her chin, both hands wrapped around it. "He never married."

"Marriage is overrated," he said.

"This from a man who still—" she began, but then stopped herself. "I'm sorry. I didn't mean to go there."

He shrugged. Looked out the side window. And saw the dirty brick wall of the convenience store. "Are we thinking of pulling out today?" he asked.

"Mother asked if we could hang around a while longer. Everybody else is leaving today, and she could use some help closing up the house. She still doesn't know what she's going to do with it."

"She grew up in that house?"

Jayme shook her head. "It was Grandma and Granddad's second home. After they became empty nesters."

"So no real emotional connection."

"Not without Grandma here."

"Did the boys spend summers here too?" he asked.

"They visited but they never stayed long. Galen and I were here the most, I guess. He was an undergrad at Berea, then went on to UK College of Medicine."

"You still stay in touch?"

"Not like we used to. But yeah, we text, we call each other once in a while."

DeMarco nodded. He watched her.

"I still miss him sometimes," she said.

He kept holding his cup even though it was empty now. Finally he set it on the table. He pulled his hands into his lap. Placed them atop his knees. "So no run today?"

"You can if you want. I mean, you're already dressed for it. But I feel so depleted. You don't mind staying on another day or two?"

"Actually," he said, "I had an interesting conversation yesterday with the librarian."

"I meant to ask you about that."

"I was invited to lunch. At least I think that's what it was."

"Aha! Do I have competition from the widow?"

"Maybe," he said. "Is she rich?"

"Probably not. Her husband was the chief of police back when the town still had a police department. It was just him and two deputies, as I recall. But that was twenty years ago."

"That's interesting," DeMarco said. "Seeing as how she also admitted to helping stage my accidental meeting with Hoyle. Any chance she was the one who suggested we jog down Poplar instead of at the high school?"

Jayme's eyes widened. "What do you think they're up to?"

"It's got something to do with the old church and those seven skeletons."

"Was I invited too?"

"I don't think she mentioned it, but you should come anyway. Some trattoria out on the reservoir road, she said."

"Zia's," Jayme said. "But I'm not going if I wasn't invited."

"You might have been," DeMarco said. "She probably meant you too."

"Who all is supposed to be there?"

"I'm guessing Hoyle too."

"A ménage à trois," she said.

"I'm sure. She probably has a thing for fat men."

"Well," Jayme said, and stepped away from the table, carried her coffee cup to the sink. "Have fun." She turned on the tap and rinsed her cup clean and set it upside down in the adjacent basin. "Be sure to let me know how it works out between you three."

"Hey," he said, and followed her into the bedroom. She dropped the blanket from around her shoulders and headed for the bathroom.

He caught her at the threshold, came up behind her, and wrapped his arms around her. "Hey," he said more softly. "Why are you upset?"

For a few moments her body remained stiff in his arms, but then it relaxed, almost sagging, and she turned and slipped her arms around his waist and leaned into him. "I don't know what's going on with me," she said. "I feel like crying again and I don't even know why."

"It's been a couple of hard days. You have every right to cry."

"I never wanted to be that kind of woman with you."

"What kind?"

"The kind who cries all the time. I've always tried to be strong around you. Nobody wants some sobbing, helpless woman to have to deal with."

He stroked her hair and kissed her cheek. "There's nothing wrong with crying," he said. "It means you feel things. You care. Tears are honest. You don't need to ever hide anything from me."

"Be careful what you ask for," she mumbled into his neck.

"I'm not scared," he said. "But let's go back to the librarian for a second. Is she rich or not?"

She punched her fist into his stomach.

"Ow!" he said, and covered up for a second punch.

Instead, she shoved him hard so that he stumbled backward into the bedroom. She smiled, waited just a moment until he recovered and smiled too and moved toward her again. Then she turned and strutted into the bathroom, closed and locked the door.

THIRTY-FOUR

Jayme's directions and his cell phone's GPS app brought him to Zia's Trattoria at 1:26 p.m. There were six other cars in the gravel lot. He pegged the silver PT Cruiser as the librarian's ride, and either the Hummer 3 or the vintage Ford Bronco as Hoyle's. DeMarco backed into the spot nearest the entrance to the highway—an old habit allowing for quick exit and pursuit. Just because he felt naked without it, and because he had learned to always expect the unexpected, he wore his pocket holster and Glock beneath the tail of a light-blue oxford, the sleeves rolled to his elbows.

The town was ten miles behind him, the reservoir and public recreation area for Lake Frances three miles ahead. Traffic on the highway was sparse. He stood outside Jayme's mother's cream-colored Milan, borrowed for the afternoon, and smelled both greenery and marinara sauce in the air. No music came pulsing through the tinted windows of the small brick building, a silence for which he was grateful.

The door opened onto a tiny lobby and a front desk illuminated by a single small table lamp with a red shade. The cool air brought a sigh of gratitude from DeMarco. Standing behind the desk, a tiny woman in her sixties looked up. "Welcome to Zia's," she said.

He glanced around the small room laid out behind her, all tables empty. At the far side of the room was the bar, where one customer sat watching a baseball game on a small flat-screen mounted above the shelves of liquor, the game's soundtrack little more than a murmur. The bartender, a young woman in her early twenties, leaned against the bar left of the beer taps, texting and smiling to herself.

"I guess I'm early," DeMarco said. "I'm supposed to meet Rosemary Toomey here at one thirty."

The woman said, "Follow me, please."

In the dimness the curtained doorway to the left of the bar was invisible until a few feet away. It opened onto a much larger room with long tables and a number of booths along the walls. Only one light, a duplicate of the table lamp at the front desk, showed their way to the large half-circle booth where Toomey, Hoyle, and another man sat waiting.

Only the stranger stood to greet DeMarco. He was a tall African American in a cream-colored suit, the sage-green shirt open at the neck. If not for the wrinkles around the man's eyes and the close-cropped gray hair, DeMarco would have estimated his age at below fifty. The man's lean, fit body and perfect posture were that of a man well below his seventy-odd years. His tailored suit and easy smile suggested an individual comfortable with a public presence.

"Sergeant DeMarco," the man said, and held out his hand. "Thank you so much for joining us. I'm David Vicente. And I believe you have already met Mrs. Toomey and Dr. Hoyle."

DeMarco took Vicente's hand and smiled first at the librarian, whose tepid smile struck DeMarco as disapproving, then at Hoyle, who nodded sleepily. To DeMarco's eyes, Hoyle's worn black suit was identical to the one he had been wearing two days earlier.

"Nice to see you again," he said.

Vicente motioned at the empty half of the booth. "Please," he said.

And now the older woman from the front desk, who had remained motionless and silent throughout the introductions, asked DeMarco, "Would you care for something from the bar, sir?"

He glanced at the others' drinks: coffee for Hoyle, water with lemon for Toomey, and either iced tea no lemon or bourbon and water for Vicente. DeMarco's first thought was that an icy cold beer would be heaven. But he had a promise to keep. "Iced tea will be fine," he said.

The woman nodded and turned away and disappeared into the dimness.

"Is Jayme arriving separately?" the librarian asked.

"Well," DeMarco answered, "we weren't quite sure whether or not she was invited. She didn't want to intrude."

"Of course she was invited," Toomey said.

Vicente said, "Perhaps you could give her a call."

"I could," DeMarco said, "but I know she plans to spend the day with her mother. Closing up the house and so forth."

"Certainly," Vicente said. "But just for an hour. If her mother could spare her."

DeMarco said, "I guess I can try. If you'll excuse me?"

He stood and walked halfway across the room. When Jayme answered, he relayed the request for her company.

"We're just getting started on the basement," she said. "I'm already covered with cobwebs."

"I get the feeling that your presence is more essential than mine."

"So what's this meeting about?"

"We haven't gotten into that yet."

"Cullen's the only one who hasn't left yet. They need to be at the airport at three."

"It's under fifteen minutes here," he told her. "Would he mind driving you out?"

"You really think it's that important?"

"I'm more than a little afraid of what the librarian will do to me if you don't show up."

She laughed. "So the romance is over?"

"Unless you can save it," he said.

Back at the table, only Vicente was still smiling when DeMarco returned to his seat. "She'll be here ASAP," he told them.

Vicente said, "I am so looking forward to meeting her."

DeMarco was glad to see the tall glass full of ice and tea on its white paper doily. He lifted the glass to his lips and took a drink, but at the first taste opened his eyes wide in surprise.

This brought a smile from Hoyle. "A common reaction among

northerners," he said. "Our sweet tea is aptly named, is it not? That liquid in your glass is twenty-two percent sugar, more or less."

"Twenty-two percent?" said DeMarco. "It makes my teeth hurt just to think about it."

Vicente told him, "Some Kentucky bourbon and mint will turn that into a julep."

"The question is," DeMarco answered, "what will it turn me into?"

Vicente lifted his own glass and tapped it against DeMarco's. "Welcome, Sergeant," he said, "to this month's meeting of the Da Vinci Cave Irregulars."

III

Love distills desire upon the eyes,
Love brings bewitching grace into the heart
Of those he would destroy.
I pray that love may never come to me
With murderous intent...

—Euripides

THIRTY-FIVE

Jayme arrived to find a display of tarot cards spread in front of the librarian, Hoyle lost in thought, Vicente and DeMarco in conversation. Both DeMarco and Vicente stood as Jayme approached the table, the older man rising to his feet more quickly to extend his hand and provide introductions. Jayme apologized for her attire of shorts, sandals, and a sleeveless T-shirt. "I probably smell like my grandmother's basement," she said.

"You smell like springtime, my dear," Vicente said. "Please, sit. Would you care for something cold to drink?"

"Zia is bringing me something, thank you."

DeMarco sat and made room for Jayme. Only then did Vicente take his seat.

Vicente wasted no time returning to the subject at hand. "As I was telling the sergeant, we three call ourselves the Da Vinci Cave Irregulars. We are all that remains of an amateur group of six, formed approximately a dozen years ago by Mrs. Toomey's husband."

"Eleven years and seven months," Toomey said. "First meeting was held in our living room in December, four months after the department was disbanded due to lack of sufficient funding. Curtis found forced retirement not to his liking."

"As have we all," said Vicente. "Together we possess a wealth of experience and personal contacts that make us well suited, not to mention temperamentally inclined, as researchers on any number of interests."

"Including the unsolved murder of seven girls," Jayme said.

Vicente nodded. "We've assisted local authorities numerous times in the past. Unbeknownst to the public, of course. But this case is special. None of our efforts thus far has borne fruit."

Zia appeared silently at Jayme's shoulder to set a tall glass of water, ice, and a slice of lemon in front of her. After Jayme's thank-you, Zia disappeared as unobtrusively as she had arrived.

Jayme said, "So. A librarian, a medical examiner…and you, sir?"

"Former professor of law at Vanderbilt University," Vicente said. "Prior to that, state's attorney general for eight years."

"Very impressive," Jayme said. "So impressive, in fact, that I have to wonder what makes you interested in a couple of itinerant state troopers."

"For one thing," Vicente said, "youth and its mobility."

"'If youth knew,'" said Hoyle, quoting Henri Estienne. "'If age could.'"

DeMarco said, "It's been quite a while since I've thought of myself as young."

"We also value your training," Vicente told them. "And your relative anonymity in the community. We've been aware of both of you for quite a while."

He smiled at Jayme. "Through your grandmother, of course. She was very much looking forward to your visit next month. As were we. My condolences for your loss. Aberdeen is less for her absence, but greater for the years she spent among us."

"My grandmother was involved with your group?"

"She and a few select other individuals have honored us with their trust over the years."

"I'm not sure I understand," DeMarco said. "You've been planning this meeting for a while? Just because we have law enforcement experience? There's no one local could help you out with this?"

Vicente held his smile for a moment, then turned to Mrs. Toomey. She looked first at DeMarco, then at Jayme.

"The clippings you sent about the Huston family. She shared them with us. We were all very impressed."

Vicente said, "'Dogged,' the reporter wrote. 'The dogged Sergeant DeMarco.'"

DeMarco frowned. "Most people back home pronounce that word with one syllable."

"And we just thought," Toomey added, "considering the difficulties you were having in your relationship, the work might help you to…"

Her words trailed off when DeMarco turned his gaze on Jayme.

She laid a hand atop his thigh. To him she said, "Grandma and I talked every week or so. And I talked to my mother. And I'm sure they shared things with each other. I just never imagined it would go beyond them. I promise you I didn't."

DeMarco was leaning forward now, squinting into the darkness between Vicente's and Toomey's shoulders. "So she enlisted you people in some kind of matchmaking conspiracy?"

He turned his chin just slightly to the right, but still did not meet Jayme's eyes. "Were you in on this?"

"No!" Jayme said. "I told her what you've been going through. What you've been dealing with. She thought that maybe if we stayed with her awhile, here in this quiet little town…"

"The subterfuge was all ours," Vicente said. "We've been stymied by this case for too long. We've tried everything we can think of, including"—he paused to consider his words—"forms of surveillance that were as ineffective as they were inappropriate. So when we saw the opportunity to bring in two new sets of eyes, two well-trained, insightful professionals committed to the ideals of justice…"

"Two troopers from Pennsylvania," DeMarco said. "What could we possibly see or know that you haven't? Who all has worked this case? The sheriff's department and state police, certainly. Probably the FBI as well. It's crazy to think we could find anything new. We'll be treading over old ground."

"Yet the case intrigues you," Hoyle said.

DeMarco placed his hand atop Jayme's, lifted hers off his thigh, and turned his body toward her. "I think we need to go now."

Toomey picked up one of the tarot cards and held it in front of him. "This is your future," she told him. "Solitude. But it isn't fixed. It depends on the choices you make."

He said, "I didn't come here to have my fortune told."

She laid that card down and picked up another. "This is your current life. Somebody is trying to get your attention."

He looked away from the card. "Jayme," he said evenly. "We're leaving."

As she started to slide from the booth, Hoyle spoke again, his voice slow and hypnotic, echoing slightly in the otherwise empty room. "When Da Vinci was a young man, before his talent was fully evident, he discovered a cave somewhere in the Tuscan hills. It was, he wrote, a vast and mysterious cave that seemed to draw him in. He was terrified that it held some monstrous beast that would tear him apart, but sensed also that it held magnificent secrets. All that is known of his experience inside the cave is that he soon afterward blossomed as an artist and thinker of staggering talent. Some suspect he was transformed by whatever he encountered in that cave. Many of his paintings, for example, when looked at through his mirror-image technique, bear striking resemblances and similarities to those of cave art discovered in southern France in 1994—art said to be some thirty thousand years old."

There was silence for a few moments. DeMarco and Jayme remained seated. Then, in a softer voice, Vicente said, "Dr. Hoyle's vast range of interests often includes the arcane and esoteric, as I'm sure you have observed. For the rest of us, our little cave here represents the place where we confront mystery and discovery—some of it, unfortunately, quite horrific. We had hoped that, at least in this one instance, you two would join us in our quest. There was no conspiracy, I assure you, except to enlist your help. I'm afraid we've become frustrated by our own limitations."

DeMarco laid his hand on Jayme's shoulder and gave her a gentle shove. She stood, as did DeMarco. Vicente stood as well.

"I apologize, Sergeant, if our methods have offended you, or if you feel you have been tricked or violated somehow. We mean no harm to anyone."

"Aside from the dark forces that beset us," Hoyle added.

DeMarco looked from one face to the other. Then he slipped his hand into Jayme's and led her away.

Toomey half rose from her seat to call after him, a third card in hand. "You are approaching a dangerous intersection, young man. Please take the time to look both ways."

THIRTY-SIX

Jayme watched his face as he drove back to Aberdeen, his jaw set, his mouth a grim, hard line. She understood what he must be feeling: betrayal. He was one of the most private men she had ever known, and maybe one of the most wounded. He held himself together through the years by wrapping those wounds in layer after layer of scar tissue, then concealing it all beneath a gruff demeanour, alternating sarcasm with stoicism. And now he felt stripped bare in front of three strangers, and at the hands of a woman who claimed to love him. For a man like him, there could be no greater humiliation.

Yet he loved her. She knew this despite his reluctance to say the word. She knew it from the way he touched her, the way he gazed at her when he thought she was sleeping. Sometimes in the middle of the night, his warm breath, quick and shallow, would play against the tip of her spine, and he would slide his hand under the sheet until his fingers lay wedged beneath her hip, needing contact, nothing more, and only then would his breath slow and deepen again, and his body relax sufficiently for sleep.

She did not know the specifics of his troubling dreams but knew he found his comfort in her. Comfort from decathexis, his unfinished grief. Ryan Jr. And maybe Laraine too. Certainly Thomas Huston. All that grief and guilt. It all kept him from loving openly and nakedly. And now he felt betrayed because a few of their secrets had been revealed. He was a man who defined himself by his secrets and by how successfully he kept them hidden.

And how would he feel if he learned of the agreement she had made with their station commander, his protégé? Doubly betrayed. She wished she had never made that Judas deal. And prayed he would never discover it.

If only she had known him before all the tragedies. What was he like as a child? Had he loved baseball and fishing, all the cop shows on TV? She knew so little about his past. Would they ever reach the day when they could lie in each other's arms and confess the hoarded secrets no one else would ever know? And if they did, could any love survive such revelations?

She said, barely louder than the hum of the air conditioner, "I don't think it's fair to blame a woman for things she said in confidence to her mother and grandmother."

He turned his head quickly, looked at her for just a moment, then faced the windshield again. The unforgiving line of his mouth never changed, but she thought she saw a softness in his eyes, though maybe it was only sorrow.

Another minute passed before she spoke again. "I'll do whatever you want, Ryan. I'll go wherever you want to go. But I don't believe, knowing the kind of man you are, that you can just walk away from those seven girls."

His right eye twitched then, the one that sometimes went slightly out of focus, sometimes watered when he was agitated or depressed. There was a tiny scar at the corner of that eye, the result of his own physical injury in the accident that took his infant son. She knew that his son was always with him, always a powerful, unrelenting ache, a wound that never healed.

As if conscious of her gaze and the thoughts accompanying it, he lifted his right hand off the steering wheel for a moment, put his index finger to the scar, rubbed it twice, then lowered his hand again. Otherwise, he gave her no answer.

A few minutes later he pulled the car into her grandmother's driveway. Put the gear into Park. Shut off the engine. And sat there staring at the garage door. She waited.

"What a strange bunch," he finally said. And then, with a little laugh, "The Da Vinci Cave Irregulars. *Irregulars* sure hits the nail on the head, doesn't it?"

She smiled. "Hoyle is exactly as you described him."

Now he smiled too, kept looking at the garage. "That librarian especially," he said. "Somebody is trying to get my attention? Do people really fall for that kind of stuff?"

She knew he didn't want an answer, he would work one out for himself. So after a few seconds she told him, "I thought that was supposed to be a lunch meeting. Where was lunch?"

Now he looked at her and offered a genuine smile. She read apology in his eyes. "Seriously," he said. "I'm starved."

THIRTY-SEVEN

That night, he dreamed of skeletons. Seven fully articulated bodies of bone assembled around his bed. Petite and feminine; bony fingers interlaced. Every bone clearly visible in the darkness, almost radiant.

He is aware of Jayme sleeping beside him. Aware of the sibilance of her breath in the night's silence. Aware of the warmth of her skin close to his. But she is a shadow, as is he. He knows exactly where he is; he is beside Jayme on a queen-size bed in her grandmother's house. Jayme's mother, Nedra, is sleeping down the hall. Jayme's grandmother is in her grave. And he knows who the skeletons are and why they have come for him.

The skeletons have no eyes or tongues but their plaintiveness is tangible. He feels it in their stillness. Their bones are white but grieving, and he knows they know that he understands their grief. They have come so that he might subsume it.

He sits up and tries to speak, but no words will issue forth. His mouth opens, tongue flicks, but he knows not what to say. And so he closes his eyes, he lies down again. He thinks, You're dreaming. And hears the skeletons collapse asunder, a moat of bones scattered all around his bed.

THIRTY-EIGHT

A t 8:00 a.m., the doorbell rang.

DeMarco and Jayme had spent the night in the guest room of her grandmother's house. After working hard into the evening sorting through family keepsakes, then packing and marking boxes and arranging for a real estate agent to show the house and oversee lawn maintenance until the property was sold, Jayme and DeMarco and Jayme's mother had fallen onto the living room sofa and stayed up till one o'clock watching Arthur Penn's *Bonnie and Clyde* on TCM.

Both Jayme and her mother kept nodding off during the movie, then waking and watching a few more minutes before nodding off again, but DeMarco, despite his physical and emotional fatigue, watched every minute of it. He had already seen the movie at least four times, but never before had he found the story of doomed lovers as compelling as he did with Jayme leaning against him, one naked ankle hooked over his. For a long time after the climactic shootout—part opera, part bloody ballet, that slow-motion fusillade of death and sensuality, a consummating orgasm for the lovers' unconsummated desire—DeMarco sat with the television off and the room dark, two beautiful women asleep at his side, their bodies limp and crumpled and riddled with exhaustion.

They all slept late the next day and were still at the breakfast table when the front doorbell rang. Jayme's mother went to the door, opened it, closed it, then returned with a large fat brown envelope on which someone had written in block letters DEMARCO & MATSON. She laid it on the table between them, then returned to her seat.

"What's this?" Jayme asked.

"Some boy dropped it off."

"A boy?" said DeMarco.

"In a little red car," Jayme's mother said.

Jayme slid the envelope toward DeMarco. "You want the honors?"

He thought, *I won't let him play us like this.* But the dream was still with him. "Be my guest," he said.

Inside were five separate packets of loose papers, each in a separate folder. Jayme removed the folders one at a time and stacked them in a pile. The folders were marked *Chad McGintey, Aaron Henry, Virgil Helm, Eli Royce,* and *Victims.*

The last thing she removed was a single sheet of pale-yellow stationery. She looked at it briefly, then held it toward DeMarco. He continued eating his scrambled eggs. "It's all yours, James," he said.

And her mother said, "Oh, isn't that dear? You call her James too. Just like Galen always did."

The color rose in Jayme's cheeks. She cleared her throat. Then read aloud: "'Again, please allow me to apologize for yesterday's insensitive intrusion upon your privacy. Perhaps we have grown so accustomed to our own desire for anonymity that our empathy suffers. The fault is ours alone, and we ask your forbearance in consideration of the matter at hand. We understand that you have other obligations and owe nothing to us or to this town, but if, at some point in the future, whether here or elsewhere, you could spare a few minutes to look over the enclosed material, and then to favor us with your thoughts, we would be most grateful. Yours sincerely, David Vicente.'"

She laid the note on the top of the stack and waited for DeMarco to look up at her.

Jayme's mother pretended to have heard nothing. She stood and carried her cup and plate to the sink. She scraped the plate clean, turned on the tap, ran the garbage disposal.

DeMarco used his fork to push the last of his eggs onto a piece of toast, then put the toast in his mouth, chewed slowly, and swallowed. He took a last drink of coffee, then turned his eyes on Jayme. She smiled.

Now DeMarco stood and carried his plate and cup to the sink.

"Nedra," he said, "is there a place nearby where we could rent a car for a couple of days?"

"In this town?" she said, and shook her head no. "But I'm sure we could find one on my way home this morning. Cullen rented his at the airport, but that's in the wrong direction. I'm headed east."

Jayme already had her cell phone out. "Hopkinsville," she said. "Eighteen point six miles. You could drop us there, then catch 68 to Bowling Green."

"Wait a minute," Nedra said. "Your grandma's car is right out there in the garage. It hasn't been run for years, so you might have to do whatever to the battery."

Jayme said, "That's okay. Ryan's good at jump-starting things. He always gets my motor running."

"Goodness!" Nedra said. "Is that the way a nice Southern girl talks?"

THIRTY-NINE

They waited until Nedra was on her way home before reading the papers Vicente had sent. The first folder they shared was labeled *Victims*.

Keesha Isaacs, 16, reported missing by foster mother 7/21/98, Lexington KY. In the photocopied photo provided (with apologies for the poor quality), her little sister's favorite, Keesha is thirteen, holding her sister Jade (eight years old) under the arms and dangling her above the community swimming pool. Both girls are wearing two-piece swimsuits, Keesha's bearing the stars and stripes, Jade's neon orange. Jade is kicking at the water, mid-laugh, her hands gripping her sister's wrists while Keesha plants a kiss atop the little girl's head. Keesha became sexually active, according to the foster mother, no later than fourteen, and soon developed the habit of staying away from home "for days at a time." She was last seen by her foster mother nine days prior to the reported disappearance.

Jazmin Wright, 18, reported missing 5/3/99, Owensboro KY. The enclosed photo shows her at sixteen years of age: the tenth-grade photo from her school yearbook. Early in her junior year she became romantically involved with a male individual five years her senior. She was last seen with him at a high school football game that fall. When she failed to return home that night, a search of her bedroom confirmed that many of her clothes and personal belongings were missing. A week later she was officially listed as a runaway. She later made contact with her parents by phone on three separate occasions, but always refused to reveal her location.

LaShonda Smalls, 16, reported missing 3/10/2000, Nashville TN. Raised by grandparents since the age of three after suspicion of sexual abuse at the hands of her mother's boyfriend. Disappeared after leaving her home to spend a weekend at her mother's apartment; the mother, unfortunately, forgot that her daughter would be visiting, and was out of town that weekend. Grandmother later received a Mother's Day card from LaShonda, mailed from Nashville zip code 37206, but no other communication was forthcoming.

The others, Vicente wrote, followed more or less similar scenarios:

Tara Howard, 15, released from Shelby County Juvenile Court Detention Facility 2/29/2001, Memphis TN. No known contact after that date.

Debra Jordan, 17, reported missing 11/26/2002, St. Louis MO. Alleged to have been a sex worker since the age of fifteen, addicted to heroin. Began advertising online as an escort in the summer of 2002, was reported missing by roommate four months later.

Ceres Butler, 16, failed to return home from a friend's house the night of 12/2/2003, Louisville KY. Friend reports they got high on marijuana and mushrooms. Ceres then wanted to "go downtown"; friend declined, so Ceres continued alone. Was not seen or heard from again.

Crystal Woodard, 19, reported missing 11/19/2004, Memphis TN. Escort for at least three years; advertised online. Reported missing by a colleague.

All victims were of African American or mixed African American descent. All considered light-skinned. All were dark-haired, slight, and delicately built, between five feet and five feet four. Some were last seen days, weeks, and on at least one occasion, months before the disappearance was reported. All but Ceres Butler, as noted above, had been out of touch with their immediate families for sixty days or more; their specific dates of disappearance are therefore unknown.

No definitive cause of death has been established for any of the victims. The hyoid bone was broken in one victim's remains, suggesting strangulation as a possibility. The same bone was missing from two other victims' remains. However, four of the victims' hyoid bones were intact. All victims' remains were missing a few or more small bones. Several victims' remains showed signs of previous but older traumas, none sufficient to cause death. Evidence of moderate osteomyelitis, osteopenia, and dental deterioration, suggestive of opiate addiction, was discovered in victims Woodard, Wright, and Jordan.

In other words, cause, date, time, and place of death: undetermined. Times seven.

FORTY

THE SUSPECTS

Chad McGintey, 48, served 172 days at the Green River Correctional Complex for statutory rape of a fourteen-year-old minor. The girl, now nineteen, currently resides with McGintey and one other self-styled anarchist, McGintey's older brother, Lucas, in two mobile homes in a wooded area three miles shy of the Mississippi River. Approximately three years prior to the church discovery, Lucas McGintey was convicted of possessing with the intent to sell two kilos of methamphetamine, for which he served twenty-seven months at the Green River Correctional Complex. A third member of McGintey's group, a homosexual male, resided with McGintey and the others at the time of the discovery at the church, but died in a motorcycle crash nearly two years ago.

All three current individuals, despite their avowed allegiance to a no-credit-card, barter-only lifestyle, receive government assistance, and had, for a short while after Lucas McGintey's release, been under surveillance by the FBI. An unknown informant had outlined the group's plan to assassinate an unspecified law enforcement officer so as to start a war with all law enforcement agencies, which they viewed as pawns of a military-industrial cabal. They were subsequently deemed a non-threat to the government of the United States when their single automatic weapon "voluntarily discharged," breaking windows and perforating the siding of both mobile homes. All three of the group suffered minor injuries from broken glass. A pit bull, shot in the hip, had to be euthanized. Lucas McGintey was charged and subsequently convicted of reckless endangerment and illegally discharging a firearm. He served sixty days and paid a fine.

In recent years several complaints have been filed against Chad McGintey for "leering at," "talking to," and otherwise "bothering" girls walking home from the local middle and junior high schools. On all these occasions he was accompanied by the previously mentioned nineteen-year-old female with whom he resides.

Aaron Henry is a disgraced and divorced former high school social studies teacher, currently age forty-six, fired from his position after sixteen years of service when an eighth-grade student admitted to her parents that she had had sex with Henry on several occasions. She named two other students who had also allegedly engaged in inter-course with the teacher, but they refused to corroborate the first girl's claims. During the subsequent investigation, several other students volunteered hearsay testimony that the teacher's sexual solicitations, often involving offers of money, were common knowledge among the student body. Two days prior to the Carlisle County district attorney's controversial decision not to prosecute Henry for second degree rape because of insufficient evidence, Henry attempted suicide by ingesting an undetermined quantity of over-the-counter sleep aids and aspirin. Upon his release from the hospital, he agreed to a plea bargain of corruption of a minor; as punishment he was barred from any further employment by the Carlisle County Board of Education, five years of supervised probation, behavior modification therapy, and registration as a sex offender. A

civil suit resulted in a settlement of $25,000 to the plain-
tiff, to be held in trust for her until the age of eighteen.
Evicted from his parents' home, Henry currently resides
in low-income housing in the city of Bardwell, where
he earns a modest living buying and selling estate sale
antiques online.

Virgil Helm was the former part-time caretaker and
handyman for the Aberdeen First Baptist Church. He
was hired by Pastor Eli Royce as a replacement for Chad
McGintey, who left that position upon his brother's
release from prison. Helm devoted twenty hours per
week to the church property, where his duties included
not only landscaping but also maintenance of all electrical, plumbing, and heating concerns. He was last seen on
the church grounds an hour or so prior to the discovery
of possible termite infestation of the church building; a
more thorough examination and treatment were sched-
uled for the following day, at which time the remains
were discovered.

Despite extensive interviews and queries of Helm's
employer and all other known associates, the handyman,
now thought to be approximately forty years old, has
never been located. He has no history of criminal activities of any kind, sexual or otherwise, was said to be an
individual of temperate habits and nature, was not known
to drink alcohol, gamble, or speak ill of others, gener-
ally kept to himself, enjoyed playing guitar but never in
public, and, according to all reports, seemed ill at ease in
large groups. He was unmarried and not in a relationship at the time of his disappearance. He claimed to have
been honorably discharged from the United States Army
(after at least one tour of duty in Iraq), but a search of

military records has turned up no proof of that claim, or that Helm ever held military service.

Eli Royce served as pastor of the Aberdeen First Baptist Church from October 2000 through July 2014, at which time the termite control project resulted in the discovery of seven skeletons concealed behind a false wall on the church's northern side. Several of Royce's former parishioners have confirmed that their pastor, although married at the time, was well-known for having affairs with several female members of his congregation (none known to be under the age of consent, which, in Kentucky, is sixteen years of age), some of whom readily admitted to the liaisons and now speak proudly of their affairs with the man who has since become a television evangelist and outspoken advocate of equal rights and opportunities for "oppressed minorities."

Hearsay evidence suggests that Royce impregnated one Antoinette Coates, sixteen, who, unfortunately, subsequently moved from Aberdeen with her mother and father, leaving no forwarding address.

Royce's cooperation during the homicide investigations was never more than reluctant, and often flagrantly antagonistic, though he did request and pass a polygraph test administered by an independent polygraph expert. Now a resident of Evansville, Illinois, Royce continues to own several rental properties in and around Carlisle County. He is currently sixty-five years old.

In 2014 the First Baptist Church of Aberdeen was 154 years old. National media coverage of the discovery of the human remains brought the building to the attention of the Kentucky Historical Society, whose research established the church's role as a stop along the Underground Railroad. Escaped slaves were said to be sheltered in the church before being conveyed by wagon to a point along the nearby Mississippi River some fifteen miles west, or to the Ohio River an additional ten miles northwest, where they were then conveyed farther north by packet boat. The Historical Society then began a campaign to preserve the church as a historical landmark. Unknown citizens of Aberdeen, however, who had no wish to have their town permanently associated with the discovery of seven skeletons of murdered girls of color, burned and bulldozed the church within a week of the discovery. The empty lot is now property of the municipality. Current proposals for future development of the property include: a community garden, a rental storage facility, or a memorial to the victims and the church's history.

FORTY-ONE

Jayme finished reading the information in the folders before DeMarco did, so she refilled her coffee cup and his, then sat at her grandmother's kitchen table and watched him as he read. He paused often in his reading, cocking his head a little so that his gaze went off to the side while he considered what he had read. She wished she could plug a cord into his brain and hear what he was thinking. She wanted to know every thought and emotion that passed through him, even those he kept pushed way down deep in his silent well of darkness. Maybe especially those.

Of the men she had truly loved—her father, grandfather, three brothers, and him—none had been so guarded and private as DeMarco. She had never found it easy to love men other than her family, mainly because their gender was so flawed by testosterone, their virtues so blunted and warped by it. A blood bond ameliorated that flaw. But her attraction to DeMarco had been immediate, and after all the years of their acquaintance was yet to fade. When on duty he had frequently been either gruff or sarcastic, but there was little of that to their relationship now. Every smile he gave, even the sad and sheepish ones, was received as an unexpected gift that made her chest fill with hunger for more of him.

Still, she was mystified by why he, of all people, held her in such thrall. She knew all about the dopamine and oxytocin that floods the brain whenever Cupid strikes, bringing feelings of elation and satisfaction, and the endorphins that produce a heightened state of serenity when she lies in his arms. But all that was the *what* of love, not the why. Why was Ryan DeMarco the one to set those chemicals surging? And how long would the tap stay open?

As a younger woman she had wondered about her capacity to love.

She harbored no shortage of compassion, no lack of empathy, no deficit of libido or fondness for sex. But love had seemed out of her reach
and possibly an illusion. As a trooper exposed to less goodness and
virtue than base, narcissistic indulgence, she had come to view most
human consciousness as no more than a blunt instrument, an animal
skin stretched taut over a hollow stump. The skin would resonate and
sound no matter what object struck it. But only the hand of love, when
she finally experienced it, produced music—the long, graceful fingers
and delicate touch, the gossamer strings needing only to be stroked,
only to be breathed upon, and a melody would course through the
body, go skittering through the blood. Sometimes with DeMarco it
was birdsong, and sometimes the trees were full of crows. Sometimes
a melodious hum and sometimes a chorus. Sometimes rank upon rank
of white-winged angels, or the piercing cat cry of an electric guitar.

Now he closed up the final manila folder and laid it atop the
others. He picked up his coffee cup, but too briskly, causing some of
the coffee to spill over his hand.

"What a slob," she said, her smile full of music, the air warm in the
kitchen, the house otherwise still.

He looked down at the cup. "Did you fill this up?"

"No, you did."

"I got up and went to the counter and filled my cup without
realizing I was doing it?"

"You filled mine too," she said.

He nodded, then wiped his hand on her T-shirt. "That's what you
get for lying," he told her.

Then he kissed her cheek. "So what do you think?"

"You're asking me who did it?" she said. And shook away the
comforting stillness.

"My money's on the anarchist," she answered. "His proclivity is
well-established. His alibi rests solely on his own little group of nut-
balls. And if none of them use credit cards, it would have been fairly
easy to travel two, three hundred miles without leaving any tracks."

"According to Vicente, there was no sign of the group's vehicles on any surveillance cameras."

"They're professional paranoids, Ryan. You think McGintey would kidnap a girl without being aware of cameras?"

DeMarco shrugged. "He did have access to the church. If his duties were the same as Helm's."

"And why wouldn't they be?" she said. "Besides, we don't know if the girls were kidnapped or went with the murderer of their own free will. Teenage girls can make decisions on their own, you know."

He nodded, thought for a few moments, sipped his coffee.

"On the other hand," Jayme said, "the handyman's glaring absence has to put him at the head of the list. Despite what my gut tells me."

"Yep," said DeMarco. "Did you get a sense, though, that whoever put this information together has a hard-on for Eli Royce?"

"Do you mean hard-on in the good way?" she teased, and slipped her hand along his thigh.

"You know I can't think straight when you do that."

"One of your most endearing qualities," she said.

He put his hand on hers, moved it to his knee, and held it in place. "I know Hoyle has a tangible dislike for the man. I suspect that Vicente does too, and I think these are his words," he said, and tapped the folders.

"Personally," Jayme said, "I have a tangible dislike for every one of these jerks. What a Pandora's box of nasty behavior! They all should be behind bars. Royce, however, is the only one without a criminal background."

"Royce and Virgil Helm."

"Yes," Jayme said, "but Helm's disappearance has to implicate him. He knew what was behind that wall. Why else would he disappear the night before a termite inspection?"

"Then why didn't he remove the bodies before the boards got torn off? He had plenty of time to do it."

"Maybe he put the bodies there that night."

"Maybe McGintey did," DeMarco said. "He and Royce must have hated each other. A white anarchist working for a black anti-white supremacist?"

Jayme said, "Imagine the dynamics of that relationship."

DeMarco shook his head, blew out a long, exasperated breath.

She raised her hand to his shoulder and lightly massaged the muscle. "You think we should talk to Vicente again? Get the Irregulars together for another fun-filled lunch with no food?"

"Vicente maybe. Not all three of them at once. Unless you're looking to get your fortune told."

"She's just dying to do a reading for you. You know that, right?"

DeMarco pushed his chair away from the table. "She is the scariest little woman I've ever met."

"Scary how?"

"Something about her eyes. The way she looks at me."

Jayme leaned close. "She's peering into your soul, my love. All your secrets revealed."

DeMarco flinched, then moved away and stood. He went to the sink, emptied his coffee cup, and rinsed it clean. Then glanced at the clock on the stove. 4:27. "We need to check in with local enforcement before we start poking around," he said.

"Not Vicente?"

"I'm trying to remember what Hoyle said about Pastor Royce. He called him a charlatan, I remember that. And something about... 'No responsibility for the crimes has yet been assigned,' he said. When we were talking specifically about Royce."

"As if he believes Royce responsible?"

"That's how it sounded to me. He also said that one of his colleagues is *certain* Royce was involved. And I'm betting that colleague is Vicente."

"Okay," Jayme said. "Let's just say it *was* Royce. Maybe he used McGintey and Helm to acquire the girls for him. Maybe there were drugs involved. Both men worked for Royce."

"But only one of them disappeared," DeMarco said.

"Or *was* disappeared," Jayme added.

DeMarco nodded, lips pursed. Then he pointed a finger at the papers. "Those were written with a lawyer's touch. And lawyers manipulate. I say we talk to the sheriff's department and the state boys. And get the skinny on the Irregulars while we're at it."

"So we're doing it?" Jayme said. "We're taking it on?"

He blinked. Looked momentarily stunned. "Damn," he said. "What about New Orleans? Key West? Gumbo and Key lime pie?"

Jayme came up behind him, set her cup in the sink, slipped her arms around his waist. "Whatever you choose, babe. I'm with you all the way."

He covered her hands with his. "That's Sergeant babe to you, Trooper."

She nuzzled the side of his neck. "It's nice having the house to ourselves, isn't it?"

"And without Richie standing outside the window, listening to you moan."

"I am going to miss that," she told him. "Hey, you want to make a video for him?"

FORTY-TWO

As a boy walking the tracks, Ryan would sometimes come across a black snake or copperhead sunning itself on a crosstie or shedding its skin on the rough cinders. He saw possums and groundhogs, raccoons and stray dogs and feral cats, on occasion a red fox, and twice a black bear. White-tails were always jumping up from the tall grass and crashing through the mountain laurel into the woods that grew along the side of the hill. Once he came upon some kind of eagle perched atop a rusted rail and tearing chunks of pink meat out of a sunfish that kept trying to wriggle free from the talons. He liked to explore the ruins of old station houses and tipples and knew which ones the older kids used on summer nights for their beer and sex and weed parties.

One day he saw an odd shape rising up from the heat shimmer coming off the cinders and on closer inspection encountered some bizarre kind of snapping turtle, its shell as large as a barrel hoop but ridged with thick spikes just like those running down its long tail and broad head. He held a dried stick to its beaked mouth and the turtle grabbed hold and snapped the stick in half.

When he was thirteen he found a loaded revolver wrapped in a dirty piece of burlap in the corner of an abandoned boxcar. He had been afraid to touch the burlap except with his foot, and then afraid to peel away the oily flap of cloth, and then for a while afraid to pick up the revolver. But he did all those things despite his fear and then he looked out the boxcar door in all three directions and then climbed down and ran into the woods with the revolver held hard against his thigh.

A mile or so from home where the hardwood forest gave way to red pines he stopped to catch his breath. There he could smell the pine needles but also the smoke from the steel factories and the soot of the city. He stood in the pines in a small patch of dusty sunlight and examined the revolver. It was heavy in his hand and the barrel was pitch-black and smooth and the handle had dark wooden panels on each side. There were four bullets in the cylinder and two empty spaces.

Only at home in his room when he knew his mother was sleeping did he shake the bullets out of the cylinder and experiment with the hammer and trigger. He learned how to release the safety and how much pressure was needed on the trigger to trip the hammer.

Sometimes when his father was out in the kitchen screaming and cursing at his mother for something or other, Ryan would lie on his bed with his hand under the pillow on top of the loaded revolver. Sometimes he would slip his finger into the trigger housing and think, Anytime I want to.

When he was fifteen his father was found dead at 3:00 a.m. in the parking lot of his favorite bar. It was his favorite because he could walk to it in twenty minutes and there was always somebody around who would stand him a dollar beer. He always drank close to home because he didn't have a car and wasn't allowed to have a driver's license. The boy thought his mother would get happy again without somebody to beat her around all the time, but she got even sadder and sometimes wouldn't leave her bed except to go to the bathroom. He would open a can of soup and heat it up in the microwave and serve it to her in a coffee mug, but she never took more than a sip or two and it was always on her nightstand the next morning with dried soup caked around the rim.

When he was in Panama with the army, the Red Cross notified him that his mother had used a razor blade to cut long slits down the insides of both elbows to the palms of her hands. At the funeral some woman he did not recognize told him, She didn't fool around with it, did she? I've got to admire her for that, and he had felt an odd sense of pride that his mother had showed so much determination, when for as far back as he could remember she had never followed up on any of her promises.

FORTY-THREE

The sheriff of Carlisle County was a tall, sinewy, burr-headed man in his midsixties, his skin leathery and tanned but jaw still firm, steel-blue eyes still clear, his cheeks sporting a day or two of white stubble. He sat with his back to the sunlit window, holding both Jayme's and DeMarco's business cards between the same finger and thumb, the cards extended to catch the morning light as he leaned back in his office chair, relaxed, unhurried. He wore faded blue jeans and an olive-green cotton shirt with light-brown buttons and flaps on the breast pockets. The sleeves were rolled neatly to the elbow, forearms and hands peppered with age spots.

"This number will get me your station commander?" he asked.

DeMarco had decided to let Jayme do the talking initially. Her smile was more fetching and likely to charm.

"Straight through to Captain Bowen," she said with a smile.

The sheriff nodded, then waved the cards at the two chairs facing his desk. Jayme and DeMarco sat.

"And how is it you two come to be involved with David Vicente?" the sheriff asked.

"Well," Jayme began, but DeMarco found he had small patience for charm.

"I'm guessing you were already filled in on that," he said. "Vicente wouldn't have given us your contact information if he hadn't talked to you first."

The sheriff laid the business cards aside, then rubbed his finger and thumb together. His smile reminded DeMarco of a cat his wife, Laraine, had adopted many years ago. It had a habit of bringing chipmunks into the living room, then setting them free, and watching, smiling, until a dazed and saliva-soaked rodent mustered the nerve to flee, at which instant the cat would pounce and seize it again.

The sheriff said, "You're in a hurry to get at it, are you?"

"Not particularly," DeMarco said. "We're doing this as a favor. Mr. Vicente is hoping we might be able to see things from a fresh angle. Personally, I doubt we'll have anything new to contribute. I fully expect we'll be treated like a couple of Yankee carpetbaggers nosing around where we don't belong."

Jayme flinched at the word *carpetbaggers*. But she held her gaze and her smile on the sheriff. "Anything interesting we learn, we'll pass it on to you ASAP."

The sheriff picked up the cards again, tapped them against the top of his desk. "I'll be counting on that," he said.

DeMarco said, "Vicente's file seems fairly comprehensive. Except for any disclosures about him or Dr. Hoyle or Mrs. Toomey."

"What kind of disclosures are you looking for? They're good people," the sheriff said.

Jayme did not fail to notice the subtle change in the sheriff's expression. It had been fleeting, too brief to say if it occurred at the corner of the man's eyes or in a momentary dip of his smile, but she recognized it and knew DeMarco did too, had seen it happen a hundred times in others, that moment when a question strikes a nerve, just before a lie or half-truth is offered as deflection.

"I'm sure they are," DeMarco answered. "But you know that feeling you get when you suspect somebody is setting you up? I've been getting that feeling lately."

The sheriff shrugged, smiled. "What can I say? Everybody plays everybody. That's life, isn't it?"

"There's nothing about their agendas, their motives, that might help me understand why they want us looking at this case?"

"The way I see it, Sergeant, we all have the same motives. Truth, justice, and the American way. Am I right?"

"Sounds like a job for Superman," DeMarco said.

"If you run into him," the sheriff said, and held out his hand, "tell him to come by. I'll put him to work."

Minutes later, on their walk back to the car, Jayme said, "What is it with you and authority figures? Why can't you just get along?"

"I didn't like his smile," DeMarco said.

She knew it was more than that; it was always more with DeMarco. He reduced complex emotions to glib statements. What he had not liked was the sheriff's supercilious attitude, as if he were the gatekeeper and arbiter of all countywide justice, and the way he had looked Jayme up and down. DeMarco saw himself as an instrument of justice, and he took umbrage at any concealment of information, any response short of full, enthusiastic disclosure. What puzzled and intrigued her was why he felt that way yet was so guarded himself, and why he cloaked his own raging need for justice beneath a sarcastic demeanor. He was an intelligent and keenly observant man who, in an instant, could relegate an individual to friend or foe, a response she had learned to read especially in his eyes. People he liked and trusted were met with what she called his smiling eyes—a relaxed, open gaze. The sheriff of Carlisle County had been regarded with a tight squint throughout the entire conversation.

DeMarco's past was a mystery to her. He was more literate than most people she dealt with, sometimes startlingly so, as the time nine days earlier when he had quoted her favorite writer from high school. They had been waiting for a table at a restaurant in North Carolina rated by Zagat's as best in the state for barbecue. The lobby was crowded and loud, the vinyl bench seats packed with talkative adults and raucous children. After twenty minutes he asked if she would mind finding another place for dinner, and outside on the sidewalk, she asked what was wrong with the place. He gave her a look that seemed to say *How could you even ask that question?* but answered only with, "Hell is other people."

She said, "Do you know where that line comes from?" And he had answered, almost blithely, "*No Exit*. Jean-Paul Sartre."

She had been delighted by the prospect of a literary discussion. "And do you also know what he really meant by that quote?" To which DeMarco had said, ending the discussion, "I know what I meant by it."

Most times when she asked about his family, his vocabulary shrank even further. Strangers who made the mistake of trying to engage him in desultory conversation were often answered with silence and a narrowing of his eyes. She knew from her own experience as well as through her study in psychology that people are born with certain proclivities, but that the real catalyst for personality development is environment. She tried to envision him as a boy. When, and why, had he become so insular? She longed to find the key that would throw open the doors and fill him with light.

She said, "There's a history in the South that makes some people more than a little sensitive at times. You understand that, right?"

He said, grinning, "You think 'carpetbaggers' was a bad choice of words?"

"I think it was a deliberately bad choice. Wasn't I supposed to be doing the talking?"

He laid a hand against the small of her back. "You can drive if it makes you feel any better."

"Don't patronize me, DeMarco, or you'll be riding in the trunk."

Their visit to the local Kentucky State Police barracks went, as expected, more smoothly. Nobody reminded DeMarco of his estranged wife's cat. A young trooper named Warner confirmed the contact information for all the suspects on Vicente's list and cautioned, politely, to tread lightly around Eli Royce unless they wished to appear in his next televised sermon as the latest perpetrators of "white folks' smear campaign against this century's Elijah."

"To be honest," DeMarco told him, "Royce is at the bottom of my list as a suspect. There's not a single bit of hard evidence to implicate him."

"I agree," said the trooper.

"Just between us, I sense a strong personal enmity between Vicente and Royce. Would you know anything about that?"

"You mean the defamation suit?"

"Come again?" DeMarco said.

"It's been working its way through the courts for several years now. Royce is suing for thirty million dollars or some such figure. He alleges Vicente publicly defamed him on several occasions. That's why Vicente lost his position at Vanderbilt, you know."

"We were told he retired."

"I guess that's the polite way of saying it."

Back at the parking lot, DeMarco and Jayme waited outside the car while the air conditioner ran full blast, gradually diminishing the greenhouse effect inside the car. DeMarco looked across the simmering roof at her and shook his head.

"What are you thinking?" she asked.

"Run," he said. "What are you thinking?"

"That a man like you would never run from anything."

He gritted his teeth and snarled. "I hate you," he told her, and popped open his door.

She opened the other door and climbed inside. "You disgust me," she said.

FORTY-FOUR

In the deep woods just outside the confines of the Columbus–Belmont State Park, a narrow washboard road twisted northeast from the Mississippi River, then suddenly west again, then made a final turn north before ending at a rusty pipe gate covered with hand-lettered signs.

PRIVATE PROPERTY!

Keep OUT or be SHOT!

If the PIT BULLS don't get you,
SMITH & WESSON will!

A hundred yards beyond the gate, two battered mobile homes sat side by side, both with empty lawn chairs alongside satellite dishes atop the roofs. The clearing also held two pickup trucks, one bile green, the newer one neon blue, plus one compact black sedan, one wheelless convertible Jeep Wrangler mounted on cement blocks, one capsized and doorless refrigerator, sundry plastic barrels, and three large dogs, all brown and tan, each chained to its own stake, each animal now stretching its chain taut and raising a chorus of saliva-spewing barks.

DeMarco, in the passenger seat, popped open the glove compartment. "Looks like Anarchy Central to me," he said. From the compartment he retrieved his gold Pennsylvania State Police badge, which he affixed to his belt.

"That's not going to do any good," Jayme told him.

He handed her the other shield. "Not up close it won't. But first we have to get up close."

"Isn't that, uh…"

"Misrepresentation?" He slid the Glock into his pocket holster, then popped open the door. "Not until we misrepresent."

"Oy," Jayme said, and reached for her own weapon.

They stood behind their open car doors. Jayme hit the horn with three long blasts. The dogs went crazy.

Thirty seconds later a trailer door swung open and a man in jeans and a wifebeater peered out, squinting. Then he disappeared for just a moment and returned with a pair of binoculars, which he raised to his eyes.

DeMarco pulled the hem of his knit shirt away from the shield.

Again the man disappeared from the doorway, then emerged wearing a pair of flip-flops. He came striding down into the scraggly yard. "Sit!" he screamed at the dogs, and they sat.

"Ah, sweet silence," DeMarco said.

Jayme smiled. As much as she adored him in his gentle mode, she loved this mode of DeMarco too. Fearless, ready to rattle some cages.

The man came to within ten yards of the gate and said, louder than necessary, "What?" He stood maybe five foot eight, close to two hundred pounds, most of it in his chest and belly. His head was shaved, face scruffy. His eyes were bloodshot, his fists clenched.

"I'm Sergeant Ryan DeMarco and this is Trooper Matson. We'd like to ask a few questions of Mr. McGintey, please."

"Which one?"

"Mr. Chad McGintey."

"In that case you're shit out of luck. He ain't home. And don't bother asking me where he is. Even if I knew I wouldn't tell you."

"It would be in everybody's best interests, Mr. McGintey, if we didn't have to come onto your property and conduct a search."

"A search for what? You got a warrant?"

"We don't need a warrant to fly a chopper over your property to do a scan. You do grow your own weed, I assume."

McGintey flinched. "That's what this is all about? You've come all the way out here to hassle us about a little weed?"

"Your brother is a registered sex offender. We're here to see how that's been working out for him."

McGintey stood motionless for a few moments. Then he said, "Fuck you sideways," turned and spit on the ground and strode away.

Jayme waited until McGintey was out of earshot. "As smooth as ever," she told DeMarco.

He looked at her and grinned. "We've tried sideways, right?"

He climbed into the car and shut the door. When she was inside and delicately turning the vehicle in the narrow space available, he told her, "When we get back to where the road makes that last sharp turn before the highway, slow down and let me jump out. You go on ahead a ways, find a place to pull over, and wait for my call."

"What are you expecting?"

"Fun and games," he said.

FORTY-FIVE

D eMarco hunched down behind a thick oak, his head weed-high. The *bumpty-bump* drone of Grandma's car was fading. But a similar sound was fast approaching from the opposite direction.

The bile-green pickup truck. DeMarco pressed himself to the tree and lifted his head a few inches higher. The truck came speeding past, trailing a cloud of road dust. But before the dust engulfed DeMarco, he had a brief but telling look into the truck's cab. The driver was a McGintey but not the older one. Beside him sat a female approximately nineteen or twenty years old. Crowded in beside her, up close to the passenger window, was another female, noticeably younger. He held up his phone and said, "Call Jayme."

She answered with, "A green truck just now blew past me. One male, one female."

"Were you visible from the road?" he asked.

"If they had their eyes open, yep."

"Then two females and a male," he told her. "One was scrunched down. Follow them and see where they go. I'll call Warner and report what I saw. Take note of who gets out of the truck when it stops, and let Warner know where to find them. Then come back and get me."

"And what will I find you doing?" Jayme asked.

"Swatting mosquitoes," he told her, and slapped the one sucking from his neck.

FORTY-SIX

On their way to Bardwell to make an unannounced call on Aaron Henry, the disgraced, divorced, and reclusive predator of eighth-grade girls, Jayme and DeMarco discussed how they would handle their conversation with him.

"How come you always get to be the bad cop?" Jayme said. "The bad cop gets all the good lines."

"I'm a better actor than you are," DeMarco said.

"Except that you're not acting. You're nasty by nature."

"All the more reason, then."

"Maybe we should both be the bad cops."

"You have to give a cornered rat a place to run," he reminded her. "Otherwise he fights back."

"Fine. He can run to you."

"Jayme," he told her, "think about it. He's a heterosexual. A perverted one, but still…"

"Nope," she said, and shook her head. "I'm taking this one."

DeMarco scowled at the windshield, but only so as to conceal his smile. None of the other troopers back in Pennsylvania had ever talked to him the way Jayme did. Nor did he want them too. But with Jayme it had always been different. She was his equal, and they both knew it. More than his equal. Intellectually, emotionally, psychologically…in every way except experience, she beat him by a furlong. And he liked that. But hoped to keep her from knowing it.

They were coming into Bardwell when his cell phone rang. The screen lit up with *Call from Bowen*. He held it up for Jayme to glance at while she drove. She pursed her lips and wrinkled her nose.

DeMarco grinned and answered the call. "Hey there, junior," he said. "You calling to brag that your pubic hair finally came in?"

"I'm calling to ask what the hell you're up to down there in Who-knows-where, Kentucky. I just had a call from the sheriff of Carlisle County."

"I hope you told him your command is in shambles without me there to hold your hand."

"I told him you're borderline insane and I hope you never come back. What's this about you and Matson taking part in some kind of investigation?"

"Do I question what you do for fun? By the way, how is that mama sheep you keep in the closet? What do you call her—Brenda?"

Jayme snickered and slowed to read a street sign.

"Listen," Bowen said. "Don't forget you're on medical leave. If you're receiving compensation of any kind—"

"Pro bono," DeMarco told him.

Jayme's phone rang then. She slipped it from her shirt pocket, looked at the number, and wheeled the car into a Food Lion parking lot. She punched the answer button and said, "One second, please." She shut off the engine, climbed out of the car, shut the door, and said, "Trooper Warner, how'd it turn out?"

"She was underage, all right. Two months shy of fifteen. She's not saying much at the moment, but we're hopeful to get McGintey with at least sexual abuse in the second, and the older girl for unlawful transaction in the third. At the very least we've got McGintey for supplying alcohol to a minor."

"So it was Chad and not the older brother?"

"It was Chad all right. We're waiting now for their lawyer to show up."

"Sergeant DeMarco and I would sure like a few minutes with Chad if we could."

"Give me a call in an hour or so. We'll do what we can for you. Personally, I don't think he's the guy you're looking for, but you never know, do you?"

When she finished the call she climbed back into the car.

DeMarco was waiting, his own phone pocketed. "Bowen says hello," he told her.

"Warner picked up Chad McGintey, the girl he did time for, plus a fourteen-year-old."

"Hot diggity. They were at the motel where you last saw them? In flagrante delicto, I hope."

"Don't know about that," she said. "He said they—" Her phone, still in her hand, beeped and vibrated again. She glanced at the screen, which read *Call from Capt B.* She silenced the phone and quickly pocketed it.

DeMarco said, "Boyfriend?" and she told him, "Mom, asshole."

She started the engine and moved out onto the highway again. "Anyway, about McGintey. Warner's going to get us a few minutes with him. We'll know in an hour or so. But he doesn't think he's our guy."

"And why's that?"

"Didn't say. Maybe because the older girl is still alive. And Caucasian. Both are Caucasian. Plus it sounds like the fourteen-year-old was there of her own free will."

"Fourteen-year-olds don't have free will," DeMarco said. "Or they do, I guess. Just shitty judgment. That's why we have laws to protect them."

She nodded. "We're looking for Carson Avenue, by the way."

"You're looking for it," he told her. "I saw it two blocks back."

FORTY-SEVEN

Aaron Henry's three-room apartment on the seventh floor of the low-income high-rise looked like the home of an octogenarian who had never thrown anything away. The living room was crammed with small antique tables, every surface covered with Hummel figurines, vases, bowls, faux Tiffany lamps, and other yard sale purchases. The only furnishings suggestive of the current century were a small flat-screen TV and a laptop computer. The room smelled of fried onions.

Aaron himself looked twenty years older than a man in his late forties. His face sallow, unshaven and haggard, a pair of reading glasses on a chain perched near the end of his nose. He answered the door dressed in red-and-black-checkered lounge pants, brown socks, and a pale-green T-shirt speckled with coffee and mustard stains.

He sat nervously at one end of a cloth-covered sofa, DeMarco at the other end. Jayme stood with her back to the window, arms crossed over her chest.

"They still haven't found that guy yet?" Henry said. "It's been how many years now?"

DeMarco smiled sympathetically. "The wheels of justice sometimes grind slowly, I'm afraid."

Trooper Matson said, "Tell us about any trips you made between the years of 1998 and 2004."

Henry looked startled by the question. "I was in college back then. Undergraduate, graduate school."

"That doesn't answer my question, does it? In fact, it avoids the question."

Henry looked to DeMarco. "Anytime I ever left town back then, I had my wife and kids with me. My wife," he said, "my ex-wife, she already told the police all that."

DeMarco nodded. "I know, I know. We just need to go over this again. It's for our benefit, since we're new to the investigation."

"And where is your ex-wife now?" Trooper Matson asked. "Where are your children? Why would she move them to North Carolina if she has so much trust in you?"

"Listen," Henry said to DeMarco, "those girls. The ones from my school. I never hurt a single one of them. I was *good* to them."

"Is that why you went to jail?" Matson asked.

DeMarco said, "We're not accusing you of anything, Mr. Henry. We're just trying to get an idea of who hurt those other seven young women. You, in the past, displayed a proclivity for females of similar age. So if there's anything new you have to tell us, it's better we hear it from you. You understand? Better that we don't have to find it out on our own."

"And we will," Matson told him. "You better believe that we will."

Henry sat there doubled over, elbows on his knees, his head shaking back and forth. "I take Depo-Provera," he told them. "I have behavioral therapy every week. My computer is monitored, I can't get a job, I'm ashamed to show myself in public."

He sat back and spread his arms out wide. "This is my life," he told them. "This! This is all I have left."

"If you ask me," Jayme told him, "it's a lot more than you deserve."

Henry bent forward again, arms tight across his belly, eyes squeezed shut.

DeMarco took a business card from his pocket and laid it on the sofa cushion. He then stood and laid a hand on Henry's shoulder. "If you remember anything at all that might help us out," he said, "if you hear anything at all, I'll be very grateful for a call."

On her way past Henry, Jayme leaned down and whispered in his ear. "I'll be looking forward to seeing you again."

On the elevator, going down, DeMarco turned from the button panel and faced her. "Any chance you might have enjoyed that a little too much?" he asked.

"No way," she told him, grinning. "I enjoyed it just the right amount."

FORTY-EIGHT

You up for heading north?" DeMarco asked as they approached her grandmother's car.

Jayme checked the time on her cell phone. 1:44. The missed call alert from Captain Bowen remained on the screen.

"It's two hours minimum to Evansville," she told him, and handed him the car key. She glanced at the sky. Battleship gray. With ominous deeper gray squall lines moving in from the west. "And there's rain on the way."

He popped open the passenger door for her. "We have a roof and we have air-conditioning."

"So does Grandma's house," she told him.

He crossed to the driver's side, climbed in, started the engine and air-conditioning, but left his door hanging open. "I figure we wrap this up today. Debrief Vicente tomorrow. Be on the road to New Orleans in the afternoon."

She held her face close to the air-conditioning vent. "I told Warner we want to interview McGintey. It would be good to talk to the females too. If there's anything more to find out about their boyfriend, they're the ones most likely to tell us."

He sat there staring through the windshield, left hand on the steering wheel.

She asked, "Are you that anxious to talk to Royce, or just anxious to be done with this?"

He shrugged. "It's not really our problem, is it? We agreed to help is all."

She leaned back in the seat. Studied his posture, his face. His index finger softly tapping the steering wheel.

"I know you, Ryan. You'd don't really want to walk away from this."

He inhaled deeply, then blew out a breath. "I do and I don't."

"Why and why?" she asked.

"Because it's just one more case in a never-ending series of cases. So what if we put one more bad guy in jail? There are thousands and thousands more out there. And there always will be."

She leaned across the console and laid a hand on the back of his neck. "Preprandial depression," she said. "You need a small cheeseburger and a big salad."

"A chocolate milkshake wouldn't hurt either."

"I'm pretty sure there's a Steak 'n Shake just before we hit 24 north."

His face turned toward her hand, and he kissed her palm. "You say the sexiest things sometimes."

They drove northwest holding hands, her fingers laced in his. She wondered if he had driven like this when he was married to Laraine. In fact, he was still married to Laraine. He didn't wear the ring anymore but they were still married. Does that bother you? she asked herself. And answered, Not so much yet. But it might start to.

First she needed to get him healthy again. Get him right in the head and the heart. He made her healthier too. Made her want something normal. Something she had never wanted before. She was maybe too old for children but how old was too old these days? And what did it mean that she was longing finally for a normal relationship, one that wouldn't be universally condemned? When she was with him she seldom thought about the other one.

She had been surprised by her interchange with Aaron Henry. Surprised to feel the anger welling up inside. Surprised by the pleasure she took from his abject shame. Surprised by how badly she wanted McGintey to shrink from her in fear and humiliation.

Outside, the sky was darkening. Heat lightning spiderwebbed soundlessly in the west.

She scanned the road ahead. "Steak 'n Shake dead ahead on your right," she said, and hoped her voice sounded steady.

"And none too soon," DeMarco answered.

She squeezed his hand and wanted to cry.

FORTY-NINE

Jayme was in seventh grade and already taller than all the boys in her class when the girl across the street took an interest in her. Usually Jayme followed the girl when they got off the bus after school, MaryKyle fifteen and a natural blond, shapely, pretty and popular, always with two senior high boys walking beside her, Jayme following five yards behind, limbs too long, feet too big, breasts too small. MK was who Jayme wanted to be and wished she could grow into. That self-assured walk. That fluidity and grace. Where did such confidence come from? Jayme was confident too but never in public. In fact, only in her own bedroom, where she was as confident as a hurricane. Surrounded by others, she would stare at the floor.

Then one day MK fell behind the boys walking her home from school, shushed their complaints, and told them to move on. With a nonchalant Hey, she fell into step beside the younger girl, Jayme's heart a startled rabbit, wildly quivering. You have such beautiful hair, MK said, and lifted a handful with her fingers. The sun just glimmers in it. You're so lucky not to look like everybody else.

Jayme blushed red hot, pale skin aflame.

I don't like most red hair, MK continued, but I'm so jealous of yours.

All Jayme could think to say was Thank you.

Do you ever curl it? MK asked. If you want to come to my house I can curl it for you. See if you like it that way.

And for the next three years they met once a week or more. Like Jayme, MK had no sisters, only a brother already in college. They did each other's nails and styled each other's hair and MK told hilarious stories about how weird the senior high teachers are and how gross and conceited the boys are. She took Jayme to Victoria's Secret where they nearly died laughing while trying on colorful panties and bras.

Every touch from MK's fingers made Jayme quiver and blush. And when MK taught her by sucking on Jayme's arm how to give the perfect blowjob—Life is so much easier if you know how to do it, she said—Jayme felt a hot trembling rush between her legs. A rush that at first frightened her, made her worry for a week that something bad had happened down there. But the next time they met MK asked, Do you know how to make yourself orgasm? And then told her where to touch herself, Something else every girl should know, and to practice they sat on the bed and touched each other, Because this makes life a whole lot better too, especially on those nights when nobody calls. And it did. Easier and better and brighter and more promising.

Until Jayme was almost sixteen and MK's boyfriend crashed his car coming home from the prom. King and queen dead on arrival, the princess-in-waiting awakened by the screaming sirens at 3:00 a.m., still awake when a police car pulled into the house next door. Then too numb to breathe, too sick to eat or go to school. She lay dully in her bed for days at a time, sobbing until she had sobbed herself numb again, her body a too-long board, every thought a splinter. Two or three nights a week she would call her brother Galen, whisper to him with her head under the blanket and beg him to come home. She had no appetite, no interest in school. At her father's insistence she spent eight weeks in therapy, but told no one why she was rotting away inside. Only when she talked to Galen or thought of MK and touched herself did she feel a quiver of life again, but only briefly, then dead once more, gagging on despair.

The house next door grew as still as a grave. MK's mother moved out, and again Jayme cried, as if the mother were a form of MK, last vestige, lingering shadow. Why does she have to leave? Jayme asked, and her own mother told her, Grief is like that, honey. It makes people sink down deep into themselves sometimes. Sometimes so deep that people never come back out again.

Jayme came back out by sneaking into MK's room when the father was at work. She knew where the key was kept, she knew his lonely hours. In MK's bedroom she would write little notes and hide them under a pillow, in a shoe in the closet, inside a book on a shelf. Everything else in the room was the same. *I miss you*, Jayme wrote. *Life sucks. Please come back.*

She would lie on MK's bed and place her mouth on her arm where MK's mouth had been. She would inhale MK's scent, which was everywhere in that room.

Jayme stopped seeing the therapist. The only therapy she needed was MK's room.

The last time she went to MK's room was a Friday in March. MK's father came home from work early. Jayme hid trembling in the closet, deep inside MK's scent, until she heard the shower running. Then she sneaked out of the room and down the hall. But instead of escaping she paused outside the master bedroom, she did not know why. Maybe she wanted to see MK's father again, up close, not waving sadly to each other from across her yard and his. He had always been so nice to her, they had all been so nice, mother gone, MK gone, only the father remained. She heard him come out of the bathroom and with a heavy sigh lie down on the bed. All was silent for a while and then the soft noises began. No words, just short, soft groans. She peeked around the doorjamb and saw him naked on the bed, eyes squeezed shut, mouth frowning. She watched him masturbate and felt both sad and aroused. What he must be feeling, she thought, and then he laid the bath towel over his belly and his hand quickened and he raised his head and watched himself as he spurted onto the towel, and she watched him watching himself and imagined going to him and crawling up beside him and saying I'm sorry, I'm sorry. But then he folded the towel in half and cleaned his penis and then folded the towel in half again and then tossed it to the floor. He rolled onto his side and faced the bathroom. It was when he started crying that she went to him, walking in noiselessly and leaning onto the foot of the bed so that he looked up startled, ashamed, and she told him *Shh* and put a hand on his ankle. She told him *Shh* and eased down beside him, kicked off her shoes and stretched out beside him, and molded her grief and her body to his.

FIFTY

While DeMarco waited for their order, watching from the booth as rain fell in thunderous gray sheets at the far edge of the parking lot and then came closer and closer and finally hammered hard against the glass, making him feel like some kind of Bizarro World fish in a dry aquarium, Jayme leaned against the lavatory in the restroom, cell phone to her ear.

"This is good for him," she told her station commander. "I know it is. He's almost like his old self again."

"His old self was a pain in the ass," Bowen said.

"Well, do you want that one back, or that quiet, morose, chronically depressed guy?"

"Are those my only options?"

"He needs this," Jayme told him. "He needs to feel useful again. He needs to feel like he's doing some good. And he is. He will. He won't say as much, but I know he's loving working a case again. We're on our way to the third interview of the day."

"All right then," Bowen conceded. "But I don't want some Kentucky fried sheriff or, God forbid, the Kentucky State Police commissioner raking me over the coals because of my loose cannon. So it's up to you to keep him on the straight and narrow."

"About that," Jayme said. "I'm really not comfortable in this position you've put me in."

"And which position is that?"

"Your spy!" she told him. "Can't you just take me off the payroll for a while? Do you know how this makes me feel, collecting a salary for being your informant?"

"You can't think of it that way. You're using your vacation time."

"I'm your stool pigeon. Your snitch. Your rat. And I'm not going to do this anymore."

"We have an agreement, Trooper, and I—"

"I'm done!" she said. "I am officially on vacation. I'll talk to you when we get back. If we come back." She ended the call before he could say anything more. Then stood there trembling, waiting for the phone to start vibrating again. But it didn't.

She took several deep breaths. Checked herself in the mirror. Put on a smile and walked out to join DeMarco.

FIFTY-ONE

The Resurrection Baptist Church on Evansville's Lincoln Avenue was a huge glass-and-faux-stone complex that reminded DeMarco of the top half of a partially squashed geodesic dome. Out of the indented peak rose a three-story spire that also served as a transmission tower. The parking lot alone covered most of a block.

Fortunately, at four thirty in the afternoon, only eight cars sat in slots near the front entrance, all late-model Cadillacs and BMWs. Their sleek, gleaming reflections in the wide, tinted-glass panels gave the church a look, DeMarco thought, not unlike an upscale car dealership.

The security guard just inside the door flinched at his brief glimpse of DeMarco's badge and holstered weapon. He asked DeMarco and Trooper Matson to wait, disappeared through the rotunda and around a corner. Three minutes later he returned and led them down a dimly lit hall to a door marked in gold script, *The Reverend Eli Royce*. He opened the door without knocking, allowed DeMarco and Matson to enter, then closed the door again and stationed himself outside.

At the rear of the deep room, sixty-six-year-old Eli Royce sat on a red velvet and black leather swivel chair behind an impressive three-sided desk of thick black mahogany, a bank of floor-to-ceiling, tinted windows on his right. Three somber and steroidal African American males in matching plum-colored suits stood against three matching walls of subdued yellow. Two stunning females, neither older than thirty, in spike heels and bright, floral dresses, sat on chaise lounges opposite the glass panels, long legs crossed at the knees, their brightly painted toes rhythmically stabbing air.

Royce wore a black pinstripe suit and lemon-yellow tie. The coat's shoulder pads made him look four feet wide. He lowered the black-rimmed glasses from his eyes and let them hang from his neck on a diamond-encrusted chain.

Royce said, "You say you're with the Kentucky State Police?"

DeMarco smiled. "I did not say that, no."

Royce flashed a wide smile full of brilliant-white teeth. "You're not Sergeant Ryan DeMarco with the Kentucky State Police?"

"We're working with the Kentucky State Police," Trooper Matson said. "In an unofficial capacity."

"Unofficially, then," Royce said, still smiling, "why are you here? And briefly, please. My associates and I are in the middle of a business meeting."

DeMarco let his gaze wander across the high, wide room. "Business is good, I'd say."

Royce's smile drooped a little at the corners. He leaned back in the chair and laced his fingers atop an ample belly.

Trooper Matson told him, "We're investigating the incident at the former Aberdeen Baptist Church."

"Still?" he said. "You mean to tell me that a state full of law enforcement personnel hasn't closed that case yet?"

"You probably would have heard if they did," DeMarco said.

"Of course it is Kentucky," Royce said, which caused his five associates to chuckle.

"Where you still own several businesses," DeMarco said.

Royce waved a hand through the air. "I scarcely know what I own anymore. My accountants handle all that."

"In any case," Matson told him, "we would like to fill ourselves in on the details of the discovery at the church. Your recollection of exactly when and how you learned about the bodies behind the false wall."

"Skeletons are hardly bodies, Trooper."

"You learned about them how?" DeMarco said.

Now there was no smile on Royce's lips. His eyes narrowed. "An unofficial capacity, you said? Did David Vicente send you here to harass me again?"

DeMarco said, "I understand there's some relationship between you two?"

Royce slowly pushed his chair away from the desk. Then he leaned back nonchalantly, thick hands hanging limp over the ends of the armrests. "I have already been questioned ad nauseam on this matter, Sergeant. So unless you are carrying a subpoena, you should refer to all extant documentation. Have a nice drive back to Kentucky."

With that he pulled his reading glasses back into place and leaned over a sheet of paper on his desk. One of the plum-suited triplets came up silently behind DeMarco and gripped his arm, turning him toward the door.

DeMarco turned more briskly than the man expected. Nose to nose with him, DeMarco said, "Right now you have committed simple assault. Would you care to try for aggravated?"

Jayme's hand went to her pocket holster.

Royce stood behind his desk. "Whoa now," he said.

DeMarco never blinked. He stepped closer, bumping chests with the man still holding his arm. "You have two seconds to get your hand off me," DeMarco told him.

The man looked at Royce, then withdrew his hand, and stepped out of the way.

DeMarco turned, smiling, to face the desk again. "I can't say you make a good first impression, Pastor."

Then he looked at Jayme. "Trooper," he said, "what say we go have another look at those police reports. My gut tells me we might have overlooked something."

DeMarco and Jayme headed for the door. Royce came around his desk to follow them. "You can tell Vicente I hope he's enjoying his retirement! Tell him we've got some fine lakes up here for fishing if he needs to put his time to something useful for a change!"

Both DeMarco and Jayme smiled all the way out to the parking lot. When the door fell shut behind them, she said, "How about the arm candy? What's their job, you think?"

"Choir," he said.

"Really? They looked more like organ players to me."

Grinning to each other, they climbed inside the car, DeMarco behind the wheel. He started the engine, turned on the air conditioner, but made no attempt to move the car. He was no longer smiling.

Jayme pushed her hair behind her ears. "What do you think he's hiding?" she asked.

"Maybe nothing," DeMarco answered.

"So this was a wasted trip?"

He turned to her, leaned back against the door. "Think about it," he told her. "What do you know now that you didn't know when you woke up this morning?"

She ran her memory through the day's events. "I know that Chad McGintey is still messing around with underage girls."

"Check," DeMarco said.

"I know that Aaron Henry is a pathetic, self-loathing man full of emasculating chemicals, and probably not worth any more of our time."

"Agreed. And check."

"And…I guess I know that Eli Royce is a self-important narcissist with a wild hair up his ass for David Vicente. Who, by the way, just might be exploiting us in some personal vendetta against Royce, whether it has anything to do with those unfortunate girls or not."

"Check and check again," DeMarco said. "Question is, what's our next move?"

She thought for a moment, studied his eyes. Then she answered, "A couple more burgers for the long ride home?"

"You are so freaking brilliant," he told her, and patted her cheek, "I just can't stand it."

FIFTY-TWO

There were two people supposed to be his grandparents living somewhere outside of Youngstown, too far away for a boy to walk. Ryan saw them only twice, both times when his mother talked their neighbor Paul into driving them there. Ryan was so small the first time that he had to get onto his knees on the backseat to watch the factories and warehouses going by, the huge metal walls and rusted roofs, then the big, pillared brick houses and then the row houses and a couple of playgrounds, and then small, dirty-white houses and the houses with buckled siding, and finally the fields and trees and then his grandparents' place.

It was an ugly, unpainted house but three times bigger than the trailer and with a small, unevenly mowed yard enclosed inside a huge unmowed yard where the chickens nested and hid their eggs. Inside the house the linoleum floors bulged in several places as if a family of monster rats had tunneled underneath, and half of the living room ceiling sagged like a balloon full of water.

While his grandparents talked to his mother, Ryan explored the upstairs with his uncle Nip who had one leg shorter than the other from polio or something and who had a whiny way of talking as if the words were coming out his nose like air squealing out of a balloon. He seemed to Ryan more like an older boy than a full-grown man. He showed Ryan the magazines full of naked women he kept under his bed, and then he asked, You want to see something funny?

They went outside into the big part of the yard where a dozen or so chickens were sitting down resting or else pecking at bugs in the weeds, and Nip said, You ever seen a chicken fly? Ryan said Sure even though he had only seen them on the television, and then Nip said, You ever seen one fly without its head? Ryan said, It couldn't see where it was going, and Nip said, That don't matter, and went running awkwardly after a chicken and finally caught one by its leg.

He carried it back into the mowed part of the yard where there was an old stump with a rusty hatchet stuck in it. Hold this thing down for me, Nip said, and showed Ryan how to pin the chicken down with one hand behind its neck and one on its head with its wings flapping and legs digging air like crazy. And then before Ryan had a clear idea of what was coming, Nip whacked off the chicken's head, narrowly missing Ryan's fingers, and grabbed the still-twitching body and heaved it up into the air with a spraying stream of blood spurting out of it. The headless bird flew straight into the nearest tree and bang into a branch some twenty feet up, and then it fell tumbling and bouncing down through the branches all the way to the ground where it lay convulsing and flapping for another couple of minutes.

When it was still, Nip put his hand on Ryan's shoulder and said, Now don't say you never seen a headless chicken fly, and Ryan looked up at him grinning and said, I guess I won't.

FIFTY-THREE

Exhausted from their day of interviewing the suspects in the Aberdeen Church case, DeMarco and Jayme agreed to save their visit to Chad McGintey in the county jail until morning. Also on the next day's agenda was a conversation with the minor girl, and a visit to David Vicente.

"Maybe we should talk to Rosemary and Hoyle before Vicente," Jayme suggested. "Forewarned is forearmed."

"You have nice forearms," DeMarco told her.

"And you're so tired you're getting goofy."

After that they lapsed into silence for the final hour of the drive. When DeMarco parked the car behind the RV in Grandma's driveway, Jayme laid her hand atop his. "You've been quiet a long time," she said. "What have you been thinking about?"

"Old stuff," he told her, and smiled wearily.

"Anything you'd care to share?"

"I'll tell you what I'd rather share," he said, and gave her a look she recognized.

She said, "You sure you have the energy for it?"

"I will after a quick shower."

She leaned closer, rested her head on his shoulder. "We don't have to have sex every night, you know. Just in case you're trying to prove something to me."

"It isn't that," he said.

"Good. Because you don't have anything to prove."

"I know."

"Don't get me wrong," she said. "I like that you like me so much."

He kissed her hair. "To me it's not just sex," he told her. "I mean it is sex. But it's a lot more than that too."

She laid a hand to his cheek. "You're not going to lose me, if that's what you're afraid of. You're never going to lose me, baby."

He turned his head a few degrees and whispered into her palm. "Famous last words."

FIFTY-FOUR

B y eight the next morning they were at the county jail in Bardwell. The deputy on duty, with whom Jayme had spoken by phone earlier that morning, brought Chad McGintey into the interrogation room where DeMarco and Jayme were seated side by side at a metal table, a large cup of Dunkin' Donuts coffee and a folder thick with paper in front of Jayme, two cups of coffee in front of DeMarco. As McGintey sat across from them, DeMarco slid the third cup his way.

DeMarco waited to speak until the deputy exited the room. By then McGintey had downed half of his cup. "Looks like you had a rough night," DeMarco said.

"This is bullshit," McGintey said. "I never touched Charlene. Ask her yourself if you don't believe me. She'll tell ya."

Trooper Matson said, "That's not our concern, Mr. McGintey. We're here to talk with you about another matter."

He took another long sip of coffee. Leaned back in his metal chair. "I don't own none of the property," he said. "It's all in my brother's name."

"Again," Matson said, and smiled, "not our concern."

McGintey waited, but they said nothing more. "Then what the hell?" he said. "You drag me out here just for the coffee? Where's the doughnuts?"

DeMarco leaned toward him, elbows on the table. "Aberdeen Baptist Church," he said. "July 2014."

"Great," McGintey said. "That shit again."

"According to our information," Matson said, and opened the folder, "you were employed to maintain the church property until… some time the previous year."

"I mowed the grass," McGintey said. "You going to arrest me for that too?"

"And why did you leave that position?"

"Because I got sick of mowing the freaking grass," he said.

Again Matson and DeMarco waited. They smiled and sipped their coffee, but said nothing.

"My brother came home," he told them. "Bought that property up near the state line, asked me to give him a hand with it."

"A hand doing what?" Jayme asked.

"Whatever he asked me to do," McGintey said. "I'd rather take orders from him than from some fat asshole preacher."

"You didn't get along well with Pastor Royce?" DeMarco asked.

"Get along?" McGintey said. "How do you get along with somebody's never satisfied? Somebody hates you for how you look?"

"Because you're a Caucasian?" DeMarco said.

"Because I'm a white man and proud of it," McGintey said.

"In other words," Matson said, "he's the racist, not you."

"It ain't being a racist when you're right," McGintey answered.

DeMarco sipped his coffee.

Jayme smiled, then leafed through the papers. "It says here you recommended Mr. Virgil Helm as your replacement at the church."

"If that means I told him there was a job open and he was welcome to it, yeah, I guess I did."

DeMarco asked, "You were well acquainted with Mr. Helm?"

"What's it say in those papers you got?"

"I'd rather hear it from you," Jayme said.

"Yeah, well," McGintey said, and turned his empty cup upside down atop the table. "I'm all out of coffee, so we're all out of time."

DeMarco said, "Any idea where Mr. Helm is now?"

McGintey stood up, leaning forward with one hand braced against the edge of the table, his other arm extended, hand fluttering through the air. "Gone with the wind," he said.

He crossed to the door and pounded on the metal frame. "Next time bring doughnuts," he said.

The guard opened the door, and McGintey exited.

DeMarco blew out a breath. "Remember the good old days when people were afraid of the police and didn't talk back? Didn't jerk us around and ask for favors? Didn't have a lawyer on speed dial?"

"No," she said. "Do you?"

"Not really," he said.

FIFTY-FIVE

On their return to the front of the county jail, DeMarco and Jayme found the sheriff seated on the edge of a deputy's desk, watching their approach. "Learn anything?" he asked.

They paused a full stride from the sheriff. DeMarco told him, "He has no fondness for Eli Royce, that much is clear."

"That's a fairly common sentiment among white supremacists."

"Which doesn't explain why David Vicente seems to feel that way."

The sheriff gave a little shrug and looked away briefly. Then he said, "Vicente's a good man. He's not shy about the truth no matter what color its skin is."

Trooper Matson asked, "So just what is the truth in this case?"

The sheriff smiled. He helped himself to another look up and down her body. "Well," he said, "Vicente has the freedom to say what he likes about Royce. Folks like us, if we condemn a black man for being a liar and an exploiter of his own people, we get tarred with the same brush as somebody like McGintey back there."

"You wouldn't care to elucidate on that characterization, would you?" DeMarco asked. "I don't remember reading any of that in Vicente's debrief."

"I suspect he's probably hoping you'll come across the information on your own."

"All I know is it would sure save the trooper and me a lot of gasoline and perspiration if somebody would just be up front with us. I'm beginning to feel a bit manipulated here. It's not a feeling I tend to appreciate first thing in the morning."

The sheriff held his gaze on DeMarco a moment longer, then moved it to Jayme. She met his gaze and kept her own face emotionless. He looked to the floor, then rubbed the stubble on his cheek.

He said, "Royce held the maintenance contract on the church back in those days. Part of his deal as the pastor. Of course the job of mowing his own grass was beneath him. So he'd take up a special collection every Sunday. And used that to pay McGintey. Same with his replacement."

"Virgil Helm," Matson said. "The disappearing handyman."

The sheriff nodded.

DeMarco said, "What about this lawsuit Royce brought against Vicente? This happened when—before or after the girls' remains were found?"

"Most of a year before," the sheriff said. "It had something to do with a claim against Royce of statutory rape. One of his parishioners."

"Royce was charged with rape?" Matson asked.

The sheriff shook his head. "No official charges were brought. Aberdeen had its own municipal force back then. Town police chief and a couple of part-time deputies. The chief had a private little conversation with all the parties involved, including the girl's parents, who just happened to be tenants in one of Royce's rental properties. Next thing you know, the family decides it's all been a misunderstanding. Turns out the girl's not pregnant at all, just trying to get some attention."

"So was she or wasn't she?" Matson asked.

"Belly bump suggested she was. That's what got the mother to start demanding answers from the girl in the first place."

DeMarco said, "And she named Royce. And that led to the confab with the chief."

"Couple days later," the sheriff said, "somebody spots the family driving out of town in a brand-new Buick. Pulling a little U-Haul trailer behind them."

"This is all in a police report?" DeMarco said.

Again the sheriff shook his head. "Nobody wrote it up. As far as I know, the only mention of it in print was Vicente's letter to the editor calling for Royce to resign his position. Royce refused. Sued Vicente for libel and defamation of character, challenged the entire town to prove he'd done anything wrong."

"But they couldn't," DeMarco said, "because the family was gone, and the police chief never filed any paperwork on the incident."

"There you go," the sheriff said.

Matson asked, "The family couldn't be tracked down?"

"Who's going to pay for it?" the sheriff said. "Aberdeen Town Council? There's no charges pending, no outstanding complaints. People want to move on, they can move on. And move on they did."

"Vicente's a lawyer," DeMarco said. "And apparently a good one. Why would he write an editorial that could get him sued?"

The sheriff shrugged. "There's no merit to the suit," he said. "Even Royce knows that. But his pockets are a lot deeper than Vicente's. And they keep getting deeper month after month, year after year."

"Deep enough to cost Vicente his teaching job?"

"You tell me."

DeMarco thought for a few moments, trying to make the pieces fit. "And less than a year later," he said, "seven skeletons are found in the wall of Eli Royce's church."

"At least they weren't found in the pulpit," the sheriff joked.

Trooper Matson squinted her eyes and thought for a moment. "So as of today," she said, "where does your office stand on all this?"

"The homicide case remains open," he said. "The girls have all been identified, the remains returned to the families. We're keeping our eyes and ears peeled, as are the local state boys. Four of the victims came from across state lines, so the FBI's been involved as well, mostly background checks, database searches, things like that. We've been handling the bulk of the ground game. But, you know, the way state budgets keep getting whacked, none of us has the time or money to invest in a stone-cold case most people would just like to forget about. Hell, most of those girls were runaways. Their families gave up on them long before their bones ended up in Aberdeen."

"What about Virgil Helm?" DeMarco asked. "From where I stand, he might just be the linchpin in all this."

"Might be," the sheriff said, "and might not. For all we know, he's dead too. We just haven't found the grave."

FIFTY-SIX

The sheriff provided the address of Charlene, the fifteen-year-old girl who had most recently been living with McGintey, but he also suggested that no beneficial information would be forthcoming from her.

"We're dealing with a certain kind of mentality here," he said, "from the girl and her family both. To that mentality, fifteen is high time a young woman got herself a man. If he feeds her, keeps a roof over her head, maybe buys her a pair of shoes now and then, not much else is expected. If he has a ready supply of drugs for the rest of her family, all the better. It's a different way of thinking than you all are probably used to."

"We get our share up north as well," DeMarco told him. "Thing is, none of that is relevant to the church case, is it? You're dealing with the present, and we're dealing with the past. All I want to know is if McGintey ever told her anything we might find useful."

"Good luck with that," the sheriff said. "I just don't see McGintey sharing that kind of information with anybody but his brother. If he even has it to share. I mean you're welcome to try, but in my opinion, you'll end up knowing about as much as you do right now. Maybe even less."

On their way back to Aberdeen, Jayme asked the question already running through DeMarco's head. "Is it possible Vicente could have planted the skeletons to incriminate Royce? Is that idea even worth considering?"

"You read my mind," DeMarco answered. For the past fifteen minutes he'd been watching the trees through the passenger window. He liked the greenery, the wide expanse of blue overhead. The land was flatter than he preferred, with not a single rounded ridge along the horizon, but there was plenty of sunlight and unpopulated space where a man could spend his days wandering a dirt trail or grassy path.

"The first question," he said, "is whether Vicente could even have known about the false wall. Why would he? He didn't live in Aberdeen then. Didn't attend that church. His life was elsewhere."

"Okay," Jayme said. "Is there a second question?"

"Even if he knew, would he do such a thing? He's ticked off, sure, but that's a long way from planting bodies. The bodies of young girls that first have to be snatched off the street—"

"Or persuaded to go with him."

"Or persuaded," DeMarco said. "And not just the bodies, but the skeletons. Skeletons that, according to Hoyle, had been meticulously cleaned of all flesh. Think about that for a moment. Think about the kind of person who would do that."

"Sick," she said. "Very, very sick."

"You'd need a private place to do something like that. Vats. Tubs. At the least, a fifty-gallon barrel."

"Jeffrey Dahmer kept bodies in his refrigerator and freezer. Brains and genitalia in jars. All in an apartment in the city."

"But there were no cut marks on the girls' bones. The limbs weren't severed. Our guy kept the bodies intact until the bones fell apart."

"What are you suggesting?" she asked. "That he treated the bodies with…some kind of weird reverence or something?"

"Who knows?" he said. "Maybe he was too squeamish to cut them up, so he just dumped them in a vat. Or buried them a while, then dug them all up later. The explanation could be situational as well as psychological."

She frowned and made popping sounds with her lips.

"What can we know for sure?" he asked her. "Psychologically speaking."

"For sure? Not much. When it comes to that kind of madness, the possible permutations are infinite. The roots of your garden-variety homicide lie fairly shallow; once the players are identified, motives and causes become clear. But the roots that anchor a serial killer to his or her particular depravity are a lot more difficult to trace."

"But there's a template, right? Basic serial killer traits?"

"There's the Macdonald triad," she said. "Behavioral character-istics said to be predictive of violent tendencies. Cruelty to animals, bed-wetting, and an obsession with setting fires. But that theory is far from universally accepted."

"Plus there's no national database on bed wetters," he said.

"The sad fact is," she told him, "every serial killer is his own kind of animal. His own species. You can't name him until you catch and dissect him."

"And you went to college for this?" he teased.

"I went to college for the hunky professors."

"Too bad you graduated."

"No worries. I kept the phone numbers."

He couldn't beat her; never would. She was quicker and more clever than him. It made him chuckle. Then he brought himself back to the matter at hand.

"We need to have a long conversation with Vicente, no question about it," DeMarco conceded. "He could have told us about his beef with Royce."

"And about the pregnant girl."

"We've been spinning our wheels because of him."

Jayme nodded. "So let's get organized here. Who might have had the opportunity? Who might have known about the false wall?"

"Eli Royce. Chad McGintey. Virgil Helm."

"McGintey has no love for Royce. Might he have done it to get back at his boss?"

"Possible," DeMarco said. "Except that he has displayed no prefer-ence for girls of color."

"But maybe he knew Royce did. And chose black girls for that reason."

"Possible," DeMarco said. "Maybe even plausible."

"And then there's Royce," she said. "He's definitely a manipulator. Loves having power over others. Is a known womanizer. And has had at least one relationship with a teenager."

"Allegedly," DeMarco said. He watched more trees go by.

"Which means," Jayme said, "that we have opportunity *and* motivation for both McGintey and Royce."

"Umm," DeMarco said. "A fondness for young black women is not in and of itself a motivation for killing them."

"Ugh," Jayme said.

She slowed the car as they entered Aberdeen's municipal limits. *35 MPH*, the sign said. *WATCH OUT FOR CHILDREN.*

"Also," DeMarco wondered aloud, "why would Royce keep the bodies right there under everybody's nose if he was involved in their deaths?"

"Pathological," Jayme said. "There's no other explanation."

"Like Dahmer keeping skulls and other body parts in his house?"

"In his freaking *refrigerator*," Jayme said. She slowed again for the driveway, pulled in behind the RV.

"So what is your gut telling you?" DeMarco asked.

Jayme shut off the engine. The air conditioner's fan went silent. They could hear the engine clicking under the hood, giving up its heat.

She said, "It's telling me to forget about Aaron Henry. McGintey... back burner for now. Maybe try to find out where the girl who Royce allegedly made pregnant is. Sheriff said they left town in a new car, and they rented a U-Haul. Whose name was used for that purchase and rental? Maybe we can track them down through that. Also, we need to find out what happened to Virgil Helm. Who's going to tell us that?"

"This is your town," DeMarco told her, "not mine."

"It's hardly my town. I spent three summers here. And weekends while I was in college."

He thought for a moment. "So those seven, eight years," he said. "They roughly correspond with the years of the girls' disappearances."

"My God," she said. "They do."

"So you might have been here when some of it happened."

"Oh my God, Ryan."

"And there was no talk? No whispers?"

"I ran with a very small group of people," she said. "Very…preppy."

"Very white?"

"There was nothing intentional about it. My grandparents belonged to a country club. Most of my socializing revolved around club activities."

"It's getting warm in here," he said, and popped open the car door. She climbed out too.

As they walked to the front porch he said, "I'm having a hard time picturing Richie as a preppy. From country club preppy to clerk at Cappy's bait store?"

"Meat, Milk, and Bait Mart," she said as she unlocked the front door. "Besides, Richie wasn't part of our gang. He was barely even an acquaintance. I'd see him around town sometimes. We used to joke that he was like that creepy guy from the Joyce Carol Oates story. Except with none of the charisma."

They walked into the foyer, shaded and cool. DeMarco crossed to the living room, sat in the stuffed chair by the window, took his cell phone from his pocket. "He certainly had his eye on you," DeMarco said.

"He was a walking erection. What boy wasn't at that age? So were you, I bet."

DeMarco sat there staring at his cell phone. Jayme said, "What are you thinking about?"

"I'm thinking I climbed into an RV a while back, had a couple weeks of the best sex in my life, and climbed out in Crazy Town."

She swung a leg over his knees and sat down. "That's what's so great about Crazy Town. The sex just keeps getting better and better."

"This is true," he said. "Even so, I think we need to talk to Richie."

"You can't be serious. You really think I'd ever let a guy like him touch me?"

"About what was happening here back then. The kind of things nice girls like you never heard about."

"Oh," she said. She tossed the car keys onto the coffee table. "How do you know his number?"

"Vicente first," he said, and punched in the numbers. "Where do you want to do lunch?"

FIFTY-SEVEN

Lunch options were limited in Aberdeen, so Vicente recommended a small place in Mayfield in the center of Graves County. He sounded tired to DeMarco, and did not question why another meeting was required.

"I'm sure he senses what's coming," Jayme said after DeMarco pocketed his phone and reported that another short road trip was necessary. "Your tone wasn't exactly ebullient."

"No?" DeMarco said. "Then why does everybody call me Mr. Ebullient?"

She laughed, pushed herself up from the sofa, and reached for his hand. "Come on. I need another quick shower."

He raised their hands to eye level. "This isn't the way to get a quick one," he said.

Before leaving town they stopped for gas at Cappy's. DeMarco filled the tank while Jayme went inside for bottled water. He watched her through the dirty front window, watched Richie's eyes following as she crossed to the cooler, then Richie coming out from behind the counter to walk up behind her, tap her shoulder. She turned, smiled, he said something, she laughed, and then they stood there talking with her back to the open cooler while the gas pump murmured and the subtle vibrations of gasoline rushing through the hose made DeMarco's hand tremble, and after a full minute of this, the stink of gasoline made him turn toward the pump and watch the cents roll over into dollar after dollar.

He was in the car, waiting behind the wheel, fiddling with the radio, when she returned, grinning to herself. She set their bottled water into the cup holders, shut the door, and pulled on the seat belt. He started the engine, checked the mirrors, drove away from the pump. "Looked like Richie recognized you," he said.

"He did! Said I hadn't changed a bit, which is a lie. I never would've recognized him, though, I'll tell you that. He looks a good ten years older than his age."

"That's ancient," DeMarco said.

She chuckled and nodded but did not answer.

Taking a stroll down memory lane, he told himself. He felt the tightness in his body, the fierce grip on the steering wheel. He kept glancing in the rearview as if something or somebody were following.

FIFTY-EIGHT

The only school social event Ryan ever wanted to attend was the ninth-grade Christmas dance. That year he had gotten to know a girl named Sarah who shared his table during the library period. She was small and quiet and wore brown-framed glasses the same color as her hair. Also at the table were Sarah's friend Emmy and Emmy's boyfriend, a good-natured farm boy called Buzz who had been held back for a year and already had his driver's license. When the dance posters went up around the school, Buzz said, Hey, whyn't we four of us go together, and before Ryan even understood what was happening, he had a date with Sarah and began to realize how pretty she was in her shyness and how nice it would feel to slow dance with her hands atop his shoulders and his around her slender waist.

The night of the dance, when Buzz and Emmy and Sarah pulled up in front of the trailer in Buzz's parents' station wagon, Ryan was still in the bathroom fussing with his hair. His mother saw the headlights in the kitchen window and stepped outside into the cold and waved for the kids to come inside. She had made Christmas treats for Ryan out of peanut butter, instant rice, and condensed milk, had rolled them into little balls and dusted them with powdered sugar. They were intended to be celebratory treats she would share with Ryan when he came home later and would sit and tell her all about his first date and the decorations and the music they had danced to, but when the kids came inside she took the treats out of the refrigerator and set them on a plate and said, You must be chilled to the bone. I'll make up some hot chocolate real fast to warm you up while you're waiting for Ryan.

In a saucepan she dumped the rest of the milk and several spoonfuls of Nestle's Quik and was standing there stirring the milk when Ryan's father, who had walked home from the bar, came in and squeezed in beside Sarah as she sat huddled and nervous with her coat still wrapped tightly around her.

Ryan came out of the bathroom feeling nervous but happy, looking forward to the most wonderful night of his life, and found his friends seated stiffly around the little table, squashed close together by the bulk of his father. Two of the little treats had already been eaten, a third squashed flat beneath somebody's thumb. His father with his dirty ski cap pulled down over his ears, face unshaved, body stinking of beer and smoke, turned to Ryan and said, Hell, I didn't think you'd even went through puberty yet, and here you are with a girl. You even know what to do with a pretty little thing like this?

On the ride to the dance Ryan and the girls were quiet and Buzz tried to laugh it off, but after just one dance Ryan could not shake the stiffness from his limbs and the stinging tight pinch of the skin around his eyes. He told Sarah he was sorry and, without any other explanation, turned away and retrieved his coat and walked home the four miles with the snow spitting against his face like hot ashes flicked from a cigarette. He went into the trailer with his hand around a large rock in his coat pocket, but the trailer was empty, his mother at Paul's trailer probably and his father off scrounging up another Christmas drink somewhere, the plate of treats empty except for three that had been squashed flat, and the pan of burned hot chocolate dumped out in the sink.

FIFTY-NINE

The restaurant Vicente had chosen was inside a brick storefront that looked as if it might have formerly been a hardware store. The large open room smelled of scrambled eggs and bacon and buzzed with a dozen conversations. Many of the customers sat with plates of waffles, pancakes, and omelettes in front of them; others were enjoying burgers, club sandwiches, white enameled bowls of homemade soup.

From a small table near the front window, DeMarco and Jayme watched Hoyle's black sedan cruise slowly through an unmetered handicapped slot across the street, and into the adjacent metered space. By degrees he climbed out from behind the wheel, closed and locked the door, approached the meter, dug in a pocket for coins, and inserted four coins in turn, double-checking the parking time available after each coin. The entire lugubrious operation lasted four full minutes, including several long pauses to gaze at various parts of the sky.

DeMarco said, "Not only should we have gotten a bigger table, we should have ordered. This is like watching paint dry."

"Don't be nasty," she said. "Think how long it must take the poor man to get into that black suit every day."

"Who says he ever takes it off?"

"Seriously, Ryan? Give the guy some credit. He could have parked in the handicapped spot but didn't."

"Kudos to him for not being an asshole."

And no kudos to you, she thought. She was learning to recognize the subtle nuances of his expressions and silence, how rigid his jaw, how narrow his eyes, whether the line of his smile was forced or relaxed. His most telling gesture was the refusal to look someone squarely in the eyes. It meant he was beyond annoyed, teetering on the verge of anger, and managing to hold himself in check only by not yet facing the target of his anger. He was a man who long ago had adopted stillness as a mask, probably so that those unschooled in the delicacy of his camouflage would be kept off balance, unable to discern an advantage. It was also, she sensed, the way he controlled himself and kept at bay the full range of emotions he had come to see as weaknesses.

Now, as Hoyle made his way through the too-narrow door and looked in their direction, DeMarco stood, shoulders tight, eyes alert, right eyebrow slightly higher than the left.

But instead of turning toward the table, Hoyle hooked an index finger and flicked it toward the back of the room, then continued on without looking back. DeMarco did not move. He watched as Hoyle approached the nearest server, a clean-cut young man in starched black slacks and a crisp white shirt, and pointed to a circular table for six that had not yet been cleared. The server immediately set about removing plates and cutlery, soiled napkins, and glasses.

Only after the table had been wiped and Hoyle seated with his back to the rear wall did DeMarco turn to Jayme. He inhaled slowly through his nose, exhaled, then picked up their glasses of iced coffee. Now his eyes were narrow, and now his mouth was hard.

Jayme stood and followed him to the table, her hand riding lightly against the small of his back. "The coffee is for drinking," she reminded him. "Not for throwing."

DeMarco placed their glasses side by side directly opposite Hoyle. Then he held a chair out for Jayme. She sat, smiling at Hoyle, who greeted her with a slow nod. The moment DeMarco sat beside her, her hand went to the top of his thigh. Four soft pats. He inhaled again, blew out his breath, then leaned back in his chair, and only then lifted his eyes to Hoyle.

DeMarco said, as if he already knew the answer to his question, "Will Mr. Vicente be joining us soon?"

The server reappeared then to lay fresh place mats, napkins and cutlery. After rearranging his place mat and napkin to his own satisfaction, Hoyle said, "Have you ever wondered why the holder of a juris doctor degree is seldom referred to as 'Doctor' in this country?"

Jayme felt the muscle tighten in DeMarco's thigh. She broadened her smile. "I don't mean to be rude, Dr. Hoyle, but we're on a bit of a tight schedule today. And we have some questions in regard to the brief *Dr.* Vicente provided."

Hoyle cocked his head as if in reaction to an anomalous noise. A moment later he said, "Of course. Forgive me. The subject at hand."

They were interrupted again by the server, this time carrying a water pitcher and glasses. DeMarco closed his eyes momentarily. Jayme was sure she detected a low growl coming from his throat.

The server filled each of the glasses and set a small bowl of lemon wedges beside the pitcher. He then laid a laminated menu beside each plate, then stood motionless next to Hoyle. Hoyle waved a hand beside his ear. The young man turned and walked away.

Hoyle nodded to himself. "The subject at hand. Vicente. Tainted," he said. "And understandably so. But still. Therefore, here I sit, his surrogate."

DeMarco leaned forward, elbows on the table. Eyes narrowed. "Tainted," he repeated.

Hoyle unfolded his napkin and used it to lift a wedge of lemon from the bowl. He then squeezed lemon juice into his glass and returned the mashed wedge to the bowl. "How much did you learn?" he asked.

"We'd like to hear it all," DeMarco answered. "In chronological order."

Hoyle nodded, lifted the glass, sipped his water. He then spoke for several minutes, his tone unemotional, words as precise and carefully chosen as if he were recording the details of an autopsy.

"David Vicente was born of one of Aberdeen's poorer families," he said. "Father a day laborer in the forge that used to exist there. Mother collected laundry to be washed and ironed in her own home while tending to her four children. David the oldest. Everybody worked. Everybody carried his or her own weight. David was bright, won partial scholarships for undergraduate work and law school. Took a position in Louisville, put his siblings through college. All have done well for themselves, their children, their grandchildren. Strong work ethic. Abiding belief in the American Dream. David served as appellate court judge, retired with honor and distinction, accepted a teaching position with Vanderbilt School of Law."

He paused for a sip of water. "Circa 1990, Eli Royce, formerly of Chicago and then unknown by David and the rest of us, accepts pastorship of the First Baptist Church. At which time David's youngest sister, Elysia, and her family are parishioners. Soon Elysia is voicing concern to her brother that Royce's sermons are growing increasingly vitriolic. Race-baiting, in her words. All of this, you understand, in the wake of the racial conflagrations ignited in Chicago in the late eighties, and still, even now, alive and smoldering. Then came the Mount Pleasant riots, the Crown Heights riots, the Rodney King riots. Royce's sermons cease to be reflections on life eternal and become incendiary invectives. At the same time, he forcibly recruits church youth, among them David's thirteen-year-old niece Shawna, into a pseudo-Bible-study group called Youth for Black Jesus. Ninety percent of whom are young females who are required to meet privately with Royce twice a week for tutorials. Eventually the group will be encouraged by Royce to protest any and every alleged incident of racial bias in the vicinity. The football team is racially biased because it has never had a black quarterback—even though only eight percent of the county is black. The yearbook promotes racial prejudice because too many whites are showcased. Black Art Month at the elementary school is blatant discrimination because it segregates blacks instead of showcasing them as part of the larger population. Et cetera. David's sister and her family eventually move from Aberdeen because of increasing hostility against them for refusing to participate in Royce's machinations."

Hoyle paused only long enough for a sip of lemon water. "David, however, remains concerned, not just for Aberdeen but for the country. He pens editorials for the Carlisle County newspapers. Not specifically mentioning Royce but clearly alluding to him. Royce responds with editorials denouncing Uncle Tomism and other traitorous activities. Names are excluded until a family of Baptist Church parishioners contacts David for advice: their fifteen-year-old daughter, a Youth for Black Jesus, has allegedly been impregnated by Royce. David advises contacting the police about criminal charges, and he recommends a lawyer to prepare a civil suit. The process begins but is short-lived. No charges are filed, and the family leaves town with no forwarding address. And here David allows his indignation to get the better of him. He openly denounces Royce in an editorial. Royce charges slander, libel, and defamation of character. There is no shortage of Chicago and Evansville lawyers and activist organizations eager to assist him. Several such organizations, well-funded and not without political influence, succeed in having David's teaching contract revoked. To this day, he continues to defend himself against Royce's legal claims, but with continually diminishing financial reserves. Which returns us to the here and now."

He picked up the menu. "Ah, the veal chili is available today! One of my favorites."

SIXTY

Vicente, Hoyle explained, had not wanted to prejudice the troopers in regard to Eli Royce's possible participation in the homicides, and so had kept his personal history with Royce out of the brief. Also omitted was information pertaining to the summer reading program Rosemary Toomey had conducted for eleven years until Royce's Youth for Black Jesus shut it down with clamorous protests and chants, demanding a wholly separate program featuring only black writers and poets, and the removal from the original program of titles such as *The Adventures of Huckleberry Finn* and *To Kill a Mockingbird* because of their racial slurs and promotion of white supremacy, *Fahrenheit 451* for its depiction of Bible burning, *Gone with the Wind* for its glorification of slavery, and all books authored by Charles Dickens for his support of colonialism and slavery during the American Civil War.

Toomey had appealed to Royce, by phone call twice and once in person, offering to incorporate several novels of his choice into the program, but he refused to be assuaged. She offered him a time slot of his choice to conduct his own program for an integrated audience. But his only interest, it seemed, was to shut down her program, which the Youth for Black Jesus did quite effectively with a belligerent protest line that frightened her program attendees away.

"Two Irregulars down and one to go," Jayme responded. "What do *you* have against him?"

"Not a shred of personal animosity," Hoyle said. "Though I do loathe the type. Opportunistic, self-aggrandizing, one who provokes for the sake of provoking, deliberately divisive, preferring confrontation over compromise, and quick to excuse any murderer, rapist, looter, or other criminal by virtue of skin color alone."

"But nothing personal," Jayme said.

"Correct. I loathe him on a purely ideological basis."

DeMarco had been quiet for a while. Now he looked into his glass of coffee, ice melted, color diluted. "Motive is shaky at best. A known womanizer, but not exclusively of minors. All apparently consensual relationships. No history of physical violence. No forensic evidence to link him to the crime."

Hoyle looked around for the server, caught his eye, and motioned him forward. "Six of the raspberry macaroons, please. To go."

The server nodded and looked to the troopers. Jayme said, "No thank you."

DeMarco continued to stare at his coffee, eyes narrow, mouth hard.

"Proximity, however, suggests opportunity," said Hoyle.

"Which means nothing without motive."

"Sir," said Hoyle, "might I suggest that—"

Now DeMarco's head snapped up, eyes leveled at Hoyle. "Might I suggest, sir, that we've spent two days crisscrossing two counties on this snark hunt of yours and Vicente's. Yes, Royce is contemptuous on many levels. Yes, Aaron Henry is a certified pedophile. Yes, Chad McGintey is a first-class lowlife. But not one of them can be connected to the murders. Just what have you and your group been doing for the past how many years?"

Hoyle smiled uneasily, his cheeks flushed. "Is it not the nature of a cold case for the evidence to be elusive?"

Despite Jayme's hand massaging his thigh, DeMarco pushed away from the table and stood. He crossed to the approaching server and intercepted him halfway to the table. They spoke quietly for a moment, then DeMarco handed the young man two twenties, took the box of macaroons, and returned to the table.

He set the box beside Hoyle's plate. "Enjoy your dessert, Doctor."

He then looked to Jayme, already rising from her chair. He touched her only lightly on the arm, turning her from the table. Careful now with every movement, he escorted her toward the door.

The moment the sunlight hit their faces, she pulled away from his touch. "What the hell, Ryan?"

"I'm tired of being jerked around," he said.

She turned to stand in front of him, blocking his movement. "Who's jerking you around?"

"Vicente, Hoyle...all three of them."

"They asked for our help. They want justice for those girls but they don't know what to do next. How is that jerking us around?"

He said nothing. Kept his gaze above her head.

She put a hand to his chin, pulled his gaze down to meet hers. She said, "Who do you *really* think is jerking you around?"

He looked away, off to the side.

"Who are you really mad at here?" she said.

He would not look at her.

"Ever since I came out of Cappy's, you've been pissed. Not before, but ever since. So why don't you just say what you want to say?"

He stood rooted in place, eyes adamantly distant, face as blank as stone.

"Juvenile," she finally said, then released him and turned away, taking long strides toward the car.

SIXTY-ONE

A t the car she remained on the sidewalk even after he had climbed inside and popped open her lock, started the engine and the air conditioner. She stood there staring down the street but not seeing any of it. What she saw was anger and jealousy, dissolution and loss. She despised the first and feared the last. For a while she had hoped DeMarco would be a different kind of man, the kind to put love above all else. For a while he had shown potential, had been gentle and considerate, seemingly attentive to what they were becoming together.

Then he had witnessed her two insignificant minutes with Richie, and how had he reacted? Everything changed. He was irritable, angry, guarded, closed off. Ready to take it out on Hoyle or anyone else. Where was the self-control that had always been so precious to him?

In the meantime she had seen too how much he needed his work. It energized him, gave him purpose and drive. For their initial two weeks in the RV, with no arrests, investigations, or domestic disturbances to settle, he had been calmer, yes—but had it truly been calmness or just indifference?

But why would he react so jealously to Richie if he were indifferent to her?

She couldn't help comparing DeMarco unfavorably to the two men who had loved her completely. Her father and oldest brother. Neither had ever asked a thing of her. Never attempted to thwart or define her in any way. Made their own needs second to hers. She had striven to do the same for them, and for DeMarco as well. Was reciprocation too much to expect? Could love exist without it?

The passenger window went down; she felt the cool air across her arm. DeMarco was leaning over the console, looking up at her. "You coming?" he said. His voice was no longer angry, his eyes soft.

She climbed in and closed the door, pulled the seat restraint across her waist. He raised the window, checked the traffic, pulled out onto the street.

Ten minutes passed. They rode in silence until he said, "I think the handyman is the key to all this. He has to be. Otherwise there is no key."

She did not answer. He glanced her way, saw her sitting with her head back, eyes closed.

She opened her eyes only when the car pulled into her grandmother's driveway. Jayme was quick to unbuckle and open her door. She stood and slammed the door and crossed to the front porch. DeMarco sat alone in the car for several minutes.

Then he seized the gearshift, and jerked the lever into Reverse.

SIXTY-TWO

From the car DeMarco called Trooper Warner at the local barracks and asked for twenty minutes of his time. The trooper readily conceded, and five minutes later, DeMarco was seated with the trooper in a small conference room. Spread across the table were four sheets of photocopied paper taped together to form a single rectangle. Printed on the paper was a black-and-white map of portions of the five states contiguous with western Kentucky. The numbers one to seven were printed in blue ink at various places on the map, and below each number was the name of a victim. A yellow marker had been used to highlight the numbers and names.

Warner and DeMarco stood side by side, peering down at the map. "Most of the investigation was handled through the sheriff's office," Warner said. "But turns out we did have a copy of the original map. I made this one in case you want to take it with you."

"Appreciate it," DeMarco said. "David Vicente gave me a list and brief profile of each of the girls, but this helps. I'm not sure how yet. Just visually, I guess. Whatever that means."

"As you can see, every city is within thirty miles of a major artery."

"And all within a couple hundred miles of Aberdeen."

"Yes, sir."

"And the girls were all homeless? Runaways?"

"All but Ceres Butler, the next-to-last victim," Warner answered. "The rest weren't all living on the street, but where they were living, nobody would really call a home. Even Ceres, according to her friends, didn't have much of a home life."

"Which means their dates of abduction are anything but precise."

"If they were abducted," Warner said.

"Do we know how many were sex workers?"

"Again," Warner said, "we're relying on the individuals who reported them missing. Most of the time it wasn't family. Most of the girls had already been separated from family by the time the missing person reports were filed."

"Society's castoffs."

"Sadly, that appears to be true."

A few moments later, both men straightened. DeMarco lifted the map off the table and carefully folded it twice. "Any other commonalities you can think of? Interests they shared? Hairstyles? Pets? Drug of choice? Anything at all?"

"Light-skinned black girls, all petite, fifteen to nineteen. That's about it."

DeMarco shook his head. "You know that feeling you get when you run into a brick wall?"

"Intimately," Warner said.

SIXTY-THREE

D eMarco parked at a wide spot along the shoulder of the highway, climbed out and crossed the road and made his way through the light brush to a sliver of rocky shore. Across the shallow stream, thick woods rose steeply all the way to the stone mansion on the bluff Jayme had pointed out when they first came to Aberdeen.

He hunkered down and peered up at the mansion and wondered what it must be like to live that way, as rich and solitary and impervious as a god. He doubted he would like it but thought it might be nice to try some time.

When his neck grew stiff he lowered his gaze to a hawk gliding back and forth over the water, seldom flapping its wings, finding the warm lift with a slight turn, then rising, gliding, descending and turning and rising again. Smaller birds swooped only a foot or two above the water, the bug snatchers, flitting and darting, as quick as dusky flames.

No wonder Da Vinci was fascinated by birds, he thought. How magical they must have seemed to him. How magical they are.

As a boy he used to spend hours sitting beside a river deeper but not much wider than this stream. Slow-moving water calmed him, the drift of a twig or leaf on the current, the hush of movement as water moved back and forth along the shore.

Why had the sight of Jayme talking to Richie upset him so much? He hadn't been vulnerable to jealousy since high school. Such an immature emotion. He was embarrassed by it, and could not understand why it had assailed him out of nowhere, a hot wind that made his skull tight, his lungs incapable of holding air. To discover this weakness in himself—he blushed hot just remembering it.

He slipped a hand into his pocket, closed his hand around the disk of cool metal. He wished he knew of a cemetery nearby. Could probably find one by GPS if he wanted to. But it wouldn't be the same. No one but strangers there. How many Sundays had he missed? Was his little boy aware of his absence? Or was it all darkness and silence where he was? All *nada y nada*.

For some reason a memory came back to him then, himself as a boy. He was eleven years old, a hot midsummer day, walking through an unfamiliar neighborhood. A fairly new housing development of neat two-story homes, all with new vinyl siding of soft yellow, cream, gray, or white. Blue or maroon or sage-green shutters on all the windows. Wraparound porches. Two-car garages. Wide, lush lawns of manicured green.

He walked up one street and down another. Tried to picture his mother and him living in one of those homes. He liked the yellow one with green shutters. The basketball hoop on a black metal pole on the edge of the concrete driveway. He would practice there every night, perfect his dribbling, his shooting, learn to jump high enough to touch the rim. His mother would watch from the kitchen window while making dinner, a pot roast, macaroni and cheese, and a chocolate cake. She would be dressed in a yellow summer dress and have a string of pearls around her neck. His father would be nowhere.

But he could not stand there and stare like a homeless boy and so kept walking, up another street, down another. A sign in a yard said *Free Puppies!*

A long-limbed boy maybe seventeen years old came out of the garage carrying a puppy in his arms. The boy was barefoot, wore cut-off denim shorts, no shirt. The puppy was white with black splotches, short-haired, its dark eyes alert.

"This is the last one," the boy said, and held the puppy out to him. "It's yours if you want it."

Ryan petted its snout, felt the coolness of its nose. "I don't know," he said.

"Sure you do," the boy told him. "Go ahead and hold him." He pressed the puppy into Ryan's arms.

Its body was warm against him. It looked up at him, squirmed to lick his face. He could feel the quickness of its heart against his own.

"I'm supposed to get rid of them before my dad gets home," the boy said. "This is the last one. Go ahead and take him; he likes you."

Ryan held the puppy and felt its love and his love for it and knew he would not be allowed to keep it. But the boy was already walking away, crossing into the green yard and toward the wide, clean porch. "He's a great little dog," the boy said. "You'll see!"

And he was a great little dog for the few hours he was Ryan's. Until his father came home in the middle of the night and heard the puppy mewling and found it under a bundled blanket atop Ryan's bed, then seized it by the scruff of its neck and carried it outside with Ryan pleading and pulling at his father's shirt until his father slammed the puppy's head against the side of the trailer and then threw it into the weeds behind the neighbor's place.

And now DeMarco watched the birds and the water and tried to push down his anger. Tried to ride the air like a hawk. Tried to move like the water, slow and soundless against the shore, and then away and then back and always drifting downstream, always the same and always new, elusive and cool and untouchable.

SIXTY-FOUR

On his way back to Jayme's grandmother's house, DeMarco decided a peace offering was in order, but after spotting not a single liquor store, he discovered through his phone's voice search function that the nearest alcohol was twenty miles north in Ballard County. He returned to the house empty-handed except for the folded map, which he carried into the house. He found Jayme lying atop her grandmother's bed, fully clothed.

He paused on the threshold, waiting to be invited inside. "I was hoping to find a bottle of pinot grigio for tonight. Turns out the county is dry. Feel like going out for dinner? There's a restaurant in Mayfield that serves wine."

She sat up, feet together, knees splayed out, hands clasped and resting atop the mattress. She said, "How many years have you and your wife been separated?"

"Thirteen," he said.

"Do you get jealous knowing she's sleeping with other guys?"

"No," he said.

"Why not?"

"I don't know."

"Maybe you ought to think about that."

"I will," he said. "I'm sorry."

"Why don't you come right out and ask me if I ever fucked him?"

"I don't need to know that."

"You don't *want* to know."

"Maybe I don't," he said.

"So instead you just get jealous and all pissy and ruin the day."

"I am sorry," he told her. "It just hit me, is all. I can't explain why."

She said, "You can't explain much of anything lately, can you?"

He looked at her a few moments longer, then stepped into the room and laid the map on the corner of the bed. "Maybe you can see something in this I can't," he said, then turned and walked away.

She leapt off the bed and went to the threshold. "There's plenty of beer and wine left from the funeral," she called. "Knock yourself out!"

Then she closed and locked the bedroom door.

DeMarco went into the living room and sat on the brocaded sofa. Except for the furnishings, he felt he had returned to a familiar place. All the old anger and guilt and self-pity were there with him again, all the suffocating darkness despite the sunlight through the curtains. He wished he knew how to make it all go away.

It wasn't her fault, no matter what she had done or not done in the past. He was wholly to blame. His problem was that he either kept everything locked up tightly inside, or he opened himself to emotions over which he felt no control. Nor did he know how to remedy the affliction.

SIXTY-FIVE

The second time Ryan saw his grandparents he was almost twelve.
Nip was dead then from a bad heart from the polio, his mother
said. Everything else including the buckled linoleum and sagging ceiling was pretty much the same except that he wasn't allowed to go
investigating upstairs this time because the floors up there weren't safe
anymore. His grandmother, during their visit, uttered only a few quiet
words, but mostly just sat there small and silent in a worn-out stuffed
chair covered with a striped bedsheet. This time she looked tiny to
him, no bigger than a little girl.

Ryan thought about asking his grandfather what had happened
to Nip's magazines but that didn't seem like a very good idea. It was
hotter inside the house than outside so he sat as motionless as possible
on a little footstool beside the torn cloth chair his mother was sitting
in. Paul stayed outside in his car, same as the first time, except this
time he was listening to an Indians game on the radio.

This time his mother asked her father if he had a little to spare,
and all of a sudden the old man was angry. Does it look like there's
anything to spare around here? he said. And he said, Where's that
husband of yours anyway? What's he doing if you need a little help
so bad? And Ryan's mother said, He works when he can. He had
a roofing job last May but work's been scarce since then. And his
grandfather said, What's he ever known about putting on a roof?
And Ryan's mother said, It was a factory job. Just a tar and gravel
roof is all. His grandfather said, That sounds like his speed all right,
and for a while then nobody said much of anything. Then Ryan's
mother took his hand and said, Come on, I'll get you a glass of
nice cold spring water, and as they were getting up his grandfather
said, Just empty out a bucket of tar and push it around for a couple

hours. That's all he's ever been good for, you want to know the truth of it.

Out in the kitchen Ryan's mother bent down and whispered to him. There's a coffee can beside your grandfather's bed that's full of silver dollars. Do you think you can sneak in there and get it and take it out to the car without anybody seeing you do it? It's going to be heavy, and I'm not sure you're strong enough yet. He straightened up and stood a little taller and told her, I'm strong enough. She said, If you can do that for me I'll be awfully proud of my big little man, and he said, What if he sees me doing it? and she said, I'll yell at you a little bit and drag you out to the car and we'll get our sweet asses out of here.

So when his mother went back into the living room and started bragging about how well he was doing in school, which wasn't true at all, Ryan peeked around the doorjamb and saw his grandmother sitting there looking at her little birdlike hands and his grandfather staring at the wall like he wanted to put his fist through it the way Ryan's father sometimes did. Then Ryan scurried down the short hall and into the bedroom and there was the yellow-and-black Chock full o'Nuts coffee can with its yellow lid right there pushed up tight beside the bed.

Ryan peeled the lid back and darn if it wasn't crammed almost to the top with big silver coins just like his mother had said. He snapped the lid back on and picked up the can with both hands and wasn't sure he could get it out the open window and onto the ground without dropping it. For one thing there was a screen on the window. So he stood there thinking about it and then he told himself, The first thing to do is to get the screen out. So he studied the screen and saw it was held in place by two buttons, one on each side of the frame. He could pull the buttons out of the metal screen frame but not all the way out, but far enough that they came out of the wooden window frame. Then there was the problem of getting the coffee can down onto the ground without dropping it.

So he thought about that awhile and decided maybe if he took his shirt off and wrapped it around the can, he could lean out over the sill and lower the can most of the way to the ground. He was surprised but proud when it worked with only a dull clunk from the can being dropped the last foot or so. Then after putting the screen back in place he sneaked back to the kitchen and outside and went around to the side of the house and picked up the can with his shirt still wrapped around it, and he walked hunched over and knees bent as fast as he could to the car.

He got into the backseat and set the can between his feet. Paul had been sleeping with a cigarette burning in his hand and the Indians still on the radio, but he woke up when Ryan set the can down with another dull clunk. He looked back over the seat and said, What's that you got wrapped up in your shirt? Ryan looked out in the yard and didn't see any chickens, so he said, It's a chicken in a can my grandmother made for us.

Paul sucked on his cigarette then blew the smoke out the window and said, Is your mother making any headway in there or not? Ryan didn't know what to say to that so he didn't say anything, and then there was his mother coming out the door at a quicker pace than she usually walked. Before she climbed into the front seat she looked at Ryan through his open window and asked him with her eyes if he had the can or not. He answered with a smile and then his mother smiled too and he felt very proud of himself for making his mother happy for a change.

Then they were driving back into the city and Paul said, Is that like a boiled chicken she gave you? and Ryan's mother looked at him and said, What are you talking about? Paul said, In that can between your boy's feet. My mother used to can chicken too. Though she'd put it up in Mason jars. I never heard of nobody canning chicken in an actual can of any kind. I don't see how it could go long without spoiling canned like that. Ryan's mother told him, Oh, we'll have it eaten long before it can spoil, and then she turned and looked back at Ryan and said, Won't we, baby?

They drove a while longer and then Paul looked at her and said, Well? Did you do any good or not?

She shook her head no. That man's so tight he stinks.

Then Paul looked angry for a while too, so Ryan settled back against the seat and tried to move out of the rearview mirror. Ryan's mother leaned over close to Paul and touched him somewhere Ryan couldn't see and said, Don't worry. At least I still have what I owe you. That made Paul smile a little, and for the rest of the trip he kept looking over at her every now and then and giving her more of that smile.

After Paul parked in his driveway Ryan's mother went inside Paul's trailer to pay him for the ride, she said, so Ryan carried the can over to their own trailer and into his bedroom where he stood by the window, hoping a car wouldn't come along anytime soon with his father in it.

After what seemed a long time his mother came rushing into the house grinning and laughing and found him there in his bedroom and she said, Where is it? He had it hidden under a pile of his dirty clothes. She knelt beside it and dug her hands into the coins and said, How many do you think are in here? He said, A couple thousand at least, and she said, Oh, I doubt that much. But it's a lot more than we had yesterday, isn't it? Ryan looked out the window again and said, What if Grandpa comes looking for it? And she said, For one thing, he doesn't have a car anymore. And for another thing, he's too damn cheap to pay anybody to drive him.

Ryan said, How much did you have to pay Paul? And she said, You don't worry about that, my little hero. You're a regular Clyde Barrow, aren't you? He didn't know who Clyde Barrow was but he liked the way she squeezed him and how happy she was. She took the can outside to hide it underneath the trailer where his father would never look.

When she came back in, she had two silver dollars in her hand, and she put one in each of his hands and said, Whatever you do, don't let your father know anything about that can. You promise? He did and never broke the promise, not even when his father slapped him hard a couple weeks later when he saw the necklace Ryan had given his mother. It was just a cheap little heart on a cheap chain but his father demanded to know where Ryan had stolen it and Ryan said, I bought it at Goodwill with the money from picking up bottles along the road.

His father slapped him and bloodied his lip and called him a lying little bastard. Then he made Ryan's mother give him the necklace so he could return it to the store. Ryan was sure the store would tell his father the necklace wasn't stolen, but after his father left that night, they didn't see him for the next three days, until there wasn't anything in the house to eat, so she sent Ryan around to the bars to find him, and when he did his father was sitting on a stool beside some woman who looked old and not half as pretty as his mother and was wearing his mother's necklace.

His father told him to get back where he belonged if he knew what was good for him, but the woman reached into her purse and brought out a five-dollar bill and gave it to Ryan to buy some food. He bought a carton of orange juice and a loaf of Wonder Bread and half a pound of chipped ham, and he gave his mother the rest of the money, and so she wouldn't start crying again he told her it was from his father, and he never once asked where all the silver dollars had gone.

SIXTY-SIX

Jayme spread the map over the foot of the bed and stood for a while looking down at it, her gaze disregarding chronology to move clockwise from the nearest victim to the farthest. At first her head was still full of DeMarco, such a frustrating man, a thick, steel vault that refused to open. But then the names on the map began to displace her annoyance, made room for empathy, the slow, sad music of sorrow.

Jazmin from Owensboro.

Ceres from Louisville.

Keesha from Lexington.

LaShonda from Nashville.

Tara from Memphis.

Crystal from Memphis.

Debra from St. Louis.

Jayme's breath grew short, her body heavy. She moved to the bed and sat cross-legged with the map spread before her. How desperate a girl must be, she thought, to run away from home and all she knew! How frightened. How steeped in despair. But not, the eyes in the girls' photos had told her, without a lingering glimmer of hope.

Most of the photos in Vicente's packet had been taken well before the girls abandoned or were chased from their homes. Therefore missing were the probable bruises, the needle marks, the sunken cheeks, the hollow eyes they would later acquire. They were still girls in the photos, children of poverty, children of abuse of every type imaginable, yet each still clinging to aspiration, to the slippery tail of a dream. How had they looked on the days they disappeared? Had they given up their dreams of being starlets, pop stars, teachers, mothers? Had they been stripped of all hope for a life just a little bit better?

"Better" for those girls would not have been more of anything, but less. Not more clothes or more cars or more dances or jewelry or boyfriends or plush pillows for the bed. But less violence. Less fear. Fewer beatings. Less ugliness and pain.

And so they'd fled. Not far; just a few blocks was all. Out of the projects and onto the street. Where had they slept? With a friend? In somebody's car? Under a viaduct? Had they prayed for a bed in a shelter?

Did they stand in line at soup kitchens? Scavenge from Dumpsters? Steal? Shoplift? Beg?

When you run from your family, feel safer as an orphan on streets filled with junkies and wolves and vampires of every ilk, how much are you worth? Twenty dollars? Maybe fifty if you don't have needle tracks up and down your arms. If your nose isn't red and scabbed. If you have a place to wash up. If you don't smell of the filth you now consider yourself to be.

Had they ever felt loved? Ever felt truly wanted? Or had misery been their only constant?

"Oh God," Jayme whispered, and lowered her head, placed her hands atop the map, and spread her fingers to cover the names and numbers one through seven. "Give them comfort," she whispered, "please. Please give them peace."

SIXTY-SEVEN

When she emerged from the bedroom carrying the map by a corner, finger and thumb tips only, as if the paper itself were imbued with all the sadness she wished to shed, DeMarco was lying awake on the sofa, the late afternoon sun slanting in through the window as he stared at the ceiling. He turned his head at her approach, saw the redness of her eyes, and sat up.

She handed him the map. "I don't think I'm emotionally equipped for something like this."

He took the map from her hand, laid it atop the coffee table, and folded it closed. "It's hard, isn't it?" he said.

She sat close beside him and took his hand in hers. "I grew up without ever thinking about girls like this. It makes me feel so ashamed. They would be close to my own age now."

"I've thought of that too," he said. "Sometimes I look at you and wonder what they would look like now."

She leaned against him, turned her face into his shoulder. "That doesn't make me feel any better. In fact, it makes me feel guilty."

He stroked her hair. "Maybe that's how we all should feel. Not enough of us do."

She cried softly a while longer, her hand against the side of his neck. He had shaved that morning but the stubble was palpable again, like the finest of sandpaper, a feeling that gave her comfort somehow, the warmth of his flesh, the movement in his throat when he swallowed.

She said, "So what do we do now, boss?"

He said, "We do what nobody else has done. We find Virgil Helm."

She sniffed and nodded, did not want to release him yet. "Any ideas where to start looking?"

"I know exactly where to look," he told her. "Everywhere nobody else has."

SIXTY-EIGHT

For the next fifteen minutes he filled her in on his conversation with Warner and discussed what was known about Virgil Helm. All of Helm's known associates, which were few, had been questioned multiple times by both the sheriff's office and the state police, all to no avail. He had been a ghost even before arriving in Aberdeen, allegedly a vet with no records or traceable history, a man who sometimes displayed difficulties in breathing and moving about, an introvert who kept to himself.

"What about Richie?" DeMarco asked, and felt a stiffness return to Jayme's body. "He's a good twenty years younger than Helm would be now, so he maybe never knew him. But he's of the right social class, if you know what I mean. He might know somebody who knows somebody."

"Somebody the police never questioned," Jayme said.

"Exactly."

She hesitated before she spoke. "Are you sure you'd be comfortable talking to him?" she asked. "Or having me talk to him?"

"I'm good," he told her. "Really."

She smiled and squeezed his hand. "You know you have nothing to worry about, right?"

"It's not worth talking about. The past is past."

The past is never past, she thought. Every second of their pasts lay gathered inside them. Every incident of their pasts had constructed their present, every cell interlocking, layer upon layer. The past is omnipresent.

She moved away from him slightly and turned to look out the window. As always during the day, there were a couple of butterflies visible, one at her grandmother's summersweet bush and another in the neighboring yard. She found herself more than a bit startled by the brightness of the flowers, the radiance of the sunshine. She said, "Do you know how a caterpillar changes into a butterfly?"

"I always figured they go into their cocoons like Superman in a phone booth. He comes out wearing a cape and blue tights, they come out wearing wings."

She smiled. "Close, but not quite. The caterpillar digests itself."

"Excuse me?"

"It excretes an enzyme that reduces the entire caterpillar to a soup. Only a few cells survive. Those cells start building and growing and duplicating. And the result is a butterfly."

"It's amazing," he said. "What made you think of that?"

"Death," she answered. "Those poor girls."

Now he turned too and gazed out the window. "It's funny," he told her, "but that's how I like to think of them too. As seven perfect butterflies. What could be better than that?"

SIXTY-NINE

After dinner at the kitchen table—leftover lasagna and a salad of romaine, radishes, sweet peppers, and cherry tomatoes from somebody's garden—they decided on a walk through town to make up for some of the jogging they had missed in the previous three days. It wasn't long before music could be heard wafting through the neighborhood, a female's voice singing, a guitar, piano, and drums filling in, then a brief saxophone solo.

"Oh my gosh," she said, "I forgot—it's Friday! Concerts in the park!"

"Just like back home," he said.

"Yes, but we've never gone to them. Why haven't we ever gone?"

"We'll go to this one."

"My misanthrope doesn't mind?"

"If I'm not mistaken, that's 'The Girl from Ipanema' I hear."

"There's ice cream too," she teased. "And homemade pie."

"Lead the way," he said.

Soon they were walking hand in hand down Main Street, past small shops and stores and offices, being drawn by the music into a park of at least two well-groomed acres. Soft yellow and white lights were strung from the fringes of a half-dozen canvas canopies, beneath which local residents, mostly middle-aged women, sold slices of pie wrapped in cellophane, blocks of homemade fudge, bottled water, and cans of soda. A carnival wagon was doing a brisk business selling sno-cones and cotton candy. At the volunteer firemen's kiosk, two men served up hot dogs and sloppy joes. On a raised bandstand, five musicians and a female singer in a blue, sequined dress serenaded an audience of two hundred seated in lawn chairs or on blankets with standards from the forties and fifties.

"It's like walking back in time," DeMarco said. Everyone they passed stared at the couple; most nodded and smiled. DeMarco recognized several of the faces from Jayme's grandmother's funeral.

"Here comes the pie," Jayme said. "What will it be?"

An eight-foot table was crowded with pies of every berry, fruit, and pudding variety.

"No contest," DeMarco answered. "Pecan pie with two scoops of vanilla."

"Apple à la mode for me," Jayme said. "I'm an all-American girl."

As a smiling woman unwrapped their orders and dug into a container of ice cream, a man's voice, loud and brusque and angry, drew their attention to the carnival wagon. The man, maybe five and a half feet tall in thick-heeled boots, with a thick mop of black hair combed over his forehead, stood berating two girls, one approximately ten, the other a couple of years younger. The man's face and muscular arms were deeply tanned, his nose wide and flat, his squat neck stretched tight, an artery bulging as he shouted at the girls.

Both girls stood rigid but for their sobbing and trembling. A woman DeMarco presumed to be the girls' mother stood head down behind the girls but did nothing to comfort them or curtail the man's verbal assault.

DeMarco turned to the lady holding out his pie. "You mind keeping that on ice for a minute?" he said, then crossed to the shouting man.

When he laid a hand on the man's shoulder, the shouting abruptly stopped. Startled, the man turned to look up at DeMarco, who was standing very close now, so close that DeMarco could see the man's unnaturally low hairline and the differences in color and texture where the toupee gave way to lightly graying, less dense hair. "Could I have a word with you, friend?" DeMarco said.

He gave the man no chance to refuse, but took him lightly by the arm and escorted him out onto the sidewalk, where both turned their backs to the attentive crowd. On the bandstand the sequined woman kept singing "Green Eyes."

DeMarco said, "I couldn't help notice what a beautiful family you have there. Your wife and daughters, I assume. You're a lucky man."

The man's face made a slow change from tight-lipped anger to a sycophantic grin. "They're a handful though. Was I a little too loud back there? Sorry about that. I was just trying to make myself heard above the music."

"Sure," DeMarco said. "The music is loud. Thing is…they're still just children, you know. Humiliating them like that, it's just not appropriate behavior. Public or private."

"Ah, they know it's all bark. You've got to get their attention sometimes, am I right? You're not from around here, are you? I don't think I recognize you."

DeMarco smiled and leaned a bit closer. "There's this term called child abuse you should become familiar with, my friend. Those of us in law enforcement don't look kindly on it."

The man's large eyes came open wider. Before he could ask the question DeMarco knew was coming, DeMarco gave his shoulder a firm squeeze. "Sergeant Ryan DeMarco, State Police. Enjoy the concert. And allow your family to do the same."

He turned and left the man behind on the sidewalk, Jayme still talking quietly to the woman and her children. The girls would not meet her eyes, but looked only at their mother, all as cowed as before. DeMarco returned to the pie table and dug into his pocket for a five-dollar bill.

Jayme joined him there a few moments later. They carried their plates and plastic spoons to a small parcel of grass at the back of the crowd. They sat cross-legged to eat their pie. "Sort of takes the edge off my appetite," he told her.

She spooned a bit of ice cream into her mouth, let it melt away, and swallowed. "You know why he was screaming at them?"

"I didn't ask," DeMarco said.

"Because they wanted separate sno-cones. He told them they were greedy and fat and had to share one."

"Lots of calories in ice," DeMarco said. He scanned the crowd for another look at the girls. "Fat?" he said. "Stand them side by side, they're not as fat as his head."

"Take a breath, baby."

"How about that hairpiece?" DeMarco said. "Looks like a hairy cow patty."

Jayme smiled and waited for the rest.

"I bet he's had that nose flattened a dozen times. I wanted so badly to just punch him in the face."

She patted his leg twice.

"Pygmy Neanderthal," he muttered, then shook his head from side to side.

Thirty seconds later he inhaled slowly, a long, deep breath, then exhaled through his mouth.

DeMarco blinked twice, trying to get his focus back. "Sorry if I embarrassed you," he said.

"You don't embarrass me. A part of me wishes you could turn your radar off once in a while, but the other part… God, baby. Why do people have to be so cruel?"

He nodded. "Those seven girls are starting to haunt me too."

She sighed. "Let's just listen to the music, okay? This is the kind of stuff you old folks like, isn't it?"

He smiled. "My mother did."

The look in his eyes then, so distant and melancholic, made something catch in her throat.

"Eat your pie," she told him. "The ice cream's melting."

SEVENTY

Over the summer after ninth grade, Ryan shot up to a full six feet. Earlier that year, on a chilly night in April when the temperature dropped to nearly freezing, his father had been found dead in the gravel parking lot of a raucous shot-and-beer bar, a small-caliber bullet near his heart. He was found with his zipper down, penis still out. The blood trail indicated he had stood up against the rear of the building to urinate, then had turned when the shooter approached, and was shot point-blank. He then crawled to the side of the building, a distance of fifteen feet or so, where he subsequently expired. The shooter was never identified.

Ryan could not help but see a connection between his growth spurt and his father's death, as if the weight of his father's presence always pressing down on him had finally been lifted. That summer Ryan took a job laying asphalt driveways with a crew of mostly hungover middle-aged men who moved through the day as if their bodies were made of the same slowly hardening tar as the product they spread. His job was to carry what needed carried and to shovel what needed shoveled. Each day as his jeans grew shorter, his T-shirts got tighter, his muscles growing hard and strong.

As the youngest and lowest paid member of the crew he brought home more money each week than his father ever had, and he filled the refrigerator and cupboards of their trailer with food and treats he and his mother had long been deprived. He tried to get his mother to quit smoking and to take better care of herself, but her only concession to that campaign was to not smoke in the trailer when he was there, and, when he was, to stand on the front step with the door open at her back and blow the smoke out across the scraggly yard as if the smoke was all he objected to.

He imagined if she were younger she would be transformed too by his father's absence, made happy again, a woman who sang along with the radio, and who after a glass or two of wine would pull her son into the narrow space available and dance with him, but instead, she adopted a lost and frightened look in her eyes as if the light had turned green but she had forgotten how to drive. She spent more and more evenings drinking with Paul, whose voice could sometimes be heard screaming through the thin walls of his trailer, but who, when Ryan banged on the door to check on his mother, always laughed and said he was screaming at the television.

On Ryan's first day of his sophomore year he witnessed an older boy in the hallway yanking on a girl's arm to drag her away from a group of friends, and when she squealed in pain and started crying, Ryan, without knowing he would do it and even surprised as it was happening, seized the boy by his own arm and twisted it behind his back and flung him crashing against the painted cement block wall.

When the boy got up barreling head down in a murderous rage, Ryan stepped to the side and clubbed his back with fist and forearm, then yanked him to his feet and slapped him hard six or seven times until the boy was bloody-nosed and blubbering just as Ryan had when he was a child.

Minutes later Ryan sat in the principal's office getting alternately chewed out and threatened by the chubby balding principal who stood behind his desk with the phone at his ear, waiting to inform Ryan's mother that her son was being suspended and, pending school board review, possibly expelled and maybe even arrested. But the phone kept ringing unanswered and eventually the vice principal came down the hall and peered in through the plate-glass window and stared at Ryan briefly before coming inside and telling him, Stand up here a minute.

The vice principal, who was also the football coach, measured his height against Ryan's and to his delight found himself coming up two inches short. What have they been feeding you all summer? he asked, and before Ryan could say he'd been feeding himself, the vice principal turned to the principal and said, So what's the verdict here? To which the principal said, Two weeks minimum and maybe the entire year unless you have a better idea. To which the vice principal turned grinning to Ryan and said, I need a fullback. How do you feel about banging into other big fellas for the next four months? Ryan looked at the principal, who was still scowling and listening to the phone ring, and Ryan said, I guess I could learn to enjoy it.

SEVENTY-ONE

They spent a little over an hour listening to music in the Aberdeen park, but although DeMarco found himself enjoying not only the amateur band, but also the Mayberry ambiance of oldsters in the audience singing along, mothers and fathers holding sleeping babies, little ones running laughing between the lawn chairs, his mind kept returning to the seven sets of remains wrapped in their plastic sheeting and duct tape cocoons. The skeletons had all been reassembled on a laboratory table years ago, dental records and DNA matched to family members, the remains reverently returned to families he hoped had accorded them their due respect, yet their story was unfinished. The writing of that ending had now fallen to him and Jayme.

For the last thirty minutes they had been sitting on the grass, no longer watching the band but gazing into the darkening sky or following the winking light of a firefly. Now he ran his hand down her arm, and she, smiling, turned her palm up to receive his, fingers slipping between fingers. He wondered how such a simple gesture could send so much information from one body to another, what kind of chemical and electromagnetic magic could transform mere touch into comfort, love, longing, and gratitude.

He leaned close to her and whispered, "Ready to go?"

"If you are," she said.

He gathered up their empty paper plates and spoons. They stood and made their way around the periphery of the crowd. At the nearest receptacle he deposited the trash. Across the street, in a bank's drive-through, Richie was leaning against the side of an ATM, talking to another man. DeMarco watched him take a drag on a joint then pass it to his friend.

"That's Richie over there," DeMarco said. "Mind if we say hello?"

She followed his gaze, then gripped his hand tight and stopped walking, bringing him to a halt. "Don't start this again," she said.

"It's about the handyman. Maybe he'll know something."

She paused for a moment, then said, "It's been a nice night, Ryan. Please don't ruin it."

He gave her hand a quick squeeze, leaned close, and kissed her cheek. And started them walking again.

Seeing their approach, Richie pinched out the joint and slipped it into his friend's shirt pocket while muttering a quick message. The friend slipped around the ATM and crossed quickly behind the corner of the bank.

Richie smiled at DeMarco first, then at Jayme. "The music's not much," he said, "but you can't beat a Southern night like this one, can you, folks?"

DeMarco released Jayme's hand, answered only with a half smile. "July 2014," he said. "You were living here back then, is that correct?"

Richie sniffed and tried to look unworried. "I was," he said. "Why do you ask?"

"How well did you know the Baptist church's handyman, Virgil Helm?"

"Know him?" Richie said, and appeared to be trying to remember. "Can't say I really did."

"But you know who I'm talking about."

"I mean he'd come into the store every now and then, like most everybody else in town. Fill up a gas can, get something cold to drink. He rode a motorcycle, as I remember. I'm pretty sure it was a Yamaha. Black. Kind of beat-up. '96, '97? A Virago, I think. Good little street bike."

"But you didn't engage in a lot of conversation, is that what you're saying?"

"Not for lack of trying," Richie said. "The man didn't talk much, simple as that."

DeMarco nodded. He maintained easy eye contact with Richie,

kept smiling. Allowed the pause to make Richie uncomfortable. "Any idea where he might be now?"

"Me?" Richie said. "How would I know that?"

"A man doesn't disappear into thin air without a bit of help. Somebody in this town knows something. And I figure you for the kind of guy on the receiving end of a lot of secrets."

Another pause. Richie shifted his weight, broke eye contact, rolled his shoulders so as to lessen the tension. "What's a couple of Pennsylvania staties care about what happens down here?" he asked.

DeMarco smiled. Jayme said, "We're assisting local law enforcement, Richie. Just trying to grab a lead or two. Can you help us out?"

"I would if I knew anything," he said.

"You must have heard something over the years. Rumors, gossip… Anything you can tell us will help a lot."

He turned his gaze to DeMarco again. "Lemme think on it a day or so, okay? See if I can come up with anything."

When DeMarco stretched out his arm to clap Richie on the shoulder, Richie flinched, flattened himself against the wall of the ATM. "Much appreciated," DeMarco said. "So we'll talk tomorrow. Enjoy your evening." He turned and stepped away.

Jayme gave Richie a final smile, then caught up with DeMarco. She slipped her arm into his. "Do you think he wet his pants?" she asked.

"God, I hope so," DeMarco said.

SEVENTY-TWO

DeMarco had a hard time falling asleep that night, neck stiff and legs tense. So he climbed out of bed and sorted through his belongings until he found a set of earphones. Back in bed he plugged the earphones into his cell phone and searched the internet for a talk radio program that might stop his mind from racing. Before Jayme came into his life he had often tuned in to a show called *Coast to Coast AM* that discussed everything from angels to men in black to star children to shadow people. On this night the subject was cryptid canines, with a special focus on the chupacabra, a large doglike creature famous for sucking blood from livestock.

He fell asleep with the program still playing. In his dream, he awoke to see a boy, twelve or thirteen years old, standing beside his bed. The boy, wearing blue jeans and a yellow shirt, white sneakers with one lace undone, smiled, gave a nod, then walked to the bedroom threshold, his smile encouraging DeMarco to follow.

DeMarco looked to Jayme. She was sleeping with one arm thrown over her eyes. So he slipped quietly over the side of the bed, found himself fully dressed but for his feet. Apparently he had gone to bed in khakis and a short-sleeved shirt. No shoes, no socks.

The boy had stepped beyond the bedroom threshold now, into what seemed an encroaching gloom with an indigo hue. He motioned with his hand and mouthed, *Come on. Hurry up.*

DeMarco took a last look at Jayme. Still sleeping, a princess in her bed.

Then he followed the boy, hurried to catch up.

Beyond the bedroom the rest of the house was gone, nothing but a single narrow tunnel with a ceiling so high and black it could not be seen. As DeMarco quickstepped after the boy, the indigo darkness slowly descended, enveloping him so completely he could no longer see his own hands or feet. Beneath his bare feet the earth felt damp, just hard-packed dirt. The boy, however, some ten yards ahead, remained fully visible, neither brightly lit nor muted in feature, though all around him was darkness. Still, he smiled. A wave of the hand. *Come on. Hurry up.*

DeMarco quickened his pace. The dampness of the earth worried him. What if he slipped and fell? What if he lost sight of the boy?

Then, off to his right, approaching from the rear, a pattering. He glanced over his shoulder. And now the tunnel wall to his right was no longer solid but a thick metal grate rising into darkness. On the other side of the grate, a large animal trotted along behind him. Its features were unclear, nothing visible but a shadow, but DeMarco thought *chupacabra* and quickened his pace.

The animal growled and bared its teeth, loped along easily behind him. The faster DeMarco moved, the faster the animal, its eyes visible now, icy blue. From time to time the animal lunged at DeMarco and snapped but was stopped by the grate. Each time DeMarco looked at it then looked ahead to relocate the boy, the boy had receded farther into the distance.

DeMarco ran, the diminishing figure of the boy his only guidepost. Darkness ahead and behind but for the boy, full darkness to his left, and to the right the grate, the beast, a milky gray as of false dawn.

DeMarco sprinted hard, holding fast to the figure of the boy. The beast began to fall behind.

DeMarco pushed even harder, ran faster than he knew he could, ran as if he were a boy again alone out along the railroad tracks, running for the pleasure of movement, the illusion of escape.

And finally, a light. DeMarco grinned at the cliché, the light at the end of the tunnel. Within that light the boy stood waiting, but with a smile diminished. What's wrong? DeMarco thought. What's happening?

The end of the tunnel drew near, the boy outside the mouth of it now, enveloped in the milky dawn but no less visible than before. He turned his back as DeMarco approached, raised an arm, and pointed into the muted light.

Out of breath, lungs on fire, DeMarco paused at the mouth of the tunnel. Out there in the glaucous dawn an individual seated in profile to him, naked, knees raised, arms wrapped around her knees, sad and cold, so terribly cold. DeMarco could feel her hunger in the air, her fear and emptiness, the chill of despair running through. He began to cry, hollowed out by her grief, too weakened to move.

Look! came the boy's voice loud in his head. DeMarco glanced to the rear, the beast surging forward now, eyes fiery, jaws open. In a few more seconds it would be upon them.

Hurry! said the boy.

DeMarco confused, uncertain, which way, hurry where? Save the girl? Save the boy? Retreat back into darkness and save himself, back to Jayme still waiting in her bed? But was she waiting? DeMarco was unsure, so far away now, it was years ago, he could not think straight. Was she only a dream?

The beast was nearly there, two seconds from clearing the grate. DeMarco could smell its breath, the stink of rotten meat. He reached for the boy but found himself alone. Squinted ahead, heard a baby crying in the fog, lunged forward with the animal's teeth ready to bite down, and he fell, sliding into a slippery darkness...

He awoke gasping for air, hands raised, palms spread, bracing for impact...

Soft moonlight through the curtains. Jayme breathing rhythmically at his side.

He lifted himself into a sitting position. Worked hard to slow his breath. Looked about the room, still expecting to see the boy somewhere. The blue numbers on the clock on the bedside table read 3:36.

Minutes later, still uncertain. Was this reality or the dream? Bit by bit he eased himself from bed. Boxers and a T-shirt. Okay, all normal. He retrieved his weapon from atop the dresser, slipped it from the holster. He crept to the threshold, looked beyond. The upstairs hallway, Grandma's house. Familiar scents. Familiar carpet on the floor.

Downstairs then, creeping along in muted light. He went to the front door, opened it quietly, uncertain what might lay beyond.

A normal night. The yard in moonlight, the scent of summersweet. The air not cool but refreshing nonetheless. The heavens in their place.

SEVENTY-THREE

Jayme awoke to find the other side of the bed empty, the sheet cool beneath her hand. She climbed out of bed, pulled on an oversize T-shirt, and walked quietly downstairs, listening for some sign of his presence. The house was silent all around her, no lights to brighten the natural dimness. She found him asleep at the kitchen table, head on his arms, laptop open a few inches from his head but the screen dark, yellow legal pad beside it. His Glock in the center of the table. The only window faced north, so the light at not yet six was soft and indirect. She leaned over his shoulder to read what he had written.

Clarence Earl Coates 132 West Pine Elizabethtown KY
Antoinette/Toni 4617 Clifford Heights Carbondale IL
Shawnee Hills Family Dentistry 438 Maxwell Drive

Quietly she jiggled the mouse and woke the screen. MapQuest, the route from Aberdeen to Carbondale, Illinois. Seventy-eight point three miles.

She went to the counter and dumped the remainder of the previous day's coffee down the sink, rinsed the carafe, and soon had fresh coffee dripping into it. There were only three eggs left in the refrigerator, but also a thick ham steak. As she reached for the eggs, a chair scraped the floor. She turned to see DeMarco rising. "Hey there," she said.

"Umm," he answered, and shuffled out of the kitchen.

By the time she had the eggs beaten, the sound from the shower upstairs could be heard, the gurgle of water draining from the stall and down through the pipe in the wall, so she cleaned and sliced a fat baking potato and set the slices to frying in her grandmother's cast-iron skillet along with chopped onions and sweet peppers. When these were ready she scraped them onto a platter and slid the platter into the oven on low heat. By the time the ham was ready and in the oven with the potatoes, DeMarco's footsteps could be heard going back and forth in the bedroom, old boards creaking, so she wiped the skillet clean, melted a spoonful of butter, then added the eggs.

She was spooning cheesy scrambled eggs onto the platter with the ham and potatoes when DeMarco came downstairs slicked down and shaved and fully dressed but for his shoes.

She handed him a large mug of coffee and kissed his cheek. "Couldn't sleep?" she asked.

"I slept," he said. "Just vertical, more or less."

"What brought you downstairs armed and dangerous?"

"Bad dream," he said.

"Want to talk about it?"

"I'm fine." He pulled out a chair and sat down. "Is this all for me?"

"If you can eat it all."

"Maybe you should join me."

"How sweet of you," she said.

She gathered two forks and a steak knife from the drawer and set them on the table, then took the seat next to his. She slid the platter midway between them and asked, "Planning a trip to Illinois?"

He leaned close to the platter and inhaled. "Mmm," he said.

"As in?"

"Mmm smell good. Me like meat."

She picked up the knife and began cutting the ham into small chunks. Conversation could wait. Over the past couple of weeks she had learned that both of them usually woke quickly, were fully alert within a few minutes of opening their eyes each morning, but that he required a more gradual entry into human interaction than she. She had once heard him tell their station commander, when it was suggested that DeMarco interact more with the younger troopers, that "human interaction is highly overrated." She remembered that comment now and smiled as they ate their breakfast.

For a man, she thought, he was a quiet and careful, almost meticulous, eater. No heaping forkfuls, no loud chewing or lip smacking. His mannerisms were almost feminine, the way he sank his fork into a bite of ham, then speared a bit of browned potato to accompany it into his mouth.

Maybe someday she would ask him where he had come by such manners. The mother, she guessed. She still knew little about his family, only that they had been poor and lived in a rented trailer, that his father was frequently absent and at other times abusive, his mother loving and attentive when not depressed or drinking. He had lost his father at fifteen, shot in the chest, assailant unknown. His mother committed suicide five years later, shortly after Christmas Day 1989, DeMarco in Panama, a soldier, a boy with a gun.

When he talked about these incidents it was in broad strokes only, dispassionate, "one of the neighbors found her body," and "things were crazy in San Miguelito then, so the news didn't reach me till the twenty-seventh."

She watched him surreptitiously now and tried to envision him as a child. Quiet and unnaturally still, she supposed. Keenly observant, but with little external sign of that trait. Stillness and alertness as a survival skill.

He finished eating before she did, drained the last of his coffee and leaned away from the table. Now, if he was ready to talk, he would talk.

First he stood, took the carafe from the coffeemaker, and refilled both of their cups. When he was seated again, after a preliminary sip, he said, "I'm ninety-nine percent certain Eli Royce is not responsible for those seven girls."

"And yet?" she said.

"I need to get rid of that final one percent. Before we can leave him behind with Henry and McGintey."

"You're ready to dismiss McGintey too?"

"You're not?" he asked.

"For the most part. I would like to spend a few minutes with the two girls, though. The ones in the truck with him."

"We can do that," DeMarco said.

"Who's Toni in Carbondale?"

"The girl Royce made pregnant the year before the bones were found. According to her Facebook page, she's a dental hygienist now. Mother and father live east of here."

"Elizabethtown," Jayme said. "It's in your notes."

He nodded, sipped his coffee.

"How did you track them down?"

"Telephone call to Vicente. Very grumpy man at oh-four-hundred hours."

"Why didn't they just give us that information in the first place?"

"All he had was the father's name. I got the rest from the DMV. Other information from Antoinette's Facebook page. Daughter is nearly five now. Anya Sage Coates."

"Pretty name. But not Royce."

"Not Royce."

"And you think we should talk to her? Antoinette, I mean."

"I think you should."

"And here I thought I might sleep all day."

He stood, gathered up the dishes. "I'll clean up breakfast, you clean up you. Deal?"

She leaned her head back to look up at him. "And how am I dressing for the day?"

"I'm thinking we head straight to Carbondale to chat with Antoinette."

"After which we either jettison Royce from the list or tighten the screws on him?"

DeMarco paused a step from the sink, plates and cups precipitously balanced, and said, "If it's all the same to you, I'm for tightening the screws no matter what. Just for the fun of it."

"So I dress for empathy in the morning," she said, pushed back her chair, and stood. "Then a little sadism in the afternoon. The leopard-skin capris are out, I guess." She stood with her bare feet apart, one hip cocked, still wearing nothing but an oversize T-shirt.

DeMarco sucked in a breath at the sight of her. "That's a fairly sadistic outfit right there," he said.

"You have fifteen minutes to load the dishwasher," she told him, then spun away, slowly hiking up the hem of the T-shirt as she walked.

"I can do it in three," he said.

SEVENTY-FOUR

They arrived in Carbondale with the last rush of morning traffic, Jayme at the wheel. They had an unspoken agreement that she handled heavy traffic better, became less rattled, less likely to engage in the strange St. Vitus dance that seized DeMarco at such times, foot to accelerator, foot to brake, accelerator, brake, heel of fist to horn. He preferred speeding along rural asphalt one- and two-laners, taking the straightest line through hard curves. Speed and open roads relaxed him. His only relaxant in city traffic was to have Jayme at the wheel.

He glanced at the yellow legal pad on his lap, then spoke into his cell phone. "Shawnee Hills Family Dentistry." Within seconds, the navigator function, in the voice of a prim New England schoolmarm, suggested a left turn approaching. "You catch that?" he asked Jayme.

She nodded and flipped on the turn signal, then glanced at the digital clock—8:47. "Do dentists open at eight or nine?" she asked. "All my appointments are in the afternoon."

"I have a feeling our Toni gets an early start."

He had used the ninety-minute drive to gather a few facts indicative of Antoinette Coates's standard of living. Her four-story apartment building of sand-blasted red brick had once been a high school. The photo showed a circular drive at the front of the building, flagpole newly painted silver, a banner proclaiming *ALL NEW UNITS!* frozen in midflutter. Rent for a two-bedroom unit topped out at eight hundred per month.

She drove a 2010 Chevy Cobalt.

She availed herself of low-cost campus day care for Anya Sage.

The dentistry business was located in the center of an eight-unit strip mall. Approximately half the parking slots in the lot were filled. One of the cars was a red Chevy Cobalt sporting an SIU commuter sticker. Three doors down from the dentist's office was a small bakery with two wrought-iron tables on the sidewalk, both empty.

Jayme parked facing the bakery.

"I'll grab a table," DeMarco said as he climbed out.

She unbuckled, climbed out, and locked the door. "And a dough-nut, I bet."

"Verisimilitude," he said.

A few minutes after Jayme entered the dentist's office, she returned to join DeMarco at the table. He wiped doughnut glaze from his lips and handed her a cup of coffee. A third cup, capped, with two cream-ers beside it on a napkin, sat at the center of the table.

"She's with a patient," Jayme said as she sat. "How was the doughnut?"

"Sugar free. Just the way I like them."

"Right," she said. She placed her cell phone face up on the table, opened the voice recorder, then turned her chair to face the dentist's office. They sipped their coffee, watched the traffic, and said nothing more for the next three minutes. Then a pretty girl in a pale-green lab coat over black slacks and a white blouse stepped out of the dentist's office and looked their way. Slender and of medium height, she wore her hair in thin dreadlocks cut to shoulder length.

Jayme waved, pressed record on her phone, turned the screen to the table, and stood. DeMarco picked up his coffee, stood, and walked leisurely toward the far end of the strip mall.

"Hi, Toni," Jayme said, and extended her hand. "Thanks for meeting with me."

Antoinette Coates stopped three feet short of the table. She said, "Who are you? Is there something wrong with Sage?"

"No no no," Jayme said. "Everything's fine. I just need a couple minutes of your time is all. Can you sit down? I bought you a coffee."

"I don't drink coffee. And I have a patient who'll need me in about five minutes."

"Then I'll only take four," Jayme said, and smiled. "Can we sit?"

After a few moment's hesitation, the young woman pulled a chair from the table. She sat on the edge of the chair, ready to rise at any second.

"So I'm Jayme," Jayme told her. "And you're wondering who I am and why I'm here."

The only response was the hum and whoosh of traffic going by. She continued, "My friend and I are on our way to talk to Pastor Royce in Evansville about a couple of matters, but the only one relevant to you is the matter of child support. We just want to make certain that you and the pastor's daughter are being sufficiently provided for. Anya Sage is a beautiful name, by the way. Did you pick that out?"

The young woman's almond-shaped green eyes narrowed. "Who ever said she's the pastor's daughter? I never said that."

"No, but it's common knowledge, right? And I've never heard Pastor Royce deny it. So…we're here just to make sure he's meeting his obligations to you. Are the payments on time? And are they sufficient to meet your needs?"

"They are what they are," Toni said.

"Well, what if I told you that I can maybe get you an increase? Would that help?"

"Of course it would help," Toni said. "But how you plan to accomplish that?"

Jayme smiled. "I'm thinking three thousand a month. Does that sound reasonable to you?"

"In child support? No way he'll agree to that. Triple what I'm getting now? No way you can do that."

"I'm not sure you fully understand your rights here, Toni. You've never spoken to a lawyer about this, have you?"

"He made us promise not to. Told my daddy he'd take us to court if we did."

Jayme frowned and shook her head. "You're the one who should be suing him. Besides the child support, did he pay for all the medical bills before and after Anya was born?"

"She goes by Sage. And yes, he did."

"Is he providing for her future? A college fund? It takes a lot of money to raise a child, doesn't it?"

"If you want to do it right, it does. And I'm doing it right."

"I know you are. You pay your rent every month, you drive an eight-year-old car, you take classes at the university. You are doing a good job, Toni. An excellent job. The question is, is he doing his share?"

"How do you know all that about me?"

"It's our job to protect young women like you. That's what we do."

Toni was silent for a moment. Then she sat a bit straighter. "I need to be getting back to my patient."

"I understand. One last question though. Has he ever become violent with you? Has he ever abused you—physically or verbally—in any way?"

"I haven't seen the man in three, almost four years now. And I don't care to either."

"Did he ever show any tendencies toward violence when you were with him?"

"He's a man, isn't he?"

"In other words, he did."

Toni shrugged. "He'd grab me by the arm, scare me a little. The man does what he wants, doesn't want to hear no argument about it." She shifted in her chair. "I got to be getting back," she said, and stood.

Jayme stood too. She reached for Toni's hand, covered it with both of hers. "Here's what I'd like to do," Jayme said. "If I send you a telephone number of somebody to talk to—"

"What somebody?"

"A lawyer. Somebody local. Someone you can trust. It won't cost you a cent. But you need to know what your rights are, Toni. What your options are. For you and Sage both. The man has a net worth of eight point six million dollars."

"You're not serious," Toni said.

"I am dead serious. Can I send you a telephone number? I'll call the secretary in your office—will that be all right?"

"It won't cost me anything?"

"Not a cent. Do it for Sage, okay? And do it for yourself. You both deserve better."

"And what about what he'll do to me and my family?"

"He's a public figure. He can't risk bad publicity. Trust me; you're the one with the power here, Toni. Within twenty-four hours I will call your office with my phone number and the number of a lawyer. And you can call me anytime you want. Okay?"

She squeezed Toni's hand.

Toni said, "This isn't some kind of sick joke or something? You just appear out of nowhere and tell me all this?"

"It's what somebody should have told you a long time ago."

Toni looked toward the dentist's office, then back at Jayme, and withdrew her hand. "I gotta get back," she said, and turned away.

Jayme watched her into the dentist's office, then turned to see DeMarco approaching. "You damn men," Jayme told him when he arrived.

"I know," he said. "I apologize for my gender and my species."

SEVENTY-FIVE

DeMarco drove the hundred miles from Carbondale to Evansville so that Jayme could research lawyers and advocates who would handle a child support case on contingency or pro bono. In the meantime he used an earphone to listen to Jayme's recording of her conversation with Antoinette Coates.

By the time DeMarco pulled into the sprawling parking lot of the gleaming Resurrection Baptist Church, Jayme had telephoned the Shawnee Hills Family Dentistry office with the contact information for two firms. Thick charcoal clouds were reflected in the church's glass panels.

Jayme closed and stowed the laptop. "So what's the protocol, Sergeant? Seeing as how we're not exactly doing police work now, are we?"

"We're not that far outside the parameters," he said. "One last good shake, just to see what falls out."

She sensed that he was changing, albeit subtly. Before Huston's death he was known as a by-the-book officer. But it was no secret that his report covering the final twenty-four hours of Huston's life contained numerous improbabilities. During the following months he had retreated even deeper into himself, save for the weekends spent with her. But even then he'd been guarded and kept a tight rein on his emotions. Of late, however, those emotions had begun to show themselves, like bursts of smoke and ash from a sleeping volcano. Jealousy. Heightened aggression. And, at least as far as Royce was concerned, a thinly veiled desire for something like revenge.

She unbuckled, then popped open her door. The dense, humid air rushed in like a backdraft. "Nice and polite, same as always?"

He retrieved his Glock and pocket holster from the console. "I know no other way."

They were kept waiting in the anteroom for ten minutes before being permitted entry into Royce's sanctum. He looked flushed, his forehead shiny with perspiration. The arm candy was visibly absent, no other persons present but for the two goons who, after closing the door behind them, followed Jayme and DeMarco as they approached Royce's desk.

"Still on vacation from Pennsylvania, I see," Royce said. "Have you come seeking salvation?"

DeMarco smiled. "Truth is salvation, is it not?"

Instead of pausing in front of Royce's desk, he strolled leisurely about the room, looking first at a photo of Royce and the governor on the desk, then at books on a bookshelf, pictures on the wall, matching vases on pedestals on opposite sides of the room. One of the goons followed DeMarco wherever he went.

Jayme stood motionless at parade rest, hands clasped loosely below her back. She wanted to keep an eye on DeMarco, but instead held her gaze on the pastor, alert for any tells.

"The truth shall set you free," Royce answered.

"Or send you to prison," said DeMarco. "Speaking of which, are you still in the habit of manhandling young women, Reverend?"

Royce's lips closed on his smile. "You're a bit far removed from your jurisdiction, aren't you, Sergeant? Can I assume this is a social call? Have you come to make a donation to the cause?"

"Take me back to the day the infestation of termites was discovered," DeMarco said. "You were on site at the time?"

Royce leaned back in his chair, rocked a couple of times. "You understand that I have no obligation to answer your questions."

"I certainly do understand that."

Royce nodded. He released a slow breath. "I am assuming that you already know I was there. It was the day of our summer picnic."

"But it wasn't you who discovered the infestation."

"One of our deacons. Who was alerted to it by a parishioner."

"And the name of that parishioner?"

"That I can't recall. Though it must be in the records. Other buildings along that street had been treated earlier in the summer. Private homes."

"And after you were informed by the deacon, what did you do then?"

"I checked it out, of course. And found there was cause for concern. Holes in the wood, mud tunnels, a couple of live ones clinging to the wall."

"Who contacted the exterminator?"

"I did," Royce said, his irritation increasing. "And I then telephoned our sexton to let him know a full inspection and treatment would be held in the morning."

"You're speaking of Virgil Helm," DeMarco said. "And how did he react to that news?"

"With few words, as always. I told him to be at the church at 7:00 a.m. sharp, and he said he would. But obviously wasn't. Which makes me wonder why you keep beating all these empty bushes around here and don't go find yourself the one man you should be looking for."

"If you did make the call," DeMarco said. "That's never been corroborated, has it? Which sort of makes me wonder if Virgil Helm disappeared of his own free will."

By now DeMarco had made a full circuit around the room. He stood at the corner of Royce's desk, fingertips balanced atop the glassy edge.

Royce looked past him to Trooper Matson. "Is he always this humorous, or is he having an especially good day?"

She chose not to answer.

"Was Chad McGintey present at the picnic?" DeMarco asked.

"Why in the world would I allow that fool at a picnic for my parishioners?"

"Did the two of you part on bad terms?"

"I was pleased to be rid of him. Man was lazy to the bone. I'd have to tell him six times before he'd get anything done. Stoned out of his mind most of the time."

"And his reason for leaving your employment?" DeMarco asked.

"Claimed he had other work. From what I heard later on, it involved his brother and their own grass, though of a different variety than what grew in my churchyard."

"To your knowledge, was McGintey aware of the false wall?"

"Now how could I have any knowledge of that when I myself had no knowledge of a false wall?"

DeMarco nodded, pursed his lips, thought for a moment. Then he leaned toward the pastor. "How long has it been since you last saw Anya Sage, Reverend? I hear she's a beautiful little girl."

Royce pushed himself erect, seemed on the verge of standing up. "I believe it's time for you to leave," he said.

"You should put her on TV with you this Sunday. Maybe have her sing a hymn or two. Unless you're afraid your audience will look at her mother and do the math."

Royce stood. "Your time is up," he said. The goon behind DeMarco stiffened.

DeMarco grinned. "I believe yours might be up too, sir."

He turned, and found himself facing over two hundred pounds of scowling goon. DeMarco kept smiling. The goon slipped a hand inside his jacket.

DeMarco said, "I'll show you my gun if you'll show me yours."

A few scowling seconds passed. Then the goon lowered his hand and stepped aside. "Trooper," DeMarco said, "do you remember the way out?"

"Like the back of my hand," she said, and walked with him to the door.

In the lobby she finally turned to look at DeMarco—a long, hard stare.

"What?" he said.

She waited until they were outside and headed for the car. The air was even heavier and hotter now, the sky uniformly dark. "Why would he call the exterminator if he knew the skeletons were there? Obviously he didn't put them there."

DeMarco used the remote to unlock the car. "Where's Virgil Helm?" he said.

They popped open their doors and climbed inside. He started the engine, cranked the air conditioner to max. She said, "He fled. Because *he* knew."

DeMarco buckled up, put the gearshift in Drive, and headed out of the parking lot. "Probably," he said. "Or not."

SEVENTY-SIX

Earlier that morning DeMarco and Jayme had made plans to finish their day with visits to Chad McGintey's nineteen-year-old companion, currently being held in the county jail in Bardwell, and the fifteen-year-old minor, at her grandmother's home a few miles east of the city. But their plans were changed when DeMarco received a call from a blocked number. The caller introduced himself as Special Agent Kevin Erdesky of the Federal Bureau of Investigation.

DeMarco pulled the car to the side of the road and put the phone on speaker. The agent said, "I was wondering if you and Trooper Matson could meet with me for a couple of minutes."

"How's tomorrow morning work for you?" DeMarco asked.

"Today works better. What's your location right now?"

"About twelve miles north of Bardwell."

"Perfect," Erdesky said. "You know where the dog park is on Templeton?"

Jayme had her own phone out and started thumb-typing. DeMarco glanced out the window. Sheet lightning bloomed across the sky. He said, "If I'm not mistaken, we're about to get a downpour."

"There's time," the agent said. "How do you take your coffee?"

"Is the Bureau into meteorology now?"

Erdesky laughed. "Doppler radar. The cell is still thirty minutes out."

"Then I guess we'll see you at the dog park. Iced for me. Cream, no sugar." Jayme nodded. "The same for Trooper Matson."

"See you there."

DeMarco hit End Call.

Jayme asked, "What do you think that's about?"

DeMarco shrugged. "You can bet it's not about dogs."

SEVENTY-SEVEN

A s expected, the dog park was empty. A few streetlamps had come on in response to the early darkness. Thunder rumbled as DeMarco and Jayme made their way through the park.

"There he is," Jayme said, and nodded toward a bench outside a large fenced-in area, where a man in blue jeans and a black sport jacket sat beside three clear plastic cups of coffee lined up in a row. Visible behind the coffee was a sign affixed to the fence: *Large Dog Run*.

"Do you think that's a coded message?" she asked. "He's letting us know he's the big dog here?"

"As if we didn't already know," DeMarco said.

The agent stood and shook their hands. He was balding, maybe five ten, maybe forty years old. "Sorry for the short notice," he said. "I'm out of town first thing in the morning, so this was my only shot at meeting you in person."

DeMarco picked up two coffees, handed one to Jayme. "Why do I get the feeling you know a lot more about us than we know about you?"

Erdesky picked up the final coffee, popped off the lid. "I need to ask you to take a couple steps back in regard to the good reverend."

DeMarco said, "You have somebody on the inside?"

"What I can tell you," the agent said, and sipped his coffee, "is that the Resurrection Baptist Church is under investigation for several matters not relevant to your own investigation."

"Our investigation of the good reverend is over," DeMarco told him. "I don't anticipate having to speak with him again."

"That's good to know," the agent said. He took another sip of coffee and seemed to relax. "Which leaves you where?"

"In our investigation?" DeMarco said. "Virgil Helm. The last card we have to play. He's not one of yours, is he?"

Erdesky smiled. "Good luck with that. From what I hear, the man's a ghost."

"And you're sure Royce had nothing to do with turning him into one?"

"Reasonably certain. If you learn otherwise, I'd appreciate hearing from you." He reached into his jacket pocket, brought out a business card, and handed it to Jayme. As she took it with finger and thumb, a raindrop splashed down on the back of her hand.

"Looks like it's time to head for the cars," Erdesky said. "Thanks again for the meet. Enjoy your stay in Kentucky." With a final smile, he turned and walked away.

DeMarco took a step back and sat on the park bench. A flash of lightning lit the park momentarily, and was followed four seconds later by a long rumbling boom. Jayme said, "Now you sit? That lightning is less than a mile away."

"The car's only fifty feet away," he said. "I like this kind of weather. You notice how it smells now? Fresher. Even in a dog park."

"You're sitting there on a wrought-iron bench in front of a chain-link fence. You're going to get fried."

DeMarco smiled. "Sometimes you get fried, and sometimes you get magical powers."

SEVENTY-EIGHT

Before Ryan started school, back when his father still went to his job in the rail yard most days, back before the drinking and violence became more than just a weekend affair, his father would sometimes prop a lawn chair up against the trailer on summer nights to watch the stars and to look at the moon with a pair of old hunting binoculars. If Ryan was especially quiet he could tiptoe up to where his father sat and ease himself down onto the ground without disturbing him and being sent back inside. They would sit there together without talking, and sometimes Ryan would fall asleep and later wake to find himself in bed.

Ryan's father especially liked summer thunderstorms, when he would move his lawn chair to the rear of the trailer where a short overhang protected him from most of the rain. Many times Ryan sat on his knees on his bed beside his mother as she put her face to the window screen and urged Ryan's father to come inside before he got hit by lightning. His father would laugh and sip his beer and say, It can hit me just as easily inside as it can out here, and eventually Ryan and his mother would move to the table where they would play Old Maid while the rain hammered the metal roof and the thunder rattled the glass and the lightning filled their little home with a sudden and terrifying brilliance.

One time after a particularly frightening blast when the light and sound simultaneously shook and stunned them, knocking out the power, Ryan in the shivery, pattering darkness asked, Why isn't Daddy afraid of the lightning? His mother whispered, Because he's crazy. He thinks if it doesn't kill him, he'll come away with magic powers of some kind. Ryan asked, What kind? and his mother said, ESP or something. Like he'll be able to see into the future. And then

Ryan understood why his father sat in silence summer nights staring through binoculars at the moon. He was looking for a future, something better, a different family maybe, a different life, a different son, and he wanted it all so badly, he was willing to risk death to get it.

SEVENTY-NINE

'm exhausted," Jayme said. "Okay if we just pick up a pizza for dinner?"

"Pizza is always okay," DeMarco said.

She called in the order as he drove slowly through the rain, a downpour the windshield wipers could not cope with even at their fastest speed. The pizza shop was at the end of Aberdeen's Main Street, a quarter-mile-long strip of mom-and-pop storefronts, all now dark but for dim interior glows barely visible behind the rain sheeting off the edges of the roofs. DeMarco squinted hard through the blurry windshield, and frequently glanced out the side window to make sure he didn't veer from the proper lane. Fortunately there was little other traffic to contend with.

A block from the pizza shop he slowed even more, then came to a full stop as he leaned close to the side window.

"You're not there yet," Jayme said.

He said, "Isn't that Richie over there?" Three men stood beneath a canvas awning, two of them smoking.

Jayme leaned across him to peer out the window. "Okay," she said. "And so?"

"We need a lead on where to look for Virgil Helm. He was supposed to come up with one."

"Supposed to?" she said with a little laugh. "He just told you that to get you off his back."

"Only one way to find out," DeMarco said. He slipped the gearshift into Park and cracked open his door. "You want to grab the pizza and pick me up on the way back?"

"It's only a question if I have a choice," she told him, then shoved him toward the door. "Go get wet."

He jumped out, slammed shut the door, and sprinted across the street.

Jayme climbed over the console and settled behind the wheel. All the way to the pizza shop she kept shaking her head back and forth.

EIGHTY

The three men smelled of sweat, beer, tobacco, and marijuana, individually distinctive odors that, dampened by the rain, merged into a wet dog stink DeMarco had smelled a thousand times before, from Youngstown to Panama to Iraq to Pennsylvania and now to Kentucky. Upon his sudden arrival, the three fell out of their short line parallel to the street and reformed in a tight grouping perpendicular to it, with DeMarco alone a yard away.

Richie did not introduce DeMarco to his friends. There were no introductions.

"Gentlemen," DeMarco said, and wiped the rain from his eyes.

Only Richie managed a tentative smile. "Evening, Sergeant," he said. Immediately, the two others seemed to shrink within themselves, their shoulders tightening, heads dipping an inch lower. "What's brought you out on a night like this?"

"Pizza run," DeMarco said. "Then I spotted you. Thought I'd stop and see what news you have for me."

"News?" Richie said. "About what exactly?"

DeMarco looked at each of the other men. Hard, wiry, wary. One staring down at his feet, the other out through the rain.

"Local real estate," DeMarco said. "Don't you remember we talked about that last night? You said you'd have some suggestions for me."

"Yeah, well," Richie said, "I haven't had much time to give that any thought."

"I have a minute," DeMarco said with a wet smile. "Why'n't you go ahead and think about it now. Meantime, who are your buddies here?"

The nearest one said, "Listen, I shoulda been somewhere a half hour ago. I'll talk to you tomorrow, Richie." And off he went, loping through the rain.

"Yeah, same here," the other one said, and then he was gone too.

Richie watched them disappear. DeMarco waited half a minute before he spoke. His voice was pitched low, barely louder than the thrumming rain. "You and me, Richie," he said, "we're never going to be best friends. But what you don't want is an enemy."

"I don't know what you want from me," Richie said. "That guy... all that business with the girls? I heard about it, yeah, but that doesn't mean I know anything."

DeMarco took a step closer, faced the street as Richie was doing, but held his hands loosely clasped in front of him whereas Richie's hands were shoved deep into his pockets. DeMarco could feel the contempt rising in his chest, the encroaching anger. He knew the feeling well but not the reason for it. He had dealt with men like Richie before, many times before, and had always been able to muster a semblance of compassion for them, individuals not blessed with special talents or ambition, cursed by circumstance, limited by their own imaginations to hardscrabble lives of inevitable misfortune. So why this animus for Richie—this virulent disdain growing more poisonous ever since their very first meeting?

"I've known people like you all my life," DeMarco told him. "You do a little of this, a little of that. You skirt the law whenever you can, but you're never far outside the line. You tell yourself you're some kind of outlaw, but you don't really have the balls for that, do you? You had a little taste of lockup and you know it's not a picnic. It's not something you ever want to taste again, not even a month here, a month there. But you always keep your ears open, right? Always looking for something you can use to your advantage someday."

DeMarco turned, faced him directly. "Well, now's your chance, my friend. I'm your advantage. Or I'm your enemy. Take your pick."

He watched Richie swallow. Even imagined he could hear the rocks tumbling in Richie's head. The rain was slowing now, lapsing into a steady patter. The scent of cooler, newly washed air. The small-town stillness.

Richie kept his head down, looked at DeMarco out the corner of his eye. "From what I hear, there's a half brother nobody knows about over toward Pottsville. Just across the West Fork."

"Name?" DeMarco asked.

"Stumpner. First name Walter, I think. He's Amish or something."

"I appreciate this, Richie."

"I ain't saying he knows anything. But he's the only person who might. If he's even still alive. All I know is what people were saying back in the day. I don't even remember who I heard it from."

DeMarco laid his hand on Richie's shoulder. "Now I owe you one," he said. "You see how this works?"

Richie held his breath for a moment, then released a long breath. "Man," he said, "I don't even know why you're fooling around with this shit. You're not even from here. If I had a sweet piece waiting for me at home like you got—"

In an instant DeMarco's hand slid up Richie's shoulder and around his throat, and he drove Richie hard against the glass, heard Richie's head bang the glass and felt the vibration down through his arm, heard himself thinking *Don't do this* even as his hand was tightening and pushing Richie's chin up, Richie's mouth puffing air and his hands pulling at DeMarco's hand, feet shuffling atop the concrete...

The sound of the car horn seemed to come at DeMarco from a distance but grew louder by the instant until it was there just behind him, steady and shrill and insistent, and he came back to himself and felt the tightness of his hand and arm and shoulder, and he pulled away, released Richie, then turned to face the headlights. Jayme was inside those lights, he knew, though he could not see her. And he realized what he had done.

"It was a compliment!" Richie was saying, coughing between words. "I only meant it as a compliment!"

DeMarco walked head down out into the rain. He opened the passenger side door, picked the pizza box off the seat, climbed in, and held the box atop his lap. Peripherally, he could see her staring wide-eyed at him, could hear the echo of the horn ringing in the stillness.

Finally, she yanked the gearshift into Drive and pulled away with a squeal of tires. The heat from the pizza was burning the tops of his thighs, but he dared not lift the box, dared not so much as flex a hand lest the awful stillness shatter.

EIGHTY-ONE

I'm becoming my father.

The thought horrified him. Why was it happening now? The absence of a uniform? The absence of regimen and routine? He thought he had outlived that possibility, had driven it too deep to ever surface again. Why now?

She meant too much to him.

EIGHTY-TWO

He waited in the car for almost an hour, long after the rain had stopped, pizza box on the driver's seat. No stars outside the still-streaked window; no moon.

Taking pains to be quiet he climbed out of the car, pizza box in hand, and pushed shut the door. Then onto the porch. Front door unlocked. House silent and dark. She was probably upstairs. He hoped she had eaten something, hadn't gone to bed hungry. He put the pizza in the refrigerator, shoved in lopsided so it would fit.

Go upstairs or not?

What would he say to her? *I'm sorry. I didn't know it was going to happen. He made a remark.*

What kind of remark?

He said it was a compliment. I didn't think so.

What does it matter what he says? Why does it even matter to you?

I don't know.

You think I fucked him, that's why.

It doesn't matter.

What, you never fucked anybody?

Please don't.

You think you're the first man to fuck me? What are you—sixteen?

Please stop saying that word.

You want me to tell you every man I've ever fucked? Is that what you want? Sit down, get comfortable; I'll tell you every single one.

Or maybe it wouldn't go that way. Maybe she would cry. No, she wouldn't cry. She had a right to be angry.

I'm afraid I'm becoming my father, he would say.

Oh, for God's sake, Ryan. Grow up.

The keys to the RV were on the counter. He picked them up, jiggled them in his hand.

Okay, he would go to bed hungry too.

EIGHTY-THREE

Gray light through the window. 5:17 a.m. The RV was already growing hot, the air stuffy. He should have opened the window over the bed, but too late now. Sleep was impossible.

It was almost humorous, that he was afraid to face her. But there was no humor in being ashamed of himself. He'd let her down, that was the thing. He wasn't the man she'd imagined him to be. He'd always known that truth, and now she knew it too.

He tried to remember something he'd read one time, something about a human's capacity for self-reflection, our main distinction from the animals. In the heat of an animal response we have the ability to pause, reflect, turn away from a bestial desire or impulse.

He hadn't done much reflection over the past dozen or so years. Too much reflection in the year prior had burned out the circuitry. He chose a less painful tactic and buried all desire, all impulse deep in the sand of grief. Reflection was permitted only in the line of duty. All business, nothing personal. In the morning he wound himself up with coffee and routine, went to work, then came home. He ate a sandwich, downed a couple of beers, sipped three or four whiskies while the TV numbed him into sleep. The hell with the circuitry. Who needs self-reflection when the motherboard is dead?

Well, that was then. Now he was self-reflecting up a storm. A funhouse mirror in a hurricane.

He needed something to do. Throw a blanket over the mirror before he made himself crazy from squinting and staring into it. Maybe give Jayme time to decide how she felt, whether he was worth the turmoil or not. Give himself time to figure himself out.

Go find Virgil, he thought. *Show her you have some value after all. But not just for her. For the seven girls too. And be honest about it: for your own sake as well.*

Okay then. Either mop up this mess in Aberdeen or admit failure and walk away knowing you did your best, or tried to anyway. Then one way or the other, alone or with Jayme—please, God, with Jayme—get the hell out of Dodge.

EIGHTY-FOUR

T he sun had barely cleared the trees, but was high enough to throw a glare of harsh light slanting into his stinging eyes as he crossed the West Fork Mayfield Creek. A few miles later he turned due east toward Pottsville and had to pull his sunglasses on. Soon his phone's navigator informed him that he should make another left in one mile. On both sides of the road lay wide green fields of corn and little else.

"In a quarter mile, turn left," his navigator said.

Still nothing but corn, acre after acre standing at least as tall as him. Only when he was nearly upon it did a small structure emerge from the glare, a wooden stand with a wide opening, a single glassless window facing the road. Small boxes of fat tomatoes, cucumbers, squash, and other vegetables were lined up on a counter below the window. A teenage girl wearing a small blue bonnet stood behind the boxes, arranging them in perfect alignment.

"Turn left," the navigator said. "Turn left."

Just beyond the roadside stand, a long, dirt lane ran perpendicular to the highway. DeMarco would not have seen it but for the dark-blue pickup truck parked close to the intersection of lane and highway, its tailgate open. A middle-aged woman in a long blue dress and tight-fitting bonnet was unloading a box of green and red sweet peppers from the bed. A bearded man in baggy jeans, a blue work shirt, and a yellow straw hat stood watching, then slammed the tailgate shut and climbed into the truck. He was driving away, disappearing behind the corn, just as DeMarco pulled onto the shoulder.

DeMarco powered down his window and shouted to the woman. "Would that be Walter Stumpner by any chance?"

She gave him a look, then continued on to the front of the stand, where she hefted the box up onto the counter.

DeMarco climbed out, crossed to her, smiled broadly. "Good morning," he said. "That man who just now drove away. Was that Walter Stumpner?"

The woman ignored him for a moment; the girl stared.

DeMarco tried a slower approach. "These are great-looking tomatoes," he said, and picked up one as big as his hand. "How much are they?"

"A dollar fifty for two," the girl said.

He took two bills from his pocket and handed them to her. She said, "I'll let you have a cucumber for fifty cents."

"Deal," he said.

And now the woman faced him. "What is it you're wanting with Mr. Stumpner so early in the morning?"

"Just have a couple of questions," he said.

She looked to the RV. "You won't be getting that thing down the lane. Not less you're planning to drive the ditches."

"I don't mind walking," he told her. "I could use the exercise."

"If you're wanting some wood cut," she told him, "he won't be able to get to it until the fall. Leave me your number and he'll give you a call tonight."

"It's not about that," he said. "It's about his brother. Virgil."

She looked at him a moment longer, face expressionless, then turned to the girl and extended an open hand. The girl reached into an apron pocket, pulled out a cell phone, and passed it over the counter. Without a word the woman crossed to the rear of the stand and into the corn.

DeMarco smiled at the girl. "Will she be coming back?"

The girl grinned, blue eyes clear and lively. "She's calling him."

DeMarco nodded. "I thought Amish didn't use such things as cell phones and pickup trucks."

"We're Mennonite," the girl said. "Where are you from?"

"Aberdeen, for now. But my home is back in Pennsylvania."

"We've been to Lancaster," she told him.

"That's across the state from me. Did you like it there?"

"It's busy," she said. "But I enjoyed it. Though I wouldn't want to live there."

"I don't blame you. This here is about as beautiful as it gets."

"If you like corn," she said.

And now the woman reappeared out of the corn. She came back to the stand, handed the phone to the girl. To DeMarco she said, "He's getting ready to take the tractor out. If you can get there in the next five minutes, you might still catch him."

"Thank you," he said. He picked up his tomatoes and cucumber, carried them to the RV, and laid them on the seat. Then he started down the dirt road. A quarter mile ahead he could see a white farmhouse, a barn, and several outbuildings. "Oh joy," he said, and broke into a heavy-footed jog.

EIGHTY-FIVE

S till fifty yards from the farmhouse, DeMarco could jog no farther.
He hunkered down over a shallow drainage ditch, panting, trying
to decide if he needed to throw up or not. Moments later the rumble
of a diesel engine overpowered the pounding in his ears. He cranked
his head to the left, saw a large John Deere tractor making a turn away
from the barn and heading his way, Stumpner's straw hat bouncing to
the wheels' heavy rolling *thrump thrump thrump*.

Three deep breaths, then DeMarco pushed himself more or less
erect and walked toward the tractor. It soon pulled alongside him.

Stumpner cut the engine, looked down. His face showed neither
surprise nor fear. "You fellas sure took your time getting here," he
said. "Who you with?"

DeMarco guessed his age at sixty or more, face hardened and
browned by sun and wind, hands thick from years of toil, beard and
hair threaded with gray. "I'm just helping out," DeMarco told him.
"As a favor. I'm visiting from Pennsylvania, with the state police there."

Stumpner nodded. "We been as far as Lancaster. Seen Gettysburg
too."

"So I heard." He moved closer to the tractor, laid one hand on the
thick tire. "Am I really the first person to speak to you about Virgil?"

Stumpner put a hand to his chin, lightly stroked his beard. "Me
and him never spent much time together. His mother left the church
just after he was born."

"So there are probably no public records to show the family
connection."

"We keep our own records," Stumpner said. "Keep our business
to ourselves."

DeMarco nodded. Then looked down the road, scuffed his

sneaker atop the hardpan. Secrets everywhere, he thought. Piety is not immune.

In Pennsylvania he had dealt with several young Amish women over the years, all runaways due to incest, rape, or physical abuse. For every girl who ran away there were probably five who stayed behind and suffered in silence. Their church tended to blame the girls for tempting the men, often their own brothers and fathers. As a result DeMarco had little respect for Amish piety. The men hired themselves out to those they call English, demanded high wages, and even charged unsuspecting clients a day's wages for the drivers who delivered them to work in air-conditioned vans and SUVs. Nearly every Amish family had a cell phone or two registered in the name of a non-Amish neighbor. Some kept their own vehicles hidden in garages a few miles from the Amish community. He knew one man who also owned a twenty-seven-foot walleye boat kept at a marina on Lake Erie.

At least most Mennonites had dropped the pretense of avoiding engines and electronics. He wondered how much information he could gather from Stumpner, and how best to fish for it.

Stumpner shifted in his seat, rolled his shoulders. "There's places I got to get to," he said. "If you have something to ask me, better ask quick."

"When was the last time you saw Virgil?" DeMarco said.

"I only seen him twice in the last dozen years or more. When he got back from that war in Iraq, he spent a night at the house. Then back in July 2014. He stopped by one night to ask could he get some canned meat and such. That's the last I seen or heard from him."

"Did he say where he was going that night?"

"Did not."

"Do you have any ideas on that?"

Stumpner stroked his beard again. "Let me ask you a question now. How sure are you he done that awful thing?"

DeMarco considered his answer. "He had what we call opportunity.

At least in regard to where the bodies were found. As for motivation…so far, there's not a sliver of evidence he was the type for it."

Stumpner nodded.

"And you?" DeMarco asked. "I'm sure you've thought about it. Could he have done it?"

"That's not for me to judge. Only God can say what's in a man's heart."

"And yet we have to find out, don't we? For the girls' sake, if nothing else."

Stumpner let only a few moments pass. "We done?"

"You know which way he headed, don't you? You would have watched him leave. Probably even asked where he was going."

"Weren't my business to ask," Stumpner said.

Now it was DeMarco's turn to wait. He stood gazing up at the man, eyes soft, encouraging.

And finally Stumpner spoke. "'And I will make with them a covenant of peace, and will cause the evil beasts to cease out of the land: and they shall dwell safely in the wilderness, and sleep in the woods.'"

DeMarco asked, "And where might those woods be?"

Stumpner put a thick finger and thumb to his eyes, pushed at the corners. Then lifted his head and looked toward the sun. "His mother's family is supposed to have come from out that way originally. Mountain folks. Just about the only real woods and mountains you're going to find in this state."

"Any chance you could get a little more specific?" DeMarco asked. "And remember, I have no jurisdiction in this state. All I'm looking to do is talk. Get Virgil's side of things."

Stumpner sat with one hand on the ignition key, another on the gearshift, his foot on the clutch. He blew out a soft breath. "Said he wanted to be buried with his mother. He was having some health problems from being in that war."

"You have an idea where she's buried?"

"I do not."

"You know her name?"

The man stared at him a long time.

DeMarco said, "Just so you know, Mr. Stumpner, I'm more or less obligated to pass on any information I collect to the county sheriff. More or less."

"Meaning what?" Stumpner said.

"Meaning I realize how important it is to your lifestyle, your religion, to not get involved in the ways of the English. I'm not sure the sheriff would care about that, however. I suspect he won't. So when I say I am more or less obligated to report everything to him, I'm saying I've been known to suffer a bit of amnesia from time to time. Such as how I learned Virgil's mother's name."

Again Stumpner was silent. His expression betrayed no emotion.

Then he said, "Leah Grace." He leaned forward a bit to take the ignition key between finger and thumb. "Summerville," he said. He turned the ignition key, and the engine boomed to life. He let out the clutch, and the tractor lurched forward with a startling growl, nearly running over DeMarco's foot before he jumped to the side. Then out the lane it went, raising a small cloud of yellow dust to swirl around DeMarco as he watched the machine pull away.

EIGHTY-SIX

S he slept poorly throughout the night, waking, it seemed, every hour or so to the sound of a door closing, or footsteps coming down the hall, or the feel of the mattress being pushed down from the side, as if he were easing himself into bed beside her. But when she reached out he was not there, nor when she sat up to listen and looked around the dark room for his moving shadow.

When she awoke she was surprised to find the room so warm and full of light. She picked her phone off the end table—7:29. No indentation in the pillow beside hers. No warmth lingering on the sheets.

She went to the window and looked out. No RV. "Sonofabitch," she muttered.

When the tears started, she returned to the bed, curled up, and cried with the cell phone clutched in one hand. And then she was angry at herself for crying, and stopped for a while, and pushed the phone away.

She could not remember a time when men had not disappointed her. If they lost themselves for a few minutes in the act of love, afterward they would be apologetic and filled with guilt, or else arrogant and self-satisfied, or silent and closed off. Even her father, her first love, had let her down again and again. Every clement Saturday morning he and the three boys would leave early for eighteen holes of golf at the country club. Why had he never asked her to go along? Why had he never taken her instead of one of the boys? She played golf with her mother sometimes, always in an all-female foursome, and by the age of fourteen was outdriving and outscoring all of them. But what she had longed for was the company of men. She wanted to see how they acted with each other, if they laughed freely and unselfconsciously then, if they hid their emotions, bragged about their talents, or sought commiseration for their shortcomings.

It never happened. They remained a mystery to her. A frustrating, maddening mystery.

She loved them all, loved them still, yet felt somehow alien from her father and brothers. Even Galen, whom she had loved the strongest. And now DeMarco. Another disappointment.

She wondered if maybe he was a kind of surrogate for the love she felt denied by her father. Maybe Galen had been too. Which would make DeMarco a surrogate for both her father and Galen.

Love is so messed up, she thought.

She hated them all, singly and collectively. All just a bunch of assholes. She hoped he never came back.

Well, that was a lie. He'd come back sooner or later, tail tucked between his legs. Until then she was giving him nothing. Not a single word. No way was she going to call or text with a pitiful *Where are you? When are you coming back?* Let him sweat for a while. Give him time to realize the error of his ways.

And when he did come back, things were going to be different. No more deference on her part. They were civilians now. Equals. Except that she was more than equal. She outranked him in intelligence. Sexiness. Jogging. Let's see if he could give himself a blowjob. *Oh, you want to have sex now? So go fuck yourself—how about that?*

He was lucky to have her. And if he expected to keep her, he had better be ready to open up with her. No more secrets. No more half-truths. It was going to be all or nothing, buster. Save that strong, silent, hard-ass persona for everybody else.

"Damn straight," she told his pillow, and gave it a punch. Then, for good measure, she hammered it twice with her fist. "Screw you!" she told it. For extra good measure she turned off her cell phone, vowed she would not turn it on again until nightfall.

Then she buried her face in the pillow. Smelled his scent. Felt herself go hollow and weak. And decided to try to sleep through it all, to sleep as long as she could. With luck she would wake up sane and single again.

EIGHTY-SEVEN

F rom his air-conditioned captain's seat in the RV, surrounded by cornfields and a sky turning pale with sunlight, DeMarco Googled *Kentucky mountains*. Elevated prominences ranged across the state, but the highest were part of the Daniel Boone National Forest in the lower Appalachians south and east of Lexington. The entire mountain range lay like a long, gnarled finger, knuckles wrenched and broken and swollen, across parts of Georgia, Tennessee, Kentucky, and up through Pennsylvania into New England, as wide as three hundred miles in some places, and over fifteen hundred miles long. The Kentucky component comprised a mere seven hundred thousand acres.

"You've got to be kidding me," DeMarco muttered.

He sat up and peered through the windshield's glare. How could he possibly find a man inside all those trees? Especially a man who neither the local police nor the FBI had been able to trace.

He must have been using an assumed name, DeMarco told himself.

Would he carry that name with him to the grave?

The Department of Veterans Affairs online gravesite locator showed no record for Virgil Helm. DeMarco had expected that result, seeing as how no military records for Virgil Helm seemed to exist. The graves registry displayed Helm graves scattered all over the state, including along the southern range of Kentucky's forested mountains, but listed no individual names.

He'd wanted to be buried next to his mother, Helm's half brother had said.

DeMarco tried the gravesite locator again. No Virgil Summerville. So he was either alive or hadn't been buried with a government marker, or hadn't used that name.

A search of military records found eleven Virgil Summervilles, but none of them came close to matching Virgil's age.

Maybe, DeMarco thought, he'd made up a first name too. Which would make further searching statistically impossible.

Now what?

Stumpner had indicated two things: that Virgil had fled to the mountains and wilderness, and that he wanted to be buried with his mother. Which implied that she was already deceased.

Leah Grace, DeMarco thought. Find her grave.

The national graves registry showed Summervilles planted all over the country, of course, including throughout Kentucky. *Which one is yours, Leah Grace?*

Back to a map of the forest. Wilderness and mountains, DeMarco told himself. Wilderness and mountains...

A section of land between London and Corbin seemed to fit the bill. Only a few county roads in and out. No large towns. No major tourist attractions. Hard up against an eastern edge of the Daniel Boone National Forest.

Back to the graves registry. Five Summervilles buried in a little town of Blue Goose.

Five hours from his current destination, MapQuest said.

Five hours there, five hours back, he thought. A day of searching. Two days minimum.

What was Jayme doing now? If awake, she would know the RV was gone. And him with it. Was she worried?

He checked his phone. No texts, no missed calls.

Okay, she wasn't worried. Still pissed off, no doubt. Maybe permanently.

DeMarco considered his options. He could return to Aberdeen, beg forgiveness, be forgiven or spurned. He put the odds against for-giveness at six to one. Which would leave him exactly where he was at that moment, facing east alone. Jayme would follow at her leisure in her grandmother's car. Back in Pennsylvania he would sell the RV and split the money with her. She would return to her job and bright future, and he would…

What? he asked himself. You will do what?

One text, he told himself. If he received a response that did not consist of only expletives, he would turn around, hightail it back to her, do whatever was necessary to patch things up. Until then, he wasn't going to just sit there staring into the morning sun.

What was the original quote old Horace Greeley had borrowed? "Go west, young man, and grow up with the country."

So okay, a different variation for me, he thought. Go east, old man, and grow up already.

With his index finger he typed out a text: *Got a pretty solid lead on Virgil Helm, need to follow it up. Should take two days at most. Will stay in touch. I hope you know how sorry I am. How much you mean to me.*

Should he say anything else? Add a smiley face?

No, not a good idea. He hit Send. And waited. If she responded, if she wrote *Come back*, he would go back.

Five minutes. No reply. He checked to make sure he had service out there in the country. Checked to make sure the text had been sent. Waited five minutes more. No reply.

He shut off the idling engine, climbed out of the RV, leaned against the fender, looked out across the field of corn.

Watched the slowly scudding clouds, gray destroyers and frigates.

Listened to the insects buzzing. Watched three buzzards circling to the north.

No reply.

No reply.

So okay, he thought. You have clothes in the drawers. Hiking boots in the closet. Coffee and some food in the cupboards. Jayme's backpack and sleeping bag. As for Jayme…she's not ready to talk. Give her some time.

He climbed back into the RV. "East," he told himself, and turned the key.

EIGHTY-EIGHT

He pulled over at a rest area north of Keavy, Kentucky, the town nearest tiny Blue Goose on the eastern edge of the mountain range. Using his laptop he pulled up the white pages for Keavy, plugged in *Helm*, and came up with six entries. Called all, nobody knew Virgil. Back to the white pages for Summerville. Seventeen matches. None of them Leah Grace, L.G., or any variation. Explanation: Leah Grace no longer had need of a phone.

He started calling again, the first of the two initialled Summervilles with Blue Goose in the address. And struck pay dirt on the first try. A woman, not young. She formed her words slowly, every syllable trembling. "I do. I do know Grace. I knew her well. Might I ask the nature of your inquiry?"

"Actually, I am trying to locate her son. I believe he went by the name of Virgil."

The woman took a long time to answer. When she spoke, her words were more certain. Absent the slow delivery, the tremolo quickened. "Why, he passed away over there in that war. I'm sorry to inform you." She hung up before he could ask another question.

He tried the same number again, but this time received no answer.

Next stop, the cemetery.

EIGHTY-NINE

The town of Blue Goose lay at the bottom of a shallow valley surrounded by fields and second-growth forest. DeMarco entered at the southern end and drove slowly past a half-dozen mobile homes and small houses, then, on both sides of the road, a tight grouping of early-twentieth-century and older two-story buildings that had once housed prosperous businesses, but now either stood empty or had been converted into low-income necessities—a laundromat, Dollar Store, drive-through beer distributor, plumbing business, Rent-A-Center, styling salon, urgent care center, drive-through bank depository and ATM, plus several mom-and-pop enterprises with apartments on the second floor, including an eatery called Donna's Dinette. Homes on wide yards were spread out on streets behind Main, more than he expected to see in a place called Blue Goose.

Having long ago eaten the tomatoes and cucumber acquired from the roadside stand that morning, plus a peanut butter PowerBar from Jayme's snack stash in the RV, DeMarco took a side street and parked the RV in the gravel lot behind Donna's. He climbed out, knees stiff and shoulders sore, to the scents of grease and garbage, the first emanating from the clacking vent fan mounted on the rear wall, the second from the overflowing Dumpster beneath the fan.

If this were a Hollywood movie, he told himself, Donna would either be a seductive blond in her thirties, or a world-weary yet golden-hearted fading beauty who dispenses sweet nuggets of wisdom with the best coffee in the county. Either would be welcome after five hours at the wheel.

Three customers, all old men, sat alone, hunched over their plates, in three different booths. They all looked up as DeMarco entered, as did the woman visible through the open window behind the short counter. She gave him a little nod then went back to scraping the grill.

He chose the center stool of the five at the counter. Music from somewhere in the kitchen came softly through the window, a female singing "when she saw them together, she said goodbye to forever…" He turned the thick, enameled coffee cup right-side up and studied the menu on the paper placemat.

A minute later the woman from the kitchen came toward him, glanced at his cup, then grabbed the carafe from the coffeemaker. Her hair was black going gray, hips wide, fingers as thick as a man's.

"Grill's closed," she said as she filled his cup. "But I can do you a bowl of chili and a cold turkey sandwich if you want."

"Sounds perfect," he said, and smiled.

If she had any smiles, she kept them to herself. "Mild or hot?"

"Ma'am?"

"The chili."

"Leaning toward hot," he said. "Lettuce, tomato, and mayo on the sandwich?"

"Wouldn't serve it no other way." She looked past him then. "You boys all right?"

Two of the old men nodded; one lifted his cup. "I could use a refill when you get a chance."

"What's left in the pot is for him," she said, and jerked her chin toward DeMarco. "You had enough already."

DeMarco said, "I don't mind if he—"

"I do," she said. "He'd set there all day if I let him." She turned sharply and went back to the kitchen.

DeMarco shrugged, sipped his coffee. It was strong, astringent, with an undernote of burned. So much for Hollywood, he thought.

The chili, when it arrived, was too greasy for his taste, but he ate it anyway, along with the white-bread sandwich with its thick slices of dry turkey breast. Individually his three courses verged on unpalatable, but together they worked perfectly, the chili coating his mouth with a lingering film and slow-burning fire, the sandwich soaking up the grease and cooling the fire, the coffee scalding his mouth clean so that he could start over and do it all again.

Fifteen minutes later, hunger sated, DeMarco glanced at his bill— $10.42. He placed three five-dollar bills beneath his cup. He wiped his mouth, stood, and said to Donna, who was seated in an empty booth now, staring out the window and smoking a vapour cigarette, "That was excellent. Thank you."

She gave him half a nod and faced the window again.

DeMarco said, "Can any of you fellas point me in the direction of the cemetery?"

Now Donna turned away from the window. "Who you looking for?"

"An old buddy from the army."

"What's his name?"

Before DeMarco could come up with a response, the old man who had asked for a refill scuffled out of his booth. "I can get you there," he said. "I'm going that way myself."

Donna said, "He wants you to drop him at the bar. Don't you do it."

The old man said, "What's it any of your business where I go?" He shuffled past her and up to DeMarco. "It's just a couple minutes up the road."

"I'm warning you," Donna said. "The minute you're out that door, I'm calling Chelsea on you."

The old man grinned, raised his hand in the air, and pretended to pull a train whistle. "Toot toot!" he said. "All aboard!" Then he was out the door and headed for the sidewalk.

"Don't you dare give him any money," Donna said to DeMarco.

"Have a good day," DeMarco said.

NINETY

Y ou live in this thing?" the old man asked. He seemed childlike in the captain's chair, dirty brown loafers barely touching the floor mat.

"Part of the time," DeMarco said.

"Looks like you got plenty of room here. A little castle on wheels, you ask me. How many beds you got?"

"Just one."

The old man turned in his seat, scanned the interior. "What about that nice couch there?"

"What about it?"

"Somebody could sleep on that easy enough."

"I guess somebody could. If I were looking for company. Which I'm not."

"I wouldn't be asking you to marry me," the old man said.

"What about Chelsea?"

"Chelsea's a pain in the ass."

"Your wife?"

"Granddaughter. Barely thirty and thinks she knows what I need and don't need."

"You live with her?" DeMarco asked.

"Her and Numbnuts. Plus two squealing babies don't do nothing but eat and shit and sleep."

"Sounds like a nice little family," DeMarco said.

"You wanna switch rooms, just say the word."

DeMarco smiled to himself.

"Cemetery's up there on your left. You can drop me up the road a piece."

"We'll talk about that," DeMarco said, and flipped on the turn signal. As he drove slowly down the asphalt lane onto the cemetery grounds, he glanced in his side mirror, hoping to see a vehicle following. Nothing yet. "So this person I'm looking for," he said. "Last name Summerville. First name Leah Grace."

The old man chuckled. "Buddy from the army, my ass. Old flame of yours?"

"You don't recognize the name?" DeMarco asked. As he drove he scrutinized the names carved into the memorials closest the road.

"Summerville, you say? She go by Leah or Grace?"

"Which one is familiar to you?" He turned to look out the passenger window, and caught the old man eyeing the coins and crumpled bills stuffed into one of the console's cup holders.

The old man looked up at him. "Lemme think on it a minute or two."

DeMarco pulled the RV onto the shoulder and shut off the engine. "I'm going to get out and walk around a bit. You're welcome to join me, or to stay put."

"I'm sorta in a hurry to get on up the road there. Won't take you more than two minutes."

DeMarco smiled and said, "I'm sorta in a hurry to find Leah Grace." He popped open the door and stepped down. Just then a blue compact came wheeling into the cemetery, moving slowly at first, then making a beeline toward the RV.

The old man, again eyeing the cup holder, said, "You won't be needing this loose change in here, will ya?"

DeMarco turned back to him. "It's for toll roads," he said.

The old man grinned. "None of those to worry about around here!" he said, and stuffed his hand into the holder.

The mud-splattered blue car pulled up behind the RV then. DeMarco turned to walk back to it. A young woman in gray sweatpants, a black T-shirt, and pink flip-flops jumped out, loose brown hair, petite frame, no makeup, brow furrowed and lips pursed. Twin babies were strapped into car seats in the backseat, one of them screaming. The woman left her door hanging open.

"He's sitting up front," DeMarco told her.

"Has he been drinking?" she asked.

"Just coffee, as far as I know."

The young woman's expression relaxed. "Last time put him in the hospital for three days. And we got a high deductible."

DeMarco smiled. He held out his hand. "I'm Ryan DeMarco. You must be Chelsea."

She took his hand, but cautiously. "Donna said you looked like a rich doctor or something."

"I should have left her a bigger tip."

She smiled. "I'll get him out of your vehicle for you. Sorry for any trouble he caused."

"No trouble," DeMarco said.

She went around the passenger side and popped open the door, startling the old man. "Oh, for crying out loud," he said.

"Come on, Paps, let's go. Miley's already crying and Miranda's about to start up any minute now."

The old man climbed out, slowly easing himself down from the high seat. DeMarco waited at the rear of the RV.

Chelsea smiled as she walked past him. "Thank you," she said.

"My pleasure."

The old man paused beside DeMarco, showed the money clutched in his gnarled hand. "You gonna want this back?"

"No toll roads around here, right?"

The old man grinned and shuffled toward the car.

"Be safe," DeMarco told him.

The old man looked back as he stuffed the money into a pocket. "What's the fun of that?" he said, and kept chuckling to himself as he climbed into the blue car.

NINETY-ONE

D eMarco asked himself, Is it weird that I'm enjoying being in a cemetery again?

He had been walking for twenty minutes or so under clearing skies, the sun warm on his face and arms, his hand squeezing the silver locket. The battleship-gray clouds had all drifted north, leaving behind a smoky patina that gentled the sun's glare and tempered the heat by a few degrees. The newest part of the cemetery was the farthest from the highway, a full hundred yards from the RV, and within a stone's throw of a stand of tall, thick hardwoods. Here, for the last few minutes, he had been kneeling close to a pair of small, beveled gravestones, each no bigger than a large boot box, identical but for the words and images inscribed on the polished face.

The one to his left read *Leah Grace Summerville, Beloved Mother, 1959–2011.* Two angels had been carved in the upper corners. The marigolds somebody had planted in front of the stone were no longer in full bloom, with several brown or dying flowers mixed in with the yellow and orange, but were not so old as to appear neglected. DeMarco slipped the locket back into a hip pocket, then cleaned away the spent flowers and leaves from the front of the gravestone, careful not to disturb the healthy ones.

He had passed other Summerville markers on his way to finding these two, but all were much older, some of them by as many as a hundred and fifty years. He guessed that these two had been installed only a day or two after Leah Grace had passed away.

The ground in front of the second stone showed no signs of mounding, no indication of having ever been excavated. The stone read *Emery Elliott Summerville, Beloved Son, 1977–.* The top corners were decorated with matching engravings of a guitar.

DeMarco brushed a dusting of dirt off the top of the stone. "Hello, Virgil," he said.

NINETY-TWO

O n his way out of the cemetery, DeMarco passed the caretaker's equipment shed and noticed the spigot on the side of the building. He paused there to rinse the dirt from his hands. Tacked to the locked door was a laminated card listing both the caretaker's number and the address and number of a company that supplied gravestones. He used his phone to take a picture of the information, and returned to the RV. Along the way he double-checked his phone for a text or voice message from Jayme. Nothing.

He opened the RV door to let the interior cool while he called Trooper Morgan back in Pennsylvania and asked him to contact the military's National Personnel Records Center in St. Louis. Morgan was the least talkative of the troopers back home, the one least likely to ask questions. "I heard you were working a case down there," he said. "What do you need—a DD 214?"

"Correct," DeMarco answered. "Last name Summerville. Emery Elliott."

Then he called the number listed for the caretaker, who answered on the third ring. Unfortunately the caretaker had no access to the records of plot purchases; those were held by the cemetery association, which had no office. The files were stored in the home of the secretary, a Shirley Wynkoop, who was currently on vacation with her family at Epcot Center.

He had better luck with the manager of Pogue Memorials in Keavy. "I probably should ask for some proof you are who you say you are," the man said after DeMarco's introduction.

"I can give you the number for the Kentucky State Police," DeMarco told him, "or my station commander back in Pennsylvania. Both if you want them."

"That's all right then," the man said. "Give me a minute to pull up the purchase order. Summerville, you said?"

"Correct. Two stones. One for Leah Grace, one for Emery Elliott."

He listened to the man typing. Then, thirty seconds later, "Got it," the manager said. "A matched pair of the small slants. Paid for in cash. What do you need to know?"

"Is there an address for the purchaser?"

"Yep. Emery Elliott Summerville. RR 2, Box 12, Blue Goose, KY, 40738."

"Box 12, 40738," DeMarco repeated. "How about a phone number?"

"Nope. Like I said, he paid in cash."

"By any chance, do you remember him?"

"Purchase order was initialled by Nancy. She's not with us anymore. Husband got a job up north."

"Okay. The address will have to do. I appreciate your assistance."

"Have a good one."

DeMarco's cell phone guided him to a run-down cottage two miles east of Blue Goose on a pot-holed macadam road. The house sat at an angle to the road, with three wooden steps leading to a tiny porch and wooden door. The door, like the rest of the house, was a chalky white much in need of a new paint job. The roof shingles were buckled, the lawn overgrown, the wider front porch blocked by what appeared to be three or four houses' worth of used hot water heaters, water filters, and furnace parts. Two dogs, one an overweight beagle and the other a German shepherd mix, both chained to the front porch, watched him as he climbed out of the RV and approached the side door. Soon the beagle broke into a shrill, yodeling bark.

The door sprang open just as DeMarco raised a foot to the first step. A barefoot, bare-chested man in baggy jeans stood on the threshold, wiping grease-stained hands with a paper towel, a dark, thick smudge of grease across his left breast. He was maybe fifty years old, wore thick black-framed glasses held tight to his head with a red Croakie.

"Afternoon," DeMarco said. "I'm looking for an old army buddy of mine by the name of Emery Summerville."

The man scratched his chest, leaving another black smudge. "No Summervilles around here for a while. I bought this place from them most of six years ago."

"You must have bought it from Emery," DeMarco said. "His mother died in 2011, I believe."

The man sniffed, looked away, looked back. "That sounds about right."

"Any chance you'd know where Emery is now?"

"Not a one."

"He didn't leave an address on the seller's contract?"

The man grimaced; cocked his head. "Who'd you say you are?"

"Old army buddy. We served in Iraq together."

"Truth is," the man said, and looked away again, out toward the RV this time, "I don't really recall ever meeting the fella. Seems to me some lawyer or real estate agent handled the whole transaction."

"That sounds unlikely," DeMarco said.

The man's eyes narrowed. His gaze came back to DeMarco. "Well, however it sounds, I can't help you any. I got stuff to do." With that he stepped back and closed the door. A dead bolt clicked into place.

NINETY-THREE

H e's close, DeMarco told himself. If he intends to be buried beside his mother, he's got to be fairly close.

Standing in the shade of the RV, DeMarco looked up and then down the lane. Three other homes, one sixty yards or so farther down the lane, two back toward the highway. Three sets of neighbors.

He didn't want the bespectacled man watching him go from house to house and calling to alert the neighbors. He might already be phoning Emery. So DeMarco climbed into the RV and drove slowly in the direction of the main road, checking out the two houses along the way. The one nearest the highway had a bright-red swing set in the side yard, and what appeared to be newer shingles on the roof. Its front door was closed. The other house and yard were neat, with two small flowerbeds off the front porch, but seemed a bit more drab to DeMarco's eyes, as if the siding could use a good cleaning. The porch was empty but for a single bentwood rocker, with a basket of ferns hanging over the porch rail, a hummingbird feeder on a slender pole stuck in one of the flower beds. The front door was not visible behind the screen door, and so, he reasoned, must be standing open.

"That's your best bet," he told himself.

He parked the RV just short of the highway, half on the lane and half on the shoulder, at an angle that did not give a view to the former Summerville home. Then waited, hoping the bespectacled man would return to his greasy work. Five minutes into the waiting, his cell phone buzzed with a call from Trooper Morgan.

"Emery Elliott Summerville, Specialist E4," Morgan said. "According to his DD 214, home address at time of entry and at separation are the same: RR 2, Box 12, Blue Goose, Kentucky. MOS, mortuary affairs specialist. Good Conduct Medal. Looks like he did four years active duty, a little over two years in Reserves, and then was granted a medical discharge, 15 October 2004."

"Mortuary affairs," DeMarco said. "That means corpse recovery, right?"

"To the best of my knowledge," Morgan said. "Anything else I can do for you, Sergeant?"

"This is great," DeMarco told him. "Exactly what I needed. How's everything going in the frozen north these days?"

"Eighty-six and sunny. How about you?"

"A hundred-twenty in the shade. How's Captain Bowen holding it together? He have a nervous breakdown yet?"

"Just a couple of little ones," Morgan answered. "We got a new guy out of the academy to fill in while you and Trooper Matson are gone. A cross between Speedy Gonzalez and Nurse Ratched."

"You boys teaching him how to be humble?"

"You bet," Morgan answered. "But we're not as good at it as you are."

A pang of nostalgia washed over DeMarco then, and he realized how much he missed his dysfunctional family. They all had their idiosyncrasies and quirks, but they all had their virtues too. Together they kept the quirks in check and multiplied the power of the virtues.

"Give everybody my best," he said.

"Ten-four, Sergeant. And the same to you. We're looking forward to having you and Jayme home again."

NINETY-FOUR

Corpse recovery, DeMarco told himself. That accounts for the illness. Those guys got the worst of it. Filthy desert air, radiation poisoning, breathing in bacteria and chemicals with every breath. Gulf War disease in triplicate.

However, DeMarco thought. If he enlisted in '98, five or six of the victims were already dead by then.

DeMarco noted the dates and their implications in a small spiral notebook Jayme kept in the console. Then sat there staring at what he had written. And thought, It still doesn't rule him out. Assumed name. Disappeared before the bodies were found. Neighbors covering for him.

He tucked the notebook back into the console, popped open the door, and walked briskly across the lane, skirting the edge of the nearest house to cross into the rear yard and past the swing set to the side door of the other house.

Music was playing in a room not far away, country gospel. He recognized the harmonies: the Gatlin Brothers. He knocked twice before the curtain over the door's glass panel was pulled back, and a small, round face peered out at him.

He smiled and mouthed hello.

The door came open, held in place by a safety chain. With it came a stream of air-conditioned coolness. He saw, at chest level, one rheumy eye, a fleshy cheek, half of a cotton ball of white hair. "Good afternoon," he said. "I'm Ryan DeMarco, with the Pennsylvania State Police."

"Oh my," the woman said.

"No, no," he told her, and flipped open his wallet to show the badge and photo ID. "There's nothing wrong, nothing to be worried about,

I promise. I'm just going around the neighborhood, trying to gather some information. Do you have a minute or two to talk with me?"

She continued to peek out at him long enough for three more blinks of the visible eye, then finally unfastened the chain and opened the door wider. The full sight of her brought a smile to his face. She stood less than five feet tall in a pair of loose gray chinos, a T-shirt screen-printed with a huge yellow sunflower, and a pair of blue, non-slip hospital socks. Black-framed reading glasses hung around her neck on a beaded chain.

"What kind of information are you looking for?" she asked.

"How well did you know Leah Grace Summerville?"

The question brought another blink. "Why, I knew her very well. We were neighbors for most of twenty years."

"So you knew her son Emery too?"

She smiled. "He used to come down here when he was little. Always singing a tune of some kind. I have a cherry tree out back, and he loved nothing better than to climb up into that tree and sit there eating cherries and singing his little heart out. I called him my little canary."

DeMarco nodded. "So you knew him later too, I guess. After he came back from Iraq."

"Oh, that war!" she said. "It was like he was a different person. Hardly ever wanted to sing anymore. And he had such a lovely voice too. Reminded me of Jimmie Rodgers. You probably don't remember him."

"My mother listened to him sometimes. Didn't he have a song about a honeycomb, or something like that?"

"'Oh honeycomb,'" she sang, shuffling her little feet, and continued singing all the way through the chorus.

"That's the one," DeMarco said.

And then her face grew serious. "I don't believe for a minute what some people say about him. You heard about that business over west, I take it."

"Sad, sad business," he said.

"A boy as sweet as Emery could never have done something like that. Never."

DeMarco nodded again, remained silent for a few seconds. "So anyway," he said. "I was told Leah Grace's family originally came from the mountains somewhere around here."

"Wildcat Ridge," the old woman said. "That's what Leah called it. Her family was loggers there until the government shut them down."

"Would you have any idea how I might get to Wildcat Ridge?"

She blinked again. "What are you looking for up there?"

"I'm just researching the family," he told her.

"A policeman doing that?" she said. Then, sternly, "If that boy's as smart as I think he is, he's long gone from here by now."

DeMarco asked, "When was the last time you saw him?"

"When he came back home to bury his mother, that's when. And he was just as kind and sweet to me then as he ever was. I wish you people would just leave that family alone."

With that she shoved the door closed. DeMarco felt the push of cool air hit his face, and then it was gone.

NINETY-FIVE

W alking back to the RV, DeMarco had to grin, remembering how Wally Stumpner had not so much as blinked at the name of Virgil. Virgil Helm. Emery Summerville. Every time DeMarco had said, "Virgil," did Stumpner have to make a shift, think *Emery* before he answered? It would be like translating from one language to another.

And beyond Wally Stumpner, closer to Aberdeen, had any of those people known Virgil's real name? Probably not.

But how about Royce, his employer? Wouldn't he have to know?

Not if he paid Virgil Emery under the table. Avoid paying taxes. All that paperwork.

But if Emery Virgil is still alive, DeMarco pondered, he'll be receiving checks from the military, right? The man is sick, probably even sicker now than when he left Aberdeen. Bronchitis. Migraines. Intestinal problems. Memory loss. Sexual dysfunction. Joint and muscle pain. And thanks to the depleted uranium he would have been exposed to, even cellular and DNA damage.

DeMarco had known three such vets back in Pennsylvania. All but one eventually gave up on medical treatment and simply waited for the inevitable. One of those two no longer had to wait.

Emery, DeMarco suspected, had probably given up on treatment too. Was that why he became Virgil Helm? To distance himself from not only the war but also the country that had turned its back on him?

DeMarco climbed into the RV, turned on the engine and air conditioner, and called Trooper Morgan again. "Would you mind running a check on Emery Elliott Summerville for any outstanding warrants and arrests?"

"I thought you might want that," Morgan said. "He's totally clean."

"Dang. Are you at your computer?"

"Yeah. What do you need?"

"Pull up his file again. Medical. Date of last treatment."

"Hold on a minute."

DeMarco waited. The air was blowing out of the vent fast and chilled now, so he pulled the door shut, settled back in his seat. Except for the cost of gasoline and the difficulty finding a parking space, he was beginning to enjoy his land yacht. Half of which, he reminded himself, belonged to a seriously ticked-off Jayme.

He wondered how she was doing. How was she spending her day? Almost seven hours had passed since he'd sent his text. Maybe he should resend it. But what if she was in the cooling-off stage now—would another text fire her up again? This relationship thing was trickier than ever these days thanks to cell phones and email. Last time he dated, a phone call every three or four days was all anybody expected. Fewer if calling long distance. Now, apparently, expectations ranged from—

"2014," Morgan said. "April 9."

DeMarco snapped back to the present. "That was only three months before he disappeared."

"So he's a fugitive?" Morgan asked.

DeMarco chose not to answer. Instead, he thanked Morgan again, hung up, and reached for the notebook.

"All right," he said aloud, needing to hear his thoughts fall into place. "Let's say he stopped going to the VA, started going to some local doc. Or stopped seeing anybody. Chances are he kept his disability checks coming, but how did he receive them? Maybe somebody forwarded them to him. Or maybe he switched to a P.O. box somewhere."

"Or maybe direct deposit," he said. "But which bank?"

He knew that not a shred of paper or anything of evidential value had been found in Virgil's apartment in Aberdeen. It was as clean as a whistle, he had been told, and looked as if nobody had ever lived there.

"But how does this relate to the name change?" he wondered.

"Okay," he said. "If we start by assuming that he's responsible for those girls, then the change of identity is a no-brainer. He needed to stay anonymous or risk getting caught. If we start by assuming his innocence...

"It's harder to explain.

"Harder," he told the rearview mirror and the eyes looking back at him, "but not impossible." The deceased vet he'd known in Pennsylvania had done three tours in Iraq. The more his health deteriorated, the more he hated the government for sending him over there. He stopped treatment. Said he would have stopped his disability checks too if not for his wife and kids. Toward the end, all he wanted was to load up a couple of magazines and take out every government employee at the VA hospital. But he was in a wheelchair then, and his wife refused to drive him to the hospital. So he took himself out instead.

DeMarco blew a heavy breath against the window. He drew a circle in the fog. Drew a diagonal line through the circle. He gazed through the circle at the mountains to the east. "Wildcat Ridge," he told himself.

"Roger Wilco," he said a half minute later. And buckled his seat belt.

NINETY-SIX

DeMarco told his GPS app, "Directions to Daniel Boone National Forest." The pleasant female voice with sometimes humorous pronunciation indicated that the nearest entry point was in London, fifteen miles north. But the little voice inside his head, which wasn't really a voice but an often bothersome nudge, tug, or scowl, said something along the lines of *Unh-uh. Too far.* To get to London, DeMarco would have to drive alongside fifteen miles of forest and, he suspected, past Emery's probable egress from the forest when he wanted to visit his mother's grave.

Every good investigator relies heavily on gut feelings, and DeMarco was learning to trust his more and more, vague though those feelings often were. For most of his career he had been reluctant to credit these hunches, and heeded only the particularly strong ones while, and frequently to his detriment, ignoring the rest in favor of logic. But during a conversation with Thomas Huston he had learned of research indicating that the heart is a sensitive sensory organ producing its own electromagnetic field five thousand times stronger than the brain's, and has a nervous system capable of learning, remembering, and communicating with and influencing the brain. Since then, because he had trusted Huston and admired his intelligence, DeMarco had been trying to listen more carefully to his heart's brain, even when it spoke from the gut. And now it was telling him *Unh-uh. Too far.*

So instead of driving fifteen miles to London he drove three miles to Keavy and parked in two spaces across from a hardware store. Before going inside he took an inventory of the camping equipment Jayme had packed but that they hadn't yet used. A ground tarp and sleeping bag. An orange backpack on a metal frame. Two metal water bottles, a Bowie knife with a ten-inch blade in a black leather sheath, a kit including a collapsible metal cup, metal plate, and spork, safety matches in a waterproof plastic tube, a little camp stove consisting of a can of Sterno beneath a ten-ounce pot resting on a frame, a pint jar filled with coffee beans, plus the remaining eleven PowerBars and an unopened bag of beef jerky.

"More than enough," he told himself. He expected to spend one night at most in the forest. The highest point, well south of where he would be hiking, had an altitude of only four thousand feet. If he could find no sign of Emery by midmorning tomorrow, he would come back to the RV and call in the infantry and air support. The only reason nobody had found Emery by now was because they had been searching for Virgil Helm, a nonentity. Apparently several people had been keeping Emery's true identity secret. What other secrets were they keeping?

DeMarco wondered if anybody had ever cared enough about him to keep such a secret. His mother had. So many secrets they had hidden from his father! And Jayme would. At least he thought she would. At least he hoped.

He considered calling her again. Held the phone in his hand. Lifted it closer to his mouth. All he had to do was tap his finger.

But no. She didn't like to be pushed. She *hated* being pushed. Push her, and she pushed back harder.

Let her be, his heart's brain said. Or so he imagined.

NINETY-SEVEN

In the hardware store he asked the manager, an agreeable middle-aged man with a pot belly and bare, shiny skull, if he had heard of a place in the forest called Wildcat Ridge. "Far as I know," the man said from behind a counter near the back of the store, "there's no place around here officially named Wildcat Ridge. People tend to give places their own names, though."

Beside him a can of paint was being vigorously shaken by a noisy machine that made the plank floor vibrate beneath DeMarco's feet.

"What's up there you want to see?" the man asked in a low shout.

"I heard it's a good place to hike," DeMarco said.

"Most people stick to the Sheltowee Trace. Lots to see along there."

"I'm looking to avoid most people," DeMarco said with a smile. "Privacy, you know?"

"Well then," the man said. He reached down and shut off the paint shaker. The vibration and rapid-fire thump lingered in DeMarco's ears for another thirty seconds. "Seems to me the only times I heard anybody speak of Wildcat Ridge, and that's been a while back, it was one of the old-timers. Fellas used to do some logging there. And as near as I can remember, it was somewhere north of the lake. But with a good view of it."

"Which lake would that be?" DeMarco asked.

"Laurel River Lake," the man said. "We're just off the northern tip of it right now. Head due west from here and keep yourself north of the lake. Any high point you see from there could very well be Wildcat Ridge."

"I appreciate it," DeMarco said. "Is there any place nearby I could park an RV overnight? It's a twenty-eight-footer."

"Campground not three miles from here off 312. You can pick up a couple of trailheads there too. Get you situated before you go off trail. You got a compass?"

DeMarco smiled. "If I get lost, just walk downhill, right?"

"In theory," the man said. "Me, I'd take a compass."

"Got one on my phone," DeMarco told him. "What's the weather report for tonight? Any rain expected?"

"Warm and clear tonight," the man said. "How long you plan to be up there?"

"Not long enough to get wet," DeMarco answered. "Thanks for your help."

NINETY-EIGHT

J ayme reread, for the third time, DeMarco's text. *Should take two days at most.* The words swam before her eyes. Two days? He was leaving her behind, just like that? As if a few words of apology solved everything? Was that all the more she meant to him?

What she should do is pack up her grandmother's car, lock the house, and leave without a word. No texts, no notes, not a single word to indicate where she had gone.

Good plan.

But where would she go?

Anywhere! Anywhere she pleased.

And, for a moment, that thought was exciting, to be so free and unfettered, sailing down the highway like in that YouTube video she loved, Van Morrison's "Philosopher's Stone" playing across the green hills, a slow river of music coursing along the valley.

But then the emptiness hit again, and she missed him. Missed him so badly her stomach felt like a huge stone of emptiness, cold and hollow and as heavy as lead. And just above that leaden nausea her chest burned, heart swollen with misery.

DeMarco was the only man she had ever loved in a full-blown, insatiable, romantic, and normal way. She still loved the first man but had learned to contain that love in a deep unlit corner of her heart just as he had asked her to do. He had put a thousand miles between them specifically to make that containment easier for both, and because he was exhausted from struggling against the moral consequences of their relationship. He had learned from many years of experience that mere willpower would never keep them apart, especially since Jayme had never struggled against any rationale, moral or otherwise. She did concede however that anything you had to keep hidden from universal condemnation was probably doomed. She could quote biblical exceptions to that disapproval and had for a while, but stopped because no argument softened the deleterious effects he suffered. It had never been a public love anyway. According to him, her love was an immature addiction. He promised that she would have lots of boyfriends when she outgrew her gawky stage. But being held by those boyfriends never felt as fulfilling to her, never stilled the other hunger for long. She'd kept hoping it would shrink in significance and fade into a fond, though secret memory.

It showed no signs of doing so until she met DeMarco. She'd been surprised to find herself thinking so frequently of him. It had something to do with proximity, of course, with DeMarco visible five days a week and the other man not even permissible through Skype, which they discovered would inevitably lead to cybersex that left neither feeling soulful or serene.

And maybe that was the difference DeMarco brought to the table. Their lovemaking always left her feeling serene and safe and clean and fulfilled. Even now she had to admire him. It wasn't as if he was out chasing another woman, or had cheated on her or abused her in any way. He was working for those seven unfortunate girls. Chasing down a lead. He was a lot like a wolverine in that regard. A badger. A snapping turtle. Once he got his teeth into something, you had to beat him with a stick to make him let go.

He'd been jealous, that's all. Was a little jealousy necessarily bad? A little insecurity in a relationship? Every man has a bit of the beast in him. But there's a time and place to let the beast run free. He needs to learn the proper etiquette, that's all. She couldn't have him going nuclear every time a man smiles her way.

So now it came down to a battle of wills. A little suffering will be good for him.

But what if he isn't suffering?

What? DeMarco not suffer? DeMarco is a first-class sufferer. Among the men she knew, he holds the heavyweight belt in self-induced suffering.

So she needed to keep herself busy a while. Not lie around moping. There were things she could do too. McGintey's girls should be interviewed. If they had any information, she could squeeze it out of them. Maybe even put them on the right track for a change. Teach those poor girls about a thing called self-respect.

NINETY-NINE

At the campground, DeMarco hoisted up the backpack, loaded down now with all the equipment and supplies from the RV. He was sweaty, exhausted, and hungry already, but felt no inclination to remain in a noisy campground, his RV a mere ten feet from the one next to it. Some time alone in the woods would be invigorating. Atop the first summit he would make a cup of coffee, eat some jerky, spread out the tarp and sleeping bag, and wait for the stars to appear. The weather forecast, posted on the campground's bulletin board, called for clear skies and a low of sixty-five degrees.

He expected to hear from Jayme sooner or later, and then he would do his best to patch things up, and would then be able to pass the night in blessed stillness, with nothing but the scents and sounds of nature for company. Tomorrow he would find Emery Elliott Summerville. Or he would not. The rest he would play by ear. Listen to the heart brain. Listen to the murmurings of seven unfortunate girls—seven unloved babies whose presence, ever since he'd started loading up the pack, seemed to be hovering near.

He couldn't get out of the campground fast enough. The pack was heavier than he'd expected it would be. Or you're weaker, he told himself. With the Glock 27 concealed beneath his T-shirt, he was carrying an extra thirty pounds or more, much of it clanking with every step.

On his way to the trailhead he passed a cement pad with a basketball hoop mounted at each end, all of it enclosed by a chain-link fence. Playing a game of one-on-one were two young men in jeans, no shirts, white socks, their arms and faces deeply tanned, chests and backs pimply and pale. Their hair was shaggy but not fashionably so. Factory boys, DeMarco assumed; late teens or early twenties. Their boots were lined up against the chain-link fence, each beside a tall-boy can of beer. They played basketball clumsily, crouching low to dribble, lunging forward to hit the backboard from twenty feet out, the ball's trajectory flat, with no chance of sailing through the rim.

He watched them and felt sorry for them, a couple of life's under-dogs, no special talents, no grand ambitions. He knew their type well, felt their sadness in his bones. He thought about joining them for a while, a couple games of Horse or 21.

But that wasn't what he really wanted to do. He wanted to have a talk with them. Tell them to never give up on hope. Never give up on love. Keep firing at the rim. Just put a little more loft on the ball. Employ a lighter touch. Life doesn't have to be a constant slugfest, he would tell them.

But would they appreciate such a conversation? Would he have at their age?

Hard to say, he thought. With a different kind of father maybe.

A man like Tom Huston would have a made a world of difference in his life; he knew that much for sure.

And then he saw the trailhead and the opening in the trees, a gaping black mouth four feet wide and twelve feet high, a tongue of packed dirt, a hole full of shade.

IV

Unless you have chaos inside, you
cannot give birth to a dancing star.

—*Friedrich Nietzsche*

ONE HUNDRED

The dimness of the forest surprised him. He had been counting on a good four hours of daylight, but the light in the forest came in stray slender beams, broken and alive with drifting motes of dust. What sunlight wasn't blocked by the high canopy some forty feet above was caught or deflected by the second canopy of saplings and slender trees maybe a dozen feet high. For the first twenty minutes, until his eyes adjusted to the dimness, he held to the trail, but after encountering his tenth or eleventh day hiker descending with nothing more than an empty water bottle or a dog on a leash, every dog too eager to sniff DeMarco's trousers, he thought *Enough of this* and veered straight uphill and slightly to the right of the switchbacking trail.

Here his pace slowed by more than half. But after he had put sufficient distance between himself and the trail walkers that their shouts and laughter faded into whispers, and then no longer registered on his ears, he did not mind the pace, and felt his body attuning itself to the climb, his senses attuning themselves to the more nuanced sighs and scents and sounds of the forest.

And his days as a boy in the woods came back to him then, that old calmness and acquiescence to a deadfall or protruding boulder. What he had taught himself as a child was that if you fight the woods they will weaken and defeat you, but if you attune yourself without resentment to their demands, you can find pleasure and reward wherever you look. His gaze was never more than six feet up the slope now as he walked, and was frequently trained on the understory or ground cover, from the squat shrubs and ferns to the fungus clinging like cantilevered stairs to a tree trunk, the moss and lichens and ground-hugging vines that would snake around his ankles and excoriate his skin with their barbs if he wasn't respectful of their space.

Frequently he had to pause to catch his breath and allow his pulse to even out. He wasn't a boy anymore with unlimited stamina, able to walk and climb all day without rest. But the advantage of age is the ability to endure greater pain, to accept it as concomitant to life, so that the straps pulling on his shoulders and the ache in his calves could be recognized and accepted without bitterness.

In this manner he continued for another two hours, picking his way through a boulder field and detouring around a jagged outcropping of sandstone plates, climbing over deadfalls with spiky broken branches, descending shallow ravines slippery with old leaves, inching under low-hanging limbs. He paused to admire an exposed rock strata polished by the elements so that it resembled an ocean wave carved in stone, and was stopped for several minutes by the sunlight splotches thrown across the forest floor like lemon paint on a Pollock canvas.

Like Jackson Pollock on a pogo stick, he told himself. He stood there smiling, imagining a half-drunken Pollock, cigarette dangling from his lips, bounding through the forest on a pogo stick, its tube filled with yellow paint, every leap squirting out a quart or so onto the forest floor. Of course he would have been knocked silly by the first branch he struck, DeMarco thought, but that wouldn't have damaged the art any, would maybe even improve it.

He was walking a pathless path now, no blazes on the trees, no indication on the ground that anyone had ever walked there before him. He allowed the path to choose itself, moving according to feeling, *this way*, then *this way*. A scent could stop him in his tracks—was that cigarette smoke? The scent of meat frying? The perfume of honeysuckle? He paused frequently, not just to catch his breath and rest his legs but to listen for a sound, a feeling coming from somewhere inside, or maybe coming to him from the woods, he did not know which. But who said he had to keep walking until he exhausted himself? He could walk a while then stop, enjoy the light through the branches or the anomalous surprise of a tiny purple flower growing between two rocks, then walk a while longer and stop again, have a drink of water, take a bite from a PowerBar. The mountain was not infinite, he would reach the top sooner or later. One foot in front of the other, that's all it would take. But nobody said he had to do it without rest. Even the bones could respect that. Keesha, Jazmin, LaShonda, Tara, Debra, Ceres, Crystal. He knew they were in a hurry; he sometimes felt those seven pairs of hands against his back. But sometimes their pressure on him relented too, stopped driving him forward, a lighter touch, as if they were all out walking together, enjoying the day.

Sometimes a sound like a young woman's laugh whispered from the dimness behind him. Sometimes a few footsteps following. Then silence. Not so much as a bird chirping, a squirrel scurrying through the leaves.

He thought it strange that, though he was walking uphill most of the time, except when cutting laterally around an obstacle in his path, a lack of urgency had settled into him. Not even the attention of the insects bothered him for those first hours in the woods, the shrill mosquitoes and silent gnats buzzing around his head, the stealthy spiders and beetles and bugs that somehow made their way onto his trousers, the little green worms that fell out of the trees and onto his shoulders or head.

The constant, barely audible rumble that used to plague him was silent now. Had it stopped because he had climbed above it? Or because this was a different kind of walking than he had engaged in daily as a trooper, when from morning to night he always felt as if he were walking against a wind, a thickness of air trying to hold him back. It had been like swimming against a slow current, nothing so forceful you could not make progress but just strong enough to require greater effort. That was how he had walked through his days for the past thirteen years—as if trudging through a swamp. But in these woods near the end of the day there was a strange lightness to his step despite the heaviness of the pack. He knew he would stop soon, find a place to lie down and sleep for a while. But it was not difficult to keep walking if he decided to do so. No force of opposition blew against him. If he felt anything at all it was a force from behind lightly urging him upward. Maybe he had simply gotten used to the walking, had found the right rhythm, entered into the flow. Whatever was happening, it was a nice feeling. A good feeling. He hadn't felt this good about himself for a very long time.

ONE HUNDRED ONE

He decided on no fire. Had nothing to cook anyway, and felt no need for coffee. Anyway, too tired. He had spent the last twenty minutes bypassing a half acre of brambles by descending and then ascending a steep, deep ravine slippery with dry brown leaves on top, damp decomposing leaves underneath. By the time he reached the top, every muscle was burning.

After clearing the sticks and roots from a small, nearly level shelf of ground several feet from the edge of the ravine, he laid out the tarp and then the sleeping bag, then removed his hiking boots and socks and lay looking up through the leaves. The leaves were dark with the sun below the hills, but here and there a dim star shone through. He could not remember what phase the moon was in, but saw no sign of it climbing the wall of the sky. He chewed a few pieces of beef jerky and sipped the last of the first bottle of water.

He thought back over the past many years, ever since the car accident that had taken his son away. The only times he had not felt alone, had not felt torn in half, were when he was alone with Jayme. Where didn't matter. In a vehicle, his bedroom, walking across a parking lot. How could one person change things so dramatically? Well, Ryan Jr. had too. And before him, Laraine. No one before them. No one. And who was left? Only Jayme. And maybe that was ruined now too.

If only she hadn't flirted with that lowlife. Now everything that had been good and pure between them was tainted, poisoned because of Richie.

And then he told himself that was all nonsense. Purity is a product of love and trust and not past experience. There was certainly nothing pure about his own past. For a long time after his mother's death he had not allowed himself to feel anything but anger and fear and grief.

In Panama and then in the States after Iraq, he had been with women but only to blunt the physical need. The other need was always there and as sharp as a spear, but he would let nobody touch it. He had grown accustomed to the darkness inside and believed he deserved it, so would not allow it to be dispelled, and even doubted it could ever be dispelled.

The fistfights of his youth were nothing compared to what he had done in uniform, and he had come out of those places sick to death of violence. Sick of grief and suffering and loneliness and despair. And one bright day with his heart black with misery he had sought out a dark room so as to contemplate what to do with his shameful life, and bought a ticket into a movie house and sat in a rear corner to work up the courage to do what he wanted to do, and was surprised to get caught up in a movie that gave direction and the promise of purpose to that life. And afterward he was blessed with moments of purity, thanks wholly to three people in his life—moments with Laraine and then little Ryan, and now finally with Jayme.

The truth, he told himself now, is that nobody ever gets to be pure except through love. And if you're not yet old enough or smart enough to realize that, DeMarco, you never will be.

All right then, he thought. You know what you've done, and what you've failed to do. It can never be undone, but maybe you can use it and learn from it, become a better man, a better partner for Jayme. You can open up more. Give her more of what she needs. Maybe you can take what you're feeling up here in these woods and carry it back down the mountain with you.

God, how he missed her. Wished he could share all this with her, the stillness and the forest and the breeze through the leaves. The scent of night. Her scent. That fresh, soapy, warm, filling scent she gave off.

The night was beautiful, fragrant and still and almost sacred in its peacefulness. But even that felt empty without her.

He rolled over and reached for his pack. Rummaged through

it, took out the phone. Screen dark. Battery dead. Why hadn't he remembered to charge it before leaving the RV? Why had he ever been jealous? Why did something as beautiful and wonderful and rare as love feel like broken glass in his chest?

S leeping, he heard the footsteps approaching. He knew those shuffling footsteps, heavy and slow. He knew that presence, knew the
stench of its breath, and was assailed by a paralyzing fear, an inability
to breathe, a thundering of his heart. A pit of darkness enveloped him.

But then a realization: *You're not a boy anymore.* And the fear
bloomed into anger, such a roar of heat flooding his body that he sat
upright, fists clenched, and would have leapt to his feet were he not
waking now, not yet fully awake but eyes open and straining in the
darkness, the blackness all around him but smelling of forest now, the
air thick and moist on his face.

It took him a while to unclench his fists, to separate the dream
images from the real. The night was pitch-black, just like some nights
back in the trailer, but his father, he now recognized, was not a part
of it. Yet the image of his father standing close, hand reaching down,
was difficult to dislodge.

In his dream he had been small, and that was how he'd always felt
around his father. Then, the summer after his father's death, a growth
spurt. On the football team he was feared for the ferocity of his play,
feared by teammates and opponents alike. In gym class DeMarco
found himself to be faster and stronger than his classmates, able to hurl
a soft, fat dodgeball at lightning speed to pin a cocky opponent against
the folded-up bleachers. He often stepped in front of the weakest
member of his team to intercept balls, catching and returning them to
nail the rival in the chest or head.

But sports could only slacken the boiling pressure, never extinguish
it. Even when he sat motionless at his desk, classmates felt DeMarco's
heat. Teachers avoided calling on him, treated him delicately, afraid
of unleashing whatever force simmered within. DeMarco was amused

by it all. They thought him full of indiscriminate fury, half-orphaned son of a murdered man. How could a boy from such upbringings feel anything but rage?

Only he knew that what he felt was liberation. Infinite possibilities. A caged pigeon freed to become a falcon. They all feared him, and he liked it.

Now, in the woods, still chilled from the dream of his father, he felt nothing but shame for those years, and for the years that followed. Until Laraine and then Baby Ryan he had cultivated and polished an intimidating persona, used it whenever called for, and just as often when not. Laraine and his son then stripped that all away. She was two months along when they learned she was pregnant. Ryan Jr. was still a baby when he died. Call it thirteen months altogether then. Thirteen months as a better human being—gentle, nurturing, all gratitude, all joy. Then the car accident. DeMarco reverted full force. Silent. Brooding. Unreachable. And truly filled with rage.

He lay on his side now, stared at the dark bark of the nearest tree. He had become, he realized, a version of his own father. A bully. A punisher. Bearer of a soul so hard and small and mean.

He despised that man. Wanted rid of him forever. Wanted to cut him away clean, shed him like a skin.

Jayme was the key. He could not do it without her. His last chance to open up, be the man the boy in him had always wanted to be. The man the boy who loved the woods had often felt himself to be, only to return home to the trailer, to poverty and fear and helplessness.

You're not helpless now, he told himself. There's nobody now to blame. You have to change yourself.

The bark of the nearest tree was darker than the darkness, almost shiny. The bark lay in thick black scales, ridged, fissured, overlapping layers. Beautiful in its way, brilliant in its construction. To think of it as an accident, a product of mindless evolution... Can't be, he thought. Just cannot be.

The fall of leaves, the seasons' change. The humus, the earth, the fragrant fecundity. Why had he forgotten all this? Why had he ever allowed this feeling, this certainty of life, conscious and observant, meticulously made—why had he ever let it slip so far away?

The dream. His father's shadow hovering over him. It needed to go. But how?

Rewrite the dream, he thought, and, remembering this, he smiled. Took a long, slow inhalation, and released it just as slowly.

He had asked Thomas Huston one time, after Tom had confessed to the plague of nightmares that tormented him, "How do you deal with such dreams?" And Tom had said, "I rewrite them. I sit there half-awake, but awake enough to know I've been dreaming, and I rewrite the dream. I come through the door before my mother is shot, and I tackle the guy and knock him down. Or I pull out a revolver and put a bullet in his head. Or I shoot him through the window.

"It doesn't change reality," Tom told him, "but it keeps the dream from haunting me all day long. It keeps the dream from making me crazy."

DeMarco bunched up the top of the sleeping bag into a pillow, wiped what felt like a cobweb off his face, and lay on his back again, looking up. The leaves were black and the sky was black. Everything around him was black. He closed his eyes and imagined himself as a boy in his bed on a night as black as this one. He let the footsteps approach, but this time the boy was not afraid. The door to the bedroom opened, and it was he, DeMarco, and not his father who entered. DeMarco walked quietly to the bed, saw his son sleeping peacefully. He bent low to kiss the child's head, and the boy smiled in his sleep.

He awoke to a chorus of birdsong, and lay awake listening in gray light. The crows were easy to identify, as were the shrill jays. There were at least two warblers calling back and forth to one another, plus more sparrows and nuthatches than he could distinguish.

His back hurt from sleeping on the hard ground, but he knew the ache would fade after a few minutes of walking. All in all he felt good about the day ahead.

He had a drink of water from the second bottle, and thought about making a small fire to heat water for coffee. Then decided against it. Walking would wake him and was healthier than coffee. He looked up the hill. Maybe an hour to the summit. He would climb to the top, hope for a clearing, a wisp of smoke, some sign of human habitation. If he saw nothing, he would turn downhill, return to the RV, call the local authorities, and let them find Emery Elliott Summerville.

He saw now how foolhardy he had been to imagine he could do this on his own. Such vanity. It was laughable, really. As stubborn and stupid as always, he told himself.

After putting on his boots and socks he shook out the sleeping bag and tarp, rolled them tight, and secured them to the pack's frame. Worked the Glock in its holster into a hip pocket. Picked up the pack, ready to slip an arm through the strap and swing the pack onto his back. But first looked uphill again.

In his heart he knew there was nothing to gain by continuing. Yet he didn't want to quit. Throughout the afternoon yesterday he'd had a peculiar feeling that the girls were with him. Seven weightless spirits marching along beside him. Now he felt nothing. No presence. No hands resting lightly on his back, urging him forward.

Just finish it, he told himself. Get to the top, have a look around.

Rest, eat a PowerBar, and then head back. You'll make the RV by noon, be back in Aberdeen by dark.

But first he had to take a leak. He leaned the pack against a thick oak, took a long step away from it, and faced a smaller tree before pulling down his zipper. Fifteen seconds later, just as he was zippering up, bark exploded off the tree, peppering his face and sending a blast of wood dust into his eyes. An instant later the crack of the gunshot reached him. Blinking and squinting, nearly blinded by the dust, he lunged for cover behind the thicker oak, at the same time grabbing for the gun on his hip—a stumbling, lurching motion that brought his left shoulder into contact with the oak and sent him tripping forward another six feet, then tumbling and rolling and sliding all the way to the bottom of the ravine.

ONE HUNDRED FOUR

H e remembered coming down hard and the brief explosion of pain when his head struck a rock, and then nothing till he opened his eyes and found himself on his back in the leaves. Now, in addition to the throbbing ache at the base of his skull and the pulse of what felt like liquid fire in his left leg, his spine felt strange…cooler than the rest of his body, cool all the way up to the shoulder blades.

He lifted one shoulder, tested for paralysis. Okay, he could move, at least from the waist up. Wet, his back was wet. But blood would be hot. Water underneath the leaves. Stream bed.

For a while then he lay there listening for the crunch of footsteps that would bring his death. All the while the pulse of pain in his leg grew and flourished, flaring rhythmically from ankle to knee, throbbing like a tortured heart. He did not know if he could move his leg or not and was afraid to try. Afraid to look at the damage. Everything hurt.

Just do it, he told himself.

He jerked his left heel closer, bending the knee, and pain ripped up through his leg like a serrated blade, searing hot and nauseating, into his anus and testicles and stomach and chest, so sudden and strong that it choked off his scream and mushroomed inside his head where it snuffed out every thought.

He opened his eyes. Felt his chest rising and falling with every breath. The pain was still there, ubiquitous. The little patches of sky overhead were not yet scalded by light, so he had not been unconscious long. There was a vague memory that might have been a dream of somebody standing above him, looking down, but the figure was all shadow, accompanied only by the sound of a distant chainsaw, lawn mower, the nebulous scent of engine exhaust.

He put a hand to his pocket, felt the holster still there, empty but for the leaves crammed inside. Without the Glock he was defenseless. Defenseless and broken. Now there was nothing to do but to wait for the shadow's return. Wait for one more gunshot.

He slipped his fingers into a pocket, worked his hand down deep. One fingertip touched the silver metal disk. Still there. He nudged it higher, into his palm, and closed his hand around it.

A scrape of leaves. He lay motionless, listened. Heard nothing more. "Is that you, Emery?" he said. His voice was unfamiliar to him. Fearful and hoarse.

He thought maybe he should pray. But what would he pray for— forgiveness? That was probably out of the question. Too much to forgive.

What he regretted most were all the years with no one to love. After his mother died, there was no one until Laraine. And then he was doubly blessed for a few short months, a wife and son. Then the accident, and again he was bereft.

And then, out of nowhere, another gift. Jayme. A godsend, undeserved. And he had treated her poorly, allowed a weakness to beset him. He had not embraced the gift as the clemency it was.

So here he was alone again, the leaf-matted sky almost black overhead, the decaying leaves damp and cold. His leg felt huge with pain. Sometimes a scorching heat would shoot up the ankle and scald his testicles, so that he had to grab them and squeeze to keep from screaming. Sometimes the pain would flare all the way up his spine, burning every vertebrae and disc, then up the back of his skull to set the skin and hair on fire.

He was going to die in these woods. Bones dragged off and gnawed by scavengers. Shreds of clothing buried beneath another season's leaves.

None of that mattered to him. What mattered was that he had so irremediably screwed up his first chance at happiness. And his second. He had never told Jayme how he truly and deeply felt. Always wanted to, always intended to, but the words when they began to form in his consciousness always sounded somehow like a betrayal of Laraine and Ryan Jr.

All too soon more leaves would fall in the fleetness of time. He'd imagined he could surmount these woods and their mountain. He'd thought he could find justice for the seven unfortunate girls. More vanity. Whoever had fired into the side of that tree would at any moment return to finish him off.

He closed his eyes. So empty. So tired. "Our Father," he began, but then stopped himself. Father had never worked for him. Father was anger and punishment. Mother was nature and often gentle, soothing, but just as frequently neglectful, lost in her own torrents of despair. So he could not pray, not even now. Not until he found somebody or something different to pray to. But what else was there?

Images flashed across the back of his eyelids. Faces of people he knew. Strangers. He heard his heavy breathing, the soft moans, they did not seem to belong to him. He felt his body sinking into the leaves, carried along by the stream beneath the leaves as if he too were just another fallen leaf among the vastness of billions.

H e opened his eyes to birdsong, the air warm and heavy and full of the loamy scent of earth, dead leaves, rotting wood. The wet chill moved up and down his back but seemed gathered at his shoulders.

The birdsong meant he had been lying there in the leaves long enough for the birds to calm. As a boy he used to test the birds and other animals. Used to sit motionless against a tree, waiting to see how long before the woods accepted him.

And now they had. The light through the canopy was brightest at an angle of maybe sixty degrees above the plane of his body. He had come into the woods from the east. The sun was still in the eastern sky. Midmorning. He had slept—or passed out; the distinction seemed irrelevant—for at least two hours.

Which means what? he asked himself.

It means that whoever took that shot at you isn't coming back.

It means you aren't dead yet.

Though you're still pretty much fucked.

As long as he lay perfectly still, the pain in his leg lay still too, but as tight and ready as a constrictor coiled around his leg from ankle to knee. But this snake was also a viper, had already bitten him once, its venom hot in his blood. Any movement would bring another attack, like fangs sinking into the bone.

Other options? he asked, then told himself, None.

He would have to get to his feet somehow, find a branch to use as a crutch, and hobble back downhill until he could go no farther. Maybe luck onto one of the marked hiking trails.

He turned his head a few degrees right, a few degrees left. Soreness, but movement. Most of the pain in that region emanated from the back of his skull. He could feel the knot like a walnut of tenderness embedded in his scalp.

You need to get up, he thought.

A mosquito was busy near his ear, whining like a dentist's drill. Another was having breakfast on his forearm. A small cloud of gnats hovered over his face, almost touching. He blew out a breath and they backed away, then returned. One crawled into the corner of his eye. He dislodged it by squeezing shut his eyes, blinking hard.

Then slipped both hands into the muck beneath his buttocks and gradually pushed himself into a sideways sitting position, right elbow braced against the ground. His left leg, the injured one, did not appear unnaturally turned. But it hurt like hell. Another attempt to bend it at the knee sent a flare of hot pain radiating up from the ankle. So he raised the other knee instead, canted to the side. Sore but uninjured. He slipped his right foot under the left knee, ran his hand down over the muddy jeans from knee and shin. No protrusion. No splintering of bone. But the lightest touch near the middle of the tibia stiffened him with sudden pain. And now he could distinguish a different color to the mud in that area, the russet spread of blood. His breath came in loud quick gasps, his face tight and hot.

Rolling slowly, a few inches at a time, he worked himself over onto his hands and right knee, keeping his left foot and leg resting atop the right. He swept his left hand through the leaves, hoping to find the handgun near his body. No luck. And the dizziness—his body wanted to tumble back to the ground.

He would need a crutch of some kind. Unfortunately there were no trees growing down the center of the narrow ravine, no stout limbs within reach. His only options were to follow the ravine either up or down, hopping along on his good leg, or to crawl up the slick slope on his hands and knees.

The latter would allow him the opportunity to search through the leaves for his weapon. The long, heavy Bowie knife should still be strapped to his pack, the pack still against the tree where he had paused to urinate. But first he had to reach it.

He faced the slope, studied the leaves. Here and there along the sloping wall he could identify where a heel had dragged, where his body had slid and scraped the leaves along with it. There was no telling how far the weapon might have been flung from his hand. All he knew for certain was that without it he was little more than a crippled duck.

And he laughed softly with the realization that he was going to crawl up that hill.

You always have to do the hardest thing, he told himself.

And answered, That's right, I do. And slid both hands forward, then pulled his body along behind, wincing with every inch gained.

By the time he reached the top of the ravine and lay panting with the side of his face in the leaves, his clothing was soaked with perspiration, his hands, lower arms, face, and neck filthy with humus. The pain in his leg had reached crescendo not far from the bottom of the ravine and abated only between pulse beats, which were coming now twice per second and felt like several pairs of huge, hot vice grips simultaneously pinching not only his leg, but also his groin and chest and neck and skull. His blood had changed to battery acid; he could taste it in his mouth.

The pain had the added effect of making him want to vomit, but his stomach was empty, so he felt the urge mostly in his throat, a periodic gag reflex he stifled with one hard, dry swallow after another.

The climb had taken more than an hour with frequent pauses to sweep his right hand and then left through the leaves. He had made contact with numerous roots and stones but no Austrian-crafted surfaces.

Now he rose up onto his elbows and looked for the tree where he had left his pack. Maybe that tree…but nothing there. Maybe that tree. Nothing there. No matter where he looked, there was no sign of anything that had not sprung out of the earth. Only DeMarco himself.

"Sonofabitch," he moaned.

He straightened his arms and went down onto his chest again.

The sweat dried on his body and his body cooled. After a while his breath came more evenly, but the leg still throbbed. It felt fifty degrees hotter than his chest. Felt as big as a barrel.

I wish I could call Jayme, he thought. Tell her about all the calories I've burned.

ONE HUNDRED EIGHT

This time he woke up shivering and feverish. The forest was darker than before, but its lines and angles crisper somehow, as if the fever had cleared his vision, and brought even his thoughts into sharper detail. He craned his eyes upward. Only gray between the leaves. Had he slept that long or was the sky overcast? It might still be morning. It might be evening.

He asked himself, Are you going to get up or not?

To lie still was to choose to die. A race between infection and starvation. Infection would probably win.

He thought of something Thomas Huston had written, that suicide is nothing more than the period at the end of *I can't take this anymore.* Choosing to live is another page, maybe a thousand more pages, all of it just one long Faulknerian sentence held together with comma splices and ellipses and conjunctions and grit.

Screw the period, DeMarco thought. I'm not at the end of my pages yet.

ONE HUNDRED NINE

He looked up only occasionally, struggled from tree to tree with the help of a crutch fashioned from a windfall branch. The crutch was a good foot too short but it helped him maintain a lopsided balance. He would hop forward on his right foot, left foot three inches off the ground, then jerk the crutch parallel, shift his weight to his left armpit cradled in the fork of the crutch, and hop forward again. Occasionally his left foot would dip and catch a toe against the ground, and the brief contact would send a bayonet of pain up through the sole of his foot and into his shin and kneecap.

Along the way a part of him removed itself from the pain and stood watching from farther ahead—detached but curious, maybe even a little amused. It wasn't an unfamiliar phenomenon. It had happened nine months ago when he had raced through a forest to the sound of gunshots, and knew that Thomas Huston was in the vicinity of those gunshots. Before that, on several occasions while sitting in his car outside Laraine's house when she came home with another man. Before that, while waiting for the ambulance to arrive and take Ryan Jr. away. And before that, dozens of times as a child and teenager caught in the glare of his father's attention.

Yet it always felt peculiar to be watching himself from a distance that way. For a long time he had believed there must be something wrong with him, perhaps something bordering on the sociopathic. Until a lunch with Huston. DeMarco had asked, with a note of envy in his voice, what it was like to live most of his life inside his own head, engaged in the godlike activity of creating and destroying people.

"You sometimes find yourself depressed," Huston had answered, "and you don't know why. You find yourself irritated, agitated, nerves on edge, and you can't figure out why. You have a beautiful life, the best family in the world, everything you've ever wanted. Why the hell are you so miserable? And then it hits you: you're living your character. Everything he feels, you're feeling it too. And he's not just messing with your head, he's all through you, because in a way he is you, a manifestation of yourself. You have your own emotions but his are stronger, they can drown yours out. So the only thing to do is to, I don't know, separate yourself from that character. You have to stand apart and just sort of watch. Let him suffer whatever he has to suffer. And try not to care."

And now, surrounded by nothing but trees and pain, DeMarco was glad he wasn't a writer. Glad he didn't have to pull himself apart this way every single day. Even gladder he wasn't God. Eight billion wailing souls inside that head. All that misery. All that desperation.

ONE HUNDRED TEN

Dusk seemed to come early. On the other hand, he could no longer trust his sense of time. Pain stretched it out. A few minutes of feverish sleep now and then reduced it to ashes. In any case it was too dark to continue. His right leg felt wooden with exhaustion, his left armpit was scraped raw from the fork in the makeshift crutch.

He thought he had reached a summit but could not really tell, was too tired and brain-fogged to distinguish if he was climbing uphill or down. And the wind was picking up, the air thicker. One moment he felt chilled to the bone, the next moment on fire.

He huddled up against a tree, hoping to put his back to the wind, but the wind was too tricky for that, it swung right and then left like a boxer, it ducked low and then came up swinging.

He stretched his left leg out, ran a hand up and down over the tear in his jeans. The blood had dried and scabbed, patched the tear shut. He remembered the denim patches his mother used to iron onto his jeans when he was small. He had hated those patches. None of the other kids had them.

He wasn't hungry but had a terrible thirst.

He closed his eyes, and his thoughts started racing again. They broke into fragments and crashed into each other. No Jayme, no television, no whiskey, no beer. Nothing to distract him from his thoughts but the trees and ground and patches of sky. The chitters and creaks and snaps. A few stars blinking on and off behind the leaves.

Nothing to do but to let them all go…

ONE HUNDRED ELEVEN

The night burst open like an electrified hell, waking him with neon-white lightning spiderwebbing above the trees, thunder exploding in sudden, startling bursts inside a continuous rumble and growl. He scooted away from the tree and leaned back on his elbows and opened his mouth. Drank the rain until his open jaw stiffened. Closed his jaw, worked it open and closed. Then opened his mouth and drank some more. Again and again until the rain stopped as suddenly as a faucet turned off.

The wind continued to whip the upper canopy back and forth, sending leaves and acorns and brittle branches ticking down through the underbrush while the trunks creaked and swayed. DeMarco scooted back to the tree, pulled his soaking T-shirt up by the hem and sucked the moisture from it. For warmth he pulled the silver locket out and clutched it between his hands.

ONE HUNDRED TWELVE

Asleep again. DeMarco is standing in an empty bedroom on the second floor of his home. There is a large picture window in the rear wall. He knows that this window didn't use to exist, but he is not disturbed by it. Nor, when he looks out the window, is he disturbed by the huge gnarled and twisted oak that now stands in his backyard, leafless and black, far taller than his house. What he finds most unusual is that a large brown cow stands calmly atop one of the upper branches.

He goes to the threshold and calls downstairs. Laraine! There's a cow in the oak tree out back!

No answer. He returns to the window, looks again, and now realizes that the cow is in fact a huge old bull with long yellowing horns. Very curious. And as he watches, the bull calmly walks out to the end of the branch, pauses for just a moment, and steps off. It falls to the ground with a heavy thump. Lies motionless. Obviously dead.

How strange, he thinks.

He turns from the window, exits the room, walks briskly downstairs to the rear door. Opens the door and steps out onto the patio for a closer look. And now sees not only the huge, motionless bull on its side on the ground, but his son, Ryan, twelve or thirteen years old, reclining on a thick lower branch like a Caucasian Mowgli. He is barefoot and bare-chested, wearing nothing but a pair of loose white trousers, and he is smiling, gazing off toward the distant hills. On the branch above him a white tiger sleeps, its legs hanging down.

DeMarco steps out a little farther onto the patio. Says as quietly as possible, not wanting to wake the tiger, Ryan, could you come inside, please? I'm not comfortable with you being out there with that tiger.

Ryan does not respond, but his smile broadens. *All is well*, his smile says.

And DeMarco stands there watching, perplexed, taking it all in, the deceased bull, the sleeping tiger, the enormous tree, the serene and beautiful boy...

He awoke to gray light, a heavy fog rising from the ground. His body was stiff and sore and shivering, clothing still damp from the night's rain, his injured leg still throbbing from ankle to knee. A few twittering birds had begun their morning greetings. The scent of the forest was strong—wet leaves and ground, ferns and greenery. He felt good despite the pain and chill of his body, felt strangely optimistic; the calm of his dream still lingered.

And then he remembered the locket, his hands empty. He froze. *Don't move.* It couldn't have gone far. He had slept lopsided against the tree, and now peered over his left shoulder and into the wet leaves, then down along his arm, moving his gaze slowly, covering every inch, and saw it there against his hip, wet and shining. Delicately he picked it off the leaves, wiped it clean on his shirt. Cupped it to his hand and raised the hand to his mouth. *If I had lost you,* he thought.

Minutes later, with the fog slowly lifting, he worked himself into a kneeling position against the tree, and gradually pulled himself erect. He leaned sideways to pull down his zipper and relieve himself. Much of the woods still lay in deep shadow, though brightened by the bluish cast of fog. But some twenty yards away in a clearing no bigger than his living room, only partially revealed in the low sunlight broken and blocked by its trip through the leaves, the silhouette of a fat little man stood against the side of a tree. The silhouette itself was not unbroken, gray light here and shadow there, but in outline it resembled nothing more than a little fat man in a peaked hat, one hand upon a hip. DeMarco smiled with the unlikeness of such an illusion. What were the chances that light would stream down from ninety-three million miles away and form itself into something so unfamiliar yet recognizable? As far as he could remember, he had never actually seen a little man in a peaked hat. Maybe in a school book when he was a child, in first or second grade. Maybe in one of the many picture books he had read aloud to baby Ryan. In any case, there it was before him, as familiar as the trees. He couldn't help grinning at it, enjoying it as a clever trick of the light.

But then the little man leaned to the side, stood, and elongated, grew into a full-sized human made of silhouette and half-light—a silhouette that now turned and walked away from him, merging into the concealing depths of the foggy trees.

A minute later a small engine roared to life, held steady and strong for ten seconds, then soon faded with distance, leaving behind only trees and fog and DeMarco and his questions.

ONE HUNDRED FOURTEEN

W here the shadowy individual had hunkered down against a tree, the ground was disturbed, leaves flattened or scuffed away. And because the ground was still damp, the trail of footsteps away from the tree were also visible, as were the tire tracks of the ATV he had ridden away on.

DeMarco studied the tracks. "Four-wheeler," he muttered. Two clear tracks left by wide, low-pressure tires. Following the ridgeline. The scent of gasoline exhaust lingering in the air.

The individual had made no effort to conceal himself. What did that mean?

It might mean, DeMarco thought, that it wasn't Emery. Or wasn't the person who shot at me. Or he thought I'd already spotted him, so didn't bother trying to hide himself.

It might mean I hallucinated him.

He looked again at the ground. Do hallucinations leave tracks?

There was only one way to find out.

ONE HUNDRED FIFTEEN

DeMarco hunkered behind a tree on the edge of a clearing of relatively level ground. Of approximately an acre in size, the clearing had not been stripped of trees but allowed for a wide patch of blue overhead, more sky than he had seen since the long trek began.

Some hundred feet ahead, near the center of the clearing, a small stone building. It stood perhaps five feet wide by eight long, was built of the same sandstone rocks he had rested upon, climbed over, or avoided with muttered curses for forty hours or more, but these were roughly chiseled into rectangles and stacked eight courses high, then topped with a steeply pitched roof of rusty corrugated panels. The end nearest him had an opening five courses high. The interior was darkness.

Another twenty yards beyond this building stood a plain but well-made cabin with a stone foundation and unpainted plank walls. Two wooden stairs led to a solid, windowless door. Two small windows on what he guessed was the southern side. No movement other than the leaves overhead, and the pulse of hot pain thrumming from ankle to knee.

He had started the climb at approximately three on Monday afternoon. It was now, as best he could figure, Wednesday. Somewhere between seven and eight in the morning. He had been stripped of everything but the clothes he wore, stripped of all means of communication and self-defense. His face had been peppered with tree shrapnel, his skull rattled and bruised, leg ripped open, body twisted and pulled in every imaginable way. He ached in every muscle and bone, was hungry, thirsty, scratched, gouged, feverish, sleep-deprived, and insect-gnawed, and now hid behind a tree while staring at his first glimpse of anything not borne of nature: a strange stone building that looked in morning light like a dollhouse mix of cathedral and ammo bunker. And asked himself, So what now?

Whatever its purpose, the building would provide good cover for observing the cabin. He limped laterally behind the line of trees until positioned in direct line with the building and the cabin beyond it. Then hurried forward as best he could, stifling a yelp each time his left foot creased the earth.

He had to duck to enter the building. Its darkness reeked of wet earth and rancid meat. The stench froze him in his crouch as he squinted to discern what lay beyond him, but with the sun still low he could see only shadow upon shadow.

The nearest shadow appeared to be hanging in the air a couple of steps away, head high and as big as a beach ball and alive with an oscillating buzz. It partially obscured the opening at the far end, a duplicate of the one he had entered. He stood motionless, breathing shallowly through his mouth, waiting for his rods and cones to adjust. And gradually he could make out the object ahead of him, the head of a deer, suspended from wire attached to the antlers, and blanketed with flies.

The sound to his rear came loud and deliberate, a clap of hands. He turned quickly, pivoting on his good leg. A gray-and-black dog as big as a wolf was sprinting toward him at full speed, and behind it stood an individual in jeans and boots, flannel shirt and ball cap, a rope dangling in one hand, a rifle in the other. The rifle was rising to the horizontal, the dog three seconds away.

DeMarco ran. But neither far nor fast enough. His first lurching step tripped a wire strung ankle-high, and two barred doors, one in front and one behind, slammed down on metal tracks.

The dog thrust its head between the bars behind him, and now it began to bark, incensed. The figure lowered the rifle and came forward. DeMarco raised his hands level with his face.

"I'm unarmed," he shouted above the barking. "And I think my leg might be broken."

But the individual, whom he now saw as a woman, though broader and nearly as tall as he, strode past the building without giving him a look.

"Come!" she called, and the dog pulled its big head out of the bars and sprinted up to her.

DeMarco watched through the exit bars as she opened the cabin door, then followed the dog inside. The door slammed shut behind them. And the world went quiet again save for the agitated buzz in the darkness of DeMarco's sky.

ONE HUNDRED SIXTEEN

He lay with a cheek to the cool, packed earth, his face to the fresher air beyond the exit bars.

He tried to work up a gob of saliva so as to spit out the foul taste of his prison. But his mouth remained dry. Meanwhile the morning passed slowly. The air grew thick and hot. The world stank of rot. He watched the cabin door until his eyes grew heavy, and then he gave up trying to remain awake. Consciousness, he told himself, is overrated.

ONE HUNDRED SEVENTEEN

In his sleep he has rolled onto his right side, back against the exit bars. The entrance bars have disappeared and the opening is full of blue fog. But DeMarco knows he cannot leave his prison, he knows that escape is impossible, so he makes no effort to get up, he merely lies there too heavy to move and looks at the man hunkered down close to him in the fog, his friend Tom Huston, his face clean and smiling and his hair neatly combed. What the fuck, brother? Huston says. And DeMarco, through his parched throat and dry lips, says, I could ask you the same thing. And Huston laughs, that sudden booming laugh of his that always catches DeMarco by surprise, that sheer unfiltered delight in a moment of existence that always brings a smile to DeMarco's face too, just as he smiles now and says, Am I a character in one of your stories, Tom? Huston says, You mean like Goodman Brown? And DeMarco answers, That's not your story. Huston nods, leans closer to lay a hand atop DeMarco's head. The hand is soothing, cool. I'm a character in one of yours, Huston says. As are you, my friend. Now DeMarco wants to laugh but is too heavy with sleep. I've never been much of a writer, he says. You'll get the hang of it, Huston tells him. Just keep scribbling. Huston grins, his teeth so white, then leans away, begins to rise, until DeMarco, seized by a sudden panic, reaches out to grab Huston's sleeve and ask, What's all this for, Tom? All this craziness. This life. What's it all about?

Huston says nothing for a moment, only smiles. Then, in almost a whisper, Sentipensante, my friend.

I don't know what that means.

Life is a poem.

How so?

Mute. As a globed fruit.

That doesn't make any sense to me.

Huston continues to smile even as his image fades, sleeve and hands and arms turning to mist, his body returning to the fog, until only the coolness of his touch remains.

S omething cool and wet against the back of his neck. Something moving, snuffling. And then he knew: the dog.

He rolled away from the bars, onto his left leg and then off again, lying awkwardly on his back with head raised, one leg bent at the knee, the pain fierce and hot all the way up his side. The dog remained with its snout poking through the bars. The woman stood behind the animal, backlit by bright daylight.

DeMarco said, "How long have I been in here? I need some water."

She stepped forward, moved her hand toward the door. A click. He raised his fists to his chest, expecting the dog to attack. She then turned away, clapped her hands one time, said "Come!" and the dog turned and followed, ran ahead of her through the cabin's open door, which she then entered too, and left the door standing open.

All was silent but for a bird somewhere outside and the buzz of flies still swarming around the deer's head. He waited for a couple of minutes, listened, heard the woman's muted voice from inside the cabin.

He rolled another quarter turn. Onto his good knee, hands to the ground. Felt around for his crutch. Propped it up, pulled himself erect.

The cage door swung open with a push.

ONE HUNDRED NINETEEN

By the time he reached the two wooden stairs leading to the cabin door, he could smell something cooking, fragrant with the scents of tomato and beef, herbs he could not identify.

Negotiating even two stairs with a crutch was not easy. With each hop his body wanted to tumble left, but the too-short crutch steadied him long enough that he finally made the threshold, stood there breathing hard.

The dog, lying now in front of the stone hearth at the far end of the cabin, raised his head, ears stiff and alert. "Stay," the woman said without looking DeMarco's way. She was seated on a bentwood rocker beside a man on a mattress atop a simple bedframe. The man, dressed in blue pajama pants, gray socks, and an untucked flannel shirt, lay on his back, eyes closed. Were it not for the skeletal hands emerging from the shirt cuffs, the thin neck, and emaciated face, there seemed to be no body inside the clothes. But his face was freshly shaven, his thin hair neatly combed.

On a small table to the right of the bed was a glass jar holding dentures, plus a plastic bottle of ibuprofen, a bottle of hydrogen peroxide, a bottle of iodine, a small yellow prescription vial, a washcloth, a jar of Vaseline, rolls of surgical tape and gauze, and a clear plastic glass full of water.

From inside the cabin came not only the scent of hot soup but an odor of smoke and ashes. Embers glowed within the small wood-burning stove, atop which sat a cast-iron pot. There was also a vague, unpleasant redolence of grease in the air, and something else as well. A nameless fetor DeMarco had experienced before, at the scene of fatal car accidents, in the home of a former colleague dying of cancer, and twice at the scenes of shootings—an odor suggesting that if the man on the bed was still alive, he would not be for long.

Now the woman turned to DeMarco and nodded toward the only other chair in the room, a worn, green vinyl chair to the right of the little table. "Sit down there," she said.

DeMarco hobbled inside, sat, looked at the glass of water, looked to the woman. She was rising from her own chair now. "Go on," she said. "It's fresh from the pump."

He drank. The water was cool and so delicious it made him dizzy and short of breath. He would drink, take a couple of short breaths, then drink again.

"There's Bactrim in the yellow bottle," she told him.

He shook two tablets into his palm and swallowed them down with a gulp of water.

She knelt before him, looked at his leg, looked down at his boot, stained black now from a mix of dirt and dried blood. "I might have to cut off this boot," she said. "There's ibuprofen for the pain if you want it."

He nodded, reached for the ibuprofen, shook out two small capsules, swallowed them down.

With the knife from the sheath attached to her belt she sliced through the laces, then laid the knife aside, pulled the sides of the boot apart. The tongue was stuck to his sock with dried blood, and the sock to his swollen skin. Delicately she worked the tongue free, taking pains to not yet tear away the sock, though that would come.

By laying the tongue the whole way out of the boot and stretching the sides of the boot as far apart as they would go, she could move the boot back and forth along the heel. "I'm gonna pull," she said. "There's no other way."

"Go ahead," he told her.

She pulled with a slow, steady pressure, left hand cupping his calf and holding the leg off the floor, right hand cupping his heel. He focused his gaze on the interior of the cabin. Counterclockwise from the bed was a round table and two chairs, then the fireplace, the wood-burning stove, a single-basin sink in a cabinet with towel racks on both sides. Next a bookcase lined with canned and boxed food, preserved vegetables and fruits and dried herbs in Mason jars. Then a smaller bookcase with a dozen or so books and, on the top shelf, a battery-operated transistor radio. Then wall pegs from which hung various jackets, sweaters, hats, a fishing vest festooned with hooks and flies, tools on leather thongs, lanterns, pots and pans, and other items. On the wall beside the door, two rifles, a shotgun, and two handguns hung from metal brackets. Below them, leaning into the corner, two fishing poles and a wicker creel.

Between DeMarco's chair and the door was an old armoire with the doors removed, and on its shelves folded shirts and jeans and other clothing. A footstool pushed against the wall. Two oil hurricane lamps and three Coleman lanterns. A battered black guitar case. The plank floor was dark with age, the ceiling stained here and there with smoke.

As his eyes moved around the room his chest heaved with every breath, muscles tensed in reaction to the pain seizing his leg as she first worked off the boot and then the sock, the dried blood crackling, bits of dead skin tearing free.

And then he felt the coolness of the air on his naked foot, then the warmth and roughness of her hand. He took a few more breaths and looked down.

She had placed the tip of the knife inside the tear in his jeans, and was slicing the pant leg open down through the hem. Now she laid the knife aside and leaned closer, fingers delicately probing despite his winces, working around his ankle, then down over the dorsal and to the toes.

"I'm sorry my foot's so dirty," he said.

"I don't feel nothing broken," she said without looking up. "But that don't mean it's not. It's swolled up with infection pretty good."

She reached for the hydrogen peroxide and washcloth. He leaned his head back against the wall. Closed his eyes. How could she be so gentle after keeping him in that cage all morning? *Women*, he thought.

And she said, "What about them?"

He opened his eyes, looked down. She was still washing his foot, cleaning the scratches around and above his swollen ankle. He told her, "I didn't know I said that out loud."

When she offered no reply, he asked, "Was that you who shot at me yesterday morning?"

"You wouldn't be setting here if I shot at you," she said. She poured peroxide over his scabbed leg. He twitched, couldn't hold back a groan. The pain made him want to urinate, but he gritted his teeth, clenched his pelvic and abdominal muscles, breathed fast and shallow through his nose.

When the sting of pain subsided and he could see again through watery eyes, he wanted to ask if her comment meant that she hadn't shot at him, or had shot but not to kill, but then decided it didn't matter. He watched her a while longer, the back of her head, the clean brown hair, her strong shoulders and hands. She reminded him a little of his mother, of those better days when he was small. But this woman was nearly as tall as DeMarco, at least as wide. Yet her ministrations were tender, with a delicacy that belied the strength of her thick fingers and arms. He wanted to lay his hands atop her head, or place them on her shoulders. He wanted to lay his hands against her cheeks. It was an urge he did not understand, and then told himself to stop trying.

When he looked up, the man on the bed was awake, head rolled toward the door, his eyes on DeMarco. DeMarco said to the woman, "Is that Emery over there?"

The figure on the bed did not fit the image of Virgil Helm DeMarco had been carrying inside his head. Virgil had been sick, yes, but only forty, so still, in DeMarco's mind, retaining at least some of a younger man's vitality. The man on the bed appeared twenty years older, wasted by illness, stripped of all strength. Only the eyes retained a semblance of the younger man's spirit.

In answer to DeMarco's question, the woman said nothing. But after a few moments, the man raised the fingers of his left hand off the bed. Held them aloft for five seconds, and let them fall flat again.

DeMarco bent closer to the woman to ask, "How long has he been like that?"

At first she said nothing. Then, "Been getting worse ever since he come here."

"Has he seen a doctor?"

She reached for the towel now, patted his foot and leg dry. Then came the iodine, more stinging pain, more clenched muscles. He said, "If you keep doing that, I'm going to pee my pants."

"That's up to you," she said. She reached for the roll of compression tape and slowly wrapped it around his foot and all the way up to his knee. Then covered the compression tape with the white surgical tape.

She stood, placed the medical materials back atop the little table. "Thank you," DeMarco said.

She stooped to retrieve a bedpan from beneath the bed, turned, and handed it to DeMarco. "Go ahead now."

He said, "I think I'll go outside if you don't mind."

"Don't be a fool," she said, dropped the bedpan onto his lap, and walked away.

She went to the sink, where she washed out the washcloth and her hands while DeMarco relieved himself in the bedpan. Then she folded the wet washcloth, took a towel from the rack, and carried them back to DeMarco. With one hand she lifted the bedpan from his lap, with the other handed him the towel and washcloth. "Clean yourself up and you can have some of that soup," she said.

ONE HUNDRED TWENTY

The damp washcloth was cold on his face, soothing to his eyes. He worked the cloth between his fingers, tried to force it under his nails. Just to sit in a chair again felt luxurious. And soon there would be soup. He loved soup. His mouth filled with saliva, and a giddiness arose in his chest, an almost drunken relief and happiness.

But then he looked again at Emery. A skeleton with wide, alert eyes. A small smile on thin, cracked lips.

"I'm so sorry," DeMarco said.

In answer, Emery raised a weak hand to his throat, touched it with two fingertips, moved his head from side to side.

The woman returned to the cabin then with a fresh bucket of water from the outside pump. She washed her hands at the sink, then filled a heavy bowl with soup and placed it on the table with a spoon and cloth napkin. She retrieved a handmade walking cane from beside the armoire and handed it to DeMarco. "Get some of that soup in you," she told him. "Then you need to get that leg looked at."

He pushed himself up, hobbled to the table. The compression tape stabilized his leg and dulled but did not alleviate the pain. After he sat, but before he took up the spoon, he turned to her and said, "May I ask your name?"

As always, she took her time answering. "Catherine," she said. Then, surprising him, "He calls me Cat."

"He's lucky to have you," DeMarco said. "So am I."

She lowered her gaze and drew away. She retrieved his water glass from the small end table, refilled it by dipping it into the bucket of fresh water, and set it before him. He asked, "Is there a trail I can follow back down? I think I took the long way up. Those woods are confusing."

She said, "Em said the same thing when he first come here. And I'll tell you what I told him. These woods aren't to be fooled with. They can heal you or they can kill you. Sometimes both at the same time."

She turned away from him then, said "Come," and briskly exited the cabin with the dog running after her.

DeMarco picked up his spoon, turned toward Emery, and said, "She seems nice."

The man's smile broadened, and his thin body quivered with a half-choked laugh.

ONE HUNDRED TWENTY-ONE

The soup was full of carrots and onions, chunks of softened potatoes, squash, tomatoes, and bits of meat he thought was probably venison. DeMarco ate quickly, head down, well aware that he was being watched by Emery. The woman, after she returned and took up her seat beside Emery, ignored DeMarco.

When he finished, after drinking off the last of the broth, he wiped his mouth on the napkin, turned to her, and said, "That was the best bowl of soup I've ever had. Thank you."

She said nothing, sat there with her chin on her chest as she stared at the floor.

DeMarco turned in his chair so that he faced Emery more directly. The pain was still there in his leg but the ibuprofen and Bactrim had extinguished much of the heat. "Cat," he said with a smile. "I like that name. Cat with a dog. Big dog."

The man smiled, blinked. He parted his pale lips, wet them with his tongue. His eyes were barely open, glistening. The odor was strong around him; DeMarco tried not to let his face show it.

"My name is Ryan DeMarco," he began, but again the man's fingers lifted. Not a wave this time. A stop. "You don't want to talk?"

Cat repositioned herself in the chair, sat more erect, placed her hands atop her knees. "Just ask what it was you come to ask," she said. The dog's claws clicked against the floor as it shifted its position, gray eyes focused on the stranger.

ONE HUNDRED TWENTY-TWO

DeMarco chose his questions carefully, knowing his time and Emery's energy were limited.

"About those girls' remains. Are you the one who put them where they were found?"

Emery's lips barely moved, his answer a slip of air. "No."

"Did you see it done?"

"No."

"Do you know who did it?"

"No."

"Did you know they were there?"

Emery said nothing, appeared to be trying to swallow. Cat answered as she stood and went to the sink to dip a fresh glass of water from the bucket. "He knew something was in there. He didn't know what."

"So he must have known," DeMarco said, thinking out loud, "more or less when it was done. And who did it."

She sat, leaned close to Emery, and held the glass to his lips, allowing just a sip of water into his mouth. "He never had the key for that place they were hid," she said.

"Somebody did," DeMarco said, and looked at Emery again. "Do you know who?"

Emery wet his lips. Then said, a whisper, "Drugs."

"Somebody involved in drugs? Was it Royce? He's already admitted he called to let you know about the inspection in the morning. Told you to be there at 7:00 a.m., right?"

Emery's breaths started coming more quickly then, four short inhalations before he held the last one and spoke. "Next call." Then he breathed rapidly again, eyes opening wider, blinking and frightened.

Cat heard the change in his breathing, leaned close, and blew softly in his face, a hand to his cheek. After a minute or so, his breath fell into rhythm with hers.

She waited until his eyes looked heavy again, face calmer. To DeMarco she said, "He can't ever get enough air into his lungs. Plus it hurts him to breathe."

DeMarco said, "Can you answer my questions instead?"

She remained with her face close to Emery's, but now cocked her head slightly, a silent question. Emery closed his eyes, a long, slow blink, then looked at her again, and smiled.

She stayed close a few moments longer. Then drew away and settled back into the chair.

"He won't tell no names," she said. "Not to you, me, or nobody. All I know is somebody called him that night before those girls got found. That's why he left and come here."

"Okay," said DeMarco, "but he said 'next call.' That means he got two calls, the first one from Royce in the afternoon. And the second one from somebody involved in drugs? That has to be McGintey, right?"

"I don't know names. I know it was whoever had the key in the first place. Some short bug-eyed guy is all he told me."

"That's not Royce and it's not McGintey either," DeMarco said.

Emery's eyes slowly closed. With every exhalation, he released a soft grunt. Cat said, "That's all he's got in him. You need to leave him alone now."

DeMarco nodded. He said, "Okay if I ask you a couple more questions?"

"Make it quick," she said.

"Obviously he told you about those seven girls. Do you believe he didn't have anything to do with it?"

Her eyes flared. "That damn war they sent him to took his health, took his peace of mind. When he heard what was inside that church, it just about made him crazy. Worse than the worst he'd already seen. Come here hoping for a little peace again. You can see how good that's turned out."

"Is that why you shot at me?" DeMarco said. "To scare me away?"

She turned her gaze on the dog. "He didn't like me doing that. Said to let you come if you were coming. Always knew somebody would sooner or later."

"Did he know I was out there in that cage?"

"Not right away. He was so mad at me for leaving you there he tried to get out of bed hisself. Almost killed him."

She stood then and retrieved the cane on the floor beside DeMarco's chair. Handed it to him. "That soup's likely to go through you pretty quick," she said. "Looks like the swelling's down some. You can slip your boot back on. There's a outhouse out behind the pump."

She picked up his soup bowl and spoon, the water glass and napkin, and carried them to the sink, where she busied herself with washing them in water dipped from the bucket. DeMarco wanted to ask more questions but knew how tenuous his position was. He also knew that she was right about the soup after his fast of forty-odd hours; his stomach felt increasingly bloated. After pushing his foot into the boot, he placed the tip of the cane against the floor, pushed himself up, and hobbled toward the door.

ONE HUNDRED TWENTY-THREE

B etween the cabin and the outhouse, he passed a hand pump and spigot, two garden plots full of vegetables and herbs enclosed in chicken wire, a cord and a half of stacked firewood, and a muddy four-wheeler. He would have liked to admire the garden longer but the urgency in his bowels pushed him straight to the outhouse.

When he exited the little building five minutes later, Cat was waiting at the hand pump. She held up a bottle of dishwashing soap and said, "Give me your hands." He cupped them in front of her and she squirted soap into his palms, which he then rubbed together vigorously, then held his hands under the spigot while she pumped icy water over his fingers and wrists.

"This is a sweet setup you have here," he told her. "It must've taken a lot of hard work."

She said, "Do you believe what he told you?"

He shook the water from his hands, then fanned them through the air. "I can't think of any reason he'd lie. Not at this stage of the game."

A few moments later he said, "I am wondering, though. Why did he change his name?"

"Didn't want a thing to do with the government no more. Didn't want them finding him. Asking questions. Poking at him. Figured he could take better care of hisself than any of them was doing."

DeMarco nodded, did not say what he was thinking. He was thinking that he had felt the same way at one time. Like little more than a meat puppet trained to kill. Cheated. Betrayed.

Cat said, "He used to be a pretty good guitar player once. That's where he got his name. You know 'The Night They Drove Old Dixie Down'?"

DeMarco quickly ran through the lyrics in his mind. "'Virgil Caine is the name,'" he quoted.

"But who sung it?"

"That was…Levon Helm. Of course. Virgil Helm."

"Used to write his own songs too, Emery did."

"I wish I could have heard them."

She looked out across the ridgeline then, the hills blue and soft in the distance, the sky as bright as the inside of an enameled bowl. And then she sang, her voice soft and pitched low. "'I have a story to tell but I don't know where to start. The beginning and the ending are about a broken heart. Somewhere in the middle it all falls apart. It ain't a very happy story but it's the only one I got.'"

She paused then, blinked once, and said, "That's the first verse. Only other one he wrote is the last."

"Do you know it too?"

She nodded. "'So I guess I'll sharpen my knives and polish my sword. The night falls down, and I'm already bored. I wish I had a pretty woman to hold my hand. I'm gonna die a lonely man.'"

There were tears in her eyes when she stopped singing.

"My gosh," DeMarco said. "Emery wrote that?"

"He never got to finish it."

DeMarco took a chance and laid a hand atop her shoulder. She flinched momentarily, but then relaxed. She nodded, sniffed once, and turned to face him.

"Get yourself situated inside that four-wheeler," she told him. "We got some riding to do, and you still have some walking left."

She picked up the dishwashing liquid and returned to the cabin.

A part of him felt almost giddy with his survival and the notion of returning to Jayme and a soft bed in an air-conditioned room. Another part of him was reluctant to leave this sanctuary high above the rest of Kentucky, this Shambhala of birdsong and solitude.

He worked himself awkwardly into the passenger seat of the four-wheeler, sitting with only his right shoulder against the backrest, stiff left leg extended out the open door. He left the cane leaning against the outside of the vehicle.

Cat returned with a red-and-black bandanna held in both hands, a length of rawhide cord hanging from a belt loop. She whipped the bandanna through the air in a circular motion, forming it into a tight band two inches wide. He saw the bandanna and knew what was coming and did not resist, but leaned toward her so she could more easily secure the blindfold in place.

"I wanted to ask you about that cage you had me in," he said. "It's a fascinating piece of work."

"Bear cage," she told him. "Hold out your hands."

He clasped his hands together and offered them to her. "You don't need to tie me up. I promise not to lift the bandanna."

The rawhide cord went around his wrists, circling it several times, tightening. "I know you'll send somebody up here," she said. "No reason to make it easy for you."

"If I did, it would just be to get Emery some medical care."

"He don't want that," she said as she doubled the knots. "Wouldn't do no good anyways."

He considered his response, but could think of nothing to say, no argument stronger than her own. So he said, "That's the most elaborate bear cage I've ever seen."

"They had them on the big estates over in Germany when my grandpap was a boy. He's the one built all this." She picked up the cane and stuck it inside against his leg. "Hold on to this," she told him.

"It's Emery's, right? I don't want to take his cane."

"He don't need it," she said.

Then in his blindness he felt her walking away from him, heard her footsteps on the wooden stairs. A minute later she returned, threw something heavy into the back of the four-wheeler, then came to the front and settled into the driver's seat. He smelled her smoky, earthy, but still womanly scent, then felt the small explosion as the engine came to life, the machine vibrating and the engine noise booming and painful in his ears. He spoke loudly, nearly shouting. "Thank you for doing all this!"

She sat motionless for a moment, then turned to face him. "Thank him, not me," she said. "I'd've buried you in the woods if it'd done him any good."

She pulled the gearshift down and the vehicle bucked forward, lurched bull-like toward the cabin only to turn sharply, first throwing him against Cat and then with another turn nearly spilling him out onto the ground, finally speeding away on a subtle decline, bathing DeMarco's face in a flood of coolness and the freshest, most redolent air he would ever inhale.

ONE HUNDRED TWENTY-FOUR

After a torturous hour or more of switchbacking and bouncing and nearly falling out a dozen times, he felt the four-wheeler climbing uphill again, and with its ascent he wondered if he had been tricked, was about to be driven to a cliff, pushed out and over the side. But then the vehicle slowed and bucked to a stop. The engine went quiet, the vibration ceased.

She climbed out. And soon stood beside him, her hands at the back of his head, undoing the bandanna. She pulled it from his eyes and stuffed it into her hip pocket.

He sat there blinking and squinting as if through eyes new to light, the sky vast and achingly blue, a verdancy of field and then, a quarter mile distant, trees impossibly green rising into mountains. The four-wheeler was parked atop a low hillock of knee-high scrub grass. He became aware then of a loud droning noise, and thought at first that the rumbling inside his head had returned. But then he recognized it as the roar of distant traffic.

He turned at the waist, faced the opposite direction. Laid out below the hill was a strip mall half as long as a football field, and just beyond its asphalt parking lot a two-lane highway, cars and pickup trucks coming and going.

She lifted something from the rear of the four-wheeler and tossed it down to his right: his pack. "You can pick the knots out of that cord soon as I'm gone," she told him.

He squinted to find her in the sunlight's glare, and when he did, she was surrounded head to feet by an aura of tiny golden sparks in a thousand radiating streams, motes of pollen or dust in unceasing and hypnotic motion.

She said, "Now get up on your feet and move away from my ride."

The nausea hit him again when he stood, and he nearly crumpled to the ground. She did not move to assist him. "Why you think I give you that cane?" she said.

He remembered it then, seized it with both hands, and planted it against the ground.

"It's all still there in your pack," she told him, "whatever you come with. We don't take what's not ours."

"I know that," he answered, standing lopsided now. "Thank you."

Still blinking and squinting, he looked around. Trees and high grass. A narrow two-wheeled track of flattened grass beneath his feet.

She nodded toward the highway. "Down there's a place to get that leg looked at. I wouldn't try getting there too fast if I was you."

He knew there was something more he wanted to say to her, but the feeling would not form itself into words.

She climbed onto the four-wheeler, sat there with her hands on the steering wheel. "Letting you out there in that bear cage," she said, "I shouldn't of done that. I hope I didn't make your leg any worse than it was."

He said, "What if we could get a helicopter up there to him..."

She shook her head no. "Just let him be. That's all I'm asking you. He's been through more'n enough already."

She sat for a few moments waiting for his answer, but he had none to offer. How to tell her what he was feeling when he could not explain it to himself? The physical pain he had endured; this moment's relief. The desire to give up and die; the decision to push on. The taste of her soup; the living corpse of Emery Summerville. The huge sun hanging low to the west yet still bright and hot on his skin.

He smiled. Nodded.

A moment later the four-wheeler's engine roared into gear and off she went, wheeling around and through the tall grass, down over the hill, back toward the line of enveloping trees.

He watched until she disappeared from sight, then longer still until the engine noise was swallowed and only the dull hum of the highway remained. Then he lowered himself down onto his good knee, then onto his buttocks. He laid the cane aside and raised his wrists to his mouth, used his teeth to pull and pick the knots from the cord.

He rested for a few moments, smiling, disbelieving. Then he wound the cord into a small coil and shoved it into a pocket. He pulled his pack close and worked a strap over his shoulder. Then reached for the cane, and pushed himself up.

Wincing with every movement, he turned to face in the other direction, saw the highway and the strip mall below, the low buildings with their flat roofs, the rectangular air conditioners and round vent fans atop the roofs, the line of mountains receding northward, verdant green melting into a distant blue. It was then he felt something wash over him and through him, something powerful and warm and bright, a wide, surging something that made him want to laugh and take it all in and fill himself with it forever.

Then he pushed himself forward and limped down off the final prominence, one lopsided step after another.

ONE HUNDRED TWENTY-FIVE

DeMarco left the urgent care facility with a new compression bandage wrapped from the base of his toes to midshin, a metal crutch adjusted to his height, a prescription for Vicodin for pain and amoxicillin for infections, a set of X-rays revealing his torn ligaments and subtalar joint trauma, and a sheet of instructions intended to limit his perambulatory activity for the next several weeks. He had been tested for concussion and almost passed, received twenty stitches to close the gash that ran from above the outside of his left ankle to midcalf, was anointed in eleven places from head to ankle for scratches and abrasions, had four butterfly bandages applied to deeper lacerations not yet scabbing, and was chided by a petite red-headed physician's assistant half his age for venturing into the woods so "ridiculously unprepared."

She guided his wheelchair out to the parking lot, where a taxi waited to convey him back to the RV. "People are supposed to get smarter as they get older," she told him.

Holding his pack atop his lap, cane and crutch across his knees, he said, "I've heard that's true."

"Can't prove it by you, though, can we?"

"Not yet anyway. Maybe from here on in."

She opened the taxi door and allowed him to scoot inside. "Just to be safe," she said, "don't go hiking alone again. And if you do…" She let the rest of the sentence fade. Then added, after a look at his sheepish smile, "Just don't."

He was surprised to learn he was only four miles from where he had parked the RV. After starting the engine and air conditioner, he dug his cell phone out of the pack and plugged it into the recharging cable.

There were nine texts and five voice messages from Jayme. The gist of the early ones was *Where are you? Are you okay?* The later ones relied heavily on synonyms such as selfish, inconsiderate, thoughtless, unthinking, self-absorbed, and egomaniacal.

After retrieving a fresh bottle of water from the fridge, and chugging a third of it, he called Jayme.

Her hello was, "Where the hell have you been, Ryan?"

Lead with the injury, he thought. "I tore some ligaments, have a stress fracture on my left tibia, a wrenched ankle, and lots of bruises, and a mild concussion, very mild, but—"

"What the hell!" she said. "What did you do?"

"Accident in the woods," he told her. "I'm sorry, I—"

"What woods? Where are you? Do you need me to come and get you?"

"I'm in the RV now. Should be back in six hours or less."

"Six hours!"

"Probably less."

"You can't drive with a concussion!"

Everything she said came with an exclamation point. He felt each one like a knuckle rap to the tender spot on the back of his head. "I'm okay," he told her, and felt suddenly very tired, but happy too, happy enough for tears.

"You are absolutely not okay, Ryan! You are not!"

"I know," he said. "I love you."

He heard only silence. Then her voice again, softer, hoarse and breathless. "You can't drive in that condition."

"My right leg's fine," he told her. "I'm on my way. Can you stay on the phone a while? I'll tell you everything that happened."

Again, a silence. She sniffed, cleared her throat. Said, "You are so, so stupid all the time."

"I know," he said. He put the phone on speaker then and laid it on the dash. Reached for his sunglasses, fitted them on. Buckled his seat belt, looked both ways, pulled the gearshift into Drive, and once again drove into the sun.

V

We came by night to the Fortunate Isles,
And lay like fish
Under the net of our kisses.

—Pablo Neruda

ONE HUNDRED TWENTY-SIX

For their first two hours together they lay on Jayme's grandmother's bed, both voices softened by their absence, every movement restrained and tender with regret. They kept the windows open for the evening birdsong, the overhead fan spinning for its cooling breeze. He told her again all he remembered about the previous three days, though this time in greater detail than he had on the phone. He held nothing back, not even the dreams.

"You knew it was your boy?" she said. "Even though he was older now?"

"No doubts. I mean I didn't think 'That's Ryan,' I just… I don't know. I just took it for granted. I dreamed about him the night before I left too. He looked the same in both of them."

"Do you think it was real?" she asked. "That he really came to you in your dreams?"

"All I can say is that he felt real. So did Tom. As real as you do right now."

He paused for a few moments, watched the blurred blades spin. Then said, "Maybe it's all real and maybe none of it is. Either way, we still have to live, don't we? Whether we're real or not."

She ran her hand up and down his chest. "What are you going to do about Virgil Helm?"

"Never met the man," DeMarco said.

"No? You never told me about him?"

"About who?"

"Okay. So I guess you what—wandered around in the woods a while? Got lost? Something like that?"

"Tried to find him," he told her. "Looked everywhere there was to look. The man's a ghost. Then I got careless, tripped and fell. Lucky I didn't break my neck."

"Okay," she said. "And you feel all right about that story?"

"Top of the world," he said.

She smiled. Kissed his chest. "I visited both of McGintey's girls," she told him.

"Oh yeah? How did that go?"

"Neither one would admit to any violent tendencies on his part. No physical abuse whatsoever. No unusual sexual practices, other than the three-ways and four-ways, which they both claim are perfectly natural and beautiful, unlike all of our bourgeois morality crap."

"I'm sort of fond of our bourgeois morality crap."

"Me too," she said. "As long as we don't get too bourgeois."

"Please let me know if I do."

"Oh, you can count on that." She hooked her naked foot under his leg. "The DA has charged Chad with deviant sexual contact with a minor, and the older girl with corruption of a minor. He's considering charging the older brother with the same thing, which would allow the police to search the entire place."

"And bring down some serious drug charges. Unless Lucas hasn't cleaned things up already."

"Precisely."

He lay there smiling and smelling her hair and the newly bathed, still-soapy scent of her skin. Sooner or later she was going to touch him in a certain way, and he would touch her in a similar way, and then they would get undressed and the world would implode and then coalesce again. But for now and maybe forever he was perfectly content just to breathe her in, just to hold her hand in his, their legs and shoulders pressed against each other.

"So what now, Hopalong?" she asked. "What's our next move?"

"Next move is to find McGintey's former partner, the one Cat told me about. Thing is, none of the suspects fits the description."

"Tell me again how she described him."

"A short, bug-eyed fella. I know a few guys like that back home, but nobody here."

"Wait a minute," she said. "Yes you do."

He rolled onto his side, facing her.

"That guy you talked to at the park last Friday night. You called him a pygmy Neanderthal."

"Caramba," DeMarco said. He blinked, and slowly inhaled. "Did you happen to get a name from his wife?"

"I barely got a nod out of her."

He inhaled deeply again, then let a low whistle slip through his lips, the sound of a distant bomb falling. "Okay, who would know? Who in this town would know just about everybody in it?"

"Bartender," Jayme said. "Hair stylist slash barber. Postmaster and/or mail carrier."

"And/or librarian?" DeMarco asked.

Jayme grinned. "Our tarot-card-reading librarian slash Da Vinci Cave Irregular. Of course! Do you want to call her or should I?"

"You, please."

And now she rolled onto her side too. "But first," she said, and laid her hand atop his belt. "If you're interested, that is."

He said, "I have four full days' worth of interest ready and waiting. So you best proceed with caution."

She unbuckled his belt, worked his zipper down, slipped her hand into his underwear. "How does this work with just one leg?" she asked.

"I lie perfectly still and you have your way with me."

"Hmm. I have to admit I found it more than a bit arousing when you talked about how Cat tied your hands together."

Her touch was alchemical, the magic of endorphins, the happy, sleepy dopiness of desire. "I am in no condition to resist," he said.

ONE HUNDRED TWENTY-SEVEN

No, just trying to connect the dots," Jayme said into her phone. "I'll let you know. Thanks again, Rosemary."

She ended the call, turned from her seat on the edge of the bed, went prone again beside DeMarco. "Todd Burl," she told him. "People call him Toad behind his back."

"I can see that," DeMarco said.

"Now here's the interesting part. Guess who he worked for back in the late eighties, early nineties."

"It's got to be the good reverend himself."

"You know how Royce owns a lot of rentals around the area? Well, Mr. Toad was his full-time maintenance guy. Did repairs, collections, mowing, whatever needed done."

DeMarco sat up. A tree peeper chirped outside the window. The room was dark now, the only illumination from the occasional headlights and a softly shrouded half-moon. "So he preceded McGintey? And, according to Emery, was McGintey's partner somehow. Involving drugs."

"I wonder if Burl was ever questioned."

"We need to find that out. And if not, why not. What's he do now?"

"Remember our drive along the river when we first came into town—that mansion up on the bluff? He's the foreman."

"We need to write this down," DeMarco told her. "Make some kind of chart. This is getting too convoluted for me."

"You're just tired is all. Let's get some sleep and start fresh in the morning."

They lay there quietly then, holding hands, Jayme on her side against him, DeMarco on his back. The air through the screen smelled clean and sweet, scented by the bushes below the window and by

DeMarco's gratitude for being forgiven and granted another chance. He smiled, remembering his dream, and hoped he would dream of Ryan again or not dream at all. The ordeal in the woods and the cage seemed a dream already, though he could call up the pain and foul pungency if he wished. He could call up the image he had drawn in his imagination of the seven skeletal girls, their seven fully fleshed and plaintive faces, the way their arms reached out for him, took his hands, walked with him through the hardest parts of the trek. His mind, he realized, was, like life itself, filled with both terrible darkness and hallucinatory light, both useful if employed effectively and in the proper dosage.

He looked at Jayme's face in the meager light and listened to her breathe, smelled the summersweet flowers, and heard the night's hushed song, the peeper's chirp, the warbler's trill, the mourning doves' lament.

ONE HUNDRED TWENTY-EIGHT

In a conference room in the county jail, DeMarco faced a shackled Chad McGintey across a metal table scarred with cigarette burns, coffee stains, and a thousand desperate scratches. Jayme leaned against the wall, unsmiling. McGintey's fists, and the handcuffs holding them together, scraped back and forth atop the table, forward and back as he talked.

"I don't know what you mean by partner. Only partner I ever had is my brother."

"That's not what I've been told," said DeMarco.

"And who told you that?"

"God whispered in my ear."

"Ha," McGintey said. "You got any 'shrooms left? I could use a couple right now."

"You're in deep shit here, Chad. You know that, right?"

"If you and God say so."

DeMarco half turned toward Jayme. "What's he looking at again?"

"Deviant sexual contact, second offense. Three to five years if he's lucky. More if he draws a female judge. Of course, he could always opt for chemical castration."

McGintey squirmed in his seat. "That ain't never gonna happen."

"Probably not," she said. "Some of your new pals in Little Sandy will take care of you first."

His eyes went back to DeMarco. He leaned forward over his fists. "This is bullshit," he said. "Nobody did nothing they didn't want to do."

"Well," DeMarco told him, "you know how well that argument's going to fly. Look, I'm giving you a chance to make a friend here. A chance to maybe help yourself out."

McGintey sucked on his tongue. "How good a friend?"

"You know that's not up to me. But I'm fairly certain the DA would rank a multiple homicide case more important than yours. You and Charlene go to jail, nobody notices. Seven young victims finally get justice? The whole country notices."

McGintey pursed his lips, chewed on the inside of his mouth. "So who's this partner I'm supposed to have had?"

"You want me to jog your memory?" Again DeMarco looked back at Jayme. "How would you describe him, Trooper?"

"Take off his boots and he's maybe five three on a good day," she said. "Wears a bad hairpiece, graying around the ears. Eyes that sort of bulge out at you. Big, flat nose and fat lips."

DeMarco added, "The kind of lips the word 'blubbering' was invented to describe. Like two giant wet grubs doing it ass to mouth."

"With a skull like a mushroom," Jayme said.

"A mushroom in a hairy condom," DeMarco added.

McGintey laughed despite himself. "Toad Burl was never no partner to me. Doing what?"

"Okay," DeMarco said. "For the sake of argument, let's say for now I have that detail wrong. You weren't partners. You never used that space behind the false wall to store anything like, I don't know, methamphetamine, coke, weed, any of the local favorites. But he was the caretaker of the church property, a position you took over from him. How did that come about?"

McGintey shrugged and looked away. "Man, that was a long time back. I guess I heard about the job and applied for it, or whatever."

"All right, you took the job. Who told you about the false wall?"

"That's something I didn't… I mean…I guess I heard about it from somebody or other. But I never had the key for it. Never had no use for it."

DeMarco leaned back. Scooted his chair away from the table a little. Prepared to stand. "Trooper," he said, "looks like we're not going to get any cooperation here. You want to go let the sheriff know so he can pass it on to the DA?"

Jayme nodded. "So all clear on adding obstruction of justice charges? Both him and Charlene?"

"Right. And find out when the search of the trailers and the rest of the property is happening. I'd like for us to be there for that."

"Will do," Jayme said, and reached for the door.

"Look," McGintey said before she could turn the handle. Both Jayme and DeMarco held their positions, faced his way.

"Yeah," McGintey said, "okay. So all I remember is that Toad got pissed at Royce about something and got himself fired. So he comes to me and says, you oughta take that job. Go see him before he hires somebody else. And that's what happened."

DeMarco stared at a water stain on the ceiling. "So you get yourself hired to a minimum wage job mowing grass. Even though you and your brother already have a fairly lucrative drug operation going. Then your brother gets busted, takes the fall for both of you, spends some time in jail. When he gets out, you pass the church job on to Virgil Helm so you can contribute more time to the family business." He lowered his eyes to McGintey. "That about it?"

McGintey's tongue wiped the front of his teeth, back and forth three times before he spoke. "I'm done answering your questions," he said. "I need something in writing. I want Char cleared of everything, and my brother too. And none of that castration shit either. That's not even an option."

DeMarco smiled. Then stood. "We'll see what we can do."

The sheriff met them in his office with a box of pastries in hand, a dozen egg-sized balls of sugar-dusted, deep-fried dough. He said, "I was just about to take these to the break room. Grab a couple each before they all disappear."

Jayme picked one up between a finger and thumb. "Cream puff?" she said.

"Poonchkey," he told her. "Spelled p-a-c-z-k-i. Filled with jelly. I think it's raspberry today. So be careful, they can be messy."

DeMarco picked one out, as did the sheriff before setting the box aside. "Help yourself to more," he said.

"I'm lucky she allowed me to have one," DeMarco said with a nod toward Jayme.

"Yes you are," she told him.

After wiping the powdered sugar from their fingertips and lips, they filled the sheriff in on their conversation with McGintey. "Interesting," he said. "I guess I'll have a chat with the DA." He carried the box of pastries to his open door, called to the nearest deputy, handed him the box, then returned to sit on the edge of his desk.

"So who was it turned you on to Burl?" he asked.

"Rosemary Toomey," Jayme said. "We were tracing back the history of Royce's employees. Turns out Burl was McGintey's predecessor. You must have been aware of that."

"We were," the sheriff said. "Checked him out right at the start. He came up clean."

"We think he deserves another look," DeMarco said.

"And what makes you think that?"

"There's more to his and McGintey's relationship than meets the eye. McGintey's got something to bargain with. We mentioned Burl, he got a little worried."

The sheriff nodded, squinted at the floor. When he looked up, he jerked his chin at DeMarco's injured leg. "You spent all that time traipsing around in the woods and never got so much as a whiff of Helm?"

DeMarco smiled. "There's a lot to smell in that forest, Sheriff, but not him."

"But if we need to know," the sheriff said, "you can tell us where all you searched in there?"

"I can tell you where I went into the woods, and more or less where I came out." DeMarco rubbed a hand over his left thigh. "If you do conduct a search, there's one particular gully I'd like to revisit with a couple sticks of dynamite."

The sheriff looked to Jayme. "Is he always that clumsy?"

"Frequently," she said.

The sheriff put a hand to his chin, rubbed his manicured scruff up and down. "You two are better than Martin and Lewis," he said. "I'll send a couple deputies out to talk to Burl again, see what we can squeeze out of him."

"About that," DeMarco said. "He strikes me as the skittish type."

"Meaning what?"

Jayme said, "We're thinking the next step should be a little more insight into Burl. First from Royce, then Burl's current employer."

"The millionaire?"

"Right," she answered. "Retired chiropractor."

"How's a man get to be a millionaire from cracking backs?"

"Six clinics along the Gulf Coast. A lot of shrimpers and oil workers with bad backs, I guess."

The sheriff shrugged. "You should know that my department's been advised to take a hands-off approach when it comes to Pastor Royce."

"Us too," DeMarco said. "But we're civilians here. Thinking about converting to Baptists. Looking for some spiritual advice, that's all."

The sheriff smiled. "He'd be the man for that, I hear."

Jayme asked, "What's the FBI's interest in him anyway?"

The sheriff glanced past her to the open door of his office: no deputies lurking outside. "Rumor is—and it's all just rumor—some of his foundation's money might have found its way into the hands of a bunch of black radicals up in Chicago. The kind that like to collect heavy-duty weaponry."

"I think I need to sit in on one of the pastor's sermons," DeMarco said.

"Oh, he's slick," the sheriff told him. "Always stays just a hair short of advocating sedition. Publicly anyway. What he advocates privately is a matter of conjecture."

"Well," DeMarco said, "I'll leave the anarchists to the big boys. Investigating sedition is way above my pay grade."

"I hear you," said the sheriff. "Between domestic abuse, sexual abuse, animal abuse, meth labs, crack houses, and poaching deer and wild boar, plus a mountain of paperwork for all of it, we've got more than enough to do around here."

"Thanks for the poonchkey," DeMarco said. "We'll stay in touch."

"Do that," said the sheriff.

Out on the sidewalk, which was simmering already at nine in the morning, bits of mica glinting like sparks, DeMarco slipped on his sunglasses and said to Jayme, "Do women really like that scruffy look on men?"

"Are you thinking of trying it?"

"Seems to me it would take longer to maintain than a nice close shave every day."

"It's okay on boys," she told him. "I'm not completely sold on the gray scruff, though."

"You know what turns me on these days?" he asked.

"It better be what I'm thinking it is. If you know what's good for you."

He grinned. Laid his hand against the small of her back.

"Who's Martin and Lewis?" she asked.

ONE HUNDRED THIRTY

Reverend Royce came striding down the corridor toward the lobby where Jayme and DeMarco had been asked to wait. Two large black men in expensive suits followed a long stride behind him. His voice reverberated off the marble tile when he asked, as if from a stage, "Is Vicente paying you two just to vex me? What's next—a plague of boils?"

"Nice acoustics," DeMarco said. Behind him, seated at his desk, the security guard chuckled.

Royce stopped two feet short of barreling straight through DeMarco. "I am in the midst of a contract negotiation with a major television network. I have no time for interruptions. And I certainly have no obligation to make myself available to individuals with no purview outside the borders of Pennsylvania."

"Yet here we stand," Jayme said with a beaming smile, "having another lovely chat."

"Because I am a righteous man, with nothing to do with the unfortunate death of those girls, no matter how vehemently Vicente wishes it otherwise. I have spoken to a dozen law enforcement personnel thus far. I have signed an affidavit. I requested and passed a polygraph test. So now I am telling you to inform Esquire Vicente, I will have no more!"

"Todd Burl," DeMarco said.

Royce's head jerked as if somebody had chucked him under the chin. "What does that vermin have to do with anything?"

DeMarco said, "I understand he was your business partner for a while."

"Partner? The man mowed my grass and fixed my toilets. In what way does that constitute a partnership?"

"Why did you fire him?" Jayme asked.

Royce glanced at the security guard. Then turned to one of his bodyguards. "Open the sanctuary."

The guard unlocked the heavy wooden doors leading into the five-hundred-seat church. He pulled one door open, and stood there waiting.

To DeMarco and Jayme, Royce said, "If you don't mind."

He followed them into the sanctuary, then, as his bodyguard closed the door behind them, crossed to half sit against the back of a rear pew, with the sprawling sanctuary laid out behind him, the row upon row of pews padded in red velvet, the wide center aisle leading to the padded kneeling rail, and behind it the raised chancel, the pulpit, and four risers for the choir, the enormous golden cross high up on the rear wall, the cameras and lights suspended over the pews.

DeMarco said, "I don't think we're in Aberdeen anymore, Toto."

"Praise God," Royce said. "As for Todd Burl?" He twisted up his mouth as if he wanted to spit. "Even his name is loathsome to me."

"And why is that?" Jayme asked.

"Have you met him?"

"Briefly."

"That should be time enough," Royce said. "But, since you asked, allow me to elucidate. He was hired, as I said, to provide general maintenance and upkeep for my properties. I had only three buildings back then, I believe. One two-unit apartment building, one four-unit, and the church, of course, which I did not own but was responsible for as per my contract. I hired Burl when I first came to Aberdeen. Before I knew the man well enough to avoid him at all costs."

"You found him unreliable?" DeMarco asked.

"Oh, he did the work. The quality of his work was, in fact, exceptional. His sycophantic harassment is what soured the relationship. Constantly attempting to insinuate himself into my business interests. Wanting to buy in with what he referred to as his 'sweat equity.' As if I would ever be associated with a man of his ilk."

Jayme said, "And by 'his ilk,' you mean what?"

"I began to hear, from my parishioners, certain rumors. First, that the man is a pathological liar. To be trusted at one's own peril. Second, that he was known on occasion to—excuse my use of the vernacular—pimp out his wife."

"Really?" Jayme said. "She hardly looks the type."

"My thoughts exactly," Royce replied. "And so I engaged him in conversation one day. Gave the appearance I was actually considering a partnership. In short, I encouraged him to run his mouth so as to see exactly where it would run. And oh, how it ran."

"Care to share the specifics?" Jayme asked.

"He claimed, among other things, to have been a Navy SEAL. To have an IQ of 140. To have a degree in economics from Drew University. To have made a fortune investing in commodities—all of which he gave away. Out of the goodness of his heart."

"Any of it true?" DeMarco asked.

"As far as I could determine, not a shred."

"And that's why you fired him?"

Royce sucked a long breath in through his nose. "He offered me his wife," he said.

"As in?" DeMarco asked.

"Imagine that if you can. A man so paranoid and insecure that he will scarcely allow his spouse out in public alone, yet offers her to another man in hopes of forging a business partnership."

"Are you saying you refused his offer?"

Royce lowered his voice but increased his adamancy. "No part of me would ever touch what that man has soiled."

"And that was the final straw for you?"

Royce nodded. "And yet, more was to come. I questioned a handful of parishioners, those who had occasion to know him fairly well, and they confirmed my suspicions. I was not the only man to whom he had made such an offer. A thoroughly contemptible human being."

Jayme asked, "Are you saying that he was prostituting his wife?"

"According to my information, regularly."

DeMarco's eyebrows lifted. He asked, "When you fired him, did you tell him why?"

Royce nodded. "I was having breakfast one morning with a couple of colleagues, that little place across from the hardware store. When in he comes. Walks up to me, lays a hand on my shoulder, addresses me as 'brother,' and in general makes a show of our acquaintance, as if we are somehow the closest of friends. I reacted poorly. Lost my temper. Enumerated his sins for all to hear. And told him precisely what a vile human being he is.

"In hindsight," Royce said, "I should not have confronted him so publicly. It wasn't the Christian thing to do."

DeMarco gazed up at the suspended cameras, a dozen microphones strategically placed.

Jayme asked, "Did you convey all this to the sheriff's department back when the investigation got started?"

"To every thing there is a season," Royce answered, "and a time for every purpose under heaven."

"Why is that season now?" DeMarco asked.

"Because I am sick and tired of being tarred by the same brush as a bunch of reprobates."

DeMarco smiled. "And how did you come to replace Burl with Chad McGintey?"

"He appeared at my home the same afternoon I confronted Burl. Said he had heard I might be looking to hire a new maintenance man. It was obvious he was down on his luck, unable to make ends meet. So I gave him a chance. Another unfortunate error in my judgment."

"How about Virgil Helm?" DeMarco said.

"Him as well. I only hired him because the man was a veteran. And obviously not in the best of health. Yet eager enough for the job. I am still astounded by the depths of his heinous nature."

Jayme said, "So you're convinced he's the one responsible?"

"You and Vicente's misguided group seem to be the only

individuals unwilling to accept the obvious. I telephoned Helm to alert him to the termite situation, and next morning, he is gone."

"Could be," DeMarco said. "Could be."

Royce now moved toward the door, wrapped his fingers around the gold-plated handle. "I trust I won't be seeing you again?"

"Who knows?" DeMarco said. "You guys still do full submersion for baptisms?"

"I will gladly submerge *you*," Royce told him with a grin. Then he pulled open the door. One of his bodyguards stepped up to hold the door.

"By the way," Jayme told the pastor, "Antoinette is a lovely young woman. I bet your daughter is beautiful."

Royce turned, eyes narrowing. "I should have guessed," he said. "Do you have any idea what that lawyer is demanding from me?"

"I can only hope," Jayme said, and walked away grinning.

ONE HUNDRED THIRTY-ONE

On their drive back to Aberdeen, after picking up a box of crispy chicken wraps and two chilled bottles of water at the nearest fast food drive-up, Jayme and DeMarco discussed the morning's information in relation to what was already known or believed to be true.

"Let's work backward from Virgil Helm," DeMarco suggested. "Emery. I wish you had met him. Unfortunately we have only my impression to go with."

"And you tend to believe him," she said.

"I can't see anything he has to gain by lying. Plus I'd probably be dead, or locked up in a cage, or still wandering around in those woods if it weren't for him. He says he never had the key to access the false wall, and I believe him."

"So then, moving backward to McGintey... Do you believe he never had the key?"

"You first."

Driving with her left hand, she took a bite of the chicken wrap, chewed slowly, swallowed, carefully laid the wrap on the napkin spread over her thigh, reached for the bottle of water in the cup holder, took a sip. "Yeah, I do. He's got some issues, no doubt about it. But I don't see him as a serial killer. You think he'll get the deal he's asking for?"

"Some variation of it. Char will walk. Brother too probably. Minimum sentence for Chad himself."

"You okay with that?"

DeMarco shrugged. "It's the sheriff's county, not mine. He'll probably figure, get Chad now, get the brother later. Clean up one mess at a time."

"Okay then," she said. "Virgil had no key, no opportunity, no discernible motive. McGintey no key, no opportunity, motive fairly murky. Eli Royce, plenty of opportunity. However…"

"Lots of howevers."

"Two big ones for me," she said. "He aced the polygraph. Plus, the man might be contemptible for a number of reasons, but he isn't stupid. Fill a church with skeletons? A church over which he presides? And then schedule an inspection that will almost surely uncover them? If he put them there, why would he not remove them before the inspection?"

DeMarco was silent for a moment. Then said, "Here's the thing. According to McGintey, he just happened to hear about the caretaker job, and applied for it. According to Royce, McGintey showed up at his house within hours of the position opening up. Somebody told him the job was available. I can't picture a guy like Todd Burl broadcasting the news about getting fired."

"Didn't Virgil tell you Burl and McGintey were partners?"

"Virgil didn't, but Cat did. Said that's what he'd told her. Unless we're chasing the wrong Toad."

"We already know that Chad McGintey lies."

"Everybody lies."

She took another drink of water. Then, "So which liar do you want to talk to first?"

DeMarco thought for a moment. "What was your read on that older girl when you talked to her?"

Jayme smiled. "Poonchkey," she said.

DeMarco laughed. "Well then, pull a huey," he said, "and let's see which way the jelly runs."

ONE HUNDRED THIRTY-TWO

The girl, Charlene, seemed older to DeMarco than her nineteen years. Hardened, ready to fight. She came into the room scowling, contempt clearly written on the hard line of her mouth and in the veiled boredom of her eyes. "If this is all you people have to do with your time," she said, "it's pretty pathetic."

She went straight to the window overlooking the parking lot, but not before picking up the cigarette and book of matches placed for her on the coffee table. The women's conference room, unlike the men's, was well-lit and more cheerfully painted, with blue walls and four padded chairs of orange or green vinyl, two of which DeMarco and Jayme currently occupied.

"This is Sergeant Ryan DeMarco," Jayme told her. "Ryan, this is Charlene."

He smiled but said nothing. Charlene did not turn from the window, but blew a cloud of smoke against the pane. "If you think I'm going to say a word against him, you're wasting your time."

DeMarco told her, "Things just got a whole lot more serious, Charlene."

She turned her head slightly, not enough to meet his gaze.

"You should know," he continued, "that we've been gathering information not only about Chad but also about his former employer, Reverend Royce, and also about his affiliation with Todd Burl and Virgil Helm. We know Chad told you about all that. We know he told you about the false wall in the church and what it was used for. That makes you a coconspirator. The charge will be felony murder, seven counts. You might never be able to look out a window again."

They sat very still then, watching the side of her face, her body. Her hand trembled as she raised the cigarette to her lips for another drag, her inhalation shallow, staccato. The fingers of her free hand twitched.

Jayme's voice was softer. "We know you didn't have anything to do with what happened to those girls, Charlene. Unfortunately, you can still be charged if you withhold what you know. That's the way the law works."

"That's messed up," she said to the window.

"It can be," Jayme said. "But if you choose to be honest with us, and confirm what we already know, there's a decent chance you can be out of here soon. Free and clear."

And now Charlene turned from the window. "Chad too?"

DeMarco said, "He'll still have to face the sexual contact charge. But that's all."

Jayme said, "We already talked to him this morning. He's agreed. Now it's up to you."

She looked to the closed door, then back to Jayme. "Do I need a lawyer?"

"You can certainly have one if you want," Jayme said. "Or you can just sit and be honest with us. We have no authority in this state. We're not here to trap you or to hurt you in any way. We just want the truth so that we can pass it on to the sheriff. He's the one who will take an official statement."

Charlene kept staring at Jayme, but her eyes were blank with fear.

Jayme said, "You have a whole life ahead of you, Charlene. I would like very much for you to live it outside of a Kentucky state prison."

And eventually the young woman moved away from the window, sat beside Jayme on an orange vinyl chair. She asked for something to drink, so DeMarco fetched a can of soda from the vending machine in the hallway. Jayme turned her knees toward Charlene, closed the distance between them, leaned closer when they talked. DeMarco kept his face expressionless, did his best to show no surprise, did not frighten her with eye contact. He sat with hands clasped between his knees, eyes down, head slightly cocked as he listened and remembered.

"Let's start with you telling me how Chad got involved with Todd Burl," Jayme said. "What was that all about?"

"I wasn't around him then," Charlene said. "I only know what he told me."

"That's what we need to hear."

"It was Chad's brother knew him first. They met in some bar, got high together. I guess Burl took him home that first night, let him do his wife."

"Todd Burl took Lucas back to his house and let him have sex with his wife?"

"That's what he said. Burl gets off on watching. And I guess that's when Burl started buying his product from Lucas."

"His product being what?"

"Weed. Burl was getting it in Tennessee before that, bringing it up here and selling it to Royce's tenants and a few other people. But he found out he could get it cheaper and closer from Lucas."

"So Burl was working for Royce back then?"

"Yeah. And selling on the side. Both the weed and his wife from what I was told."

"Was Royce involved in this?"

"In the dope? Hell no."

"And this continued for…"

"Well, after Lucas got busted and sent away, it was Burl and Chad then for a while. Until Royce got pissed about something and fired him."

"Fired Burl."

"Yeah. So Burl calls up Chad right away, and they cook up this plan for Chad to get Burl's job doing the mowing and stuff. Because Burl has a set of extra keys for the church. And what better place to sell their stuff with nobody seeing, right? I mean Royce hardly went near the place except on Sundays, too busy with whatever else he was into. Mostly pussy, from what I was told."

"Prostitution?"

"Naw, just screwing everybody he could. Plus there was shit going on in Chicago or somewhere. Black Power stuff, you know? And Royce was trying to get in good with those people."

"Okay," Jayme said. "So Burl is buying weed from Chad and selling it out of the church?"

"They were getting into some meth then too. Anything they could sell. The funny part was, Royce had his office all decked out in expensive furniture and paintings and stuff, including this big black leather couch he supposedly used to lay on while composing his sermons. Getting his inspiration from God, you know? Really it was where he banged half the black women in town, Burl said. So Burl got this brilliant idea of having his wife screw guys on that couch too. A couple times a week. Just to spite Royce is why he did it. Ever since he'd got fired, Burl was out to mess things up for Royce any way he could."

"And you're sure about Burl liking to watch? His wife with other men?"

"Absolutely. He watched Chad do me lots of times. Or me and his wife at the same time. He made this little crack in the wall, you know, so he could stand behind it and watch us go at it. That's his thing, watching and beating off. Me, I prefer the real McCoy. But whatever floats your boat."

"Okay," Jayme said, "let me get this straight. Burl has another job by this time, but he's still using the church as a place to sell dope. Does he store it there too?"

"We figured he must have. I mean, why cart it around with him? Nobody but him was ever allowed in behind that wall. One time Chad tried to pick the lock down in the basement, up on the basement ceiling, you know? Underneath one of the ceiling panels or something. But then he quit 'cause he was afraid Burl would notice somehow. And I don't know if you know this or not, but Burl's a batshit little fucker. Holds a grudge like nobody you ever seen. He was always talking about getting back at Royce someday. Messing him up good, you know? That's half the reason Chad quit that mowing job, 'cause he didn't want Burl sucking him into some craziness he cooked up."

"What's the other half?"

"Well, Lucas got out of prison and he wanted Chad back on the property full-time. Getting ready for the revolution, you know?"

"So then Chad quits working for Royce. And recommends Virgil Helm to replace him?"

"Right. Virgil had come into town and moved into the apartment above the bar and was looking for some work. Thing is, the guy was sort of a mess. Kind of reminded me of a starved cat he was so scrawny. Something wrong with his lungs apparently. But how hard is it to drive a lawn tractor around?"

"What about the day Virgil disappeared? Did he know what was hidden between those walls?"

"Nobody knew," Charlene said. "I mean somebody did, but it wasn't Chad or Virgil. Then the day Virgil found out there was going to be that termite inspection, he was having a beer downstairs with Chad, and Chad told him right away Burl's stash was probably behind those walls, and if it was found, Virgil would sure as shootin' be the one to get blamed for it."

"So Virgil took off?"

"Wouldn't you? Packed up his motorcycle and was gone. Next day the termite guy pulls off a couple boards, and that's when all hell broke loose."

Twenty minutes after their conversation began, Charlene returned to her cell, softly crying but hopeful. Jayme and DeMarco remained in their chairs, Jayme typing into her laptop, DeMarco scrawling notes in a small spiral notebook, writing fast in his typical shorthand absent of nonessential words.

When both finished, DeMarco said, "One of us needs to thank the deputy on duty. The other one can give the sheriff the call."

Jayme closed up her laptop and stood. "I'll take the deputy."

DeMarco smiled. "You just know the sheriff is going to hit on you."

"Yes I do," she said. "And I don't want you arrested for assaulting an officer."

"I've developed an empathy for the sheriff," DeMarco said. "I understand how he feels."

"Right," Jayme said. "See you downstairs."

Ten minutes later they walked out into the searing heat together. "Sheriff is having his men look into Burl's credit card purchases back in the nineties, see if any records still exist. Anything to put him in the towns where the girls disappeared. In the meantime he's happy to let us get some intel on Burl from his employer. Even offered to deputize us."

"Yippee," Jayme said.

"I declined the honor," DeMarco told her. "We have more freedom as civilians."

"Plus you can't stand the idea of working for him."

"This is true," DeMarco said. "But I do like his poonchkey."

ONE HUNDRED THIRTY-THREE

The millionaire chiropractor's estate consisted of over eight hundred acres atop a bluff high above the West Fork of Mayfield Creek, a tributary of the Mississippi River. From the road along the creek, only the main house was visible, and, a hundred feet below it, the scarred cliffside of the quarry from which the massive sandstone building blocks had been carved. Jayme and DeMarco stood outside the car on the driver's side, peering up at the building while sporadic traffic passed in both directions, every vehicle washing a warm, rumbling breeze over their faces.

"When was it restored?" DeMarco asked.

"I stopped spending full summers with Grandma when I was sixteen. So some time after that."

"The girls started disappearing in 1998."

A shiver ran down Jayme's spine. She rubbed her arms.

DeMarco said, "What do you know about the owner?"

"Not much," Jayme said. "I do know that he's very reclusive. Almost nobody ever sees him. I remember Grandma mentioning that he got married several years after he moved in. Went away somewhere and came back with a wife. She has some kind of spinal condition and needs a wheelchair to get around. Supposedly—and this is just what Grandma heard; she never saw them herself—a few times every summer he drives down to the Dairy Queen with her riding in the backseat, and he buys a couple chocolate cones at the drive-through. That's sweet, isn't it?"

"Sure," DeMarco said. "Any idea on his age?"

"In his seventies probably."

DeMarco pulled out his cell phone and checked the time. "Four seventeen," he said. "You think Burl gets off at four or at five?"

"Depends. Does he work with the animals or just the buildings? I hear they have llamas and miniature goats and peacocks up there."

"A little Garden of Eden," DeMarco said.

"Don't be jealous," she teased.

He said, "What's the difference timewise? Between animals and buildings?"

"I was just thinking the animals probably take more attention. Fed, watered… I don't really know."

"Let's wait until after five. I'd rather he doesn't know yet that we're poking around. How far is it to that Dairy Queen?"

"If you're thinking Rocky Road Brownie Blizzard, you're thinking twelve hundred calories, babe. That's twelve miles of jogging. Can you do that with a crutch?"

"I've been piling up the miles lately."

"Motorized miles don't count."

"I climbed a mountain," he said. "Spent three days in the woods. Almost no food. Got shot at. Was nearly eaten by a wolf-dog. I'm running at a calorie deficit here. Eight thousand minimum."

"Oh boy," she told him. "I'll drive. You need to save your strength. Those plastic spoons are heavy."

ONE HUNDRED THIRTY-FOUR

Jayme pressed the intercom button on the security gate a half mile from the main house. Four minutes earlier, parked within view of the private lane where it joined with the highway, they had watched Burl's blue pickup truck emerge onto the highway and proceed toward Aberdeen. Now the intercom clicked and a woman's voice said, "Yes? Hello?"

"Hi," Jayme said. "My name is Jayme Matson, and I'm here with Sergeant Ryan DeMarco. We'd like to get a few minutes with Dr. Friedl if we could."

"Is there something wrong?" the woman asked.

"No, ma'am. We're just gathering information about a case we're working on."

"Oh," the woman said. Then, a few seconds later, "William is out at his workshop, I think."

Jayme said, "We just have a few questions. It won't take long. Would you mind giving him a call?"

"He doesn't carry a phone," the woman said. "Stop at the house and I'll give you directions."

"Thank you," Jayme said. A moment later the security bar lifted.

They drove slowly past an open field and pond, then a forest of red pine, then hardwoods on both sides of the asphalt lane. Then the land to the right of the lane began to slope downward, with the lane riding a low ridge above a barn and a corral with six llamas grazing. A side road attached to the lane led down to the front of the barn. Also visible spread out below were a long, narrow greenhouse, a smaller barn, and several other picturesque buildings of stone or red brick or plank, all relatively new and in a peculiar mix of architectural styles, including a small fortlike building, an aviary, a freestanding tower complete with gargoyles, a carriage house, a rose garden gazebo, a tiny chapel, and other unidentifiable buildings, all linked by a maze of flagstone paths and shrubbery.

In front of the main house a wide circular drive enclosed a mani-cured lawn of low grass. To the right of the mouth of the circular drive was a paved parking area, empty but for a compact red coupe. The house, a three-story mansion made of polished sandstone blocks, sat just behind the drive, its white Roman columns and wide portico furnished with several wicker chairs in bold Caribbean colors. The nearest side of the house was bordered by a row of well-maintained rose bushes; a profusion of other bright varieties lined the front wall.

Jayme pulled the car in beside the red coupe, slipped the gearshift into Park, and shut off the engine. DeMarco continued to look in the direction of the small woman in an electronic wheelchair waiting underneath the portico's vaulted roof.

He said, trying not to move his lips, "She's black. You didn't tell me she's black. Is he?"

"I didn't know," Jayme said. "And no, I don't think he is."

They both climbed out smiling. He left the cane in the car, and moved gingerly at first, left leg still stiff, still wrapped tightly from ankle to above the knee.

Mrs. Friedl watched with her eyebrows knitted in puzzlement. DeMarco guessed her height at maybe five two, weight not more than a hundred pounds. Only her face showed her age, which he guessed at early forties. Her skin was a light-caramel color, hair raven black and cut short in ragged bangs over her eyes. She sat crookedly in her wheelchair, a small protrusion visible at the top of her spine.

"I don't understand why you're here," she said. "I probably should have asked for some kind of identification."

They showed her their state police credentials. She said, "From Pennsylvania?"

Jayme said, "We're working with the local state police and the county sheriff's department."

She blinked once at Jayme, once at DeMarco, her small hands resting on the wheelchair's armrests, thin legs and feet motionless.

She gave a little nod toward his injured leg. "Are you okay to walk?"

He smiled. "Just not in a straight line."

She returned his smile. "If you follow that path," she said, and pointed to her right, "the workshop is the third building. I expect he's there, but you might have to search for him some."

"Thank you," DeMarco said.

As he walked away, Jayme said, "Would it be all right if you and I spoke for a few minutes?"

"If you'd like," the woman said. "Would you prefer we go inside?"

"It's lovely here," Jayme said. "I can smell the roses. Would it be okay if I sit in one of those chairs?"

"That's fine," the woman said.

Once Jayme was seated and the woman had maneuvered her wheelchair to face her, Jayme said, "I understand that Todd Burl is an employee of yours."

"He left here not ten minutes ago," the woman said.

Jayme nodded. "What can you tell me about him? His demeanor? General personality? What kind of relationship do you have with him?"

"I don't have many dealings with him myself. He works outside the house."

"But you've had occasion over the years to form an impression, am I right?"

The woman cocked her head a little, appeared uncomfortable. "You should probably speak to my husband about him."

"Sergeant DeMarco will be doing that. I'd love to hear your opinion."

"Is he in some kind of trouble?"

"I really can't discuss that right now," Jayme said, smiling as always. "How about if we start with you telling me what his duties are here?"

Mrs. Friedl looked away and seemed to be staring at a spot on the grass inside the circular drive. Her brow remained furrowed.

When the screen door to their right suddenly opened, both Mrs. Friedl and Jayme flinched.

Out stepped a young woman in her early twenties. Jayme sized her up at a glance: faded blue jeans and T-shirt, five eight, sturdy, brown hair pulled into a short ponytail held in place with an elastic band. She looked briefly at Jayme, then to Mrs. Friedl.

"I'm sorry, Dee; I don't mean to interrupt," the young woman said.

"It's fine," Mrs. Friedl said. "Are you leaving now?"

The young woman nodded. "I finished the laundry and started up the dishwasher. You're getting low on almond milk and English muffins."

"Would you mind picking up a bunch of fresh basil too? William wants to make pesto tomorrow night."

"Will do," the young woman said and, with a quick smile, headed toward the red coupe.

Jayme waited until the young woman was inside the car and pulling away. "One of your employees?" she asked.

Mrs. Friedl nodded. "Susan. Comes by for a couple hours every afternoon. Such a sweet girl. She's putting herself through college. Her home life is…not ideal."

Jayme nodded. "So your first name is Dee?"

"Diamond. But, in my husband's words, diamonds are hard. He started calling me Dee right from the start. I've grown used to it. Prefer it, actually."

Jayme smiled. "It's such a big, beautiful place you have here. It must take a lot of people to maintain it."

"Not so many as you'd think," Mrs. Friedl said. "We try to keep it to a minimum. Most are part-time."

"Except for Mr. Burl?" Jayme said.

Again Mrs. Friedl paused, and looked into the near distance. "He's the grounds supervisor," she said. "His job is to make sure everything's as it should be. He tends to the animals, supervises the gardener and any of the building crews we hire. If something goes wrong in one of the outbuildings, he either fixes it or hires a specialist to do it."

"And are you happy with his work?"

Another pause. "My husband seems to be."

"Am I wrong," Jayme said, "or do I detect a certain discomfort when you talk about him? Is it fair to say you aren't exactly fond of him?"

The woman took a long time forming her answer. "He's…" she said, then stopped. "I don't like speaking ill of anyone. Especially when they're just feelings I have. Nothing concrete."

"It's your feelings I'm interested in," Jayme said.

"He has a certain…air about him," Mrs. Friedl said. "Proprietary, I think is the word."

"In what way?" Jayme asked.

"I often feel unwelcome in his presence. As if this is his home, and I am a visitor here. An intruder. He and William have lunch out here sometimes. I've learned not to join them. He makes me…anxious."

"I understand what you mean. I met him once. Very briefly."

"And you had the same feeling?"

"I did."

"I once made the mistake of rolling up close to the flowers after a rain. The man barked at me. He literally shouted at me that I was damaging the sod. Of course he apologized profusely as soon as he heard himself. Begged my forgiveness. But I've felt ever since that the incident gave me a glimpse into the real man."

"Did you mention it to your husband?"

The woman shook her head. "Around William, he's always nodding and agreeing, no matter what William says. Too much, do you know what I mean? Too agreeable. William doesn't see it."

"They have a close relationship?"

"I suppose," she said. "Mr. Burl was already here when I came, so I hate to say anything about him to William. But sometimes I get the feeling he's been in the house. Without William, I mean."

"What do you think he would be doing in there?"

"I try not to think about that." The woman gazed down the path toward her husband's workshop.

"William is very susceptible to flattery," she said a few moments later. "Everywhere he goes, people ask him for a contribution to something. I can't tell you how much he's given away. Even our accountant has told him—he has to be more careful with who he trusts."

"He has a reputation for being quite the philanthropist."

"Half the time, he doesn't even know where the money is going. He just loves the praise. He says he was a very homely child, didn't have any friends. I just worry that Mr. Burl is taking advantage of him."

"I can see how that would be a concern," Jayme said. "How long have you been married?"

"Thirteen years this May."

The spring of 2005, Jayme thought, then said, with a teasing smile, "You must have been a child."

A soft laugh. "There is a significant age difference," she said. "But not to me. I was twenty-seven."

And now Jayme waited. Would she reveal more? She did not seem the kind of woman who would choose a reclusive, isolated life, but one who'd had it thrust upon her.

She spoke while studying her fingernails, which were perfectly manicured and painted white. "For some people it was scandalous, marrying a man past sixty. But I used to tell them, ride a mile in my wheelchair, and then you can judge."

Still Jayme said nothing.

"I haven't walked since my teens. William was the first man to treat me like a human being. Like a woman. He means everything to me. I don't like it when people take advantage of him. He had a difficult childhood too."

"Really?" Jayme said.

"Not poor, like mine; his family was well-to-do. But he was a big child, awkward, clumsy, didn't care for sports. Not handsome in the traditional sense. But he's beautiful to me."

"And you think Mr. Burl takes advantage of him?"

"Did you see the animals on your way in?"

"Yes."

"His idea. Several of the buildings and other projects too. And of course William just writes out the checks, no questions asked. And some of the prices are outrageous."

"That's unfortunate," Jayme said. "What do you know about Mr. Burl's family life?"

"I know he's married. Two little girls. I haven't met any of them. William and I don't socialize much at all."

"Is your family local?" Jayme asked.

"My family? I'm an only child. My father…chose to move on, well before I married. My mother comes to visit at Christmas each year. She still lives in Mobile. That's where William and I met. I was his patient." She smiled proudly. "And now I'm his only patient. I don't know what I'd do without him. What a godsend he's been."

ONE HUNDRED THIRTY-FIVE

As DeMarco approached the first building along the path, a long, red-brick stable-like construction, he glanced back over his shoulder, saw Jayme taking a seat under the portico, Mrs. Friedl moving in her wheelchair to follow her. He stepped quickly to his left and crossed along the side of the building, his movements hidden now behind the shrubbery. The air was sweet with the scent of greenery and flowers. Off in the distance, a peacock cried three times in a row, a sound that struck DeMarco as eerily similar to a woman screaming, "Owww! Owww! Owww!"

The building was dark through dusty windows, but with hands cupped around his eyes he could make out a half-dozen vintage automobiles lined up in a row—long, wide, tail-finned cars from the fifties and sixties.

The second building, twenty feet beyond a long, cantilevered pergola festooned with vines and leaves and clusters of fat, blue-black grapes, was a large windowless shed on a concrete pad. The front door was held closed by a small combination lock. Tracks similar to those made by a garden tractor led off the pad and into the grass. Day-old tread marks of crushed, browning grass lay in relief atop the concrete.

Beyond this building stood a wooden Dutch barn large enough to house two school busses parked side by side, the double doors wide open, soft music breezing out, a snare drum and trumpets, Bobby Darin singing about Miss Lotte Lenya and old Lucy Brown. A red golf cart was parked near the open doors.

DeMarco crept up to the barn and peeked inside. The front half of the building was empty, nothing but an oak plank floor and the scent of fresh sawdust. A pair of sawhorses against one wall, a push broom and dustpan against the other. In the rear half of the room stood a long sturdy table underneath a fluorescent light. A scroll saw was bolted to one end of the table, a table saw at the other, and several tools scattered in between. On a shelf along the window were laid out several pieces of cut lumber in various sizes, plus a portable stereo tuned to an oldies station, the antenna leaning against the window.

Sitting in the corner on a lattice lawn chair facing the table saw was Friedl—a broad sagging face, large nose and fleshy ears, thin white hair parted on the side, thick hands and forearms. His height was difficult for DeMarco to judge but he guessed at six two or three, weight two fifty, a lot of it in the belly and hips. Clad in baggy chinos, a blue chambray shirt with sleeves rolled above the elbows, and a pair of brown Hush Puppies mall walkers, the chiropractor sat hunched forward over spread knees, reading glasses perched on his nose, hands spread three feet apart holding a large sheet of paper printed with what appeared to be a construction diagram.

DeMarco rapped on the doorframe. Friedl looked up, removed his reading glasses, squinted at the figure in the late afternoon light.

"Sorry to disturb you," DeMarco said. "Your wife told me I would find you here."

Friedl rose from his chair with some difficulty, went to the radio, and turned the music off. To DeMarco he said, "Say that again."

DeMarco came forward pulling his wallet from a back pocket. "I'm Sergeant Ryan DeMarco," he said, and flipped the wallet open to his credentials. He held it open for two more steps, then snapped it shut and pocketed it again. "I'm working with the state police and the county sheriff's department."

Friedl blinked, folded the arms of his reading glasses, and laid them atop the stereo. Then he faced the worktable and pressed the heels of his palms against the rounded edge. "Working with them on what?"

"I was hoping you could help me out with some information about your foreman, Todd Burl."

"Such as?" Friedl asked. His voice was not shaky but hesitant, with each statement preceded by a brief pause.

"How long has he worked for you?" DeMarco asked.

"Well, let's see." Friedl looked down at the table's surface, flicked a curl of sawdust onto the floor. "He's been here pretty much since the beginning. I started working on this place in the late nineties. I remember it was April. Seemed cold coming up from Alabama."

"And how did you happen to hire Mr. Burl?"

Friedl stared at DeMarco, blinked once, then again. "What does this concern?"

"The incident at the Baptist Church a few years ago." DeMarco spoke evenly, watched carefully. A quick lift of Friedl's eyebrows. A sniff.

"What is it you think he's done?" Friedl asked. But his eyes had gone unfocused; his gaze no longer met DeMarco's.

DeMarco said, "We don't think anything, sir. We're just gathering information."

Friedl stood motionless for several beats. Then he turned, moved back to his chair, hand trailing along the table. When he reached out to steady the chair and sit, his hand, DeMarco noticed, was not steady.

"I came back from the realtor's office the morning I closed on the sale," Friedl said, "and he was up here wandering around. Introduced himself and said he'd heard I might be hiring a few people."

"And you hired him on the spot?"

Friedl shrugged. "Saved me putting an ad in the paper."

DeMarco nodded, smiled, assumed a casual posture, hip against the table. "How well do you know Mr. Burl?"

"I know he shows up on time and does his work. Meticulously, I might add. Very detail-oriented. He keeps things running as smoothly as they can."

"Would you say you have a friendly relationship with him?"

"He works for me. We talk from time to time. That's about as far as it goes."

"Do you trust him? Enjoy his company?"

Friedl put his hands together, right hand gripping the fingers of his left. "I can't say I understand what you're getting at here, Sergeant."

"Would it surprise you to hear that allegations have been made regarding Mr. Burl's honesty? That he was fired by his previous employer, Pastor Eli Royce, for possibly engaging in activities involving drugs and prostitution?"

Friedl winced, squeezed his fingers. "It would indeed," he said. He switched hands now, squeezed and pulled at the fingers of his right hand. "But that was a long time ago, wasn't it? People change their ways."

"Some do," DeMarco said. "So when you hired him, you knew none of this?"

"Other than the realtor and a lawyer, I didn't know a soul in this town. He claimed to have experience as a general contractor, said he was looking to change jobs, do better for himself."

"You didn't check his references?"

"I took him at his word." Now Friedl leaned back in the chair, squared up his shoulders, and blew out a little breath. "It's possible I made a mistake, I suppose. My wife thinks I give people too much trust."

"Him in particular?"

Friedl nodded. "She's told me time and again. Gives her the willies, she says."

DeMarco studied him for a while. He seemed tired, slow-moving, weighed down by the resignation men his age often manifest. His posture had gone limp now, hands loose and quiet atop his belly. He reminded DeMarco of some of the farmers he had known up north, tired old men who had lived on hope their entire lives only to have that hope dashed season after season by too much rain or too little rain, too many pests, too many regulations—men facing foreclosure or cancer or lung disease or just another winter.

When Friedl looked up again his eyelids were heavy, gaze almost plaintive. "Is that it?" he said. "We done here?"

DeMarco said, "I'm curious, sir. What's all this for anyway?" He waved his hand toward the open doorway. "All these buildings, all the expense you've gone to. Millions of dollars, I'm sure. Seems like a lot for two people. Why have you done all this?"

Friedl's head went from side to side. "Why's a person do anything? Trying to prove something to himself, I guess. You've never felt the need to do that, Sergeant?"

Every day, DeMarco thought.

He stood away from the table. "I'm going to ask you not to mention this conversation to Mr. Burl," he said. "Or to anyone else for that matter."

"That won't be difficult," Friedl told him.

DeMarco was halfway to the pergola when the music started in the workshop again. "Summertime," Sarah Vaughan sang, her tone strangely funereal, "and the livin' is easy…"

ONE HUNDRED THIRTY-SIX

There's something off about him," DeMarco told Jayme. "He's involved somehow. I'd bet my pension on it." He was watching a stand of red pines go by as Jayme drove them off the estate. The security bar across the lane lifted as the vehicle approached.

"I don't want him to be involved," Jayme said. "What will happen to her if he is?"

"Think about this," DeMarco said. "His wife is black. All the victims were black. Light-skinned blacks, all eight of them."

She nodded. "But she's alive."

DeMarco shook his head. Then, "You had a closer look at her than I did. Was it just the way she was sitting, or…"

"Some kind of spinal deformity. She was his patient. That's how they met."

"None of the girls had a condition like that, did they? I don't remember it being mentioned anywhere."

"We didn't see the full forensic reports."

DeMarco shook his head again, thinking, wondering. "He's a part of it. I know he is."

"Oh God," Jayme said. "His wife is so sweet…so vulnerable."

DeMarco said, "We don't get to decide these things."

They rode in silence for a while. Then Jayme said, "He brought her here in the spring of 2005. After they were married."

DeMarco turned from the window; stared at the side of her face.

"It might just be a coincidence," she said.

"They're starting to pile up."

"I'm going to pray that he's not involved. For her sake."

He leaned closer, laid a hand on her shoulder. "You never told me that you pray."

"More lately than usual."

He said, "I'd like to talk with you about that sometime."

"About praying?"

"More like...to who?"

"I'm not sure," she told him.

And he said, "Neither am I."

ONE HUNDRED THIRTY-SEVEN

That night, DeMarco awoke with a panicky feeling and reached for his phone to check the date. He had felt certain that yesterday was a Sunday but the phone told him otherwise. This disoriented him even more. Why was his heart thumping as if he had been running hard, chased by something unseen? And why Sunday?

And then it came to him. He had already missed too many Sundays with Ryan Jr. He felt off balance. Needed to be close to his boy. His grave hundreds of miles away.

He slipped out of bed, careful not to disturb Jayme. In boxers and a T-shirt he tiptoed downstairs in the dark, leaning into the bannister for stability.

At the landing he paused, tried unsuccessfully to remember why he had come downstairs. Wondered if he was sleepwalking. Or had he heard a noise? Some kind of disturbance outside?

He went to the front door, unlocked it, looked out into the 3:00 a.m. darkness. The night air felt sticky on his chest and arms and in direct opposition to the artificially cooled air now washing across his back. He stood there staring into the darkness without looking at anything in particular, just seeing it all as a huge, dark pool filled with houses and bushes and trees and lawns, with sleeping, oblivious people, any number of whom could be slaughtered in their sleep or killed on their way to work or school in the morning. He smelled the summersweet bushes but also the acrid stench of creosote. Light traffic could be heard out on the main street two blocks away, anomalous dull lights moving about here and there. Nothing was clearly visible, everything shrouded in darkness.

The darkness conceals itself in itself, he thought.

Jayme touched him gently at the waist, startling him so that he stiffened for a moment. Her hands slipped around his waist and she leaned against him, mouth close to the top of his spine. "What's going on?" she whispered.

He said, after a while, "It's all just an illusion out there."

"What is?" she asked.

"This pretty little town. Every town. It might look fine from a distance but…not if you look up close."

"What do you see up close?" she asked.

He didn't answer, and she wondered where he was going with this. Maybe he was still asleep. Caught up in a dream. "Are you okay?" she said.

She felt him shiver, felt something tremble through him.

He said, "Have you read Montaigne?"

"Not that I'm aware of. What did he write?"

"'Here we sit upon the highest throne in the world, yet here we sit upon our own tails.' Something like that."

"Meaning, I guess, that we're all still animals?"

Again he fell silent. She leaned her forehead against his back, slipped her hands around his belly.

He said, "You know what I see when I look out there?"

"Tell me," she whispered.

"I see meth labs and crack houses. Men beating up their wives and girlfriends and kids. I see drunks driving cars…vermin raping little girls and little boys…politicians lying and snooping and selling us out right and left. The streets are full of them. Cockroaches selling drugs and guns and women and who knows what else."

"They're not everywhere, baby. Plus there's a lot of us trying to clean things up. Am I right?"

He laid his hands atop hers where they pressed warm against him. "We're losing," he said.

"No," she told him. She pressed her mouth to his back, kissed the ridge of bone.

"I never told you what I did in Panama," he said.

"You don't have to."

"Our helicopters lit up the sky like Christmas," he told her. "It was Christmas. Midnight Christmas night. Missiles and bombs falling as thick as snowflakes. Three days of burning down whole neighborhoods and killing anything that moved. All to get rid of Noriega. He'd been on the CIA payroll for years by then, but now he wouldn't cooperate anymore. Now he knew too much."

"About the CIA?"

"And about why we were there. I didn't even know why. Not until years later."

"You were a soldier. You did what you were told to do."

"We used flamethrowers," he said. "Then threw the bodies into pits and buried them. They just melted when the flames hit. Faces, names, families…everything. Four thousand degrees Fahrenheit. It all just melted into the ground."

She was shivering when he finished. Could feel the goose bumps on his skin too. She held him harder, pressed herself against him. "It must have been horrible for you," she said. "But, baby," she said, and wondered what she would say next, how to use mere words to extinguish the flames.

"I know it's hard to understand," she whispered. "Why things happen the way they do." Her arms tightened around him. "But you know what isn't hard to understand?" she asked. "And never will be?"

"What?" he said, his own voice now as hoarse as hers, his own throat thick.

"What's in my heart for you. And in your heart for me. That's something beautiful and full of light. Nothing out there in the darkness can ever change that."

He nodded, but remained motionless. Out in the darkness a car horn shrieked, a dog barked. After a while a whip-poor-will began sounding its call, the short, sharp whistle and the long, fading trill.

Jayme rubbed her hands up and down his chest. "Can we go back to bed now?" she said.

A few moments later he turned and smiled. Put his hands on her shoulders and gently turned her around. And followed her up the stairs in the darkness.

ONE HUNDRED THIRTY-EIGHT

He slept only briefly and then was fully awake again. His legs ached with restlessness, and after stretching and flexing and bending them several times he finally gave up on sleep and eased himself out of bed. He needed to talk to someone. Needed information he wasn't privy to. Information no minister or counselor had ever been able to provide.

He dressed quietly and crept out of the bedroom, leaving both crutch and cane behind. Downstairs he rinsed his mouth at the kitchen sink. He wanted coffee but not as badly as he wanted something else.

Ten minutes later he stood on the sidewalk outside Rosemary Toomey's house, a motionless figure in the gray preceding dawn. The morning smelled of damp grass, of trees and summersweet and the stagnant humidity of a retreating night.

He touched the button on the back of his phone, looked at the glowing screen. 5:49. Was it too early to knock?

Old people get up early, he told himself. Or they sleep late.

For once in his life, he could make no decision.

And then the front door opened.

She stood there in a fuzzy pink robe, feet bare. "Do you want to come in?" she asked.

He nodded.

"Come on then."

ONE HUNDRED THIRTY-NINE

She had him sit on the sofa, his left leg stretched out stiffly under the coffee table, his back to the wide window, the draperies open but the sheer curtains closed, so that only a meager light shone upon him.

"I can make some coffee," she told him, her voice as muted as the light.

He shook his head no. "I'm sorry to disturb you like this."

She took a seat in the wing chair to his right, a small lamp table between them. "Just say what you came to say."

He tried to gather his thoughts. "Do you remember when you told me, first time you and I met? You said somebody was trying to get my attention."

"I remember," she said.

"I'm thinking maybe…maybe that happened."

She waited for him to say more, but he only kept looking at her, his chin low, forehead knitted with creases.

She opened the drawer on the end table, and drew out a wine-colored velvet bag. "Would you like me to read your cards again?"

"I don't know," he said. "I don't think so."

"Then why did you come here, Sergeant?"

"I don't know if I believe in any of that. Don't know if I even want to."

"Do you believe that your son has a soul?"

"Did Jayme tell you that? About my son?"

She smiled, though not apologetically. "She told her grandmother, and Louise told me. She was so looking forward to meeting you. You two would have hit it off, I'm sure of it."

He nodded. Felt his thoughts scattering again, as if the wild thrumming of his heart was shaking everything.

"So you do?" she said.

"Ma'am?"

"Do you believe that your son has a soul? You must. Why else would you sit by his grave every Sunday afternoon?"

"And you got this from Louise as well?"

She smiled. "Or from Jayme's mother."

Half a minute of silence passed.

"It's okay," she told him. "You feel like it's a violation, that I know things about you. But it's okay. We're not supposed to live in isolation, you know."

When DeMarco looked up at her again she was laying out the tarot cards along the edge of the coffee table.

He said, "I wanted to think he could maybe see me somehow, sitting there beside him. Wanted him to know how much I missed him. How sorry I am for what happened."

He watched the cards go down in three sets. Watched as she studied them. She touched her index finger to a center card. "Something has changed for you. Where have you been?"

His chest hurt. Head filled with congestion. "He was older. I wasn't sure. I couldn't understand what he said."

"Are you saying he came to you?"

DeMarco nodded.

"In a dream?"

"I don't know. I guess it must have been. But I couldn't hear anything he said to me. It wasn't clear. And then in another dream he didn't speak at all."

"The language of spirit," she told him, "is symbol and metaphor. It's almost never straightforward. So you find a meaning in how you *felt*. That's what's important. How did you feel when you saw him?"

DeMarco shook his head back and forth. Some things were not for sharing. He had always hoarded his grief, his guilt. And now the beautiful sadness of seeing his son again. The joy, the aching loss. It was no one else's burden to bear.

And the rest of it; the others. His father's visit. Huston's. And those thin girlish hands upon his shoulders and back, never pushing actually, but encouraging, maybe guiding. None of it had frightened him. None had been unwelcome.

"But why there?" he asked. "Why not all the other times back home?"

"Where did all this take place?"

He did not answer, but blinked at the cards.

"He's wherever you are, my dear. You just have to get quiet enough to listen."

DeMarco lowered his head, pressed a fingertip into the corner of each eye. He sniffed, his breath quick and shallow. He tried to hold his body still as the tears ran over his hands.

"Ryan?" she said. Then, "May I call you Ryan?"

He nodded.

"I have what—thirty years on you?"

"A little less," he said.

"Even so…we've both had a lot of pain in our lives. A person doesn't get to be our age without suffering a lot of pain. Would you agree?"

"I would," he said.

"Fortunately, the older we get, the more pain we can take. The more we can live with. Because we have to. When we're young, everything is still so new to us. Anything bad that happens is a catastrophe, the end of the world. But we get older…we suffer more losses…more heartbreaks. And, if we're lucky, we eventually realize that there's nothing we can't endure."

She moved her hand now, touched a finger to a card in the third set. "And if we're truly lucky, we come to understand than even death will be transcended. It's just one more hurdle to get over. One more hill to climb."

She paused then, leaned closer, her voice little more than a whisper. "Do you understand what I'm saying?"

He nodded. "I think I do."

Quietly then she gathered up the cards, slipped them into the velvet bag. Then she stood, stepped close to him, laid a small, brittle hand atop his shoulder. "Stay as long as you like," she told him. "Come back anytime."

Then she left the room, left him telling himself to be practical about this, be a realist. Yet the tears continued to fall, and the sobs shuddered through him, and he admitted to himself that he wanted the other reality more.

He said, "You know how we're always referencing Occam's razor?"

Jayme had just walked into the kitchen, eyes not yet fully open, cheek still lightly creased from her pillow, her body naked but for one of his T-shirts. Through the window she could see morning in full light, the kitchen's overhead light also ablaze. DeMarco sat at the table with his case notes spread out across it, a yellow legal pad in front of him, an empty coffee cup atop a dried coffee ring. From his laptop came music so low she could not identify it. She squinted at him before proceeding to the cupboard for a mug.

"Who is?" she said. The pot was nearly empty. When she lifted it off the burner, the smell of burnt coffee rose into her face.

"Cops," he said.

She emptied the pot into her cup and shut off the burner. "You going to want more?"

He turned then to look her way. She was standing with her back to him, leaning into the refrigerator for a carton of almond milk. When she turned to set her mug on the table and fill it from the carton, he was smiling at her.

"What?" she said.

"I think I could look at you like that every morning, and it will always seem new to me."

She pushed a few papers aside and sat across from him. "Look at me half-asleep?" she said. "You know it's only"—and she glanced at the digital readout on her grandmother's range—"7:34? How long have you been up?"

"Since a little after five."

"And you've had almost an entire pot of coffee so far?"

"I'll make you a fresh one," he said.

"This is fine for now. Three parts milk and one part coffee dregs. I should sell the recipe to Starbucks."

He kept smiling, watching her sip from the cup, watching the way her breasts lifted and fell when she breathed, how her eyelids remained nearly closed, how her face still held the softness of sleep. "Times like this," he said, "I wish I were a poet."

"You could take an online course," she told him. "So what's this about Occam's razor?"

He tapped a finger to the notepad. "There's some strange kind of fuckery going on here."

"Fuckery?" she said. "Did you just now invent a new word?"

"I think Amy Winehouse did."

Her eyebrows rose. "You're a fan of Amy Winehouse?"

"She was a huge talent."

She leaned back in her chair. "You never cease to amaze me, Sergeant."

"Nothing amazing about me," he told her. "Just a trailer-trash boy from Youngstown."

She thought her heart was going to break. She reached out to lay her hand atop his. "One man's trash is this woman's treasure," she said.

He stood and crossed to her, bent down, and kissed the top of her head. Then he turned away and busied himself with the coffeemaker, emptying the used filter, replacing it with a new one.

She sipped her coffee. Then said, "Occam's razor?"

"This case," he told her. "Occam's razor does not apply. So what would be the polar opposite of that?"

"Well…the polar opposite of the simplest answer would be the most complex or complicated answer."

"The most convoluted?" he asked while filling the carafe with cold water.

"Sure. Why not."

"So instead of a razor, what would we have? What's a good metaphor for something convoluted and unpredictable?"

"You really expect me to think about this right now?"

"You're up to it," he told her. He emptied the water into the coffeemaker, set the carafe on the burner, and pushed the power button. Then he returned to his seat.

"How about a Möbius strip?" she said.

"Perfect. Because that's what we have here. That's what this case is."

She leaned forward to look briefly at several of the papers scattered before her. Then she reached for his legal pad, slid it her way, turned it right end up. "You've been a busy boy."

"Throwing dates at it is all. And I think I'm starting to see some connections. But I've also had way too much coffee, and tunnel vision might be setting in."

She ran a finger down the list of notations. "You're sure about this?" she asked. "The first vic disappeared less than a year after Friedl came to Aberdeen?"

"He told me so himself. The date he came to town, I mean. Which was more or less the same day Todd Burl went to work for him."

"Caramba," she said. Then, "That means, like, holy cow—right?"

"It can."

She considered another notation. "This date for the last vic's disappearance. This is from the stuff Vicente gave us?"

"Correct."

She said, "Hand me your pen." He did, and she wrote something on the legal pad, then pushed the pad and pen back to him.

He read what she had written: *Friedl brought new wife to Aberdeen May 2005.*

He nodded. "I thought that's what you told me but I was waiting to be sure."

"So no vics before Burl goes to work for Friedl, and none after Friedl's wife comes into the picture. Double caramba," she said.

She leaned back in her chair, coffee mug in both hands, rim resting against her lower lip. Her gaze went slantwise to the table but her eyes were unfocused. He waited, watching, until she looked up at him, eyes fully open now, fully alert.

"What are you thinking?" he asked.

"It's not a very enlightened thought," she told him. "From a feminist perspective."

"Let's hear it."

"His wife is a sweetheart," she told him. "That might explain everything or nothing, I don't know. It's just that…"

"Say it," he said.

"I couldn't help thinking, sitting there talking to her, why a millionaire Caucasian male chooses to marry a poor black girl who is confined to a wheelchair. She was only twenty-seven when they got married. He was in his sixties."

"So explain it," he said. "You're the one with the master's degree."

"And that makes me an expert?"

"The closest thing to one in this room."

"Were any of the victims in a wheelchair? Or have a spinal deformity of some kind? We don't know that yet, do we?"

"There was nothing in Vicente's notes about it. Forensics would have mentioned it. What we do know is that they were all small, light-skinned black girls. Same as his wife."

"So the fetish might be…broader based than just the spinal deformity," she said. "Fetishes usually take root around puberty. What do you know about Friedl's childhood?"

"I know he had one."

"Brilliant," she said. "The last piece of the puzzle."

He grinned at her. "You know you're beautiful when you're seminaked and sarcastic?"

She held out her cup. "Shut up and get me some decent coffee, Einstein."

ONE HUNDRED FORTY-ONE

They spent the next two hours with their laptops, hopscotching from one site to another. Not much personal information could be obtained online about Friedl's wife, other than her full maiden name, Diamond Cecilia Walker, and the date of her marriage to Friedl. The chiropractor, on the other hand, had been awarded several distinctions from various Rotary and civic organizations in the Gulf cities where his clinics were located, and had been profiled by a half-dozen different newspapers and two trade magazines. Father a general practitioner in Fort Myers, Florida; mother a homemaker and hometown amateur tennis champion; William Blaine Friedl their only child. Both parents now deceased.

"Listen to this," DeMarco said, and read aloud from a profile in the Fort Myers *News-Press*:

"When asked why the son of a successful general practitioner chose chiropractic as his specialty, Dr. Friedl answered, 'When I was eight or so, my mother hired a live-in maid named Idora. She had a daughter who was a year younger than me. Her name was Beatrice. I called her Bee. We became very close, and remained that way until she died at the age of sixteen. She spent most of her life in a wheelchair because of a terrible congenital disorder that causes, among other complications, deformities of the spine. Her condition touched me very deeply, and as it worsened over the years, I developed a naïve idea that I could figure out some way to cure her. I spent all my time studying bone structure and how the spine works and so forth. I was unable to save her, of

course, but by that time, my life's passion had already
been determined.'

"Dr. Friedl's eyes filled with tears as he told this touching story. It is small wonder why his patients and colleagues
speak so highly of this intensely compassionate healer."

When DeMarco stopped reading, Jayme said, "His friend's name
was Beatrice but he called her Bee. His wife's name is Diamond and
he calls her Dee."

DeMarco looked up from the screen. "It doesn't say the maid or
her daughter was black, but what if she was? That would be a big,
fat *bingo*."

Jayme's eyes were wide with the prospect of discovery. "That,"
she said, "would be bingo bango bongo."

ONE HUNDRED FORTY-TWO

He was standing in the shower, water pulsing down hard between his shoulder blades, just warm enough to be felt as it sheeted over his back, when a thought came to him. He slid the shower door open six inches and shouted so as to be heard downstairs, "Can you check Vicente's notes again?"

Jayme's answer was softer and closer. "I'm lying here on the bed waiting for you to stop using all the hot water."

He spun the dial above the faucet and shut off the water. Stepped out, grabbed a towel, half dried his body before entering the bedroom. She lay there on the bed, looking more naked to him than ever because of the smile she offered, hands placed one on top of the other over her belly, right ankle over the left.

"You're dripping," she told him.

He tried to keep his eyes on her face, his erection pushing at the towel wrapped around his waist. "What exactly did the notes say about cause of death?"

"We talked about this."

"My brain is on spin cycle now. Remind me, please."

"Nothing definitive or common to all seven," she answered. "Asphyxiation by strangulation or smothering are possibilities. As is poison. But only because of the lack of any other conclusive evidence."

"There were two with a damaged hyoid bone, right?"

"One. Two with the bone missing. But most of them had several smaller bones missing. Why? What are you thinking?"

"I'm trying to line up Burl with the cause of death somehow. You remember when we talked to him and his wife at the park?" he said. "She was wearing that long skirt, looked almost Amish? Plus a short-sleeved turtleneck. It was yellow, I think."

Jayme rolled onto an elbow and propped herself up. "You're sure about the turtleneck?"

"Not about the color, but the turtleneck, yes."

"I remember the skirt, but not the top she was wearing."

"We were focused on other things. The little girls crying. But what if I'm remembering it right? Why would a woman dress like that on a night like a steam bath?"

"So you're saying he's a guy who likes to strangle women?"

"I'm saying what I'm saying. A woman wears a turtleneck in ninety-degree weather, she's covering something up."

"Maybe it was a hickey. Maybe the result of erotic asphyxiation. Maybe she just likes turtlenecks."

He was silent for a moment, then blew out a breath. "You're right. I'm struggling for connections where none exist."

"They might," she said, and swung her long legs over the side of the bed and sat up. "She and the girls should be alone in the house by now. He'll be up at Friedl's place."

"Hmm," DeMarco said, then shook his head. "We talk to her, what's she going to do? Call her husband thirty seconds after we walk out the door. We're not ready for that. Plus there's another thing. The dates for the girls' disappearances. They all took place when?"

"They all could have taken place anytime between September and early December of the given years."

"The three that were certain," he said.

"First two weeks of December."

"What if they all actually disappeared the first two weeks of December?"

"What if they did?" she said.

"Give me a minute." He hurried out of the room, downstairs, and to his laptop on the kitchen table. Clicked through the pages he had left open on several websites. Found the one he was searching for, and hurried back upstairs just as she was stepping into the shower.

"December 19," he said, out of breath.

"Okay," she said. "Relevance?"

"Friedl's birthday."

She lifted her wet foot back to the bathmat, closed the shower stall door. Water pattered like a hard rain against the glass and tile. She said, "First you imply that Burl's wife might have been hiding neck bruises. And now you pull in Friedl's birthday. Evidence suggests that Friedl might have a fetish for black girls in wheelchairs. Those are awfully tentative connections, baby."

"But they are connections," he said with a grin. "Go ahead and get your shower. I'm going to check in with the sheriff." He started to turn away.

"And then what?"

"Then we talk to the one person I know we can turn. And we turn him inside out."

ONE HUNDRED FORTY-THREE

A few minutes shy of noon Jayme pressed the intercom button on the security gate and told Mrs. Friedl they had a few more questions to ask. Mrs. Friedl said, after a moment's hesitation, "We're just about ready to sit down to lunch."

Jayme said, "This is important, ma'am."

Twenty seconds later the security bar slowly rose, and Jayme drove forward onto the estate grounds.

Alerted by DeMarco's finger tapping the passenger window, she slowed the vehicle as the llama barn came into view in the shallow valley ahead. Burl's blue pickup truck was parked facing outward with the bed of the truck inside the barn.

"What now?" Jayme said.

"Stop up ahead where this road swings down toward the house," DeMarco said.

"You don't care if he sees us?"

"We're talking to him next. Especially if I get what I need from Friedl." He popped open the glove compartment, took out his holstered Glock and Jayme's slim, subcompact Glock 42, waited till the vehicle stopped, and handed the .380 to her.

She took the handgun. "Where do you want me?"

"In the shade under the trees on your side," he said. "If the truck leaves the grounds and heads away from here, call the sheriff's department and have them pick him up. If he comes my way, let me know. Otherwise, just hang tight till I come back for you."

They both climbed out, pocketing their holsters as DeMarco crossed, limping, to the driver's side, and Jayme to the deep shade twenty yards away along the tree line. He then pulled the car alongside her and powered down the window.

"He might or might not spook if he sees you," DeMarco said. "If he does, it's because Friedl told him about our last visit."

"If he spooks," Jayme said, "he's our man."

DeMarco nodded. "He might or might not be armed. Protect yourself. Whatever it takes."

The steadiness and intensity of his gaze made her smile. "You too," she said.

ONE HUNDRED FORTY-FOUR

'm curious about your relationship with Todd Burl," DeMarco said. He stood with his back to the southern wall of windows in Friedl's solarium. Friedl, on a wicker settee with cushions decorated in huge orange, yellow, and blue bougainvillea blossoms, was forced to gaze directly into the light if he wished to look at DeMarco, which he seldom did, and then only askance.

Three bamboo ceiling fans kept the cooled air moving as it seeped through vents near the ceiling. Tall ferns and ficus plants and four miniature lemon trees filled the spacious room with a scent of the tropics. The soft hum of the fans' motors irritated DeMarco, as did the doctor's wrinkled and humiliated presence.

"Specifically," DeMarco continued, "why you allow him to work for you. Every other person I've spoken to says he can't be trusted. One individual called him a pathological liar. Said he would sell his own children down the river if he could make a few bucks from it. I personally have witnessed him verbally abusing his children, and have seen evidence that he physically abuses his wife. In the meantime your own wife has made it fairly clear that he's been skimming money from you, yet you refuse to do anything about it. How do you explain all that, Doctor?"

Friedl said nothing, his face cramped, eyes pained.

"Okay," DeMarco said. "You want to know how I explain it? He's blackmailing you."

"No," Friedl said, but with his gaze on the marble floor now.

DeMarco waited a full minute until Friedl lifted his head a little, raised his eyes to meet DeMarco's.

"Let's talk about those seven unfortunate girls," DeMarco said.

Friedl's wince was discernible.

"Here's how I think it happened," DeMarco said. "Feel free to stop me when I get any of it wrong. You grow up with your only real friend the daughter of your family's live-in maid. Her name is Beatrice but you call her Bee. She's a very sweet but fragile black girl. With a heartbreaking condition."

He paused, giving Friedl time to correct the description.

The doctor said nothing.

"Over the years," DeMarco continued, "you grow very close. In truth, you come to love each other. And as your bodies mature, you find another way to show that love. Living in the same house, your father away at his practice all day, your mother playing tennis and socializing, you have plenty of opportunities for that. Was she paralyzed below the waist?"

Friedl sat motionless, eyes again hidden, left hand rhythmically pulling on the fingers of his right hand.

"Either way," DeMarco said, "there were things you could do. Her mother's busy cooking, cleaning, probably does all the shopping too. So opportunity is not a problem. And for once you don't feel like such an awkward, homely boy. She means everything to you."

Friedl leaned forward now, elbows on his knees. He sniffed. Started breathing through his mouth.

"After she's gone, you're all grown-up, making money hand over fist, but nothing makes you feel the way she did. Nothing makes you whole. You throw yourself into your work, buy this place, maybe restore it as a kind of monument to her. Expect to spend the rest of your life here with just your memories."

Friedl put a hand to his throat, massaged it so forcefully that DeMarco could see the skin redden beneath the doctor's fingers.

"In the meantime," DeMarco said, "you hire Todd Burl. As far as you know, he's a good guy. A little too talkative maybe. Too buddy-buddy. And one day he gets to talking about sex, a couple of bachelors sharing their secrets, that's all. Nothing wrong with that. Except that your secret is an unusual one. You're even a little ashamed of it now that you're older. But it's an urge and a desire that has never faded."

Friedl's body sank lower. He dropped his hands into his lap, pulled and squeezed his fingers.

"And Burl, he's a master opportunist. So just before your birthday in December 1998, he brings you a present. Or maybe you went looking for one together."

"No," Friedl said. "I never went. The first time was a surprise. After that…"

"After that you came to expect it. Looked forward to it, I bet."

"I never asked him to do it."

"You didn't have to ask. He knew how to keep the boss happy. I'm betting he brought her to you in a wheelchair, didn't he? Made it feel just like you and Beatrice again."

Friedl said nothing, only a nearly inaudible whimper each time he exhaled.

"How long did you keep each girl here?"

The doctor's head moved back and forth, back and forth.

"Just one night?"

A nod.

DeMarco said, "Because afterward you're too ashamed of yourself. You're not a boy anymore, you're a grown man. You tell yourself you'll never do it again. But you do. One birthday after another. Maybe you tell Burl to stop, but he won't stop, he knows exactly how to play you. He's got you now. Still, it's all just buddy-buddy, isn't it? Until you meet Dee on a trip back to your clinic in Mobile. She's the real thing. And she thinks you're wonderful. So you marry her and bring her here. You tell Burl no more birthday presents. You don't need them anymore."

DeMarco waited. By now Friedl was doubled over with his hands to his face, a fingertip in the corner of each eye, nose and mouth in the cup of his hands, breathing loud, every exhalation a small moan. "I tried to let him go," he said.

"You mean you tried to fire him?"

Friedl nodded.

"Did he have video?" DeMarco asked.

Friedl's answer was muffled in his hands. "He says he does."

"He probably does," DeMarco told him. "He found your weakness, exploited it, and now he's got you over a barrel. You and your beloved Dee."

Friedl looked up suddenly, face wet, hands trembling. "She doesn't know any of this."

"Of course she doesn't. That's what gives him his power over you."

Friedl sank back into his hunched-over posture, and covered his whole face with his hands. "Oh God," he said. "Oh God."

DeMarco's cell phone vibrated in his pocket. He took it out and read Jayme's text: *He's coming your way on golf cart. Must have seen me. Will follow.*

DeMarco pocketed the phone. "The girls," he said, his voice a bit more urgent now. "I need to know about the girls."

"They came because they wanted to," Friedl told him. "Nobody forced them to do anything."

"Does that include being killed?"

Friedl sniffed, dropped his hands. Lifted his head a bit, his gaze on the nearest lemon tree. "I gave him money for them, every time. Lots of money. I told him take them home. And he said he did. We never mentioned them again."

"Out of sight, out of mind," DeMarco said. "Until July 2014, right? You thought of them then, didn't you? Even up here in your castle, you must have heard about it."

"He swore they weren't the same girls. He said the minister must have had something to do with them."

"And you wanted desperately to believe that, didn't you? Seven girls in the church, seven birthday presents. But it was only a coincidence, right? That was the only way you could live with yourself. Especially after the news broke that they were all young black girls."

Friedl was sobbing now, more vocally than ever.

DeMarco let him sob. He reached into his pocket for his phone, intending to send Jayme a text to call the sheriff for backup. But as he turned slightly to take the glare off his screen, a movement at the corner of the solarium caught his eye, a shadow sliding across the glass. He hurried to the window, four long, lopsided strides, and saw Burl riding away on a blue golf cart, driving with one hand while looking back into the glass.

DeMarco sprinted as fast as he could with one stiff and tightly bandaged leg, but the golf cart was fading into the greenery. Only twenty yards from the house DeMarco was already breathing hard, his vision watery, pain shooting up and down his shin. As he ran he told his phone, "Call Jayme."

When she answered he said, short of breath, "I'm on foot chasing Burl in the golf cart. He's trying to hide around bushes and buildings, but I think he's headed for his truck. Where are you?"

"Still up on top but closer to the house now," she answered.

The wavering spot of blue in DeMarco's vision made a hard left off the corner of a building. "Shit!" he said.

"*What happened?*"

"He's definitely cutting back toward the truck. He'll be there in thirty seconds."

"I'm moving. I have the barn in sight."

"You have to get there before he gets to the truck! I'll call the sheriff."

She didn't reply. He knew she had kicked it into high gear, was running full-out, the cell phone clutched in a fist or shoved into her pocket. He imagined those long legs eating up yardage.

Golf cart twelve miles per hour, he thought. Flo-Jo twenty-four. Jayme maybe eighteen?

"Go, baby," he said out loud.

ONE HUNDRED FORTY-SIX

S he saw the chest-high fence, the grazing llamas, one of them now looking up at her. Burl was twenty yards below, also watching her, the golf cart bouncing over uneven ground. She screamed at him to stop but he only lowered his head and kept going.

Quickly she assessed the situation. He would have to drive alongside the fence to reach the other side of the barn where his pickup truck was parked. She could maybe intercept him by leaping the fence, charging past the llamas and into the barn from the near side. But there were lots of maybes. Maybe a foot would catch on the top rail and she would go down hard, face in the dirt. For all she knew of llamas, maybe they would bolt, get in her way, knock her down, and trample her. Maybe she would run into the barn and find her progress blocked, no quick entry into the other side.

Her only other option was to run outside the fence on the uphill side and hope she could get a shot or two off at the tires as the truck sped away.

Screw that, she told herself.

Six strides from the fence, she held her phone to her mouth and asked, "Do llamas bite?" But DeMarco did not answer. Nobody answered.

With Burl's golf cart moving past the rear corner of the barn now, the fence two seconds away, she could break stride long enough to shove the phone in her pocket, or she could—

She dropped the phone. Clamped both hands atop the rail, leaned toward her hands, and vaulted up off her left foot, right leg and then left rising as her momentum carried her up and over the fence. She landed solidly but facing the fence, spun around, and saw the llamas all at attention now, long necks stretched high, ears erect, big eyes full of wonder and fear.

As she turned and sprinted she slipped a hand under the hem of her shirt, felt the pebbled grip of her .380, simultaneously thumbed down the safety and slipped the weapon free of its holster.

She ran into the dim opening and immediately ducked and weaved to her right, then stopped short in a half crouch, weapon extended, sweeping back and forth. She was standing in a wide aisle running the length of the stalls, each with its door hanging open toward her. Maybe forty feet beyond the stalls lay the front of the barn, the walls lined with tractor attachments and tools, bags of feed and other supplies. Burl's pickup truck was parked in full light, the tailgate open, the bed of the truck backed into the barn.

And then in the dimness a few feet behind the truck she saw movement against the left wall. The girl, Susan, the college student, had turned away from a wooden funnel-flow bin, and, white plastic bucket in hand, now stood motionless, eyes riveted on Jayme.

"Get down!" Jayme screamed. "Get back here to me!" Cautiously she stepped closer to the girl.

But the girl stood frozen. "What did I do?" she said.

And in that moment Burl lurched past the corner of the barn door, yanked open the pickup's door, seized a shotgun from the rear window rack, pumped it as he pulled out of the truck, turned, and fired into the ceiling.

"Don't move!" he shouted. And pumped another shell into the chamber. The empty shell clattered to the floor.

The girl cowered against the bin. Burl moved closer to the wall and closer to the girl, put Susan directly in front of him, his shotgun now aimed just off her left shoulder, directly at Jayme.

"Drop the weapon!" Jayme called. But he was too close to the girl, Jayme's line of fire too dangerous.

Burl smacked the barrel against the girl's arm. "Stand up!" he said.

She straightened but with shoulders still hunched, hands clasped to her chest. To Jayme he said, "You drop yours. Now!"

He was almost completely shielded behind the girl. Jayme thought, *Where are you, Ryan?*

"Now!" Burl shouted, and fired over Jayme's head. Pellets rattled and ricocheted in the rafters as he pumped another shell into the chamber.

She raised her left hand into the air. Knelt slowly. Laid the .380 on the floor. Then stood with both hands shoulder high. Took a small step away from the weapon.

To the girl he said, "Start walking backward."

Jayme said, "The sheriff's department is going to be waiting for you at the security gate. You won't get off the grounds."

He said, "We'll see about that." Then told the girl, "Start backing up. One step at a time."

Jayme knew he had other options. Drive off road through the woods. Return to the mansion and slaughter Friedl and his wife. Or hole up for a prolonged hostage situation.

She was betting on the off-road option. By now he knew those woods like the back of his hand.

She said, "Let the girl go, Todd. I'll be your hostage."

He pushed the girl into the truck. "Move over!" he told her.

She crawled across the seats, huddled against the passenger door.

Burl kept the shotgun aimed at Jayme. Looked into the truck for a moment, then back at Jayme. He told the girl, "Start it up! Turn the key!"

Jayme thought, He's going to have to take his eyes off me to get into the truck. He has no choice but to shoot me first. And he's going to realize that any second now.

She made another quick assessment: Looks like a twelve gauge. Spread approximately an inch per yard. Ten yards away. Direct hit fatal.

He stood with his back against the open truck door. Raised his left foot to the running board. He kept looking at Jayme, then glanced quickly at the girl, who, after starting the engine, still lay across the seat, her head close to the steering wheel. "Slide over!" he screamed.

Jayme thought, You're not getting another one. And the moment he looked back at her, she shouted, "Get out of the truck, Susan!"

He pivoted, and Jayme dove for her weapon, seized it as she slid onto a shoulder, and fired two shots. The first pinged into the door. The second went into his right side, nipple high.

His knees buckled and he crumpled against the truck door but did not go down. He was all she could see now, everything around him blurred and dark, a man at the end of a tunnel, now slowly turning her way.

Everything in slow motion. Everything silent and nearly still. Put two in the chest, she told herself. But waited for him to turn a few more degrees, expose his body to her.

And then the truck door slammed against him, slammed him forward into the side of the truck, and everything snapped back to full speed, the shotgun banging against metal, DeMarco crashing atop Burl, ramming Burl's head against the truck bed's exterior wall, Jayme on her feet, running toward them. The shotgun slipped from Burl's hand, clattered to the floor, with Burl falling atop it.

Jayme held her gun on Burl while DeMarco climbed to his feet and recovered the shotgun, DeMarco breathing hard, trying to keep the weight off his injured leg. Burl lay on his left side, moaning and breathing quickly. With each breath, a suction sound issued from the bullet wound.

"Sucking chest wound," Jayme said. "We need to get him over. Is it back or side?"

"Your training's newer than mine. Your call."

"Back!" she said, and they pulled him away from the truck and rolled him over. Jayme yanked up his shirt and covered the bullet wound with her hand. Then shouted toward the truck, "Susan! We need your help!"

The girl climbed out, came around the back of the truck, approached them gingerly, saw the blood seeping beneath Jayme's hand, and backed away.

"I need a plastic bag," Jayme told her. "Or plastic wrap. Something not too thick. And tape of some kind. Right now!"

The girl jerked as if slapped, then spun around and raced to the rear of the building. DeMarco, still trying to catch his breath, called for an ambulance.

ONE HUNDRED FORTY-SEVEN

After pocketing the phone, DeMarco looked down at Burl, and smiled at what he saw. Despite Burl's pain, the man kept patting his head with one hand, adjusting his hairpiece.

DeMarco knelt on one knee, intending to take hold of the hairpiece and rip it away, a final humiliation.

But at the last moment, DeMarco paused, stilled by the panic and confusion in the man's eyes, the wheeze of his labored breathing, the blood under Jayme's hand. And DeMarco's contempt for Burl drained away and dissolved into something else, something like pity, as if Burl were a small, wounded animal, frightened and helpless and doomed.

DeMarco leaned away from him, raised his eyes, and looked into the trees.

When the girl returned with a white plastic grocery bag and a roll of duct tape, Jayme ripped off a square of plastic and pressed it over the wound. DeMarco took the roll of tape, ripped off one strip after another, and taped down all but a corner of the plastic. Each time Burl inhaled, the plastic was sucked tight against his skin, sealing the wound. When he exhaled, the flap jiggled, releasing air.

To Susan, Jayme said, "Go back to the house and lift the security gate. There are people on their way."

Jayme kept her eyes on the plastic, listened to Burl's breathing. She and DeMarco remained on their knees, waiting for sirens. At one point a cold shiver passed through her, and she said, "Hunh," meaning nothing, an involuntary response.

DeMarco laid his hand against her back. The warmth of her skin through her shirt was inviting; he wanted to pull her close, enclose her in his arms. But she had other things to do, so he lightly rubbed her back, touched his head to hers.

"Heck of a day," Jayme said.

"Heck of a woman," he told her.

ONE HUNDRED FORTY-EIGHT

When his father's heavy snoring began, Ryan eased himself out of bed, found his jeans and shoes, and slipped them on. In the kitchen he slid open what they called the junk drawer, the one below the silverware, where matches and straws and twist ties and other stray items were kept. Near the back of the drawer he felt the penlight's cylinder, wrapped his hand around it, and lifted it out.

In the weeds behind the trailer he moved carefully, slowly playing the dim light back and forth, parting the weeds with his free hand. The weeds were damp, the night air sticky and heavy in his chest, his father's snoring still as abrasive as a wood file grating back and forth across the boy's nerves.

The spot of white caught his eye, and Ryan dropped to his knees, laid a hand atop the puppy's small belly. It was still warm, its breath fast and shallow. Ryan shined the light on the puppy's face, saw the panic and confusion in its eyes, the blood that had run down over its snout and muzzle.

Ryan rolled onto one hip, lifted the puppy as delicately as he could, and cradled it against his own stomach. He shut off the penlight, eased down onto his side in the weeds, held the puppy against him.

After a while he opened his eyes and looked up to see the sky filled with stars. The puppy's stomach was no longer moving. Ryan climbed to his feet and without using the penlight walked into the woods and found a soft depression between the roots of a big tree he liked to climb. He laid the puppy to the side and scooped out the depression with his hands. Afterward he cleaned his hands by swishing them through the damp weeds, and then back in the trailer in his bed again he wrapped the pillow around his head and tried without much luck to silence the awful snoring.

Jayme, DeMarco, and the Carlisle County sheriff conferred in the gazebo while personnel from three county vehicles, one state police patrol car, and one ambulance went in and out of the house. Another ambulance and patrol car had already left the barn and were on their way to the hospital. Mrs. Friedl's personal nurse had been notified and arrived within minutes to administer ten milligrams of diazepam. Friedl himself, now wearing a pair of plastic double-loop cuffs, was allowed to remain in the house with his wife while the sheriff was debriefed.

"All these years," the sheriff said, and shook his head as he gazed at the impeccably manicured grounds, "and not once did anybody look in the right direction."

"Hardly anybody looks in the least likely direction," DeMarco told him. "We got lucky."

"Maybe," the sheriff conceded. He turned to Jayme. "You're fairly certain Mrs. Friedl had no involvement in any of this?"

"Hundred percent," Jayme said.

"What's your take on Burl's wife and kids?"

"They'll cooperate," she said, "given the right approach. You have a female deputy or two in your department? Somebody with patience?"

The sheriff nodded. "Plus a terrific victim's advocate."

"Search Burl's house," DeMarco told him. "Twenty-year-old videotapes."

"With what on them?"

"Allegedly he taped other men having sex with his wife. Probably also taped Friedl with the victims. You might even find something featuring Pastor Royce in a starring role."

"Good Lord," the sheriff said.

"Sweeten the deal with McGintey," DeMarco told him, "and you're likely to get yourself a corroborating witness."

"If he talks after he lawyers up."

"If he doesn't, you have Trooper Matson and me. We heard his full confession."

"You Mirandize him?" the sheriff asked.

DeMarco smiled. "Good thing you didn't deputize us," he said.

After a few moments the sheriff stood, raised both hands to a roof beam, and stretched his back. He held that position while he spoke. "Any chance you want to fill me in on what really happened in that forest out east?"

"Bugs," DeMarco told him. "A whole lot of bugs."

"Somebody put you onto Burl. Rosemary Toomey might have mentioned him as Royce's former employee, but I think somebody else pinned a target on him for you. I'm thinking that was Virgil Helm."

"I can tell you with all honesty," DeMarco said. "As far as I know, Virgil Helm is no longer among the living."

After a few moments, the sheriff nodded, then let go of the beam, and straightened his shirt. He looked at DeMarco, then at Jayme. "I'll send a paramedic to take care of those scrapes on your arms."

"They're just floor burns," she said.

"We'll get her some X-rays," DeMarco told him.

"And you too," Jayme said. "You reinjured your leg."

The sheriff watched them smiling at one another, then blew out a breath. "You two planning on heading back to Pennsylvania anytime soon?"

Jayme looked to DeMarco, her eyebrows raised in question. DeMarco said, "I think it's fair to say our plans are wide open."

The sheriff nodded once again, then stepped down off the gazebo. Without turning he said, "You mind writing all the relevant details down for me chronologically? I feel like I've forgotten half of it already."

Jayme said, "Email okay?"

He raised a hand in affirmation. Then walked away toward the house.

Jayme leaned close to DeMarco and whispered, "I think he's developing a real fondness for you."

"Tough luck for him," DeMarco said, and slipped his arm around her waist. "I like girls."

She jabbed her elbow in his ribs.

"Umpf!" he said, and rubbed his side. "I mean women. Strong and quick. And a little bit nasty."

B efore heading back to Grandma's house later that evening, Jayme called Rosemary Toomey and offered a debriefing for the Irregulars. Rosemary promised to have Vicente and Hoyle in her living room within the hour.

They were all seated around the coffee table, sipping tea, Hoyle nibbling on Rosemary's shortbread cookies, when Jayme and DeMarco arrived. The Irregulars had left the sofa vacant, so Jayme and DeMarco, after declining the offer of tea, seated themselves with their backs to the picture window. The light was soft and low outside, and glowed through the curtains like candlelight.

Anxious to avoid preliminaries and get back to the soothing privacy of Grandma's house, Jayme provided an abbreviated narrative of the events in the llama barn. Even Hoyle's eyes widened when she recounted the shoot-out. Her tone was matter-of-fact and unemotional, though she still felt herself quivering inside.

"And you, Sergeant?" Vicente said after Jayme's monologue. "While all this was transpiring?"

Jayme winced at the question; it sounded like an accusation.

But DeMarco merely smiled. "Dragging a bum leg a hundred yards."

Jayme said, "He showed up for the finale, though. Actually, the whole thing took less time than it did for me to tell you about it."

"Heroes both," Rosemary said.

Vicente sat leaning forward with his hands clasped between his knees, eyes on the carpet. His one-sided smile struck Jayme as more of a frown.

She thought about mentioning her conversation with Antoinette Coates and the increased revenue the young woman would soon be enjoying from Eli Royce, but then decided to remain quiet. If

Vicente was too bitter to enjoy the day's victory, she was not about to throw him a bone.

Hoyle said, "I am intrigued by the abrupt though fortuitous turn in your investigation, Sergeant—a turn none of us ever thought to take. What led you to Todd Burl?"

DeMarco shrugged. "Local tip about his employment history with Royce," he said, and smiled at Rosemary. "After that it was just a matter of connecting the dots."

Hoyle said, "The dots, as I recall, were exceedingly scarce."

Jayme said, "McGintey and his girlfriend were finally persuaded to be a bit more forthcoming. So as to enjoy less of the county's hospitality."

"At least they will face some punishment," Vicente said. "While Eli Royce continues on unscathed."

Jayme thought DeMarco would snap at that, and turned to watch his response. But he continued to smile. The look in his eyes seemed almost sympathetic. "The FBI is keeping a close watch on him," he said. "He'll trip up sooner or later."

A few moments of silence followed. Rosemary broke the tension by asking, "And you think Burl procured the girls as a way of currying favor with Dr. Friedl?"

DeMarco lifted his gaze to Jayme, gave his head a little nod.

Jayme said, "I would use the word 'leverage,' or even 'power,' instead of 'favor.' I think Mr. Burl views himself as a master manipulator of some kind. He has a pathological need to be in control, whether with his wife and daughters, the men who paid him to have sex with his wife, or Dr. Friedl. Initially Burl had it out for Royce, who refused to go into partnership with him. So Burl secretly used the church not only as his stash house, but also as a brothel. He took pleasure from that. From…"

"Defiling," Hoyle suggested.

"Exactly," Jayme said. "From defiling Royce's private space. Then, when Friedl appeared on the scene, I think Burl saw another opportunity for self-gain. The very day Friedl closed on the property, Burl was there waiting for him. And Friedl was easy pickings. Weak. Susceptible to flattery. Probably a very lonely man at the time."

"Interesting," Hoyle said. "So you're suggesting...an elaborate plan on Burl's part?"

Jayme looked to DeMarco to continue. "You're doing fine," he told her.

"Then no," Jayme said. "Not necessarily elaborate. In the beginning maybe all he wanted was a job. Maybe he viewed Friedl, another rich man, as a substitute for Royce. And the more he got to know the doctor, especially the doctor's fetish, the more opportunities he envisioned."

"But why kill the girls?" Rosemary asked. "Why reduce them to skeletons?"

To DeMarco, Jayme said, "Jump in anytime, Sergeant."

"At first," DeMarco answered, "maybe just for the money. Friedl said he paid each of the girls 'a lot.' I'm guessing a thousand dollars or more each. So Burl thinks, why drive four hundred miles round trip to take her home? I'm guessing he never took them off the estate. Drove out into the woods somewhere, strangled them, maybe raped them, and buried them. They're like money in the bank to him. A hedge in case Friedl ever turns against him."

"Yet they ended up inside the church," Vicente said.

"Personally," Jayme said, "I think that the church, especially that secret space between the walls, became a kind of...place of empowerment for Burl. From there he could watch his wife having sex with other men. He could leave his scent all over Royce's office."

Hoyle said, "Mark his territory, so to speak."

"Right," Jayme said. "He could easily have developed his own fetish for that place. He was all-powerful there. His own kingdom."

"Surrounded," Hoyle said, "by the spoils of his war against the world."

DeMarco shrugged. "Burl's mind is a rat's nest. For now we can only speculate as to his motives."

"I, for one," Hoyle said, and dipped a shortbread cookie into his tea, "would relish hearing any and all of those speculations."

"Things were going well on the estate," DeMarco said after a pause. "Every time the doctor wanted to put up another building, Burl was in charge. Made the purchases, hired the help, skimmed a healthy portion off the top for himself."

"Knowing," Jayme added, "that Friedl wouldn't complain. Burl knew too much."

"And one day, for whatever reason, Burl's festering resentment toward Royce flared up again. So he dug up the bodies, reduced them to skeletons, and gave them a new home. For which Royce, he figured, would someday pay the price."

"He might even have had that plan in mind from the beginning," Jayme told them. "From the first girl. He might have never stopped looking for a way to get his revenge on Royce."

Hoyle raised a finger in the air. "And yet," he said, and paused to consider his words. "The care, if I may use that expression, Burl showed to the victims' remains. The bones were washed of all dirt. All shreds of clothing removed. Even their hair. One might call such attention 'reverence.'"

"I can think of two possible explanations for that," Jayme said. "First, Burl appears to be a very possessive man. He likes to have absolute control over what he thinks of as his. What, in his mind, he owns. Dr. Friedl called him meticulous, Mrs. Friedl called him proprietary. Which could explain why he treated the remains as he did."

"In a sense," Hoyle mused, "retaining each of the victims' identities, rather than throwing all the bones together in one heap."

Jayme nodded. "The other theory has to do with arousal levels. Some research links criminality with low arousal levels in the brain. Certain individuals inherit a nervous system unresponsive to normal levels of stimulation."

DeMarco asked, "They have to up the ante?"

Jayme nodded. "High-risk activities, antisocial behavior, crime, sexual promiscuity, anything considered deviant or perverse."

"Including," Hoyle said, "meticulously and obsessively cleaning the bones of his young victims."

Rosemary shook her head. "Oh my, my. Such a mind. I shudder to think individuals like that actually exist."

"Sadly," Hoyle said, "in multitudes. Lacking only the opportunity."

They all sat silent for a while. Hoyle brushed the crumbs from his lap. The light outside the window had faded, and the room was growing dim.

DeMarco was the first to stand. He shook hands with each of the Irregulars. Jayme followed suit, ending with a long hug from Rosemary.

"Will we ever see you again?" Rosemary asked before releasing Jayme's hands.

Jayme looked to DeMarco for an answer.

He said, "'History never really says goodbye. History says, see you later.'"

"Excellent quote," said Hoyle. "Eduardo Galeano. Simply excellent."

VI

I become a waterwheel, turning and
tasting you, as long as water moves.

—*Rumi*

ONE HUNDRED FIFTY-ONE

In the evening they sat for a while on the front porch of Jayme's grandmother's house, rocking gently on the swing, feet scraping the boards. Neither felt much need for conversation, nor for anything more than the other's presence, a hand to hold, her head on his shoulder. The light faded and cooled, and in the dimness the scent of the summersweet bushes grew stronger, more redolent than on any other night.

"I must say," Jayme told him, "you seemed almost gentle with David Vicente earlier."

He shrugged. "I understand his disappointment. Royce stripped him of his job. And is still trying to bankrupt him."

The swing slid back and forth, back and forth.

Now and then a dog barked somewhere down the street, but otherwise the night seemed preternaturally still to DeMarco, almost like the October nights he remembered as a boy, when he was old enough to leave the trailer alone after dark and go wandering into the woods or in search of a field from which he could study the stars.

The call of a loon in the distance surprised both of them, its reedy wail starting low, then rising a few notes higher, then sliding back to the original note again. "That's odd," Jayme said. "Loons don't usually come through Kentucky till much later in the year."

"He's lost," DeMarco said.

"It sounds that way, doesn't it? So full of sorrow and longing."

They were quiet again for a while, and set the swing moving once more. After a few minutes Jayme said, "What are you thinking about, babe?"

"Tom Houston. And what he said to me in the dream I had in the bear cage."

"Do you have any idea what he was talking about? Or is it still gibberish?"

"That strange word he used…'sentipensante.' Turns out it's Portuguese. It means 'feeling thinking.'"

"Feeling and thinking what?" she asked.

"Not feeling *and* thinking. But a kind of thinking that comes out of feeling. Out of experience. Not something based on logic or analysis, but only on feeling. A feeling that speaks the truth. A truth that can't be expressed in words."

"Like love," she said.

DeMarco nodded. "And the 'globed fruit' line? I plugged it into a search engine, not really expecting to get any hits."

"And?"

"It's from the poem 'Ars Poetica' by Archibald MacLeash. It's about poetry. What a poem is and what it should do."

Jayme thought for a moment, then said, "Okay. And how does that relate in any way to the question you asked Thomas about the meaning of life?"

"Tom said, 'Life is a poem.' So yeah. If I substitute the word 'life' in place of the word 'poem,' it does make sense. Especially the last line of the poem. 'A poem should not mean, but be.'"

"So then," Jayme said, "it becomes 'A life should not mean…but *be*.'" She rubbed her arms. "I just got goose bumps. 'A life should not mean, but be.' Like sentipensante. The experience of living *is* the meaning of life."

DeMarco smiled. "That's pretty sweet, isn't it?"

"It really is. And also spooky."

"Unless I'm just forcing a meaning out of what was only a meaningless dream."

"What does your sentipensante say?"

He answered with another smile. Slipped an arm around her and ran his hand up and down her arm.

A minute later he said, "Do you know the song 'San Diego Serenade' by Tom Waits?"

"I don't think I do."

"Great lyrics."

"Sing it for me," she said.

"I have a better idea." He pulled his cell phone from a pocket, tapped the search icon, said, "Tom Waits, 'San Diego Serenade.'"

When the music started, he stood and held his arms open to her. She stood and stepped forward into his embrace, slid her hands around his waist. They danced slowly with their foreheads touching, the phone held close to their ears, the harsh notes of Waits's barroom piano and smoke-scarred voice softened by violins gently sliding through their glissandos, turning the loon's haunting cry into something different too, a song still bittersweet but limned with gratitude and memory.

When the song ended, Jayme whispered, "Again," and they danced with their feet barely moving, lips nearly touching, breathing each other's air.

ONE HUNDRED FIFTY-TWO

A t 3:13 a.m., his cell phone vibrated on the bedside table. DeMarco awoke immediately, rolled onto his side, and covered the phone with his hand to mute the vibration while he brought the phone closer. Even in those moments before he put the phone to his ear, he felt the gravity of the room changing, the darkness thickening all around him.

Jayme continued to sleep until he sat up and slid his legs over the edge of the bed. As he started to rise he felt her hand on his back, so he settled onto the bed again, both feet on the floor. He spoke quietly into the phone, mostly asking questions, but his tone was somber, and soon she was sitting up too, leaning forward now with her forehead pressed to his back, hands on his waist, the light from the phone unpleasantly bright.

When he ended the call, he continued to sit motionless for a while. Then he laid the phone on the table again, facedown to smother the screen's lingering brightness. Only when the screen went dark did he turn his body and pull up his legs, then, sitting awkwardly, turn at the waist to face her.

"Laraine tried to kill herself," he said.

"Oh my God," Jayme said. "How?"

"Wrists," he said.

"Where is she now?"

"Mercy General. That was her doctor on the phone."

"Who found her?"

"Some guy was there," DeMarco said. "He heard her crying in the bathroom. She wouldn't unlock the door, so he kicked it in."

Jayme said nothing, had too many questions, not the right time to ask. She reached for his hand, pulled it close, and held it against her belly.

He said, "I'm the only person who understands what she's going through. I need to go there. Need to make sure she gets some help."

Jayme nodded, but the tears came anyway. "Right now?" she said.

"Soon. Let's just lie here for a while, okay?"

They lay on their backs, holding hands, both staring up at the dark ceiling. DeMarco wished the window were open so that he could breathe fresh air. The room was cool thanks to the air conditioner, but now the air felt heavy both in his chest and atop it. Everything felt heavy in the darkness except for Jayme's hand in his, which felt light and small and as beautiful as an injured bird.

She rolled over with her face close to his and said, "You better come back."

"I promise. With a divorce agreement in hand."

"I don't give a damn about paper," she said. "I want flesh and bone."

"You have it," he told her, "always," and knew she was probably thinking, *Then why are you leaving me?*

He wished he could answer that question in a convincing way. Wished he had the words to articulate all those years of guilt and obligation, the recompense not yet fully paid. But no words would be sufficient, so instead, he kissed the tip of her nose, then her cheek, then the corner of her lips. The taste of her tears made him dizzy and want to cry too. But he was already with her in their sorrow and he did not need tears to know it.

But he needed to give her something. Even if it was difficult for him to do. Even if it cost him more than he had ever given anyone except his little boy.

"How do you feel about poetry?" he asked.

"Whose poetry?" she said.

"Poetry in general."

"I like it, I guess. Some of it. It's not something I think about. What made you ask that?"

"I wrote a poem for you," he said.

"Seriously? When?"

"In the bear cage."

"Oh, baby," she said.

"I was, you know, lying there with my leg on fire. Going a little crazy probably. So to keep from focusing on the pain, I started focusing on other stuff. Like the birds out in the trees. I started listening to their songs, and how they were calling out to each other. And, I don't know, it reminded me of you, I guess. How you make me feel."

"The birds' songs did?"

He nodded. "So the first line sort of just came to me. And then the next. And I just kept writing it like that. The way Tom said he wrote. Just working the sentences over and over until there was nothing left to change."

"Can you say it for me?" she asked. "Do you still remember it?"

"I do but…I've never written a poem before."

"Not for anybody?"

"I used to make up little songs when I was rocking Ryan back to sleep. When he'd wake up in the middle of the night, you know? I loved getting up and rocking him and feeling him sleeping on my chest like that. It was the most peaceful, contented feeling I'd ever known."

"I'm honored that you wrote something for me too. I'd really like to hear it."

"Don't laugh," he said.

"I'm not going to laugh."

"It doesn't have a title yet."

"I can live with that."

H closed his eyes for a moment, brought the bear cage back to him. Then he let the cage go and opened his eyes and stared into hers, smiling as he spoke:

"In the language of birds, your heart sings to me.
Its music lifts the leaves and makes the branches tremble.
It pulls the moon into the sky and holds the stars aloft.

"The bird that is your heart sits amid the leaves
and sings the sunlight and the rain.
It sings the blossoms open and teaches sweet fruit to grow."

She leaned into him then, sobbing, her body against his, hands pressed tight against him.

"That bad, huh?" he said.

She laughed, sobbed again, held him tighter. Her tears were warm and slick against his skin. "You better come back," she told him.

He nodded, swallowed hard, her breath feathery against him. Thirteen years, he thought, since such a feeling had held him in its embrace. That overwhelming love and trust that had filled him to completion. Ineffable. Inexplicable. The scent of his child's hair and skin, how he had breathed it in so hungrily, that warmth and trust, a beauty and gratitude too huge to bear. He had wept back then and wept now to remember it and to remember it gone, and he wept with the scent and touch and gratitude for this woman in his arms, both of them weeping now, holding each other so tightly, both so grateful and afraid.

READING GROUP GUIDE

1. What do you think would have happened if DeMarco had been allowed to retire as he had planned? Do you think Jayme's sick leave was the best option for him?

2. If you were to take two months of sick leave, what would you do with the time? Where would you go?

3. Describe Jayme and DeMarco's relationship. Do you think they are well suited to each other? What are the biggest challenges they face? How does their relationship change over the course of the book?

4. Imagine you were in Jayme's position. How would you help DeMarco face his past demons? How would his jealousy and anger issues make you feel?

5. Describe DeMarco's childhood. How do you think his upbringing changed him?

6. Compare and contrast Jayme and DeMarco. How are they similar? How are they different?

7. Describe the Da Vinci Cave Irregulars. Why do you think they are set on cracking this cold case? Why do you think DeMarco and Jayme agree to help?

8. Upon reading the initial list of suspects, who did you originally

think killed the seven girls? If you were DeMarco, who would you look into first?

9. Compare DeMarco's and Jayme's detective styles. What role do they take when they interview suspects? If you were a detective, who would you be more like?

10. What was the relationship between Royce and the Da Vinci Cave Irregulars? Why did they suspect him? Did they have reason to?

11. Do you think McGintey, Royce, and Burl get the justice they deserve? Why or why not?

12. What is the relationship between Burl, Friedl, and the murdered girls? Who do you think is ultimately at fault?

13. How do you think solving this case affected DeMarco? How have these characters changed over the course of the book?

14. If you were DeMarco, what would you do after the case closed? Would you continue on leave or return to the force?

15. What do you make of the poem DeMarco writes for Jayme? Do you think they will get a happy ending together?

A CONVERSATION
WITH THE AUTHOR

Ryan DeMarco is a very layered character. What do you think is his best quality? What do you think is his biggest challenge to overcome?

His best quality is empathy. He's a very compassionate man, especially toward those he considers innocents—children, women, and men abused or maligned by others. His role in life, as he sees it, is to protect the innocents and bring the guilty to justice.

In regard to his biggest challenge, he holds himself responsible for every abuse he failed to prevent. Consequently, he has become emotionally guarded and reluctant to allow himself any of life's pleasures. Jayme is helping him to overcome those problems.

You currently live in Pennsylvania. What research did you do to bring the South to life in *Walking the Bones*? Do you have a special connection with that region of the country?

I have a special connection with any part of the country that reminds me of the Appalachian foothills, woods, and river valleys where I spent most of my youth. For the past couple of years, each time I visited one of my sons, I would research potential sites for my relocation to a place that reminds me of western Pennsylvania but receives more than sixty sunny days each year and whose winters are less dismal than here. Other criteria for my next home is that it will be in a rural area and that I will be able to see mountains (or at least big hills) from my future front or back deck. So far, the Ozarks and eastern Kentucky seem to fit the bill.

How would you describe DeMarco and Jayme's relationship?

They are still feeling their way through it, still trying to understand each other. They have a deep love and respect for each other, but each has secrets that impact the relationship. Their physical chemistry is still an important part of their relationship, especially for DeMarco—it's one of the few times he can truly be open and unguarded and allow himself to experience the fullness of human connection.

Which character did you most enjoy writing?

DeMarco is easiest for me. I need only look a few years in the past to remember what it is like to be so guarded. But I also enjoy the challenge of seeing life from a female point of view. Fortunately, I've had some guidance over the years in understanding that point of view.

For that same reason, I also enjoyed writing Cat. She's a woman with a huge heart but with the brittle shell of a lot of the country-women I knew as a boy.

As for the other characters, I had a lot of fun with Hoyle. Everything he does filters through his intellect. His physicality is an encumbrance, so his physical pleasures are limited to the gastro-nomic. I, on the other hand, have always exulted in the physical; as a high school and college athlete, my attitude toward the physical life was akin to that of the ancient Greeks. Even though my running and jumping days are behind me now, I still retain an appreciation for the physical life, but am gradually according more and more importance to the nonphysical.

Which character did you find the most challenging to write?

Several of the secondary characters are based more on observation than on an inner understanding of what drives those characters. I find it impossible to appreciate the motives of anyone who deliberately harms another person.

Do you see any similarities between DeMarco and yourself?

Maybe. Maybe not. ☺

There are some really great twists in *Walking the Bones*. Can you describe some of your plotting process? How do you map out the events in your novels?

Typically, I don't start writing until I know the opening scene and have an idea of the conclusion. Somewhere along the way, I begin to discern future plot points that will tie the beginning to the ending, though the ending is quite likely to change before I get to it. Overall, I let the characters determine the course of the story. I set them in motion, then follow along behind and record their decisions.

If you had one piece of advice for aspiring mystery writers, what would it be?

Do I have to choose only one piece of advice? How about two?

Here's number 1: Don't assume that an MFA or any other degree will turn you into a writer. It won't. At best, a degree will expose you to a lot of good, published writers and will shorten your apprenticeship by a few years. At worst, a degree will take a lot of money and time and will homogenize your writing so that it is acceptable to the lowest common denominator of literary taste. I think an aspiring writer will learn a lot less about herself, human nature, and life by sitting in a classroom for two years than by traveling the world, or just the country, and by reading and studying every good book she can get her hands on.

Number 2: Know story structure. Know what is meant by a beginning, a middle, and an end. And understand that even that formula is only a suggestion, not a rule.

What do you want readers to take away from *Walking the Bones*?

If my readers close the book and feel they have been on an emotional journey with my characters, and if the reader says goodbye to those characters as they would say goodbye to dear friends they hope to see again, I will be satisfied that I have fulfilled my obligation.

DeMarco has suffered through a lot of tragedy, both in his childhood and adult life. Do you think people ever truly escape the ghosts of their past?

I will let Thomas Huston and Jayme Matson answer that question.

Thomas: "There's story and there's backstory. In fact, there's no story without backstory. There's no you.... There's no present without the past."

Jayme: "The past is never past. Every second of their pasts lay gathered inside them. Every incident of their pasts had constructed their present, every cell interlocking, layer upon layer. The past is omnipresent."

What do you think makes DeMarco a great detective?

He listens to his heart.

ACKNOWLEDGMENTS

My thanks, as always, to Sandy Lu, my wonderful agent, and to my stellar editors, Shana Drehs and Anna Michels, and to my gang of three beta readers/idea generators/snafu catchers, John Fortunato, Mark Hoff, and Michael Dell. What a team!

ABOUT THE AUTHOR

Randall Silvis's fiction and nonfiction books have appeared on Best of the Year lists from the *New York Times*, the *Toronto Globe & Mail*, SfSite.com, and the International Association of Crime Writers, as well as on several editors' and booksellers' pick lists. Also a prize-winning playwright, a produced screenwriter, and a prolific essayist, his literary awards include the Drue Heinz Literature Prize, two literature fellowships from the National Endowment for the Arts, a Fulbright Senior Scholar Research Fellowship, and a Doctor of Letters degree from Indiana University of Pennsylvania for distinguished literary achievement.

Cohost of the popular podcast series The Writer's Hangout (thewritershangout.com), Silvis lives in western Pennsylvania.